PENGUIN BOOKS

THE HIGHEST BIDDER

Janet Cohen is the author, under the name Janet Neel, of three highly acclaimed crime novels: *Death's Bright Angel*, which won the 1988 John Creasey Award for the best first crime novel, *Death on Site* and *Death of a Partner*, shortlisted for the 1991 Crime Writers' Association Gold Dagger Award, all published by Penguin.

Educated at Cambridge and qualified as a solicitor, Janet Cohen spent time in the USA designing war games and working as an industrial relations specialist for John Laing Construction before spending thirteen years in the Department of Trade and Industry. Now a director of Charterhouse Bank, she is their privatization specialist. She is also a director of the Yorkshire Building Society.

Janet Cohen frequently appears on radio and television, on *Any Questions*, *Question Time*, *Start the Week* and financial programmes. She started Parsons restaurant in the Fulham Road, London, and created Café Pelican in St Martins Lane, London, and its sister restaurant in the City. She is married with three children and lives in London.

D1382504

JANET COHEN

THE HIGHEST BIDDER

PENGUIN BOOKS

PENGUIN BOOKS

Published by the Penguin Group
Penguin Books Ltd, 27 Wrights Lane, London w8 5tz, England
Penguin Books USA Inc, 375 Hudson Street, New York, New York 10014, USA
Penguin Books Australia Ltd, Ringwood, Victoria, Australia
Penguin Books Canada Ltd, 10 Alcorn Avenue, Toronto, Canada m4v 3b2
Penguin Books (NZ) Ltd, 182 190 Wairau Road, Auckland 10, New Zealand
Penguin Books Ltd, Registered Offices: Harmondsworth, Middlesex, England

First published in Great Britain by Michael Joseph Ltd 1992
Published in Penguin Books 1993
1 3 5 7 9 10 8 6 4 2

Typeset by Datix International Limited, Bungay, Suffolk
Filmset in 10/13pt Monophoto Times
Printed in Great Britain by Clays Ltd, St Ives plc

For my son Henry

I

Lucy Friern covered her head with the sheet, as the lights snapped on, three wall lights throwing indirect light up to the high ceiling of the room in which an outsize double bed sat squarely and deliberately as a centre-piece. It was a big, restful room, with very little clutter, furnished only with the bed, tables at each side, a couple of chairs and a small elegant Victorian desk. Off it a door stood half open on to a glimpse of built-in wardrobes, and beyond that the gleam of pale porcelain. The Frierns' London flat was of a generous size, but then Sir Matthew Friern was a big man physically as well as a rich one.

'Matt, it's only seven o'clock.'

'And time we got up if we're going to get to this conference. Come on, Lu, we talked about it.'

He had, Lucy acknowledged, and she had agreed that she would accompany him to the conference, in some West End hotel, where a government minister was speaking. She sat up and slid out of bed pulling on a silk dressing-gown. 'What did I do with my nightie?' she inquired, peering around her, and her husband laughed.

'It's probably down the bottom of the bed, darling. Put your glasses on.' He watched, amused, as Lucy found her glasses and put them on, an incongruous sight above the clinging dressing-gown. Not that Lucy looked anything but beautiful, even in glasses, with her long, nearly black hair and wide violet eyes. She sat down again on the edge of the bed, feeling for her slippers, the dressing-gown slipping away from one long, elegant leg, as she hooked a slipper from under the chair. She really did not look like a lady who would be thirty-nine next birthday, her husband thought, with pride.

'Do we have to be there at the beginning?' she asked, locating the other slipper.

'Yes. I want to see the Minister who is giving the speech. He arrives at ten for coffee, apparently, and we ought to be able to manage a quick word then.'

'What about? The quick word, I mean.'

'I thought you weren't paying attention when I told you, but for God's sake, Lu, this is important.' Matthew got out of bed, irritably, stopped irresolute, then went off towards the bathroom. 'We're going to this conference,' he said, crossly, over the noise of running water, 'because there is a company I might want to buy. It was nationalized – taken over by Labour to save it from going bust – and our lot want to sell all those companies back into the private sector again.'

'I can't hear you very well,' Lucy said, coldly, accustomed to due deference even from a husband eight years her senior and five stone heavier, and Matthew Friern cursed.

'The company is called Prior Building Systems, but never mind the details,' he said, coming back into the bedroom, holding up his pyjama trousers. 'What I want to find out is whether this lot really are going to sell, and I want to make damn sure they know that if they are we – Friern – are interested.'

This much at least made sense, Lucy acknowledged. Friern Construction plc, of which her Matthew was

2

chief executive and a substantial shareholder, had been founded by his father as a house-building company, and had prospered as that. Matthew had diversified into civil engineering, doubled the company's size since his father's death, and was now one of the north-east's richest and most successful businessmen. Nor did he intend to stop there. He wanted to double the company's market capitalization again in the next ten years. And, after an unexpected Conservative election victory the year before, on a platform of Rolling Back the State, it also made sense that the Government would be trying to reverse at least the more recent Labour nationalizations as quickly as possible.

'Why am I coming?' she asked, bluntly.

'Our banker, dear, Andrew Eames Lewis suggested it. It turns out that the civil servant who is handling the sale is someone you both trained with. Clive Fieldman. I said I didn't know how much you'd kept up with him, but he was at that party in Dorrington last Christmas, when the Labour lot were still in.'

'Clive? Oh, really? I have seen him since then. But Andy could have talked to him – he was at Smith Butler too.'

'He only found out over the weekend that Fieldman was involved, apparently. He just thought it might help having you there too. And he fancies you, does our Andrew.'

Lucy passed this by, impatiently, too used to her effect on men to be particularly interested. 'He wants me there, I expect, because he and Clive didn't get on terribly well when we were all in Articles.'

'I expect you got on with them both, though,' her husband said, drily. 'Well, it's nice to know there was some point in your doing a year as an articled clerk. You hated it at the time, I remember.'

'It was so *boring*,' Lucy was looking ruffled at the memory. 'Nothing but loads of paper and drafts for the next morning.'

'I never saw you as a solicitor,' Matthew was laughing.

'Clive thought it was boring too,' Lucy said, with dignity. '*He* left after a year, just like me. And Andy left a year after qualification too. It wasn't just me being frivolous. It *was* actually boring, being a lawyer and I expect this conference will be too. What do you want me to do, Matt?'

'Just look beautiful, chat up Fieldman at the lunch, and get introduced to the Minister if you can. Andy and I will do the rest.'

His wife considered him carefully, pushing her dark hair back. 'I *was* going out to lunch.'

He reached for her. 'Do this for us, then, Lu.'

'I may want a treat.'

'You had one, didn't you? Last night.'

'It was all right,' she said, demurely, and he laughed.

'You'll get a treat if this comes off. It's a good company.'

'We'd better have breakfast. I can hear Bridget in the kitchen, and I'm starving. All right, Matt, but I must leave by two thirty. Fred can take me.'

Matthew Friern agreed with hardly a qualm that his wife could take his personal driver – it would be worth it to get her to the conference with her mind on the job – and they both padded down the thickly carpeted corridor to the dining-room.

*

4

An hour later, in a large, bleak office at the top of one of the towers that dominate Marsham Street, home of the Department of the Environment, another prospective participant in the conference was loading papers into a briefcase, with no particular sense of haste.

'Coffee, Mr Fieldman?'

'Thank you, Miss Williams.' The civil service is not a particularly formal or old-fashioned organization and Clive Fieldman normally called colleagues at any level by their first names, but his secretary, who was in her late fifties, had always made it quietly clear that she expected to call him Mr Fieldman and be treated herself with equal formality. Clive Fieldman, at thirty-eight the youngest of his grade in the Department and making for the very top, was sensitive to what people wanted and more than willing to try to provide it.

'No hurry, Miss Williams. The private office says that Mr Winstanley will be ready in five minutes.'

She smiled at him, knowing as well as he did that this message meant that chaos reigned up in the office of the Minister for Housing and that the talented young man who ran the Minister's office was doing his best to keep the troops posted.

'It's not very far to the hotel,' she said, reassuringly, and put his coffee in front of him, leaving him to reread the brief he had prepared and check the final amendments to the speech which his man would be delivering in just over an hour. *That* was all right; he had been over it with Winstanley the night before, but he would need to check that he had read the brief too and was prepared for the interested parties he would meet. There would be at least ten minutes in the car to go over it. Winstanley was new, appointed to the job three weeks ago to replace a colleague who had died of a heart attack, but all ministers were good at picking things up and retaining them for at least the day on which they needed to deal with the particular issue. Well, they had to be: it was either that or die on your feet.

'The private office say that Mr Winstanley is ready and will meet you downstairs, Mr Fieldman.'

Twelve minutes, he noted, unsurprised, and 'ready' a relative statement, meaning only that as escort he was unlikely to have to wait more than ten minutes in the car. Still, a gossip with the driver was always worth having; they knew everything that went on.

'Right. The Minister is doing the lunch, Miss Williams, but leaving at two, so I'll be back at two thirty at the latest.'

He waited in the car for ten minutes before John Winstanley, Minister for Housing, and a private secretary burst out of the lift.

'Sorry to keep you waiting, Clive,' Winstanley said, punctiliously, as he slid into the car, and Clive considered him thoughtfully; he was looking tired and tetchy and harassed. Got the foreman's job at last and can't keep up with it, Clive thought in his father's parlance, momentarily irritated. He decided that this was uncharitable – this one had the makings of a decent minister: he had had eight years in Shell and two in a merchant bank before deciding to stand for Parliament, so he had at least lived in the real world. And he had had a parliamentary secretary's job before becoming a minister of state. But he had only held the previous job for six months and he had been concerned exclusively with Social Security regulations. He was still on a very steep learning curve and it behoved an ambitious civil servant to be patient and to help.

'So,' Winstanley said, firmly, 'we've got five civil-engineering or building companies here, owned by the NEB, all total no-hopers. Right?'

'Well, not quite, Minister.' So much for his careful briefing, Clive thought, resigned. 'Two of them are losing money. But two are profitable, if undercapitalized, and saleable right now. The fifth – Prior Building Systems – is the one which is most difficult.' He paused to make sure that Winstanley at least had the categories clear but realized that he had lost his man.

'Why on earth are these sort of companies government-owned at all?'

'It was felt at the time – and these companies were acquired between 1975 and 1978 – that it was better to take a viable company which was going through a bad patch into public ownership rather than to lose employment and industrial infrastructure in areas of the country where unemployment was already very high. Of these five companies, three are in the north-east and the other two in the north-west.'

John Winstanley considered his civil servant covertly. The Prime Minister, whose every word he believed to be gospel, frequently urged her team to remember that the whole of the civil service had been working for a Labour government from 1974 to 1979 and had been putting their best efforts into extending the powers of the state into places where even the massive nationalizations of the late forties had not reached. Moreover, as she told them all at every opportunity, Labour policy accorded with most civil servants' instincts – they being left-wing, corporatist and personally concerned to extend their own empires. This chap was very young for an under-secretary and had been one of a wave of promotions in

7

the Department just before the change of government. The bugger had probably been involved personally in taking these companies into the NEB and was presumably ready to frustrate putting them back where they belonged in the private sector, to sink or swim on their own merits. Well, he would see.

'At any rate they need to go right back where they came from.'

'Into receivership, Minister?' Clive Fieldman had had enough of ministers who did not read their briefs, and was pleased to see Winstanley disconcerted. But he must not indulge himself, he decided a second later: this lot were here to stay.

'I meant back to the private sector,' Winstanley said, grittily.

'Yes, of course, Minister. There is no logic in these companies being state-owned. And I would think there were purchasers for most of them.'

Winstanley blinked, disconcerted at this ready acquiescence. The PM was obviously right, all you had to do was to be firm. 'You from the north yourself?' he asked, vaguely, having remarked before that this particular high-flying civil servant had not bothered to eliminate a strong regional accent. Good-looking chap, very dark, almost black hair, light, useful sevens player by the look of him.

'Yes, Lancashire, Minister, and I know these companies. I was not involved in the original decision to fund the NEB to buy them, but when I took over this division, just before the last election, I went round all five.'

Professional, Winstanley thought, grudgingly. 'Have we tried to sell them?'

'No, Minister. We were waiting to seek your views.

The brief, which you have there, proposes a sale and asks for your authority to get a proper valuation for all five.'

So it bloody does, Winstanley conceded, inwardly. And all in one page, conclusion highlighted in yellow by his office, as he had not had to tell them. 'And I should have read it.' He decided that some apology was due, and received as an answer a wide, amused, ungrudging grin from his civil servant. Definitely a good-looking chap, almost Italian with the very dark brown eyes.

'I'm always conscious that we overload ministers with information, but it's difficult to know how to cut it down at the beginning.'

'You couldn't have cut it much further. I just didn't get round to it; I went to Covent Garden last night and was too tired to get through all the boxes.' He sighed. 'What did you do before you joined the civil service, Clive? I know you were LSE, but where before?'

'Ducton Grammar School. My father was a foreman in one of the steel factories.'

'My father was in the army. Welsh Guards.'

Clive, who like all senior civil servants had looked up his minister's history, said he had heard, and asked a civil question about life in army quarters. The car ground to another halt, in thick traffic, the driver visibly sweating, and Clive decided that he had better get back to business.

'The particular company which may need dealing with first, Minister, is Prior Building Systems. One of the potential purchasers – he's had a word informally with the Permanent Secretary – is likely to be at this conference. He is Sir Matthew Friern, of Friern Construction – and he may take the chance to lobby you.'

9

'What do you want me to say?'

'Something along the lines of no reason why this company should not be returned to the private sector at a fair price. Then listen to him telling you why it's not worth more than 20p of anyone's money.'

Winstanley burst out laughing. 'You've met him?'

'I know him slightly.' Clive hesitated. 'It's one of those odd connections. His wife Lucy and I were articled clerks in the same solicitors.'

'Really? Were you a solicitor then?'

'No. I decided after a year that I didn't like it enough, so I did the exams for the civil service and got in. And Lucy Friern didn't finish the course either, because she decided to marry Matthew and have kids instead.'

Winstanley said, gloomily, he hadn't realized that there were any women left who still did retrogressive, ordinary things like that, and Clive, grinning, observed that there probably weren't any more, but Lucy would be around thirty-eight, same as he was, and women had been a bit less determined in those backward days. 'We're talking about 1964 here, Minister. Very few women in Articles altogether.'

'Was Lady Friern the only one?'

'No, we had another. A very different cup of tea. Yes, just here, Jim, that's the hotel.'

'Right.' Both men, unconsciously, put on their official faces and pushed papers into briefcases as the big car swung into the kerb. The driver made to open his door, but Clive was out, moving neatly and fast, and holding the door for his minister.

'Two o'clock, Jim, right here,' Clive said briskly. The driver waved in acknowledgement and made to pull away, but had to bring the big car up with a jerk that pushed its front wheels right down, as a taxi driven like a racing-car dived for the kerb just ahead of him and pulled up on a sixpence. A tall girl got out in a swirl of pleated skirt, revealing long legs, clasping a briefcase under one arm. 'Now, darling,' she said, minatorily, to the taxi, causing both Clive and his minister to stop in their tracks. 'Jean is there, at home. Waiting for you. You are to have a rest and *not* watch TV all day.'

Clive edged towards the taxi, momentarily forgetful of his minister, who followed him, interested. A boy of about twelve, rather pale with a pad of bandage taped over his right temple, was at the window of the taxi. He looked up, wide, blue eyes under a thick fringe of floppy blond hair, and Clive blinked at him.

'He'll be all right with me, dear.' The taxi-driver was an amused, balding tough in his forties. 'You go to your conference – I'll get him home, not to worry.'

'Thank you.' The girl bent to the child, who kissed her unselfconsciously on the lips. 'I won't be late,' she promised, watching anxiously as the taxi pulled away at the same racing speed at which it had arrived. She turned and the briefcase which she had been holding insecurely and half open slid to the pavement scattering papers. 'Oh shit,' she said, in heartfelt tones, and Clive felt a great smile spreading itself all over his face, then remembered his minister, but Winstanley was laughing.

'Time for all good men, obviously,' he said, and advanced to where she was crouched on the pavement, pleated skirt trailing unregarded on the dusty ground, her blonde hair very bright in the January sun.

Clive squatted beside her. 'Let me help, Caroline.'

She turned to look at him, a fistful of papers squashed in one hand, and he grinned at her as he trapped the remaining papers in the case and set it upright. Not a girl any more, of course, he thought, looking at the faint lines around her eyes and the hollows under her cheekbones. Well, she'd be his own age, wouldn't she?

'Clive. Clive Fieldman. Why are you here?'

And not much changed in sixteen years either, he thought, picking up the briefcase and extending a hand to help her to her feet. No cries of how nice to see you, thank you so much for your help.

'I'm with my minister,' he said, falling into the old pattern of following Caroline's lead, and deciding that he must stop doing that forthwith. 'Minister, the lady who fell on her knees at seeing you is Caroline Henriques – sorry, Caroline Whitehouse. We were articled together.' He scowled unhopefully at Caroline and was seriously taken aback to see her offer Winstanley her hand and a wide smile.

'How do you do. How kind to stop and help. It's not my day. My eldest cracked his head open scrapping with another child at school and had to be stitched up and despatched home, which made me late. I do look forward to hearing you speak.'

Clive, struggling with a sense of dislocation, considered his old friend doubtfully. Not even exactly an old friend, Caroline Henriques as was, far too well connected, too difficult and too fierce for him when they had all been 22-year-old articled clerks in the firm in which a maternal great-grandfather of Caroline had pursued a distinguished career. There had been twelve of them in Articles, all at various stages of their postgraduate apprenticeship; all except him had been Oxbridge graduates but the firm had a name as a liberal employer which accounted for him and for the fact that two of the twelve had been girls. It was different now, of course; the big City firms, under the pressure of the expansion of work in the 1970s, had given up looking to Oxbridge and instead concentrated on getting the best from any university. And up to fifty per cent of the articled clerks were girls these days, he had heard, although there were still very few among the partners. Caroline Henriques had not been given to pretty speeches – indeed, she had barely been given to civility – but here she was, charming Winstanley, who was showing every sign of willingness to stay chatting on the windy pavement all morning. Being not at all required to oil the conversation, he considered her carefully, unconsciously straightening as he watched her. She was a tall woman, his own height within half an inch, she 5 ft 8½ ins and he 5 ft 9 ins, and he shivered slightly in the cold wind as he remembered the day they had established this differential. He had been in Articles for three months and everything about the poised, Oxford-educated Caroline had made him prickly with discomfort, from her unthinking lack of deference to the most senior partners to her athletic height. Finding himself alone with her in the venerable lift one winter day, she, on her way out to play for the firm's netball team, looking perfectly at home in a short, flared skirt with tracksuit trousers on underneath, he had said, nervously, that she wasn't so tall in gym shoes. She had fixed him with that blue direct stare that had already unnerved several of the firm's clients, pulled him out of the lift at the next floor observing that they had better settle this right now, for Christ's sake, Clive, he was a perfectly *ordinary* height, and insisted on a startled fellow articled clerk measuring them against each other back to back. 'So,' she had said, grimly, 'you're half an inch taller, Clive. Is that OK now, because if so I'd better get out and warm up – I am not fit.' He had felt himself turn a slow scarlet, but that had not been the worst; the news had spread by osmosis, bringing three more of the articled-clerk gang including Andrew Eames Lewis, an elegant Etonian whom Clive had particularly disliked.

'Why are you measuring him, Caroline, darling?' Eames Lewis had asked, taking in the situation at a glance. 'To see if he'll fit in bed?'

Clive had wished for death at that point, but Caroline was unfazed. 'It isn't length from head to toe that matters in that context, Andy – didn't they teach you anything useful at school?'

'You may have to wait for her to insist on measuring anything other than your height, Clive,' Andy had observed, nodding courteously to the senior partner who was creeping round by the walls trying to get unobtrusively out of the office.

'Piss off, Andy,' Caroline had advised, equally heedless of her senior, stripping off tracksuit trousers to reveal long, brown legs, and disappearing downstairs two at a time, leaving Clive torn between rage and sexual excitement which had persisted all that day, severely interfering with the draft contract for sale with which he had been entrusted. He hadn't got anywhere along those lines either; as he had slowly come to realize, much of Caroline's unthinking confidence and directness with men stemmed from a totally secure attachment to the man she had had since she was twenty-one and later married. Ben Whitehouse had been at Harvard for most of the time that Clive had been with Smith Butler, but he remembered vividly the one time he had met him collecting Caroline from work. He had been expecting, in the language of his childhood, something built like a brick shit-house, capable of chewing nails and spitting rust, and had been seriously taken aback to find himself talking to a lightweight, who probably was not quite six foot, and was a first-class academic jurist. He had died, had Ben Whitehouse, in an air crash on the way home from a conference, at only thirty-nine meriting an obituary in *The Times* which Clive had read, shocked, and written a stilted note to Caroline. That must have been two years ago, he remembered.

'Your lad's just like you,' he observed, into a hole in the conversation, realizing as he spoke that he would have to move his minister on. 'Same haircut, too.' He was not, after all these years, about to be frightened of Caroline Whitehouse. She grinned at him, showing her even white teeth, a product of the same genetic inheritance as the thick hair and the blue eyes that had cropped up so strikingly in the boy he had just seen in the taxi.

'Actually he's just another Henriques,' she said, confirming his view. 'He looks like all my brothers' boys. My daughter now, she looks like Ben. Ought one to go in – I mean do you want to look at your notes?'

Winstanley, thus called to order, though with a great deal more politeness than the younger Caroline would have deployed, agreed that they should go in, though not without hoping aloud that he would see her at lunch. Clive was fascinated to see her dimple prettily and say she looked forward to it. She disappeared into the hotel portico, leaving Clive to explain about the late Ben Whitehouse, in answer to Winstanley's rather over-casual question.

She appeared at his side, minutes later, coatless, with

her conference folder locked under her arm. She smiled at them both. 'Caroline Whitehouse', her name tag said, 'Partner, Smith Butler'. He watched his minister absorb the information and at the same time realized that Caroline was waiting to say something.

'Perhaps you'd like to come and eat lunch with me and my partners at the old shop some day?' She gave him a business card. 'I'll get my secretary to ring – I just thought I'd say now, in case I missed you later.'

Winstanley gave him an amused, ironic look as they proceeded up the grandiose carpeted staircase to the first-floor conference hall. 'Not many women partners in city solicitors.'

'No. She was always extremely able.'

She was too, he remembered; the effortless speed with which she absorbed instructions and turned out careful, well-considered drafts had overcome the objections of even the crustiest of the older partners to her directness, fearsome bad language and total lack of deference to age or experience. She had read Law at Oxford, and done Part II of the final professional examinations before she had joined Smith Butler, so she had had a head-start on him anyway, he having read international relations at LSE.

He reached the top of the stairs, and saw, immediately, as he had expected, Sir Matthew Friern, strategically posted to keep an eye on the entrance, watching him over the shoulder of a slightly smaller man whose back was towards them. He glanced at his watch: just time for a quick handshake, then he would have to push Winstanley through to the top table. That was fine – Matthew Friern ought to be allowed his word with the Minister, but equally any substantial discussion at this stage would be undesirable. He touched Winstanley's arm.

'Minister? Sir Matthew Friern – the one who wants to buy Prior Systems – is just over there. Do you want a quick word?'

'Yes, yes. I'll do that.' Winstanley altered course, stuffing notes into his pocket so that his hands were free, and clearing his throat. Clive, clever, quick, lively and having long ago shed any residual shyness, still wondered what it must be like always to be on the qui vive, always ready to shake a hand and be civil, whatever you were feeling like. Politicians didn't mind that, he reflected; they liked it, they drew nourishment from it all.

The man to whom Friern had been talking turned as they came up, and Clive blinked. Andrew Eames Lewis, elegant as ever, looking much as he had sixteen years ago as an articled clerk at Smith Butler, was standing at Matthew's side watchful and steady, the name of a great merchant bank beneath his own on his name tag. He nodded to Clive, coolly, and stood back, eyes on Winstanley.

'Minister, may I introduce Sir Matthew Friern?' Clive said.

'I've been wanting to meet you.' Matthew clasped the Minister's hand and nodded to Clive. 'I'd like a word about a company that Labour nationalized.'

He was a big chap, Matthew, one always forgot, Clive reflected, and indeed he had done five years in some bit of the army where they hired them oversize: a Guards regiment presumably. Good yeoman stock. Blond, red-faced, a good fifteen stone, eyes set too close together. A hard man, they said, but a capable one. And married to Lucy Friern, who did not after all seem to be here with him.

'And this is Andrew Eames Lewis from Walzheims, who are our advisers, as I expect you know.' Clive watched as his minister shook hands with Andrew; these ministers would always be civil to merchant bankers of course, unlike the previous administration, who had treated them with grudging, anxious suspicion. So Andrew had jacked in the law as well; what with both of them and Lucy Friern, the law in general and Smith Butler in particular had retained only twenty-five per cent of that group of articled clerks. A merchant bank was of course Andrew Eames Lewis's natural home, rather than a middle-class professional solicitors.

He pulled himself back to the present and the conversation between Winstanley and Matthew Friern, observing that the Minister was sticking to his brief, confirming that the Department were about to appoint financial advisers who would then, with the NEB's advisers, consider offers for Prior Systems. Clive allowed five minutes, then detached Winstanley courteously, with the civil servant's acquired murmur about time, Minister, notes, chairman waiting. He caught Andrew Eames Lewis's eye momentarily, and was disconcerted to see him looking fully as maliciously amused and interested as the day on which he had found Caroline with a tape-measure. He escorted Winstanley to the top table, introduced him to the conference chairman and persuaded one of the myriad uniformed young women to check that the microphones worked and that the Minister had a glass of water and space for his notes. His last posting had been principal private secretary to the Secretary of State, the high-flier's job, and he still, automatically, ensured that all the administrative detail was in place: cars, microphones, water, notes, telephones, lavatories. He glanced over the big conference room, now full of men in good suits wearing labels, arranging themselves in rows, with, as a refreshment to the eye, the occasional woman – perhaps a dozen among over a hundred men. Most of them were dressed in a parody of the men in good dark suits, but at least you could see their legs and the pretty ones wore make-up. Caroline had been wearing black, he remembered, but that had looked extremely striking against her bright hair and blue eyes. He squinted across the hall to see where she was and a flash of colour caught his eye, at the entrance.

'Lucy,' Caroline's effortlessly clear voice rang across the hall, causing half the men to turn to see.

'Caro,' Lucy Friern, recognizable anywhere, shoulder-length black hair swinging above the collar of a violet Chanel suit, moved easily, clearing a way for herself, smiling prettily, along the front of the hall to kiss Caroline. She peered towards the platform and waved tentatively to Clive, who beamed back at her.

'Who is the beautiful girl – the other one, I mean, not Mrs Whitehouse?' the Minister asked in his ear.

'That is Lady Friern, wife of Sir Matthew. This is old mates' day for me, Minister. Lady Friern, Mrs Whitehouse and Andrew Eames Lewis of Walzheims, whom you just met with Sir Matthew, were all at Smith Butler with me. Lucy Lindfield – Lucy Friern, that is – and I didn't last the course.'

'It must have been quite something to have had both those girls in one firm.'

'Mm.' It had been, of course, in a way, if not a way capable of explanation here and now. And he was going to be spared the necessity of explaining. The hall quieted as the chairman rose, making practised introductory noises. Administrative arrangements first: John Winstanley, most honoured to have him with us, his speech to be followed by another and then by A Panel for forty-five minutes, which could not be allowed to overrun, lunch arrangements otherwise jeopardized, drinks-time cut down; nervous sycophantic laughter from the uniformed conference groupies at this point, but a stone-faced response from what was obviously an experienced audience. The chairman launched on a fulsome exposition of Winstanley's career – Clive sitting beside him watched sardonically out of the corner of one eye as his man looked professionally modest – then addressed himself warmly to the benefits that were expected to flow from the new government's refreshingly robust attitude to the Role of the State and the Future of British Industry, both of which the Minister would now address. Not exactly what the Minister's speech was about, Clive reflected, behind a professional lack of expression, but close enough; no one here would notice the difference. He watched Winstanley advance confidently on the microphone to explain the Government's intention to remove forthwith the dead hand of the State from every aspect of British life, thereby regenerating British industry, restoring the value of the pound and, for this sort of audience only, scattering the trade unions and their leadership to the four winds.

Clive, whose father had been a union shop-steward for most of his life, had succeeded in making Winstanley draw, at least publicly, a distinction between responsible union leadership and the other sort; uphill work this had been in view of his minister's unspoken but clear conviction that all union leaders and ninety per cent of their membership were bullying hotheads given to preventing little old ladies from burying their dead. Well, the union movement had brought that on itself: the prevailing image of the winter before had been of big, well-fed, sullen blokes, standing between hard-pressed people and anything they might need, like a hospital bed. The sheer gratuitous spite and sullenness with which the various disputes about public sector pay had been carried on had taken everyone by surprise, including Clive's father.

At all events, this audience was lapping it up, he observed, following his own copy professionally, ready to note where Winstanley deviated. He glanced up to where Caroline and Lucy were sitting in the third row back: Caro was looking sardonic, but attentive, Lucy was furtively reading the paper, and half the conference participants were feasting their eyes. It was *very* like being twenty-two again.

He sat, eyes on the speech in front of him, mind elsewhere as he thought about Lucy and Caroline in their youth. Superficially they had been very similar: both extremely good-looking girls, products of the same, fiercely academic girls' boarding-school, both Oxbridge graduates – Caroline being Somerville and Lucy Girton – both from the privileged middle-class, both very clever.

There all resemblance had ended. Lucy, the youngest child of a successful Newcastle businessman, who had decided to go into the law in emulation of Caroline, had managed a third at Cambridge on almost no work, but had wilted, quickly, under the ferocious pressure of the professional exams and the long hours of hard drafting.

She had, however, given a good deal of innocent pleasure all round at Smith Butler, being ravishingly pretty and gentle-mannered, before retiring to marry Matt Friern, eight years her senior, heir both to the baronetcy, bestowed on his father for massive political services to the local Conservative Party, and to a very good business. She had made a beautiful and fashionable bride and Clive had treasured for a long time the gentle comradely kiss she had bestowed on him at the wedding.

Caroline, by contrast, had been nothing that was feminine or gentle; quite as good-looking as Lucy in her way, with that aura of good health and athletic strength, the bright, thick hair and clear skin, she had all the makings of a beauty. But as Andrew Eames Lewis had said, sadly, over the umpteenth beer one evening, one might reasonably have hoped to recruit another pretty, deferential woman, suitably grateful to be let in to a man's world rather than this savage, able creature who thought that men in general and clients in particular were just a bloody nuisance who ought to be told what to do. Everyone up to and including the senior partner had had 'a word' on the occasion of various atrocities committed by Caroline without noticeable effect. They had kept her through her training on the strength of the Henriques name and, of course, as no one quite said, on the basis of her unusual ability to work without supervision: left on Maundy Thursday alone in the office, with a crisis on her hands, the relevant partner sick and the manager locked in a smoke-filled room on another major deal, Caroline had sorted out a difficult completion, leaving scars all over the other side's solicitors, but having won the lasting admiration of both her own client and theirs. Faced with a year-end problem in the trust accounts administration section where she had passed an action-packed three months, she had worked for forty-eight hours flat out, shoulder to shoulder with two management accountants, to get the last accounts disentangled and properly assembled. For every client or partner she had mortally offended there had been another who had been impressed enough to ask for her on the next job, and he supposed that in the end Smith Butler had decided that they could afford her.

He returned to the present day with a start, alerted by the unmistakable sound of a minister arriving at the peroration of a speech and found, relieved, that his hand had followed the text, whatever else his brain had been doing, and that he knew exactly where Winstanley had got to. He sat, unmoving, his face a mask of careful attention, while his man, warmed by the audience, repeated himself for five minutes before sitting down triumphantly.

2

Michael Appleton, senior partner of Smith Butler, went down two floors of the substantial Georgian building to find Mrs Caroline Whitehouse, addressed as Ms at your peril, she taking the view that one was either Miss or Mrs, both being equally honourable titles, and that Ms was a bastard, self-conscious, unworthy invention. He paused for a moment by the open door of her office and watched her, knowing that she was so deep in concentration as to be unconscious of his approach. He supposed that was how she managed to run a house and three children and a partnership at a top firm of solicitors, by concentrating savagely and exclusively on what she was supposed to be doing at any one moment. She was totally immersed in the document, hunched over it, pen in her right hand, her head resting on her left hand, the bright blonde, thick hair pushed up round her fingers. He waited till she finished the sentence she was writing carefully at the bottom of a page, then called her name and waited while she focused on him unseeingly and remembered who he was.

'Michael, I'm sorry I had to go to the fucking conference.' Both the language and the absolute absence of any civil greeting, such as 'Good Morning' were characteristic and had lost their power to disconcert him. 'I need to talk to you about Prior Building Systems.'

'Your visitors are here, Caroline.' Her secretary put cups of coffee in front of both of them as she spoke.

'They can wait five minutes, thanks, Susie. I just want to explain this all, carefully, to Michael.' Her senior partner ignored the implied insult and urged her to continue. 'Our potential client is Peter Burwood. Chief Executive of a company called Prior Building Systems, all shares in which are owned by the National Enterprise Board. Turnover about £300 million, just in the black last year, profit before tax going for £12 million this year. The NEB took it over when it went bust three years ago.'

'Why do they need a solicitor? Don't the NEB's people – it's Fleetwoods, isn't it – act for them?'

'They would normally, but they are running into a conflict of interest and the management have asked permission for the company to have independent legal representation. Thing is, Mike, it is now policy to sell out the NEB holdings, including, or even starting with, Prior Building Systems.'

'And the interests of the NEB and the company do not coincide? The NEB own all the shares, you just said.' He considered the bent head, watching her think.

'Well, Mike, I suppose it is the interests of the management and the NEB that may not coincide.' She stopped and he waited her out. He had known her for sixteen years since she was first in Articles and knew exactly when she did not feel herself to be on secure ground. She met his eyes. 'They want to organize a management buy-out, and they don't really know where to start. I met Peter Burwood at a party – oh, a couple of weeks ago – and we got on immediately.'

Michael Appleton considered her across a substantial expanse of desk, and she smiled at him, innocently. 'And he told you he was looking for a good lawyer.'

The blue eyes shifted. 'Not exactly. I told him he'd need one. And he *has* permission, Mike – I mean he can appoint us to advise the management team. The NEB have agreed to pay the costs.'

'Normal rates?' He sipped his coffee, and watched her fidget.

'Well, we may have to take a bit of a view. Fuck it, Michael, I made us a fortune on the last one of these, *and* we did most of it with articled clerks.'

He bent a disapproving look on her and she apologized. 'Just slipped out, I know I mustn't swear, the children pick it up.'

Never mind mine or the clients' views, he thought, resignedly, but the children matter. He passed it by and sat square and formidable on the other side of the table and she watched him, deciding not to press further. She had come over the years to trust his judgement on key issues, like whether to take on a client or not. She had also, more slowly, learned to accept that in a large partnership there were 'procedures', that you could not just go your own way, taking on what work you felt like, regardless of the consequences to the firm's cash flow or available pairs of hands. She remembered that there was one thing she had not told him.

'It really is the Government's intention to sell the company. John Winstanley – you know, the junior minister at Environment – was speaking at this conference. *He* didn't mention the company by name, but I checked afterwards with the civil servant. You'll never guess who it was – Clive Fieldman. He was here. Do you remember him?'

'Just. Didn't finish Articles. Chippy young man from the north. One of your admirers?'

'Not really. And not chippy any more, relaxed with age and success. He's an under-secretary, about two years earlier than anyone else, and he's coming to lunch here in three weeks or so. *He* says the company's for sale all right.'

Michael Appleton considered her, conscious of the pressure of work already in the firm, trying to balance it against a potentially interesting job, and against Caroline's perfectly justified assertion that she had made a financial success of the last one of these she had taken on. Solicitors, by convention, work on the basis of charging for their time, unlike merchant banks, who charge a fee calculated on a combination of the value of the transaction and an assumption about what the traffic will bear. Even for those tied to an hourly rate, however, it was a lot easier to charge on a generous interpretation of time spent – and a generous interpretation of whose time was being deployed – where the transaction was substantial. This would be a major job and one of Caroline Whitehouse's many useful gifts was her ability to get high-class work out of the firm's trainees, thereby enabling them to be charged at the full rate, and to accelerate their training not a little. Most of those who worked with Caroline stuck with her, since she delegated unhesitatingly and fully to any competent pair of hands she found around her. He had once congratulated her on this, and she had pointed out that if you were trying to bring up three children, assisted only by a husband who could be away for months at a time, *and* fight your way to a partnership in a major law firm, then you either found competent help and delegated properly or fell dead in the middle of the ironing. Not, she had added, fair-mindedly, that she had even contemplated ironing these many years, but the principle must be right. The conversation had left him torn between admiration and a smug pleasure in the fact that his own wife would never be asked to work quite so hard.

'Well,' he said, 'we do want to do more of these management buy-outs – it's a very profitable field. And this one is a decent-sized company. But it's very political, isn't it?'

'Oh very. But look, Mike, we also want to get into the privatization work, don't we? I wish you'd heard Winstanley talk yesterday – they do intend to sell everything. Work for us all.'

'What will they get done in five years?'

'Four years is the most you can reckon on.' An Henriques connection, he remembered, had been a not-very-successful minister for a couple of years in the last administration. 'They can do a great deal if they get started quickly. There are lots of easy bits – the shareholdings in BP and Cable and Wireless – well, they're quoted, you can just sell those – and all the bits in the NEB that got there by accident. Ferranti and Fairey, to name but two. And you probably need three sets of advisers everywhere, one for the company, one for the government.'

'And another for the NEB,' Michael Appleton said, thoughtfully.

'That's right,' Caroline gave him the sort of approving look he had seen her bestow on a child, but he was unworried by this treatment. Of course there would be a lot of work about, and the job she was trying to bring into the firm was a concrete sample. No major law firm could afford to be left out of this wave of business, as they had agreed six months ago. Indeed, at that moment they had two bids in to advise two different departments of state on the legal implications of major privatizations they were contemplating.

He walked over to the window and peered out on to Lincoln's Inn Fields; it was close to lunchtime and the Fields were full of people hurrying across in the brisk January day. A knot of girls in short pleated skirts were running towards the netball courts, giggling and bouncing the ball between them, and he watched nostalgically.

'Do you still play for the netball team, Caroline?' he asked without turning from the window.

'Michael.' He turned towards her to find her looking indulgent and exasperated. 'I'm thirty-eight. I'm a partner in this place, remember? Those girls out there are eighteen plus, six years older than my eldest child, and fit. When would I have time? How could I do it?'

'Just a thought. You don't look much older than when you first came here, somehow.'

'Kind you always were,' she conceded, grimly. 'Is all this a preliminary to telling me you don't want this customer? We *must*, Michael – don't be difficult.'

She moved slightly into the light, reminding him as she had intended to that she was indeed no longer a raw, able articled clerk, but a formidably experienced commercial partner with the lines of permanent shortage of sleep that that and her other responsibilities entailed. He considered her and saw the exhaustion hidden by the vivid bright hair and clear skin. She must have been short of sleep for years, he realized, momentarily conscience-stricken – her youngest child was only eight. He took for granted, as they all did, her stamina and ability, but the cost was beginning to show. Perhaps a

29

conscientious senior partner would turn this job down or give it to another partner.

'To be honest, I'd rather have one of the jobs we're already after. I'd rather see us acting for the Department of Industry, on British Leyland, or for Energy, on Gas,' he said, cautiously.

She nodded. 'That would be marvellous. But Michael, think for a moment. For a start we have to compete for both of these. What have they asked for? Tenders from everyone who wants to bid, then a shortlist of six. What did it cost us even to get on to the Department of Industry shortlist, by the time we had Andy and Keith flat out for a week, learning about cars and writing pages and pages of the stuff – £10,000? Yes, well, and we're only on the shortlist. Same with the Department of Energy job. And I'll tell you another thing. If we *get* either of them, well all right, wonderful, high-profile stuff, but we'll get screwed on our charges, that's clear from the invitation to tender, and at the end of it we won't have a client. Once the Government has unloaded BL, whether as a whole or in bits, it will be the solicitors acting for BL – or its dismembered parts – who have the client. Not us.'

He considered her. 'Not like you not to have said all this at the meeting when we discussed it.'

'I was on holiday, or I would have. No, Michael, I don't mean we shouldn't go for some government work, of course we should. I'm just saying that we ought to be going for a mix – some jobs we do for the Government but the really juicy growth jobs are the ones where you get a client. *That*'s why I want to do this one – if we pull it off we have a decent-sized, grateful client for ever, or near offer.'

He nodded, accepting the point. 'You're overloaded already though, Caroline. Can we pass this one on to another partner?'

'Over my dead body,' she said, as he had expected. 'Just let me keep Mark Dwyer and give me a decent articled clerk and I'll manage. It'll start slowly – lots of politics, I expect. That just takes time out of hours.'

'All right. Have you references on the people?'

'I'm doing that. They'll be OK – they look all right, you'll see. I'll bring them in for lunch if we can get into your diary.'

A sensible caveat, Michael Appleton agreed wearily. The managing partner of a major law firm has little time to himself and all his lunchtimes were booked for weeks ahead for one or other task critical to the future of the firm. On bad days he was sustained by the vision of a different life in which he lunched on a thick juicy ham sandwich and a glass of beer by himself. He discarded reluctantly this mirage and watched as she seized the phone to square a date with his secretary, reflecting that any other of his partners would have got their secretary to do this chore, but Caroline always did things herself if she thought it was the shortest route. She hooked the thick blonde hair behind one ear and he smiled involuntarily at the familiarity of the gesture; he must have seen her do that hundreds of times in the years he had known her. She was recovering, he decided, with respect; she was suddenly looking smarter. She finished the call and got up to escort him from her office and stopped by the mirror, pushing her fringe back from her face and studying the result critically. He coughed, tactfully, and she turned, startled, having forgotten he was there.

'I had it highlighted, Michael. It doesn't look dyed, does it?'

'Not at all,' he said, seriously startled. 'It looks very good – I just thought you were looking well.'

'Wonderful what highlights do. The truth is the colour has faded a bit and it makes me look tired. I noticed when I saw Timmy and me side by side in a mirror. Our hair used to be exactly the same colour, but mine had gone mousy.'

'So you restored it to its original shade,' Michael Appleton offered, charmed by this sign of humanity.

'What a good way to put it. Yes.' She grinned at him and he found himself inviting her to join the lunch he was giving, having decided weeks ago not to expose this particular gentlemanly customer to the fierce Caroline. To his relief she refused, on the basis that she was lunching with a girlfriend, and he went back to his office hoping that he had been right to take on her protégé at Prior Building Systems.

Caroline dealt with her visitors then signed off the letters she had dictated at 8 a.m. that morning, then hopped into the waiting taxi to get to lunch. She stepped out, thanking the driver, reflecting momentarily that she had practically forgotten how to pay a taxi, using actual cash, as opposed to authorizing an enormous bill when it arrived.

'Lucy,' she called, seeing her friend peering about her shortsightedly and remembering with something between affection and exasperation that Lucy never would wear her glasses; there might have been some excuse for this when they were all twenty-two, but surely now they were both thirty-eight and mothers of several children, it was no longer necessary to keep up appearances to quite that extent. Lucy Friern's looks were well worth sustaining, however, you had to concede, her black, shoulder-length hair newly washed and immaculate, falling gently to the collar of a beautifully cut woollen suit, the same violet blue as her eyes.

'But you look wonderful, Caro,' she exclaimed, rising to kiss her.

Everyone said that these days, Caroline reflected drily, and with just that note of relief. When Ben had died so unexpectedly, even her close friends had not known what to do or say; perhaps at thirty-six we were all too inexperienced with death, she reflected fair-mindedly, but even people to whom she had once been closer than a sister, like Lucy Friern, had been made awkward and distant by shock, varying between inappropriate reactions like instantly producing all the unattached men they knew or failing to invite her to anything at all. In a way the men had been easier to deal with; an amazing number of men she had known and liked as other people's husbands had made passes of various levels of crudity. Having inherited low expectations of male behaviour she had found this less difficult to understand.

'You look good too, Lucy. That's a smashing suit. And the one you were wearing yesterday was lovely too. Tell me about the boys.'

She listened, genuinely interested, to Lucy's account of her difficulties with her sons, and found that the ice was breaking. Lucy Friern was relaxing and the old footing was being re-established.

'So Mark is down for Eton, and I expect Jamie will go too. But Caro, where are yours? How do you manage?'

'With difficulty. When Ben died, I thought they'd

33

have to go away to school. I had no idea how to cope, especially with two boys.'

'You were used to brothers though,' Lucy Friern pointed out, forgetting the line of her argument in the interest of the conversation.

'*That* made me more inclined to try to send them away,' Caroline said, grimly. 'Then I remembered my idiot father, half starving us all to send us to boarding school, even those too stupid to get scholarships, and decided not to do that.'

Lucy Friern was, as always, made uncomfortable by Caroline's trenchant view of the distinguished Professor Sir Sholto Henriques. 'How is your Pa?'

'Just the same. Careering round the world giving lectures and doing bits and pieces for the Labour Party. At the age of seventy-two he hasn't got very much pension provision, and has made virtually no sensible dispositions for my lady mother.'

'Perhaps he'll go on getting jobs and won't need a pension,' Lucy suggested.

'They don't pay you for doing little jobs for the Labour Party. Or for the sort of work that considers the philosophical basis of NHS provision for kidney transplants. Interesting Sunday supplement stuff which isn't going to keep anyone, including my mother, in comfort in their extreme old age, or even provide them with enough help in the house right now.'

'Perhaps your mother doesn't mind?'

'Yes, she does, only she's never managed to say so. And she would never go out and get herself a proper job rather than being on every voluntary organization for the relief of the criminally incompetent in north London. Sorry Lu, you must be bored with my family and I digress. Timmy and Francis are therefore at the City of London School, a decent day-school. Tell me about you – it's a long time since we had a proper gossip. How is Matthew?'

'Well, you know.' Caroline watched her indulgently, as she fidgeted with her glass. 'Well, he's always working.'

This meant that Lucy, not one to stand for being in any way neglected, would be adopting her usual way of ensuring that Lucy Friern had a reasonably nice time and did not feel unloved, Caroline reflected, and bit back an observation to this effect.

'How do you manage, Caro? About men, I mean?'

Just as I, under pressure from men I like and admire, have become a little more tactful, Caroline thought, disconcerted but amused, so Lucy, under pressure from somewhere or someone, had become more direct, more inclined to get her retaliation in first.

'I don't,' she said, deciding a blunt question deserved an honest reply. 'After Ben died, I tried all sorts of things, including going to bed with three men who had been around when I decided to marry Ben. Old suitors, as it were. Disaster, or near disaster all round. Then I had a couple of one-night stands with other people's husbands. So I stopped. I've got all I can manage with three children and a full-time job.' She considered her friend kindly. 'It makes life simpler if you're not trying to struggle with a sex life as well. And I've got a lot of men friends.'

They were interrupted by a waiter wanting to take their order, and Caroline, watching the fall of Lucy's dark hair as she held the menu too close to her, was reminded of breakfast at their crack boarding school, with half the school watching Lucy, beautiful even in the unbecoming green uniform, bending to peer short-sightedly at the array of breakfast dishes, one hand holding her long black hair out of the way, revealing the clear olive skin and classically straight nose. Then as now she had never been willing to wear her glasses which had been carried around with her, reluctantly and unregarded, broken half the time or held together insecurely with Sellotape, worn only in the classroom where she conveniently considered herself invisible. Not, in practice, that Lucy had been other than instantly, dazzlingly visible to any man of whatever age or confor-mation; starting from when they were both about fifteen, an array of men, ranging from a High Court judge, old enough to be their grandfather, to the eighteen-year-old musical genius at the local boys' school, had thrown themselves in Lucy's path. They had been separated at university, Lucy having just not got into Somerville, but had visited each other regularly, and Caroline had there-fore had a grandstand view of Lucy's career at Cam-bridge which had followed a similar pattern. There, too, men had dogged her path, appearing in her room at all hours, popping up much too casually, at the same coffee-shop or bookshop where she had stopped, or bearing a wild variety of tributes further to distract Lucy from the few hours' effort a week in libraries that she found time to put in. Caroline, who had worked a professional five hours a day for a good Second, turning in all her work on time, and who, when concentrating, was unlikely to be disturbed by the outbreak of war, had simply been incredulous and, she acknowledged to herself, markedly prissy about the whole thing. Lucy, of course, had got a Third, and Smith Butler had been initially reluctant even to interview her. Something had prevailed, however, and since the partners' interviewing committee in those unreconstructed days had been entirely male, Lucy's application for Articles had been unanimously and enthusiastically supported. Lunches with Lucy had often involved a monologue about her latest man, after a courteous inquiry after her friend's health and welfare, but Caroline liked Lucy and derived considerable covert entertainment from the various histories. It was, and always had been, interesting to watch the activities of a genuine *femme fatale*.

'So tell me, Lu,' she said, bowing to the inevitable, 'who have you in your toils *this* time? Have you gone even further up-market? Royalty next.'

'No,' Lucy said with some regret. 'No, well, Anthony and I had to stop. Celia – his wife – was getting very suspicious and however cross I get with Matt I *don't* want to end up divorced, thank you, so we thought we'd better sign off. Also those ghastly people who do the notes for William Hickey were hanging about.'

Caroline grinned involuntarily at the note of innocent pride in her friend's voice. 'Well, they would, wouldn't they? Anthony being who he is,' she said, obligingly.

'Yes.' Lucy paused and considered her friend. 'So, I suppose I went down-market. You know him actually.'

'Darling, *not* one of my partners?'

'No, no. None of your partners are at all fanciable.'

'Oh, I don't know.' Caroline protested. 'Jeremy Lewis?'

'No good in bed.'

'Lu! You didn't.'

'No, of course I didn't. But I'm sure he isn't. Much too straight. Oh, thank you.' She smiled absently at the waiter, who set down her plate with trembling hands and retired reluctantly to watch her from the service hatch.

'What's wrong with being straight? No, sorry, forget I asked.' Caroline was laughing. 'Tell me about the latest. Where do I know him from?'

'Smith Butler.'

'And not one of my partners. Lu, it *isn't* one of the juniors?'

'You *are* an age snob. You know they've got more time and energy when they're young. Leo – you remember him – was one of the best fucks I ever had. No, just the mange-tout please.'

Caroline watched sardonically as the young Spanish waiter backed away, shocked but adoring. 'Got a volunteer there, Lu, if you need it.'

'You don't know where those boys have been, darling, honestly. They're mostly bi, you know.' Lucy was in no way thrown out of her stride. 'No, he isn't still at Smith Butler, but we all trained together. He was there yesterday.'

Caroline put down her fork and reviewed her day. After the conference she had gone back to the office and done what would have been a day's work for many people, then rushed home to supervise homework, then gone back to assist in a negotiation which had been going on for hours and was seriously in need of a fresh eye. Lucy, she thought, momentarily envious, had probably spent the afternoon having her hair done – or in bed with whoever it was – and the evening at Covent Garden. The Friern boys were, of course, at one of the good preparatory boarding schools, so the Latin prep and the violin practice would be someone else's responsibility. She pulled her mind back to the conference. 'Andy Eames Lewis,' she announced triumphantly, having scanned the possibilities. 'Well, only a *bit* down-market from Anthony.'

'No, not *Andrew*. I mean, we did *then*, but that was before Matt and I married.'

Caroline nodded in acknowledgement of something she had suspected at the time. 'Well, who else was there then?' she asked.

'Clive. Clive Fieldman.'

Caroline gaped at her, honestly surprised. 'Good heavens, Lu. I didn't know you'd kept in touch – sorry, I'll go back and do *that* again – I mean, I suppose I didn't think he was your sort of thing. You didn't fancy him when we were all children, did you?'

'No, not particularly. He was so awkward, if you remember.'

'Yes. Chippy. But he had something, didn't he? Knew what he wanted. He's married, I take it?'

'Divorced. Two kids. He's rather a star in the Department of the Environment, apparently.'

'That is right. He's only our age, and he ranks to under-secretary. Heavens, *Clive*. Actually, I was watching him because I've got a professional interest in what he's doing. I thought he'd come out rather well. He was always good-looking of course.' She bit back her next thought which was that they had concluded in their 22-year-old arrogance that he wasn't really dashing enough for either of them, but Lucy with the cat-like instincts of the truly feminine had caught the thought.

'That sort of thing doesn't matter any more, does it? Weren't we silly?'

'Oh, idiotic. What's *he* like in bed – Clive, I mean?'

'Well, he needed a bit of coaching. But he's jolly good now.'

'Oh, well *done*, Lu. Another man improved for the community. What a good girl you are.'

'Well, darling, someone's got to make the effort. Are you being disapproving?'

'I'm sorry, I don't mean to sound prissy. I'm jealous, I guess – I just can't pull them like you do nor do as much with them.' She considered the last sentence, caught her friend's eye and started to giggle. 'Sorry,' she said helplessly, but Lucy was laughing with her.

'No, listen, Caro,' she said, sobering. '*I*'ve got an apology to make. I feel a real bitch for not ringing you up more, for not trying harder since Ben died. I've been depressed again, but that's no excuse.'

Caroline smiled at her, touched. 'I wasn't being very welcoming.'

'Well, no, darling, but I expected *that* – I mean you've always behaved like a cornered wolf when things didn't go right for you. Or do I mean wolverine, unless that is something else altogether?'

'It's a quite different animal. And I don't know what you mean.'

'Oh Caro. When Francis and you broke up you were *intolerable*, bit everyone who came near you. That's how Ben got you: he took no notice of any of this, just went on asking you out, everyone else returned wounded, not to say shrivelled. I'm not saying you were as bad as that this time, mind, I'm just saying that I, of all people, should have known better than to stop trying because you were less than civil to me.'

'I've got much better at being civil to people. Everyone says so,' Caroline protested.

'Difficult to get any worse,' Lucy observed, with the privilege of old friendship, and Caroline smiled at her, sadly.

'I learned it originally from my mother.'

Lucy blinked, recalling clearly to mind the gracious Pamela Henriques as she had last seen her and expressed courteous astonishment.

'Yes, well, exactly,' Caroline said, with some force. 'Civil to everyone, and therefore trampled underfoot by my father and brothers because she wouldn't tell them where to get off. Do you know, Lu, that at one point my father was spending two thirds of his net income on keeping those three big idiots at Winchester while making my mother's life hell because she couldn't provide gourmet meals for six on sixpence-halfpenny a week. Instead of telling him either to stop having a lovely high-minded time as a professor in a justifiably unfashionable branch of philosophy, and earn some decent money, or send the boys – at least the two who didn't have a bloody great scholarship, same as I did – to a good day-school. She used to apologize to him and complain bitterly to me. Even at eight years old I knew she was addressing her complaints to the wrong person, but the silly old bat would not – could not – take on my father.'

'Her husband.'

'Her husband as you say. I'm surprised I managed to get married at all with the example of domestic felicity available to me.' She paused, remembering. 'Mum used to break things when she got really pissed off, which would then have to be expensively repaired, thereby adding to the poverty and general tension and causing further frightful rows. Cor, Christmas! When I look back at it, what a childhood!'

41

Lucy thought about the Henriques household which she had always found alarming though for different reasons, when spending time there as a teenager. The three boys, older than Caroline, and with the same blond good looks, physical energy and daunting intelligence, had swarmed noisily all over the house, making incomprehensible academic jokes. They had insisted on her playing hockey with them and a mixed gang of their friends, who all, like them, were children of distinguished intellectuals with none of the physical incompetence or gentle manners traditionally associated with the breed. It was true that the food had been plain and not entirely adequate, now she came to think about it, and that the condition of the house which had not seen a lick of paint in twenty years had mildly shocked her, as the indulged child of a successful industrialist.

'I suppose your mother could have got a job.'

'Of course she could. But she is a Fisher and they all do voluntary work of a bossy and interfering nature. So she organized housing for the poor of north London. It was we who were the deprived, as I used to observe as a teenager.'

Lucy who had never heard her friend speak with such force of her childhood considered her, wondering whether to distract her or let her go on, but Caroline was far away, the blue eyes slitted at an unoffending fork. She looked up, suddenly. 'Sorry, Lu, I don't know why you are getting all this. I was so desperate after Ben died and the boys were so impossible that we all went off to a family therapist, and she dug all this out. I half knew it, of course I did, that's why I've always insisted on working, but it wasn't so clear why.'

'You work too hard, Caro,' Lucy said, soberly. 'I

know what you think about me not working, but it's still true.'

Caroline nodded in acknowledgement. 'I know I do, but it is, just like they say, a drug and a consolation. And what I've always thought about you, Lu, is that you'd be happier if you worked a bit – you don't need to be a lunatic obsessive like me. Now please tell me about Clive. I can't wait to hear. Where did you meet him again?'

Lucy allowed herself to be side-tracked, falling easily into the old student relationship where she had entertained Caroline and indeed their whole gang with her latest sexual adventure. 'At a reception last year, when the Labour lot were rushing round trying to shore up the vote in the north-east. He came with the Minister – Ted Lewis – to open the new community centre, and someone gave a dinner afterwards. So there we all were, standing around in the Cumberland, lots of trade union people, all about five foot high, smoking their heads off.' She paused, flicking a glance at Caroline, who was choking with treacherous laughter. 'And there was Clive, with his minister, looking bored. I recognized him straight away, and he turned his head and saw me and took about two seconds to remember me and then gave me this huge smile. Like a little boy, you know.'

Caroline remembered suddenly an evening, sixteen years ago, when, realizing that Clive was also working late, she had collected coffee and a sandwich for him at the same time as getting one for herself and, not having a hand free, had shouted to him to open the door for her. He had appeared, blinking and pale, the brown skin sallow with tiredness and the dark springy hair flattened. He had backed away, alarmed, then lit up like a lamp at the sight of food, and his smile warmed her now, even in memory. Softened by this welcome, she had sat and eaten with him and they had talked about his family in the momentary easy companionship that comes to exhausted people finding themselves together in the middle of the night.

'Yes,' she said, rousing herself. 'I do know. Like a kid whose mum has unexpectedly appeared in a dull lesson.'

'Yes. So he came over straight away, and we got talking, and then I altered the table plan so he was next to me.' She started to laugh. '*That* caused lots of problems; I didn't know, but I'd switched things so that two mortal political enemies were sitting next to each other. But neither of us cared, we were talking too hard. He kissed me goodbye – you remember how he used to say you and I were ridiculous because we always kissed people? Yes, well, he's got the idea now, and was kissing all sorts of Labour ladies with home perms.'

'Not home perms, these days, Lu,' her friend objected. 'Everyone goes to hairdressers now.'

'Well, darling, you always knew more about the Labour Party than I did.' Lucy was sparkling and undaunted.

Caroline repudiated this promptly and explained that she had finally given up all hope for the Labour Party, when she had gone to see her mother, just before the last election and found the house full of middle-aged men with hair brushed forward over the bald spots, intoning sentences all of which started with 'That will be Oonacceptable to My Members.' Lady Henriques, to do her justice, had said to her daughter that if they went on like this trade unionists would find themselves Oonacceptable to any sane member of the voting population, it being difficult to perceive the communal benefit in having to provide one's own sheets for the sick in hospital, or bury one's own dead. And so indeed it had proved and the trade union barons, who had so badly misjudged the voting public, were still engaged in furious self-justification and internecine strife.

'So, Lu, sorry, there you and Clive are, hardly able to fall into each other's arms in the middle of a rally of the faithful in Dorrington. What happened next?'

'Well, it was the weekend, and I didn't know how to get hold of him. But he rang me on Monday and we had lunch. Then we had lunch again on Wednesday at the Tate which isn't far from his office, and he said why didn't we go and look at some pictures.'

'*Clive?* Pictures? Do you remember his views on the Nat Gall?' Caroline was unable to help interrupting, but regretted it as her friend gave her a rather cool stare.

'He's changed, I told you. Anyway, I thought we'd never get anywhere this way, so I said: "Well, Clive, I'd love to look at pictures with you if that's what you would like, but on the other hand if you'd like to spend the afternoon in bed with me we'll find an hotel."'

Caroline looked at her, open-mouthed with admiration, feeling old, staid and hopelessly out of date. 'What did he say?'

Lucy's wide beautiful mouth tucked smugly in at the edges and she pushed her dark hair behind one ear.

'Nothing at all for a minute, then he said, he'd love to go to bed with me, please, now, anywhere. So we went to this hotel in Pimlico, which *he* knew, let me tell you, so he'd done this before.'

45

'What's it called?' Caroline inquired, in the interest of research, and wrote down the answer. 'You're the only person I know who is going to tell me things like this, so I log them somewhere. Do you always go to an hotel?'

'No, we use the flat now. Matt is mostly in Dorrington during the week.'

Caroline considered her friend thoughtfully, wondering if Matthew Friern knew about any of this.

'You disapprove of me fucking Clive?' Lucy asked, catching the look.

'No,' Caroline said, unhesitatingly. 'You're actually doing the same thing as I am in a different way, not letting men make the rules. I still feel you'd be better off if you combined all this with some career. Or, even better yet, doing some painting. But let me not bore on.'

Lucy smiled at her with genuine affection and firmly paid the bill. 'And you know I think you'd be better off loosening up a bit and finding a man, even if it is someone else's husband.'

They walked together to the door of the restaurant, drawing every eye, and stopped just inside it.

'We ought to swap,' Caroline suggested, laughing as they kissed. 'Next time you fancy a man, ask yourself whether a course in interior design or landscape painting would not be better. And next time I think I'll take on one more client or a 7 a.m. class in German company law, I'll look round for a man instead.'

3

Peter Burwood, Chief Executive of Prior Building Systems, decided not for the first time that the ability to see two out of his six major sites from the office window was a liability rather than an asset. There always seemed to be something going on that could be improved just too far away for him to do anything about it. This morning, the problem was particularly obvious: the crane had not moved for fully twenty minutes on the Northchapel site. That crane should be lifting some piece of kit into place virtually continuously, therefore either the machine itself had seized up or, more likely, something had not arrived. He stood watching, a light, blue-eyed man in his late thirties, with the clear red hair which is a legacy of the Norse invaders who pillaged the coast around Dorrington.

System-building is an architect-led attempt to get the house-building industry away from the basic time-consuming activity of laying a brick measuring 9 by $4\frac{1}{2}$ by $4\frac{1}{2}$ ins on another brick. Viewed logically, houses ought to be constructed out of larger factory-made pieces. The prefabricated houses put up as temporary housing at the end of the war faithfully followed this logic. In the Arcon houses, erected everywhere from 1945 onwards, every component was factory-made in sheets, so that they could be put up in one day on a prepared site. Indeed Prior Systems in the late 1940s and early 1950s had regularly performed this operation for visitors with, as a final flourish, the foreman making a cup of tea on the stove at the end of the day. Peter Burwood had watched this particular miracle performed as a child of eight, clinging to his father's hand, and the vision had bitten deep.

The Arcon houses had been detached bungalows, each set in their own little plot, exactly what most families wanted, with a little space between them and their neighbours. They were small, true, but superbly designed inside; the bathroom and the kitchen from the Arcon Mark V were by now in the Science Museum as examples, to quote the citation, of the first time good architectural design had been applied to working-class housing.

Somewhere along the line, however, the original simplicity of the vision had got lost. Early in the 1950s the planners had decided that land-use would have to be more intensive, and, carrying this thought to its logical extreme, had caused huge concrete tower blocks to be erected, which now glowered sullenly in all large cities, the grey concrete streaked permanently with damp and rotting where it stood, the lifts and communal areas laid waste by people in protest at living in dilapidated boxes half-way up to the sky on top of their neighbours. The pendulum had swung back now to some extent, but since no local authorities had the land available to go back to building the little bungalows that people clamoured for, they had arrived at the compromise of smaller blocks of flats as the only way of meeting the demand for cheap housing.

The Northchapel site was therefore designed to be five small blocks, no more than six storeys each, plus some single houses on a particularly bleak and windswept site, with a tricky, marshy subsoil. The huddle of men around the crane, which had caught Peter Burwood's eye, was hunched into thick donkey jackets, the wind from the North Sea flattening their trousers round their knees and ankles. It was going to take more than a few tastefully arranged trees to keep that wind from blowing the windows in when the gales came; half a forest would be more like it, he observed, sardonically. He watched unmoving as the group broke up and the crane jerked into life, the whining and grinding of its gears audible even through double-glazing. The men on the ground moved swiftly and a section of wall rose slowly off the ground, checked, and came down again, the gang on the deck semaphoring violently. 'Damn wind,' Burwood said, aloud, recognizing instantly the familiar problem: the large sections were simply uncontrollable above about ten feet off the ground where the wind caught them. The site would be held up until this wind blew itself out. He sighed, still watching, listening for the phone.

He was waiting for Caroline Whitehouse to ring him, and he was nervous. She had spoken to him the night before, but had warned him she had not yet cleared her senior partner. 'I'd better tell you what I *have* done,' she had said. 'I checked the client list. We act for Mulliners and for Garfield Bryant, but they are civil engineers, of course. No problem? Good. And a couple of housebuilders, one in Bristol, one in Liverpool. I take it they aren't competition?'

'No. You don't act for Friern?'

'No.' She had sounded fractionally hesitant and Peter Burwood said so.

'No, we don't act, Peter, but Lucy Friern and I were at school together and we are still close friends. Is this a worry?'

'Friern want to take us over – I mean they want to buy the firm from the NEB.'

'Ah. That I did not know. But she's a friend, not a client, and I wouldn't discuss a client's business with her. I haven't got a problem but you have to be comfortable.'

Peter Burwood took a minute to think, lighting a cigarette.

'You still there, Peter?'

'Yes. No, that's OK, Caroline. Not a worry.'

She had rung off, in a hurry as usual, and he wished she would ring again. He had met her at a party given by a firm of executive search consultants. He had been standing by himself, resisting the hosts' attempts to introduce him to people he did not want to meet, but had been attracted by Caroline's looks and had made his way towards her, hoping she was the in-house effort at customer relations. At the moment he had arrived at her side she had been expounding, briskly, the principles of frustration of contract to a plant manager who had ill-advisedly decided to make conversation by telling her about his troubles with a Scottish supplier. Peter Burwood had listened, delighted by the clarity and impatience of the explanation. The unfortunate plant manager had vanished, leaving the two of them together. 'Prior Building Systems,' she had said, reading the label on his jacket. 'A toy company? Like Lego?' He had understood immediately that she did not suppose he ran a toy company but was simply discharging irritation with her last conversational partner. In return he had asked whether Smith Butler was an agency for the supply of domestic staff and had watched with pleasure as her head went back and she openly reconsidered him.

He had got her another drink and they had wedged themselves into a corner of the room, beating off all attempts to introduce either of them to anyone else, and he had found himself telling her about his dream of buying his company from the National Enterprise Board.

'It's a big company, though,' he had said, warningly. '£300 million turnover, give or take. I mean, it's too big for a management buy-out, isn't it?'

'If you mean could you and your mates and the wife afford to buy all the shares, no, you couldn't. But "management buy-out" is a misnomer; it's used typically to mean a deal in which management end up with say ten or twenty per cent of the equity, and financial institutions get the rest of the equity and provide all the lending.' She had seen him looking baffled. 'How much do you know, Peter, or is all this foreign ground?'

'It's all new,' he had acknowledged, promptly. 'All I know is how to run a company.'

'That's the thing you need to know. Anyone can do the whizzo financial engineering, or . . . well, not anyone, but lots of people. And you're not too big. The last one I did – which finished last week – was Alkit Engineering. You've heard of it? That was £350m turnover.'

'Have dinner with me?' he had suggested, urgently, realizing he had found the expertise he needed.

'I can't. I have three children and the nanny goes off tonight at eight o'clock so I have to be back. I could have lunch tomorrow.'

He had cancelled all his plans for the next day then and there and snapped up her offer, and they had spent two hours over lunch, talking non-stop, he soaking up information.

'What's the value of the company, Peter? £300m turn-over, £16m profit this year – profit before interest and tax.'

'Trading profit, yes?'

'The institutions use PBIT or EBIT – profit or earnings before interest and tax. It's the same thing. So, knock off the £4m interest, knock off corporation tax, get £8m odd and you're probably on a p/e of 7. Say £56m, give or take.'

'You lost me, Caroline.'

'Sorry. One typically works out the value of a company which is in profit on the basis of multiplying its fully taxed earnings by some number which gives you a price. Now, to find the magic number we look at the *Financial Times* under "Construction". Now we find under the "p/e ratio" column that all the companies are around 6 to 8 with the exception of Nelson Construction which is at 18, way out of line. That probably means a take-over bid around so the price goes way up and we ignore it. A p/e of 7 looks about right.'

He had considered her, amazed, but doubtful. 'Is that all you do?'

'Well, there are other ways. What are the assets – give me your balance sheet.' She ran a finger down it. 'Around £50m, that's what I'd expect. Whichever way you look at it it's £50m to £60m for the whole shooting match, given ordinary amounts of borrowing.'

Peter Burwood sat back and thought about it. Yes, well, the invariable civility which the company's bank manager always accorded him was unlikely to stretch to £50m. And no matter how many times he and his top team remortgaged their houses it wasn't going to make much impact on a sum like that. Caroline had warned him he would need outside investors. 'How much of the company could we get – management, I mean? And how much would we have to put up – in cash?'

'Depends. But generally in these things you can negotiate ten per cent of the equity straight away and another ten on a ratchet basis, so you get the extra 10 per cent if you do well. And the institutions will want you to put up enough to hurt if you fail. Typically they would like to know your house and children are on the line.'

Burwood bristled. 'I wouldn't do that.'

'No,' she agreed. 'I'm just telling you where they start. There's a lot of money looking for deals, and I didn't let anyone consider screwing management on the last one I did, not to worry.'

Peter Burwood took back his balance sheet and looked at it carefully, but Caroline was already reading through the notes to the accounts.

'What would be nice would be if we could get you accepted as the preferred buyer – the one with a clear run, and persuade them *not* just to put it up for sale and let everyone else bid,' she said, thoughtfully.

'We ought to be able to do that. We're the only people who can make this company pay – we know how to get those systems up.'

She looked at him, sideways. 'Oh yes? Pull the other one. System-building isn't magic. Who are your competitors? Will they want it?'

Rude, bloody woman, he thought, indignantly, but answered her question. 'Tarmac, Shaw, Friern. Tarmac won't bother – they've got more than they can handle – and I don't think Shaw is all that interested. But Friern would want it.'

'Yes, well, there you are.' She returned dismissively to

the notes to the accounts, eating spaghetti with her free hand. 'I'll need to meet your finance director soon,' she said, turning over a page.

'If we ask you to help us,' he retorted, nettled, and she had looked up from the papers and fixed him with that blue-eyed stare.

'Sorry. Am I rushing you?'

'Yes. No. I mean it's all new to me, and the three of us, that's Graham Gough, my finance director, and Martin Williams, my production man, always discuss everything.'

She pulled the papers together, handed them back to him and signalled briskly for the bill while he watched her, alarmed, trying to work out what to say. She must be his own age, he decided indignantly, despite that daunting unhesitating confidence. She looked across at him and smiled, suddenly, transforming herself from a dead-ringer for his primary-school headmistress into an extremely good-looking woman.

'Peter. You're going to need a really rough, pushy lawyer to get you through all this. You ain't seen nothing yet, there's going to be a lot of politics and there's all the negotiations with the financing institutions and the banks and so on. And there are few rougher or pushier lawyers around than me. Why don't you go and talk to Don Martin at Alkit? He'll tell you.'

He grinned back at her, melted by the smile and relaxed by the easy, matter-of-fact confidence.

'I never thought I'd have a woman lawyer.'

She scowled so sternly that he quailed and then decided that this relationship was never going to work on this basis and, taking a deep breath, covered her hand with his. 'But I know you've had to be better than a man to get where you've got, and I reckon we'll be lucky to have you. So if I can get those buggers to confirm we can have our own lawyers, I'll bring Graham and Martin down to see you. OK?'

'And if they say I'm all right, we're on.' She was laughing at him.

'That's right,' he said, stolidly, and took the bill firmly out of her hands and paid it, adding a tip generous enough to ensure him a welcome next time. 'I'll ring you inside a week,' he said, firmly holding her hand in his. 'And thank you.'

They were much of a height, he decided, but she had heels on. She looked at him carefully. 'You'll be OK,' she said, seriously. 'But it's going to be hell.' She looked down at her watch, turning the hand he was holding, and used a word he hadn't heard from a lady in many years, then giving him a swift ceremonious peck on the cheek, vanished towards her office, leaving the waiters shaking their heads in a fatherly, Italian way.

Graham and Martin had liked her from the start. Or rather, after an initial ten minutes, they had recognized her quality and were treating her as a trusted equal. There had been an uneasy moment or so, when she had told Graham he was talking rubbish – and been right – but that had passed and despite the feeling, as Martin had plaintively observed, that they had spent the last hour in a high wind, they had taken to her. Peter had, bravely he felt, taken her to task for going too fast for them.

'Sorry. I do know I mustn't,' she had said, blushing and looking suddenly about sixteen, and Graham and Martin had smiled. She should do that more often, Peter had thought, but she wasn't going to, was she?

She battered her way through, that one, and most people were just going to stand well back, thanking their lucky stars they weren't married to her.

The phone rang and he reached for it, still watching the men struggling with the crane. 'Mrs Whitehouse, Peter,' his secretary said, faint disapproval edging her voice.

'Peter? If you still want me, you're on. I've cleared my senior partner, at the rates we agreed. The clock starts as soon as you say yes.'

Nothing about how honoured we would be to have you as a client, or how we were looking forward to a stimulating relationship, he thought, grinning.

'Does it cost if you come and see the site?' he asked, demurely.

'Course it does. I fill up a time sheet every day. In half hours. Tell you what, though, I'll come on the train and work on someone else's stuff, that'll save a bit.'

'How many hours do you account for a day?'

There was a pause and he heard her laugh.

'I might have known an erstwhile production man would be on to that one. We account on the basis of a seven-hour day.'

'How many hours do you do?'

'Depends. I don't work through the night much any more. Probably not more than ten hours on average.'

'So you're costed to make a profit on seven hours and you actually do ten and charge them.'

'Very good, Mr Burwood. That's why we can afford to charge you rather less than our top rate.'

'£100 an hour isn't your top rate?'

'By no means. Are we going on discussing this, because I'm clocking up time?'

'No, you aren't. I haven't said yes yet.'

'Shit. It'll have to be logged to sales. I hate doing that.'

'Caroline! Language.'

'Sorry. Are we on or not?'

'You're on, yes. You come up here, soon as you can, but out of prime shift.' He stopped, conscience-stricken. 'What about your kids, though?'

'I have live-in help. That's why I cost so much. Nanny and housekeeper to support. Tomorrow evening then.' She rang off, crisply, leaving him laughing to himself. She was going to suit them a whole lot better than some poncey young man in a good suit.

Twenty miles away, Sir Matthew Friern was scowling at a scene much like the one which Peter Burwood had been contemplating. The wind had stopped the big Friern crane as well. He turned reluctantly from the window, a bulky man in a good suit that glossed over an incipient bow window and excess weight on the hips.

'Mr Eames Lewis is here, Matthew.' His secretary, a determined square widow in her sixties, who had been his father's right hand, called from her office.

'Thanks, Doreen. Come in, Andrew.' He considered his banker and held out a hand to the younger man with him.

'Matthew, this is John Michaels, one of my fellow directors in corporate finance.'

Brought a younger bloke to do the work, Matthew observed. He waited while coffee and his finance director arrived, then waved everyone to the table, noticing with a mixture of amusement and contempt that the indefatigable Andy was talking about football with the finance director. Had the man's passion in life been darts or ten-pin-bowling, Andy would have been talking about that.

'I want to get Prior Systems,' Matthew said, briskly. 'I want you to tell me what you think I have to offer and how you think we should finance it.' He sat back, watching the two bankers. The junior, he noticed, had several copies of a bound paper. Done his homework then. He looked at him expectantly, but the young man was watching his senior and Andy wasn't about to hand over any documents.

'We've done some calculations and comparisons and can suggest a price range. But it'll all depend on how much competition there is, and you've got a better feel for that than we have.'

Matthew considered his adviser. 'We're not planning on a competition, Andy. What we want is a negotiated deal. We'll offer them a fair price, and the Ministry ought to be bloody glad to get it off their hands.'

'That's not quite what the Minister said, Matthew, when we met him the other day.'

Matthew looked at him sharply. 'But you know the civil servant – Fieldman – well, don't you? Trained together. I mean you can talk to him. Lucy knows him a bit, if not.'

Andy nodded, patiently. 'I talked to him yesterday. He was between meetings, but perfectly straightforward. He put me on to Gruhners, who are advising the NEB – well, I was at school with John Martin, so I had a good chat with him. John tells me they already have indications of interest from us, from Shaw and from the management of Prior Building Systems.'

'Shaw won't want it. They're just around in case the company is being given away.'

'John would agree with you. The management, on the other hand, do want it.'

Matthew swallowed his coffee noisily. 'They won't have the cash.'

Andy considered his client carefully. 'Not personally, of course. But sitting management do have advantages. Buy-outs are very fashionable – there is plenty of money around in the City to finance them. And I understand from Clive Fieldman that his ministers – who, after all, are going to have to agree to all this – are likely to be attracted by a deal where employees get shares. Anything to screw the unions, as I understand the matter.'

Matthew stared at him, openly hostile to this explanation, but Andy was unperturbed. His junior stirred and volunteered helpfully that people were very keen to finance these buy-outs, as evidenced by the recent big one in engineering. Andy lifted his hand marginally from the table to silence him but not before his colleague had become a lightning conductor for Matthew's frustration.

'That ought to be illegal,' he said, red with indignation. 'I mean, if the managers want it for themselves, they've got the inside track and they're going to do their best to bugger us up, aren't they?'

The young banker glanced apologetically at Andy who had not moved at all from his position, lounging back in his chair.

'Not necessarily, Matthew. The NEB would be fully within its rights in firing the lot of them for a start, if they tried to obstruct a sale. They won't want to be too difficult with you. They're all quite ordinary chaps, aren't they? I mean with wives and children and mortgages. They won't want to be on the streets if you take

59

over. They may be quite prepared to make a deal with you, especially if they can't get enough cash together. People who finance buy-outs expect to get them cheap. They may well not be prepared to pay as much as the company is worth to you.'

Matthew poured some more coffee and thought about it, conceding that the argument made sense. 'I've met Burwood. His father was a foreman joiner for my father. I could talk to him about coming in with us. I could use him somewhere.'

'But not as chief executive,' Michaels said, irrepressibly.

'No. I've got one of them. See what you mean. He might not want to come, cocky bugger.'

Andy stirred. 'I wonder if it isn't a little early to open negotiations with Burwood, Matt? Gruhners will let us have a good look at the company as soon as they've got their papers together and you can see how bullish Burwood's feeling then. There's a long way to go on this one.'

Matthew Friern got up and walked about restlessly. 'Bloody wind,' he said, pushing up a slat of the venetian blind to peer out of the window. 'We'll lose the day on that site. So will Prior, of course, with any luck. Why don't I skip the NEB and go and see Winstanley direct and offer him a good price – say ten per cent above the odds in return for an exclusive for two months or so?'

Andy looked doubtful. 'I tried that on Fieldman, delicately. He wasn't encouraging. No harm you trying it on Winstanley, though; he was a businessman, he might buy it.'

'I'll do that.' Matthew was pacing the room, a big man, discharging energy and tension, and Andy shook his head slightly at his junior, who was poised for action.

Matthew swung round and considered them sardonically. 'I'm going to send you to one of the other sites – the wind has stopped the crane here. We'll lend you some clothes.'

Andy, who had thought he was wearing his site-visiting suit, looked mildly surprised but assented. Matthew's finance director, a square Yorkshireman, whose eyes had never shifted from the papers in John Michaels' hand, cleared his throat hopefully.

'This is very much a first shot, you understand, without having seen the site,' John Michaels said, clasping the papers to him and the corners of Andy's mouth tightened. 'I am sure Matt and George understand that. I'd like, however, to talk the whole thing through with you first.'

He collected his junior and found an opportunity to say while they were being fitted out with safety footwear – huge, welted boots – and donkey jackets, that he never liked to leave papers with a client unless they had been discussed first; against that background it was of course better not to reveal the existence of the papers unless and until a discussion could be held.

The younger man turned pink, but stood his ground. 'I thought they might be pleased to know we'd done some work.'

'We aren't paid to do *work*, John. We're paid to think. *Accountants* produce papers.'

Michaels, who had trained as an accountant wilted, but noted the point. He had fought for the opportunity to work with Andrew Eames Lewis, who was a known personality in the City, in line to be the next head of

Corporate Finance at Walzheims, and he was going to use it. The man was an arrogant bastard but he was a star and could teach him a lot. He gritted his teeth and consigned the papers, over which he and a team had worked long and late, to his briefcase.

That evening, having left his bankers at King's Cross, Matthew was eating stylishly with his wife in Thomas's, Lucy's looks and familiarity with the establishment having secured them a very good table. The place was quieter than usual, because Thomas himself was absent; Lucy was herself fond of him and usually found him vastly entertaining, but Matthew detested him and was here this evening only on her assurance that the boss himself was having a night off. Lucy had stopped to kiss several friends on the way in, and was feeling pleased with herself. Her husband waited patiently while she settled at the table and they ordered the meal. 'And we'll have a bottle of the Chablis, please, while we're waiting,' he said, and added, not bothering to drop his voice, that he always had plenty of time to get through a bottle while waiting to get something to eat at this place.

'Have a breadstick, darling,' Lucy said, firmly, smiling on the departing waiter. 'It'll keep you going. It's nice to have dinner with you, by ourselves for once, so don't complain.'

He smiled at her, charmed by her as always. 'You're looking very good.' So she was, he thought, noting the way the eyes of men and women alike were drawn to her: a vision of sleek elegance with the black hair swept back and up, and a pale cream silk dress that had undoubtedly cost him a lot of money.

'Do you want to talk about Corsica? We ought to – I know it's early but if we don't get the flight booked now we always seem to end up having to stop the night in Lyons.' She sounded unhopeful and Matthew grunted. This was an old battle; he hated going away and could never be persuaded to make arrangements in advance, preferring to be dragged away reluctantly at the last minute.

'You book for yourself and the boys and leave me to book separately when I know what I'm doing,' he suggested, and drew a withering look from his wife.

'Absolutely not. I was stuck on that bloody island with Nanny and the boys and two of their little friends for two weeks while you hung on in Dorrington. *Then* you got very angry when I had to go home with the boys at the end of the third week. And you were even more furious when you could only get a first-class ticket home. We're not doing *that* again.' She lit a cigarette and stared crossly at a table in the opposite corner of the room, her expression changing as she recognized its occupants.

'Will you sit *down*, Lucy. I do have something I want to talk about which has nothing to do with Corsica.'

She stiffened, and didn't look at him for a moment, confirming that as he had half guessed, she was up to something. He was not himself faithful to her, and had recognized when marrying the beautiful Lucy Lindfield that he might have a bit to put up with, but he did not accept anything that really inconvenienced him in the line of extra-marital activity on her part. He put up with all the carry-on, because he didn't feel it mattered much; they were basically well suited, particularly in bed where she always gave him a good time, no matter what else was happening. Indeed perhaps a better time because of her outside activities. 'I want you to understand how important buying Prior is for us,' he said, watching her sit up and sparkle with relief. 'I need to buy that company.'

She gave him her full attention, ignoring a smile and half movement in her direction from two men arriving at the other side of the room. Her husband did not often consult her on matters of business, but she was her father's daughter as well as being extremely intelligent and she usually got to hear about the key decisions.

'It's not all that big, is it, Matt?'

'Oh, it's big enough. About £300m turnover. That'd bring us up over the billion mark, take us to about £1.2bn. That's important in itself. But it's what it does that matters.'

Lucy nodded; she had been listening to conversations which went like this since she was a child. 'But we've got system-building sites too, Matt?'

'That system is going to be a winner. I know they've had a job to get it working but it's a gem.' He considered her. 'You know that the factory is even more important than the site with these systems.'

'Well, of course, it is. If it's not properly made you can't fit it together quickly. Like those kitchen cabinets Caro and I bought when we were sharing a flat after university. They would not fit – we had to get a carpenter in the end, and it cost a fortune.'

'That's right. That's the point. Mind you,' he added, sidetracked, 'you and Caro were trying to put that joinery together with the back of a knife and a bent can-opener, as I remember.'

'It *said* "Easy to assemble".' Lucy was somewhere between amused and ruffled at the memory and he smiled at her with affection.

'So the factory's very important – the stuff's better designed than ours for a start, and those Danes they got over have really made that factory produce. I mean we're trying but it'll take some time between eighteen months and never to get to their standards. They're already taking contracts off us *and* making a decent profit on them. They could kill that bit of our business.'

Lucy frowned at him in concentration. 'But, darling, weren't they making awful losses? I mean isn't that why the NEB rescued them?'

'Quite right.' He was impressed but not unbearably surprised to find her well informed; for all she was bored by the north-east she was very much part of that society and not much gossip got past her. 'But they're doing bloody well now, and with our contacts they'd clean up. The NEB don't know much about building and the chaps they've got running that company don't know anyone outside Dorrington.' He watched her to see if she had got the point, but she did not speak for a moment.

'The NEB own lots of companies, don't they?' Lucy had finished her smoked salmon and was washing it down with white wine and a piece of bread, and her husband reflected that the best thing about her was that she had all the appetites.

He watched her, eyes slightly narrowed, remembering with pleasure that they would for once be back at the flat in good time. He was getting on a bit for having the kind of rousing good fuck they both liked, if he had to start past midnight and be at work at 8 a.m. as usual.

'Yes, they do,' he said, turning back to the business in hand. 'And they've got a load of accountants and civil servants – no one who knows anything – sitting in an office in *London*.'

Lucy reflected with annoyance that he managed to make London sound like Clermont-Ferrand or Buxtehude, but he was right, of course. A young man sent up from London would never get inside the tight-knit local society, would never be accepted into the innermost cabals by local businessmen, their friends, sons and associates.

'When I get the company, I'm going to take it outside the north-east – no reason it shouldn't run sites in the Midlands or the south. That factory is only on single shift – it can go to two shifts and double its output easily. I know how to get the jobs for them.' He paused to make sure his wife was still paying attention to him but she was listening carefully. 'If we can do that, then it starts to make sense to buy a bigger flat here or perhaps even a house. I'll be here more and we'll need to do more entertaining. You'd like that.'

'Yes, I would.' Lucy had been trying to persuade her husband to buy a larger London place for years, and having Matt more often in London would not constrain her unduly; he spent all day in an office anyway. 'Matthew,' she said, firmly, chasing her original train of thought. 'The NEB owns lots of companies – I mean, I was at that boring conference and I did listen to that bit. And the Minister did say he wanted to get them back into the private sector quickly.' Matthew nodded, crunching on a breadstick. 'Well, if that's what he wants, why couldn't you offer to buy all the construction companies? I thought there were five of them.'

'There are.' He looked at her, thoughtfully. 'You were listening, weren't you? But two of them are dogs, and I don't really need the two respectable ones either. It's Prior we want.'

Lucy dimpled prettily at the waiter, who was refilling her glass, and waited for him to go. 'Could you sell off the ones you didn't want?' She watched her husband, whose eyes were fixed on an inoffensive vase of flowers on the table with an intense, slightly cross-eyed stare.

'I could,' he said, slowly. 'At least the two other profitable ones. Tomorrow. I know who wants them. And the NEB could keep the two dogs or give me the cash to close them. Lot of hassle, though, but we could get Prior cheap if we took that lot on.'

He was no longer talking to her, Lucy understood, unoffended, but away in contemplation of the difficulties, and she waited, sipping her drink, for him to emerge.

'You're more use than bloody Walzheims, you know,' he said, emerging, and she smiled at him.

'Well, Andy can do all the hassling for you, can't he? I mean he can handle the sales.'

'That's right.' Matthew straightened his back and looked around for a waiter. 'I don't know if he'll be able to handle the politics, though.'

'Well, I might be able to help,' Lucy pointed out, gently. 'What can I do?'

Her husband considered her. 'You can get next to Winstanley.'

'*Right* next to him?' She smiled at him over her wine glass.

'Might be worth it for this company. No. I didn't mean that.'

'I expect I can find a way.' She hesitated. 'We do know the top civil servant of course, Clive Fieldman.'

'He'll not be making the decision.' Matthew dismissed him from consideration but his wife persevered.

'No, of course, he won't, Matt, but he will be advising on how to get to the decision. I mean he'll be telling ministers they ought to be putting this company out to open tender, which we don't want, do we? We want to go for a negotiated contract which would be better for us.'

Matthew noted with pleasure the use of the words 'we' and 'us'. For far too much of the time the problems of the business were nothing to do with his lady wife, indeed seemed to be manufactured by him specifically to harass her or prevent her going to London. Ah well, a bit more time here would be a small price to pay if Lucy were going to use her considerable intelligence and ingenuity in the interests of the business.

'Yes, you're right. Since Clive's an old mate of yours, you could ask him to dinner with his wife, couldn't you?'

'He's divorced.' Her husband looked at her sharply, but she went on unbothered. 'I'll find him someone. Well, what about Caro? We were all trained together and she was very pleased to see him at that conference you made me go to.'

'I suppose Caroline would be all right.'

Matthew had never been very keen on Caroline, but then men were always a bit uneasy with their wives' best girlfriends, she thought.

'Well, now you know why I asked you to go to the conference. Got bloody good value for it.' He beamed at her.

'Yes. It *was* boring, though.'

'You're a good girl. A very good girl. I'll buy you a treat. What would you like?'

'That Elisabeth Blackadder picture.' She had not even paused to think, he realized; he'd walked into that one. 'We won't lose on it, Matt – she's getting very fashionable. And she is a very good painter.'

'OK.' What was it going to cost, he wondered? 'All right, you can get it tomorrow.'

'Can I call Charles tonight? I've got his home number – I just want to make sure I get it.'

He considered her, grinning. 'Afterwards.'

'You're a greedy sod.'

'But you like it.'

'That's right.'

4

At the Department of the Environment, on Thursday of the week afterwards, it was a calm, clear day, free of the wind which had been disrupting Prior Building Systems' and Friern's sites. The atmosphere in Winstanley's spacious office was more tranquil as well, though not without its tensions. Six men were gathered around a table, John Winstanley at the head of it, with his private secretary, an experienced principal in his early thirties, to take the note. Richard Watts, the new head of corporate finance at S. W. Fredericks, a merchant bank which with over a hundred years of trading in the City of London considered themselves much too grand to make any reference to their main line of business in the title of the firm, and his junior, a fellow director, sat on the Minister's right. Next to the Minister on the other side sat Clive Fieldman and the assistant secretary, James Mather, who would be involved on a day-to-day basis in any sale.

The Minister was exercising himself automatically to be liked and to have the meeting go smoothly, even though everyone else in the room was a paid adviser, but the three civil servants were watchful and noncommittal, retaining some sense of who was paying for what. Richard Watts, who, like all successful corporate finance advisers, was sensitive to the most subtle currents of feeling, was very conscious of the need to judge Clive Fieldman's reactions. His fellow director had been urgently directed to watch the civil servants, see what they did, and not, of course, to speak; this in sharp contrast to the civil service pattern, where the most junior officer present at a meeting is expected to contribute.

Clive Fieldman, sharply sensitive himself, understood very well what was happening and was amused. Something to be said for this principle; it did mean there was one man on the team who, freed from the pleasures and responsibilities of getting his mouth open, could observe what was going on beneath the words. He sat back, deciding that he would let his minister and James Mather carry the meeting while he watched, thereby neatly inverting the command structure, and, he hoped, confusing the Fredericks team.

Richard Watts had opened the batting. 'Minister, you asked us to value these five companies and to advise on their return to the private sector; this we have done, but I wanted to talk through our views with you and your advisers before we produced a formal report.'

Which might contain some piece of advice that absolutely did not suit us, Clive thought, fascinated, as Watts continued. 'These five companies are very different from each other, Minister, as you know. Two of them – O'Brien Limited and Davecat Limited – are making losses which seem to be increasing steadily. Both are specialist suppliers to builders and civil engineers. O'Brien, of course, is a plant rental firm and Davecat a manufacturer and supplier of fitted kitchens.'

'Davecat? Funny name.'

Richard Watts looked blank, and Clive stirred. 'Combines the names of the proprietor and his wife, Minister.'

'Oh, I see.' New horizons were obviously opening up for Winstanley.

71

Richard waited to see if anyone had any other contributions before going on. 'We can see no viable future for either of these, unless perhaps as part of a larger organization, but given the amount of debt in their balance sheet, we believe some restructuring would be needed before any sale would be possible.'

Clive hoped, silently, that Winstanley had retained enough from his briefing to translate this sentence. These companies had been loss-making before the NEB had taken them over and had gone into even more alarming decline since, as some over-hopeful accounting practices caught up with them. The NEB's credit was good enough for the banks to lend any amount to their wholly owned subsidiaries, but no one else was going to take these two on unless the NEB paid off most if not all the bank debt.

'Mm. And the other three?'

'All profitable in various degrees. Carrs and SLG are very profitable – for that sector – and we believe readily saleable as they stand. Indeed, we have identified the likely purchasers. Prior Building Systems, while profitable, may not be quite so readily saleable.'

'That is the one with the loss-making contracts in it?'

'Yes, Minister. But one contract is complete and the other two will be completed within two and a half years. Without them the NEB consider that the company is potentially highly profitable.'

'But it can be sold now, surely. I met a builder the other day who wants it: Sir Matthew Friern.'

'Indeed?' Richard, who had been told by Clive about Friern, registered cautious interest. 'Well, that is very useful to know, Minister. And yes, indeed, the company is saleable now, but I understand that my colleagues at

Gruhners are advising the NEB that the company could be worth substantially more in two years' time.'

'We're not waiting two years,' Winstanley said, sharply, and the whole table considered him with careful attention. 'No way. I have told the Prime Minister that we are getting *on* with this, at once. And as quickly as possible.'

Richard looked carefully round him at the civil servants and, getting no help, took a deep breath. 'In which case, Minister, we will have to try to find a way of reflecting what the NEB believe to be Prior's potential value in any sale.'

'Yes,' Winstanley said, definitively.

Ah well, Clive thought, so now we know. It really is sale time. This lot *had* absorbed the lesson that if you wanted anything done you had to do it at once, right at the start, regardless of problems placed in your way. Richard was of course treating the Minister as a client, whose views must be deferred to, whereas the civil service, allegedly there to serve ministers, never managed quite to behave like this; you told ministers what was what, and then slowly adjusted policy here and there to accommodate their party-political prejudices. But the whole idea of tailoring advice or, worse yet, policy to accommodate what a minister wanted to do was alien. Clive, who had watched Labour ministers worn down by the civil service treatment, invariably courteous but in a crunch starkly and effectively hostile, felt a sharp surge of excitement. It was a pity this lot wasn't the party he had been brought up to, but good luck to anyone who could bend a core institution of English society like the civil service to carry out a policy they disliked.

73

'So.' Winstanley had taken charge of the meeting. 'How do we get this lot back into the private sector as quickly as possible? Why can't the NEB float the whole lot on the stock market?'

Clive sat passively, knowing that his man was going to be disappointed. What Winstanley had in mind was presumably the recent publicity attendant on the sale of Amersham International, with a lucky colleague grinning from a platform at the City press, surrounded by merchant-bank advisers and pretty girls handing out application forms for shares. And pages of admiring coverage in the Sunday press. Clive and James, however, had talked to several firms of merchant bankers as part of the selection process before recommending Fredericks to Winstanley, and had told him that no one was going to be prepared unequivocally to recommend a flotation. But, obviously, he did not wish to believe his brief; well, let these highly paid bankers now earn their exorbitant fees.

He watched Richard think and was mildly impressed; very few people are prepared to leave a pause while they think their way through a point.

'The short answer, Minister, is that, even with a restructured set of balance sheets – which would mean writing off some of the debt – any flotation would be extremely difficult. This is a very mixed bag: they don't service the same customers – they're really all in different branches of the building trade. There is, in short, no synergy. And the financial state of each company is different.'

He hesitated, watching Winstanley, waiting to see, Clive realized, whether the Minister really wanted to go down this route, in which case the Fredericks team would plainly try to oblige.

'Is what you mean that we – the NEB that is – might not get the best price if they tried to float?'

'I would have to say, Minister, that they might not get this lot away at all without substantial incentives for investors, and I am sure that the NEB advisers would take that line.'

They'd have to be given away with a pound of tea, but you want us to go and take on the NEB's advisers, we'll do it, anything for a client, Clive translated to himself. He looked up to find the junior Fredericks man's eyes fixed on him and returned to contemplation of his papers. By the time they got these companies sold the fees would be astronomical. The NEB, recognizing *force majeure*, had put their merchant-bank advisers in place immediately after they had been told to liquidate their holdings. Both government departments involved with the NEB had, at first, been reluctant to add another layer to the structure, but both, after consultation with each other, had concluded that their ministers would be vulnerable without the same sort of advice in place as the NEB had available to it. 'It's a question of fighting fire with fire, isn't it?' Clive's equivalent in the DTI had said, wearily. 'No one, least of all the Public Accounts Committee, as presently constituted, is going to accept that mere civil servants can hold their own against highly paid merchant bankers.' And given the new Conservative administration's general antagonism to civil servants and their continual public statements about the need to have fewer of them, it had seemed to experienced men that expensive advisers had better be appointed as a protection for the departments, never mind the ministers involved.

'Mm. Well, all right. What about selling all five of them as a package to a trade purchaser?'

Richard Watts fished out another piece of paper. 'The same objection applies: they are a very mixed bag, Minister, as I said. We found it difficult to think of anyone who would want all of them.'

'Could we put the group out to tender?' Clive Fieldman, who had told Winstanley unequivocally that this route was unlikely to be recommended, watched Watts unblinkingly, interested to see how far he would go to try to meet a client's wishes.

'It would, I believe, have to be a restricted version of this procedure,' Richard said, after another impressive pause. 'You see, Minister, if you are selling a jewel you put out a memorandum of sale and sit back and watch purchasers scramble. But these companies aren't in that class. So I have to say this could be a very risky strategy, and you may end up with no purchaser at all and the market soured. What you need here is to find the right purchaser, one who understands the difficulties and won't resile at the last moment, when he gets close up to some of the problems.'

'So find one purchaser and negotiate with him?' Winstanley sounded doubtful.

'That is very often done, Minister, with a difficult sale. We, or rather the NEB's advisers, Gruhners, would put out a rather – well, limited memorandum of sale, the aim being to identify, say, three groups who can be offered a lot more information than one would put in a normal memorandum and then to negotiate a deal with one of them.' He hesitated, watching Winstanley carefully. 'I'm describing an ideal, of course, but in this case I do believe we are looking for a special purchaser – by whatever route.'

Well done, my lad, Clive applauded silently, and you

can form up and explain all that to the Public Accounts Committee in two years' time, when this minister will have moved on and it will be thee and me, two Christians in the lions' den, armed with a toasting fork apiece.

'Well that sounds right,' Winstanley said hopefully and Clive braced himself to destroy the general air of accord and progress. 'I think, Minister, that you will need to be advised on the effect on the price the NEB would get from selling these companies as a group, as opposed to separately. I take it that you have done a valuation on that basis, Richard?'

Richard shuffled papers, unhurriedly, and considered the single sheet he had. 'We value Davecat and O'Brien negatively, Carrs at about £70m, SLG at £40m and Prior at anywhere between £50m and £90m, depending on your view of the contract renegotiations and the company's forecasts.'

'Given that Davecat and O'Brien have £30m of debt which will have to be paid off, this values the group at £160m to £200m, Richard – right?'

Clive intervened in order that Winstanley should have time to think. 'It's a very wide range.'

The banker nodded. 'Yes.'

And anyone buying a package like that would expect to get it at the lower end of the range, which could leave me and my man explaining to the Public Accounts Committee the reason why the NEB got perhaps £40m less than it could have if it had sold the companies separately, Clive thought. He looked sideways at Winstanley, who was looking cross and thoughtful. 'Prior is the problem company, then, from a valuation point of view,' he suggested. 'And that, basically, is because they are

77

still working through some intrinsically unprofitable contracts.'

'That is entirely right,' Richard said, promptly.

'Could the company not repudiate these contracts? Where did they come from, Clive?' Winstanley was sounding censorious, and Clive stiffened, then consciously relaxed. No point in being paranoid even if this administration believed the civil servants were responsible for every idiocy committed by any organization in the last ten years.

'Prior, which was, of course, a private company at that time, took on three contracts in 1976 to build 700 units for the local authority, at what they thought to be a rock bottom price, but one on which they hoped a profit could be made. One of the problems, as I understand it, was that the particular system, which is Danish, did not actually conform to local building regulations.'

'Oh,' Winstanley said, blankly.

Clive decided not to bother him with the detail. 'So by the time the whole design had been altered to take account of local requirements, much of the advantage both of cash and ease of erection had been lost. Although some renegotiation to take account of the change was achieved, the company struggled and ran out of cash in 1978.'

'A most unfortunate history,' Richard said, smoothly, into a silence no one else seemed inclined to break, and Winstanley nodded, smugly.

Clive decided he had better go on. 'Indeed. They have now overcome these difficulties and have good, profitable contracts not only in the north-east but over the border as well.' See list in brief if having forgotten or not believing me, he thought, irritably.

'So there might be lots of companies who would like to buy Prior,' Winstanley said directly to Richard, not making it a question.

'Well.' The banker was impressively unflustered by the *faux-naïf* technique. 'Not exactly. However well they are doing now, the technology is still new, and the track record isn't impressive. It is a different management from three years ago, but it all comes from inside the company and may not carry much credibility outside. It isn't exactly a jewel in the NEB's crown.'

'But saleable.'

'Oh, yes. Indeed apart from Friern's who as you know are based in Dorrington, Shaws have indicated an interest. And so have the management, on behalf of themselves and the employees.'

'That I also knew.' Winstanley was sounding irritated and his advisers fell silent. So there it was, Clive thought, there you have it, Minister. We probably can sell this lot as a package but it'll be a special purchaser and you can't get such a good price that way, because you have a real problem with Prior Systems.

'Mm,' Winstanley said, crossly, into the respectful silence. 'So it looks as if the thing to do is close the two duff ones and sell the others separately. By tender. How long will all *that* take?'

Richard Watts just managed not to imply that Gruhners and the NEB would take a great deal longer than Fredericks and the DoE, and said, regretfully, 'Well, if started tomorrow the process could take nine months to a year, start to finish.'

Clive watched Winstanley looking sulky, as his hope of a quick, politically attractive fix ebbed.

'Not a lot more we can do today, then?' Winstanley

looked up at the clock. The bankers, acutely sensitive to atmosphere, were already rising to go, murmuring graceful farewells as the private secretary escorted them out. Clive remained behind, as always, in case the Minister wanted anything done.

'I didn't think we could get very far today,' Winstanley said, fretfully. He hesitated, and Clive waited, knowing there was something to come. 'I like the idea of negotiating a sale of the whole lot as a package, Clive. It's got its merits.'

'Oh, indeed it has. I'm just sorry it doesn't seem to be the best route.'

He gazed reflectively down at the street, seventeen floors below, and Winstanley came and stood beside him. A substantial blue Jaguar was waiting on a single yellow line and as they watched two small foreshortened figures hurried up to it, and a uniformed driver hastily got out and held the back door open.

'*They*'re working for *us*,' Clive said, drily, and Winstanley laughed. 'Better car than I get.'

'They get more money, too,' Clive pointed out.

'About six times more than me, or at least Watts does. I asked his boss at dinner last night. I don't know why we do it.'

At seven o'clock that evening Caroline looked up with a start as her taxi swung into King's Cross, skirting the hotel car park and double-parked by the side entrance to the station.

'Hang on a second,' she said, stuffing papers back into her briefcase. 'Hadn't realized we'd got here.'

'Take your time, Mrs Whitehouse.' The driver was watching a badly driven Jaguar doing a three-point turn perilously close to the taxi's paintwork and Caroline peered at his image reflected in the driving-mirror. He did look familiar, but she had been driven by Computer Cab drivers for years. 'How are you?' she asked, not wishing to be unfriendly, and he smiled at her forgivingly. 'I drove you the other day when you were coming from St Margaret's with your lad. I took him home for you.'

'So you did. I'm sorry, that was such an awful day, I've managed to forget all the details.' She had got her papers under control and was scooping up her coat and overnight bag. She crawled out of the taxi inelegantly, balancing her possessions, and put everything down on the pavement to put on her coat.

'You left a newspaper, Mrs Whitehouse. And an umbrella.'

'Oh, Christ! Sorry.' She rescued both, waved the driver away with thanks and glanced at her watch. Five minutes to the train, but as usual she had her ticket, tucked into her handbag or somewhere. She had never managed to look poised and unflustered travelling; for her as for most working women, who are also mothers, leaving home, even for the night, required many small, patient, detailed adjustments. As a result she always seemed to arrive at a station or an airport scrabbling in her handbag, mind distracted by sudden recollections about the school trip, notes to form master, prep and daily help. She had once found herself on a plane, bound for Manchester, gazing at a British Midland dinner without the slightest recollection of how she had got there, so occupied had she been with arrangements.

She went through the barrier with only a minute to spare and swung into the first carriage, turning to pull in the door.

'Don't shut it!' A tall man was running from the barrier and as she stepped hastily away from the door he swung himself on to the train with the all-in-one easy movement of a good athlete, reached out and slammed the door after him. He then leaned out to wave and smile at someone on the platform.

'Nice chap,' he said, conversationally, to Caroline, who had picked up her case. 'Let me through without a ticket.' He sounded pleased, but just faintly smug, she thought, as if it was in some way his due. She looked at him, consideringly; he was tall, very attractive, his dark brown curly hair cut very short, eyes narrowed as he looked back at her, not wearing a coat over his suit despite the weather. The face was definitely familiar, but she couldn't remember where she had seen him before. Probably a fellow lawyer, she decided, it would come to her presently. She picked her way through the first carriage till she found her reserved seat, dropped her briefcase, overnight bag and coat on it and, disencumbered, made for the dining-car. It was almost a four-hour journey; she could at least get some supper, and she needed a break before starting on the next lot of papers. She sat down at a table for two and fished out the evening paper, promising herself one drink with the meal, guiltily conscious of the relief of not having to deal with Timmy's maths prep, Susannah's violin practice or Francis's spelling. She read the City pages while waiting for the whisky she had ordered, then sipped at it luxuriously while she read the cartoons and her horoscope which promised her success in a new enterprise. She raised her glass quietly to Prior Building Systems, and settled down to think about the way ahead, reaching into her bag for the pen and paper without which she never moved outside her office.

'Is anyone sitting here?'

She looked up from the pad, startled. 'No, sorry, do have it.'

It was the man who had run for the train, and she *had* seen him before if she could only remember where. A little older than she, he could be a partner in another firm. Or more likely a barrister. He had the assurance of someone used to appearing in public and the easy, chatty manner. He was using a lot more personality on the act of ordering a drink than she had ever felt necessary, and the attendant had rushed off beaming; the chap must be a regular on this train to get this treatment. He caught her eye.

'Gerry Willshaw,' he said, briskly, extending a hand across the table and causing her to drop her paper in a courteous attempt to reciprocate.

'Caroline Whitehouse,' she said, equally briskly, hoping for inspiration.

'Here you go, Mr Willshaw.' The attendant put his whisky down carefully and smiled at him. 'Saw you on TV yesterday.'

Not an actor, surely, she thought, watching the tight lines at the edge of the wide mouth – an actor's fluency, yes, but too calculating, too decisive.

'What's that Robin Day *like*?' the attendant was asking, and Caroline, who, in an unacknowledged protest against her oldest brother, highly placed in Current Affairs at the BBC, rarely watched anything other than ITV, got the answer slowly. Gerry Willshaw was a politician of course, a junior Conservative minister. Indeed, good heavens, he was on her list of people the gentlemen of Prior Building Systems would need to know. He sat for the constituency next door, having wrested it at the election before last from a trade-union sponsored Labour MP, who had not spoken a word of sense or otherwise for fifteen years in the House, but had assumed that he could continue to command a majority of 7000 for ever.

The attendant retreated, beaming, and Willshaw turned to look at her. 'Can I get you another drink?'

'Thank you, no. I should either go to sleep or start swinging from the fixtures.'

'Ah. Well, I wouldn't want you to go to sleep.'

Quick, she thought, appreciatively. She had his full attention now and he was considering her with direct, concentrated interest. A *very* good-looking man, she thought, primly, in precisely her mother's phrasing, a little too conscious of it, but with enormous physical charm which had something to do with that restless energy that was keeping him fidgeting in his seat. Rather like her own family, she thought, in a sudden flash. Wide, mobile mouth, triangular, pointed chin, and straight nose, like her brothers' and her own, but instead of their blond hair and wide, blue eyes this one was dark with eyes between brown and green and narrowed under heavy brow bones.

'Are you going to Dorrington?' he asked.

'Yes. To see clients. I am a solicitor.'

'What sort of clients? I mean what sort of law do you do?'

'I'm a commercial lawyer. These clients run a building firm.'

'Which one? I'm in politics, my constituency covers part of Dorrington.'

'My clients are Prior Building Systems. Just outside your boundaries, I believe.'

84

'Yes, that's right. But some of my constituents work there.' He was still watching her, alight with interest. 'Are there many women commercial lawyers?'

'Not at partner level.' Caroline saw no reason to belittle her own achievement, particularly not to this audience. 'You could count us on the fingers of one hand.'

'Wouldn't even need to use all the fingers, I expect.' She laughed, taken aback and he grinned at her, openly pleased with himself. 'But the NEB own Prior, don't they?' he said.

'At the moment. The plan is to sell it back to the private sector along with everything else. Or isn't it?'

'Yes, absolutely. Do you disagree?' The directness of the approach took her by surprise and she had a moment's fleeting insight into how her own blunt tactics must often affect people.

'Not about Prior nor indeed anything the NEB holds, no. I've got my doubts about the natural monopolies, like Gas and Water and the Post Office.'

'Oh, I think we all have.' The response was automatic, and designed to carry an audience past a difficult point, and she watched him, interested. 'We would have to be very careful that consumer interests were safeguarded before deciding that those could be privatized.'

That 'we' is not just the Conservative Party, this is a man thinking forward to being top dog, she thought. Daughter of an ambitious man and sister to three ambitious brothers – however peculiar she felt their aspirations to be – she was on home ground here.

'What took you into politics?' she asked, and settled herself into a posture of admiring attention.

His eyes had never shifted from her face, she realized.

'I'd always been interested in politics. So after four-teen years in the army I decided to try it. I fought the first 1974 election in the constituency, and lost, but I cut into old Stan Flood's majority, and at the second election I took it away from him. Are you political?'

'No.' The negative came out a little too forcefully and he sat back a little. She sighed. 'Sorry. I have reasons. I come from a family which has for a long time been a major component of the Hampstead wing of the Labour Party.'

He leant forward again, amused and deeply interested. 'So we are on opposite sides?'

'That's not what I said.'

'Ah. Nor it was. Is Whitehouse the family name?'

'My maiden name was Henriques.'

'Ah. Well, I see. There *are* a lot of you, aren't there? Your father . . . would it be? Professor Michael Henriques came to lecture to us when I was at Staff College. On the politics of Thailand.'

'An uncle, not my father, who is called Sholto, and is a philosopher. Yes, there are a lot of us.'

'I have also heard your father speak. I thought him extraordinarily impressive. And, surely, I met another member of your family last night, on *Question Time*. The deputy head of Current Affairs. He joined us for supper and addressed the audience before we were thrown to them.'

'Jesus Christ!' Caroline put her glass down. '*Felix* did the warm-up? What did he give them? The Duties of the Public Broadcaster? Whither the BBC? Must have made their day, either way. He's my eldest brother.'

Gerry Willshaw was grinning at her. 'I didn't hear his speech. We were all clustered outside the studio, making nervous conversation, waiting to go on. But I did feel the audience was a bit cold and serious when we got there.'

'Bored rigid, I should think.' She smiled at him to find him still watching her, absolutely concentrated, and hurried nervously into speech: 'But what a minimalist explanation of why you went into politics. It runs, roughly, that having organized people in the Army you thought you'd go on doing it. And since the Labour Party is by definition not organizable it had to be the other lot.' She wondered if the whisky had been a mistake, and glanced nervously sideways to the table across the narrow aisle which was occupied by four solid businessmen, making serious inroads on British Rail's drinks and openly listening. The nearest man was hunched forward, waiting for his chance to get into the conversation.

'I'll tell you some time,' Gerry Willshaw said, calmly. 'Ah, food. Have some wine with me? With food you ought to be all right.'

'This is true.' She was adjusting to being gently man-oeuvred and to the implied promise for the future. She would have to watch what she drank, she thought, with an alarmed prickle of the nerves, and she was very conscious indeed of this man. She watched him deal briskly with the wine waiter and the man at the next table who had seized his moment to introduce himself, and to congratulate him on his *Question Time* appearance as a preliminary to his real business, which was to secure Willshaw to give away the prizes at his daughter's school next term. Willshaw put the same nervous force into whatever he was doing, whether being civil to a barman, or courteously and gracefully dealing with an invitation.

'Please do write to my constituency secretary either at home or at the House and I'll try to do it, but as I am sure you know I am not in control of my own life while the House is sitting.' He turned back to Caroline, having returned a satisfied customer to his own seat.

'Shall you do that prize-giving?' she asked quietly, uneasily aware that she was sounding a little like the Royal Family inquiring about the habits of whatever remote tribe they had been exposed to.

'If I can.' He poured her a glass of wine.

'Lot of voters in the audience?' She was aware she was needling, but he simply looked at her thoughtfully.

'Yes. And they'll tell me things, before, during or afterwards, about the school, or about their lives. That's what an MP is for.'

Caroline felt herself turning scarlet and put her glass down, realizing that she had deserved that. What was she doing being rude about someone else's treasured trade and particularly to a man she had just met? She found herself unable to speak, between shame and flaming anger at being so abruptly called to order. Long time since that happened to me, she thought, poise slowly restoring itself.

'Mrs Whitehouse?'

She looked up reluctantly, to see him watching her, concerned but unyielding.

'I'm sorry, I didn't mean to snub you like that.' He was speaking softly, pitching it carefully below the general background noise.

'It was entirely my fault,' she said, between her teeth. '*I*'m sorry. The Henriques clan does not cultivate constituents, it writes about policy, and discusses it, interminably, with each other, not with the voters.'

They looked at each other across the table and she felt suddenly slightly giddy.

'What does your husband do?'

She looked away. 'I am a widow. Ben was a barrister specializing in international law. He was killed in a plane crash coming home from a conference in Turkey, two years ago.'

'I remember it.' She sneaked a look at him and braced herself for any of the numerous wrong reactions to this carefully prepared statement: distress, embarrassment, pity, wariness, or the instant, hopeful flash of sexual interest that even the best men seemed unable to suppress at the use of the word 'widow'. She had learned to ignore, forgive, or work through these reactions, it was always a chill moment. But this man was doing none of that; his expression contained nothing but the most serious concern.

'And you have children?'

'Three. Timmy is twelve, Susannah ten and Francis eight. We were rather organized about it.' That, too, of course, was a prepared statement, complete with a joke to deflect any pity, distress or embarrassment that might be about, but Gerry Willshaw was not deflected.

'But that means you must be working inhumanly hard.'

That's right, of course, she thought, dully, contemplating her plate with its suddenly inedible square of British Rail pâté, right down to the choice of word: inhuman is what it is – work all day, accepting no quarter or comment, home to the kids, doing my best. No, that's not right. What is it the French say? *Je fais mon possible* – I do what is possible for me – and what is possible is to cope, to see they get to school and do their prep and get space to grow up, and soothe their nightmares. But what I cannot do often enough is to love them and nurture them in a human way. I always found it a strain even when Ben was here, God rest him, but without him to look after me I have not enough left for them. I'm too anxious and too lonely, and they want blood all the time, or that's how it seems to me. And I am not, absolutely not, going to cry in public on this train, because a stranger has found the right word. She took in a long slow breath and pulled her spine straight.

'I have a lot of help,' she said, dismissively. 'One of my sisters-in-law mixes my children with hers a lot to give me a break. And, of course, it is a long time since I did any cooking or ironing or cleaning, or anything like that.' She managed to look up at Gerry Willshaw, who met her eyes squarely, all that restless energy impressively stilled.

'But your job must be very demanding?'

'I had just been made a partner when Ben was killed.' It was always much easier to talk about work. 'And once you are a partner in a big firm, keen young men do the running about and the late nights for you. I've done very little of that in the last two years.'

'But you're here, travelling to meet a client.'

'A very rare honour for them, as they do not yet know. I just need to see their place of work in order to understand what I'm being told. But I need only do it once, I expect.'

The attendant was hovering, looking inquiringly at her uneaten pâté, but a lifelong prohibition of waste in any form caused her to wave him away and eat fast, without tasting what was in her mouth. Gerry Willshaw was still according her his unbroken attention, and she found herself able to consider him in return.

'What about you? Does your wife have a job?'

'Well, she looks after me and three children, and a constituency,' he said drily.

'That's a full-time job,' Caroline acknowledged. 'How old are the children?'

'A little older than yours. Peter is seventeen, Mickey fourteen, Miranda ten.' He hesitated. 'I would have liked a fourth but there never seemed to be the right moment.'

Caroline allowed herself to wonder, fleetingly, how his wife had felt about the matter. 'We meant to have four but I weakened.'

'I find that difficult to believe.' The wide mouth quirked, and she ducked her head in reluctant acknowledgement. Exhausted as she had been by having three under five and trying to work four days a week she would have gone on; it had of course been Ben who also wanted another child but had seen that she and the whole household were appallingly overstretched and had held back. She had been the leader in their partnership, restless, clever and driving, but he had always known how to stop her from plunging them all into disaster. When she had said they should go on, he had agreed that a fourth child would be splendid but only if she could bring herself to stop work altogether for a few years. It had taken her, she recalled wryly, about twenty minutes to decide not to go on. And just as well now; what would she have done with four children and no partnership? Something else – and it might have worked out better for the children and you in the long run, a tiny voice inside her head suggested, and she returned hastily to the present and the offered plate of Sole Colbert.

'Who was Colbert?' Gerry Willshaw asked her, evidently deciding to move off the subject of personal history.

'Louis XIV's Finance Minister. He inherited him from his mum.' She took a bite. 'I can't remember if this is what it is supposed to taste like.'

'Did you do History at University?'

'No, Law.' She glanced at him and realized he was looking very slightly discouraged. 'My good school was pretty insistent on culture. We did a lot of that sort of thing. You presumably went to Sandhurst and learned to draw maps and fire guns instead.'

'Yes I did, but actually I expect you *are* very clever.'

Oh dear, she thought, rather a lowering of the standard of this conversation, then realized that he was sounding wistful. Well, presumably, the most academic boys did not go into the regular army; how would she know, the Henriques family being uniformly academic. She realized they had been talking so hard they were well behind the rest of the carriage with their dinner, and they both speeded up, refusing pudding.

'Dorrington in half an hour,' he said, as they drank coffee, sedately discussing the weather, both of them instinctively backing away from the intimacy of the earlier conversation.

As they got up to go back to their seats Caroline reminded herself that she needed to know this man and was finding a way to suggest that she might bring Peter Burwood to talk to him, when he turned in the space between the carriages.

'Do you have a card or something?'

'Of course.' She produced her business card, deeply thankful that she had remembered to replenish the case.

Half the time she found herself writing her name and the firm's on a piece torn out from her notebook, which never left her handbag, or taking a card off the other person and getting her secretary to send hers the next day.

'I'll ring you,' he said, glancing at it.

'That would be nice. If you don't already know the Prior Systems' management perhaps you'd like to meet them?'

'I would. I'd also like to see you again.'

The speed and straightforwardness of the statement caught her by surprise and she glanced up at him to find he was watching her intently, the full power of his nervous energy concentrated on her. She wanted suddenly very much to touch him.

'I'd like that too,' she said as lightly as she could, getting her breath back, and watched his mouth relax.

'When are you back in the office? Monday? I usually come down very late on Sundays, when the House is sitting. I'll ring then. Good luck with tomorrow.' He touched her shoulder and was gone, and she watched him moving deftly through the crowded carriage.

5

Caroline Whitehouse woke in a hotel room in Dorrington, not knowing where she was, frightened, as she had often been as a child, but the anxiety eased as she recognized the hotel room. She'd had a bad night; childhood insomnia, which had slowly ebbed away over the years, had returned to plague her after Ben's death. She could always get off to sleep, but on bad nights would wake, sweating, and pursued by vague terrors at 3.30 a.m. on the dot, as if some invisible alarm had rung. In the first awful months after Ben had been killed she had confided this to the therapist who had been patiently dealing with Tim's nightmares. The woman had considered her carefully and said that her pattern of insomnia was depressive but not nearly as serious as that suffered by people who could not get off to sleep. 'Those people fear death, and are difficult to help. You have the normal depressive fears of loneliness; as the depression lifts you will sleep.' At the time she had told her coldly that she did not find this analysis helpful. She had, she now acknowledged, done the good woman an injustice; knowing that her insomnia was attached to depression had enabled her to deal with it efficiently. Instead of lying awake picking her life apart, she had learned to get up resignedly, after half an hour, and do some work. There was always work to be done, papers to write, bills to pay, and she was going to be at less than her best after a night with too little sleep anyway, but at least this way, however terrible she felt, she had several hours' start on the day. After a few days of this, sheer exhaustion would ensure her a night's sleep. And sometimes the gods relented, and after an hour's work she would find herself able to go back to bed again and sleep.

Last night had been such a night but she had got back to sleep very late which was why she felt as if she was coming up from the bottom of the sea. She closed her eyes again, guiltily, and woke up cursing and dry-mouthed, half an hour later, with only forty minutes to spare before her client picked her up. Still, a site visit was always easier to handle than a formal meeting because the client was more relaxed on his own ground.

She thought again of Gerry Willshaw, as she had in the hours of wakefulness in the night, trying to remember what he had looked like and the exact colour of his eyes. He was married, she reminded herself, and had been for a long time. She abandoned this line of thought uncomfortably and concentrated on stuffing nightdress, sponge-bag and yesterday's underwear and blouse into a bag.

She was sitting in the lobby when Peter Burwood came to collect her. He looked at home in his surroundings, stopping to greet a couple of men with the professional salesman's warm handshake, the left hand going round to clasp the other man's elbow. She rose as he came over and waited to see if she was going to get the handclasp treatment but he kissed her firmly, pleased to have negotiated a new social custom, but slightly embarrassed by the sideways looks he was getting from the contents of the hotel lobby. Evidently not much of a place for kissing people, Dorrington.

He escorted her to a waiting car and driver, and they drove smartly to the site, parking the car behind a huge new building, essentially an enormous tin shed. Graham Gough and Martin Williams were there to meet them and she grinned at them with proprietary affection as she got out of the car. Martin was ten years older than she but with his thick dark head of hair still intact, stocky and solid, a clever one as she had established, a brilliant engineer, who had channelled that gift into the design and layout of a factory process. Graham, the finance director, tall and red-headed, who still looked like the county-class swimmer he had been, and whose measure she had not yet got, was a newcomer to the company, having joined less than a year ago. She had checked up on him automatically; a quiet chat with an old friend in the big firm that audited Prior's accounts had given him a glowing reference. Both men broke into answering smiles and Martin plunged forward resolutely and kissed her. Graham hung back, extending a hand, but she stood on her toes to kiss his cheek. He reddened, embarrassed but pleased, and she mentally congratulated herself. He had wanted to be treated the same as the other two who had worked together for years, but had been having difficulty stating his demands. It had been the thoughtful, clever, observant Ben, always a little detached from his surroundings, who had taught her to observe such things, and she was much the better off and more effective for it. Oh Ben, she thought, stabbed suddenly by a longing for him, then looked back at the three men watching her expectantly, banished the memory and took Peter's offered hand to help her over the rough ground.

They headed into a Portakabin, divided into small cramped offices, papers covering every inch of the walls of each little cubicle that they passed, and stopped at the corner office which contained a table large enough for six people to sit down, and in which the paper was all pinned tidily to the walls, in the form of charts, drawings, programmes in various colours with scratchy pencil amendments.

'Martin and I will take you round the site,' Peter said, firmly. 'Graham wants to spend time with the site accountant.'

'Explain the layout to her here, Peter, so we can all get our sixpenceworth in first,' Martin, older and craftier than the other two, suggested, and passed the coffee round the table.

'I don't know how much background Caroline has,' Peter started, dourly, and Caroline sighed, inwardly. Peter, for all that he had picked her out of the pack, obviously still had trouble with women.

'Why not give me the idiot's guide?' Peter, arms still folded, defensively considered her from across the room, then abruptly unhooked himself from the wall against which he was leaning. 'Right, come over here.' He unrolled a chart and Caroline joined him promptly. 'The whole of this job is about getting the right bits here at the right time, and putting them up at the right speed. The bits come from our own factory – we'll go there after lunch.'

'Fine.'

'Well, the idea is that the big pieces – that's the walls and floors – arrive on a transporter and we take them off the transporter and put them up, with a crane.'

'I see.'

'Well, that goes wrong for a start,' he said, triumphantly.

'I was just unkindly thinking that it must,' she agreed, unperturbed, 'life being what it is. So you keep a stock.'

'We take the smaller bits out of stock anyway. It's the big bits that are the problem. It costs more to handle them twice, take them off the flatbed, pile them, pick them up again. It's crane time, you see – you can't handle these any other way. So we work straight off the transporter as much as we can.' He gestured out of the window and she gave an involuntary 'Ah' as the crane wires tightened and a panel rose from a long, low lorry into the cold January air and was then winched up fifty feet and swung across into place. She watched, entranced, as the panel moved slowly towards a waiting three-man team, who placed it, unleashed the chains and cast them out into the air again.

'We can, if everything goes right, get a storey up ready for final fixing every three days,' Peter said. 'Mind you, we depend on the factory; they can only just keep up. But we've had bad weather up here, we've been taking five days a storey, so they're well up with us, and we've got a pile of panels waiting there.'

'What rate do you price on?'

All three men exchanged glances.

'This contract was priced on three days,' Graham said, evenly.

'Really?' Caroline turned to look at him.

'This is an old one and we're still negotiating. We're competitive with anyone on five days. We average four on the sites at the moment, but we aren't telling too many people that.'

Caroline considered her clients and decided that there was a time and a place and this was neither. 'OK,' she said, briskly, 'I've got the basic principle, and I'll probably pick up enough of the refinements as we go round.' She smiled at Peter, who was looking doubtfully at her suit and high-heeled shoes. 'I always turn up looking respectable, but I've got jeans with me and wellingtons, and I can see it's a hard-hat site.'

Peter grinned back and gave her to his secretary, returning to gaze wordlessly at his colleagues.

'That is a very smart lady, Peter.'

'Got straight on to the pricing, didn't she?' Graham observed.

'I checked her out before we hired her. I told you. She's one of the best commercial lawyers in the City.'

'Too pretty for it,' Martin said.

'I don't think of her like that at all,' Peter said, surprised. 'I mean I suppose she's good-looking, but she might as well be a bloke.'

His colleagues were looking at him incredulously, when the door opened and a vision in heavy site-overalls appeared, swamped by a vast duffle coat with 'PRIOR VISITOR' written in large red capital letters on the back which came down to her ankles. A white helmet, also labelled, was jammed well down over the forehead.

'Peter,' the apparition observed, 'this *is* the only visitors' site kit apparently. What comes round this site, Martians?'

'That helmet adjusts,' Martin said, starting to laugh and going to help her, so that by the time she had been redressed, all lingering constraint was thoroughly banished, and she and the group were chatting like old friends as they went outside in the bracing February air.

'This crew is going straight through the first fixing,' Peter said, waving a hand at the six men working on various bits of the structure. 'That's wiring for electricity, inside piping. It's electric central heating of course.'

'Bloody expensive to run. It's gas country here isn't it?'

Martin sighed. 'You've put your finger right on it but this system's designed for electricity.'

'*Our* customers here want gas because it's cheaper to run and when we didn't know so much about this system we tried to redesign it for them. That destroyed all the economies in the manufacture, as we saw quite quickly, but the council has got firms willing to do anything to get work, so we had to try.' Martin had stopped in between two piles of concrete panels, hands moving in the air and struggling for words in remembered frustration, and Caroline watched him with sympathy.

'Is this the reason the early contracts lost money?' She directed the question to Peter and he sighed.

'One of them, yes. We have two contracts that still lose money. We've been trying to get a bit back but it's heartbreaking. Even going flat out all the time here we're only breaking even. And people like Friern and Shaw are ready to drop poison every time. That's not all they drop, either.' He stopped and looked at Martin. 'I maybe shouldn't be saying all this.'

'I do act for a civil engineer, so I know what you do to get a contract,' Caroline said, mildly. 'Tell me, what's happening here, after the plumbing and ducting goes in? We can talk about commercial issues later.'

Both men relaxed, being obviously uncomfortable with the subject, and took her on to the next block.

'They're working hard, aren't they?' she shouted in Peter's ear. 'No one even looks round.'

'They know I'm here,' he shouted back and she grinned into the upturned collar of her duffle coat. He was right, of course, it was like a lord of the manor. No one touched a forelock these days, of course, but maybe managing a big site gave you something akin to the pleasure a squire must have got from strolling among his haymakers, uttering encouraging words. Perhaps a slightly roseate vision she thought, as one of the beduffled, behelmeted, modern-day haymakers slid down a scaffold pole and advanced on Martin with a shouted, incomprehensible demand for information or help of some sort, which caused him to scowl and issue a complex set of orders.

'Buggeration factor?' she asked, the words falling into a sudden silence with embarrassing clarity.

'Where'd you learn that, Caroline?' he said, disapprovingly. 'Your civil-engineering client, I imagine. Now, look there. That's the electricians coming down after the plumbers, putting the wiring through ducts. Then you have the second fixers – they put up prefabricated wall panels over the whole lot. They've got holes cut for the ducting and the electric boxes, so once you've got them up, you're done – you've got a room. Bathrooms and kitchens are a bit different, but the whole issue's prefabricated in the factory and the second fixers put it in.'

Caroline watched, fascinated as men picked up panels from piles sitting in the middle of each floor and started to bolt them on.

'The crane brought these up?'

'Yes, that's right. Soon as you get the outside panels on and just before you swing the next floor up you bring the internal panels and fittings and ductings, and put them all in piles.'

'So everything has to arrive at the right moment.'

'Yes.'

'And it has to fit. Sorry, bear with me. If it doesn't fit then you have to fiddle about.'

'If it doesn't fit then you're into cost. I tell them to send it back so it doesn't happen again but they will try to adjust it.'

'Of course they do. They would in their own houses.'

Martin stopped in his tracks. 'That's right,' he agreed. 'That's what I'll tell them, that they're not at home now.' He looked sideways at her. 'You're cold?'

'Yes,' she agreed, gratefully, thinking that it would be he rather than Peter who noticed. 'But don't stop. I need to see everything.'

'You nearly have. With the next block we'll be inside.' They ducked round a freezing corner and she breathed in thankfully, free from the fierce east wind. She clattered up the stairs, her heavy pair of safety footwear skittering uncomfortably on the steel.

'Here they're putting on the internal panels which come painted with undercoat. We fit them out, put a coat of paint on and Bob's your uncle, it's done. Lino down on the floors, ready cut to size.'

'Neat,' Caroline agreed, and it was. And pleasant, compared with London council housing, she thought, even though you would be overlooking those bleak sand dunes with only distant glimpses of the grey North Sea to enliven the view.

She followed her escorts through three more identical floors, politely approving, inwardly dying for something hot to eat, preferably now, and shivered as they led the way out into the wind again, and back to the Porta-kabin. She had better warn potential investors to wear long woolly underwear if she didn't want them going sour on the whole deal; she could have done with a pair of thermal Directoire knickers herself.

She emerged hitching her skirt to be whisked off in

Peter's Jaguar to a private room in the local country club, a Georgian house, comfortable with chintz-covered chairs and an aura of money spent prudently but without skimping. Peter, she noted, took it for granted as did Martin, while the younger Graham was looking round, expanding with pleasure at being inside the place.

Caroline, sinking into a sofa, was cheered by the comfort and the flowers, but undeceived; here came the moment at which the client team needed to be convinced they were going to get value for the very considerable money they were letting themselves in for in taking on Smith Butler. Her eye was caught by a newspaper laid out on the low table and she turned it to look. 'Stock market flotation for Prior Systems', it said, and she spread it out with an exclamation that drew the three men to her side.

'Bloody hell,' Peter was looking alarmed.

'No, it's not as bad as that.' Caroline, by nature and training a voraciously rapid reader, had got through the three half columns of text in one minute flat. 'It's pure speculation, the chap hasn't talked to anyone.' She sat back, narrowly avoiding a collision with Martin, who was leaning over her shoulder reading at about a third her speed. 'I wouldn't worry about that,' she said, authoritatively. 'Really not. There is no way the NEB will find a sponsor to put it on the market, unless it's given away. So they won't float it.'

The three men drank thoughtfully.

'So they have to sell it to us?' Peter said, hopefully, and she put her tomato juice down, carefully.

'No, they don't: they have to sell it, yes; but remember these are public-sector assets we're talking about here and they have to make sure they get a good deal.'

'We'll give them a good deal,' Peter said, his clear skin flushing. 'We'll get the company valued and pay them that. You think it's about £60m don't you, Caroline?'

'Mm. If you had a company to sell, gentlemen, how would you do it?'

There was a thick silence into which Graham spoke.

'I'd advertise it. Put out a memorandum for sale. Like we did at Deloitte.' He looked at her sideways, but she was watching Peter who was still scowling. She waited.

'How do we stop them doing that then, Caroline?' he asked, finally.

'*That*'s the right question. And, if we can see no way of stopping them, what do we do to make damn sure that we are the most attractive proposition around?'

'We offer them more money than anyone else?' Martin fed her the line, and she smiled at him, but did not speak.

'We may not be able to,' Graham said, bluntly. 'Friern or Shaw could cut out a lot of overheads if they took us over. They could afford to pay a bit for that.'

Peter looked at him as if he had offered to sacrifice his eldest child. 'Are you going cold on this, Graham?'

'He is stating a commercial fact – that's what a finance director is *for*.' Caroline decided to intervene. 'Peter, you have to reckon there is someone out there who can pay more for the company than you can. Institutions don't usually pay top prices: they can't make the returns they want if they do.'

A waiter arrived to say that their first course was waiting for them and would they like to move to their table, but none of the men moved, all intent on what they were being told, and Caroline had to announce that she was both freezing and starving, to get them to their feet. She decided to eat rather than speak, hearing inside her head Michael Appleton suggesting forcibly that sometimes it was better to let the client think, for God's sake, Caroline.

'We could refuse to co-operate with the sale.' Peter was devouring *pâté maison*.

'You risk getting fired,' Caroline said, through a mouthful of potted shrimps. 'Don't even think about it.'

'So what do we do to make ourselves the most attractive bid, if it isn't money, Caroline?' Martin asked calmly.

'This company is effectively government-owned, right? Well, what else does this government want apart from money?'

'They like the idea of management buy-outs, don't they?' Graham asked.

'Yes. Yes, they do. Quite. Perhaps not enough.'

'They also like the idea of wider share-ownership,' Martin said, watching his chief executive. 'I mean, perhaps if some of the employees wanted to buy shares, that would be an attractive idea for government.'

Peter put down his fork, appalled. 'Nothing but trouble ahead if you invite the unions in. I've just got those buggers tied down. I'm not starting *that* again.'

'Well,' Martin said, 'it could have real business benefits for us, to have employees as shareholders, with their own money in the company. It's a pretty powerful message to our employees, and would do wonders for motivation.'

'The unions are against privatization,' Peter protested,

doggedly. 'You saw that chap – what's-his-name – in the papers yesterday, saying his members could not be bribed with cheap shares.'

'Rubbish,' Caroline said, briskly. 'I was brought up listening to this load of old cobblers, as perhaps you gentlemen weren't. Of course, your chaps will buy shares if it is a good enough deal – they're not stupid, whatever their leaders think.'

Peter glanced at her, but Martin was nodding. 'I agree with you. The problem is our blokes don't have that much cash to buy shares with – I mean they won't be able to afford all that much.'

'You'll still need the heavy-duty financial institutions for the real money, of course you will,' she agreed, promptly.

'They'll be attracted by the fact that employees are buying shares, though,' Martin said, hopefully.

'No, wrong. They'd rather it was just you three. They'll think employee-shareholders are a terrible nuisance – well, they think private shareholders are a bore anyway. It's one of the things that has gone horribly wrong with this country, that all the money is with institutions which are run, for the most part, by complete dorks.'

'But they aren't the audience we're trying to reach,' Peter said, having impressively managed to absorb an alien idea in twenty minutes flat, and now obviously starting to explore the angles. 'It is the government – the seller – we are trying to reach.'

'Absolutely,' she agreed, thinking there was a lot to be said for a sound training in marketing and sales.

'What we need,' Martin said, eyes narrowed, 'is to make the NEB an offer they can't refuse.'

Peter picked up the baton. 'We emphasize the benefits to them and to the government. The deal widens share-ownership, gives them a fair price, screws the unions. It's very powerful, like Martin says.'

The three men contemplated the picture, rapt.

'You guys get shares of course.' Caroline decided the time had come to drag some of the other motivations to the surface, and Peter looked at her, warily.

'Do we get them free?'

'Some of them. Like I told you, you buy some and you get more shares if you do well. It's called a ratchet. Standard practice in these things is that management doubles its shareholding against certain criteria.'

'Like increasing the profits?'

'Up to a point. Profit is all very well, but what the punters want is the cash back in their hands, multiplied several times.'

The group regarded her, inimically.

'You mean they'll want to sell us out?'

'What I said is that they'll want some cash back in three or four years' time,' she said, patiently. 'You may be able to float and pay them back, or you may be able to afford to buy back some shares at a profit by then. If nothing else works, then yes, they will want to sell you out to a trade purchaser for cash.' No point in not reciting the facts of life, loud and clear, she thought, cheerfully.

'Listen,' Peter said, urgently to his colleagues, 'if we can't float the company and we aren't doing well enough to buy back shares *we*'ll want to sell out, come on.'

Caroline made a fierce effort to keep her head still and let the others react, and her patience was repaid, as the other two thought their way through this statement at various speeds and agreed to it.

'What kind of return are these investors looking for? I mean, they obviously want more than a point over base rate, but how much more?' Graham asked, feeling for a piece of paper in his pocket, and she sighed.

'Don't even *start* from base rate. They're looking at a running return of forty per cent annually. That includes capital growth, of course, but it's pretty demanding.'

Her audience stared at her, aghast.

'Forty per cent annually? That's, well, that's *usury*.'

'They would claim that it is a fair allowance for risk, and that they need returns like that on some investments to make up for the others that are going to fall flat on their faces.'

'But how does that work?' Graham, like all the best finance directors, was writing down figures on the back of an envelope.

'Well, say the company's worth £60m now. Just for argument's sake,' she added firmly, warding off an intervention from Peter. 'So you borrow £50m – tops – take £10m from the institutions, probably £2m in equity, £8m in preference shares or loan stock. You can't afford to pay too much interest on that so the institutions get, say seven per cent on their £10m investment. They can get ten per cent on government stocks, guaranteed by the Treasury, so they will be looking for the equity to be worth a lot of money some day.'

'It'll have to be worth a bloody fortune to get their return up to forty per cent annually,' Peter protested.

'Yes, but the sort of fortune shares in these buy-outs can be worth,' she said, promptly. 'Look, you make £8.5m odd profit now, so the company's worth £60m on a price/earnings ratio of seven. If we do this, you'll spend most of your profits covering interest and dividend in year one, but by year three you expect to get your post-tax profits up to £18m. At which point you can do anything – float it, sell to a competitor or anything. Even on a p/e of seven the company would be worth £126m. Take out the preference shares and the debt, and £2m of ordinary shares turn out to be worth something like £100m.'

'And we, the managers, I mean, how much do we get?'

'You and the employees started out with ten per cent of the ordinary shares for which you paid £200,000. You double your shares if you manage to sell the company inside four years, so there you are with twenty per cent of the shares. Worth about £20m, i.e. a hundred times your initial stake.' She paused to make sure they were following her. 'It's never *that* good, of course, life being what it is, but that's the principle. Everyone laughs all the way to the bank.'

A long, dazzled pause followed, while all three men present stared into a roseate future.

'Why can't we buy more than ten per cent? At those prices I'd mortgage the kids.' It was Martin who recovered first and Caroline grinned at him.

'The institutions won't play. Remember, they don't get any capital growth on their £8m preference shares. So they will only let you buy a limited amount of what the trade calls "the sweet equity", i.e. the ordinary shares. But you're right, Martin, *that* is what the negotiations with the institutions are all about, how much of the sweet equity you get.'

Peter was sitting, hunched and suspicious. 'Why don't all managers organize buy-outs like this?'

She leant forward, hooking her hair behind her ears.

'Ah. You have to be running a company which generates cash rather than eats it, because you have to be able to pay a lot of interest. This company, for instance, ate cash until last year with heavy research and development costs and loss-making contracts running off. And *that*'s why it went bust – there wasn't any *cash*, never mind what happened to the profits. But now you've done all the capital expenditure at the factory, your loss-makers are nearly gone – and you may even get some cash back on them in a renegotiation – so virtually all the cash you generate is available to pay interest. There are very few companies like that.'

She stopped, interrupted by the arrival of four man-sized steaks, entirely surrounded by sauté potatoes, mushrooms, tomatoes and two green vegetables. Up here in Dorrington, she thought, admiringly, we put it all on t'plate where you can see it, lass, none of this *nouvelle cuisine* nonsense. Silence fell as they all worked their way through their plates.

Peter suddenly observed, through a mouthful of food, that the more they could borrow the less they would have to take from institutions, and the more of the company they could keep for themselves.

'And the higher the risks. Damn and blast,' Caroline said swallowing a potato whole. 'Interest on borrowings has to be paid, remember. It's running out of cash that busts companies. In any case, no bank will let you borrow it all – they want some nice comfortable equity in there.' Enough was enough for the moment, she realized. Her group was looking both bedazzled and exhausted and all of them were drinking without registering what was going down.

'What about a lovely factory visit then?' she said,

finishing her vegetables and the last two pieces of steak, just ahead of Peter. 'I have to have seen that, if you want me to rally investors – I can't afford to be vague about it.'

In the confusion of bills being paid, coats found, and drivers located, she found Peter at her side. 'You're sure the figures are as good as that?'

'If you halve those figures they still stack up. The trick lies in getting the deal done at all, given that other people want to buy the company too.'

'So we are going to need a lot of political help, you think?'

'I know so.' Caroline never bothered to trim to a client's feelings and wasn't going to start with this one. 'Do you know the MP for the next-door constituency? Junior minister, called Gerry Willshaw?'

'I met him once.'

'I came up with him on the train last night. I didn't lobby, obviously, but I told him who I was and what I was doing.' She paused. 'We got on all right,' she added, as temperately as she could.

'A glamour boy,' Peter Burwood said.

'You didn't like him?'

'Not a lot.'

'Change your mind, Peter. Fix it on wealth and power.'

He nodded seriously. 'I am prepared to love him. Can you get him to come and see the site? Soon as you can.' He hooked an arm over her shoulders and they stood, pleased with each other, waiting for his Jaguar to manoeuvre itself to the door.

6

Clive Fieldman sat down, heavily, and poured himself a stiff whisky, ignoring the inner voice which reminded him that alcohol was a depressant, particularly a couple of hours after you had ingested it. It had been a cold and exhausting weekend. He had driven ninety miles each way on the Saturday to see an old friend from his days at the LSE and been depressed by the experience; his old mate Alan had married a dull woman, who had produced an equally dull woman as a partner for him. On Sunday he had picked up his two children from his ex-wife's house and the day had not gone easily. His marriage had foundered for a variety of reasons; he had outgrown his wife Linda, and had been unhappy quite quickly, a nagging discontent which he had tried to cure by working hard and long, culminating in nearly two years as principal private secretary, rarely going home before nine at night and engaging in a claustrophobic affair with one of the assistant private secretaries, a clever 28-year-old girl. This had finally undermined a shaky marriage and left his wife with not much alternative other than to find someone else, a solution he had at least partially willed. He had been appalled at himself and had lost confidence. He had found that he did not want to marry his young woman, nor was she, in the event, that keen to take him on with two children and a diminished income. Linda, however, had found herself a highly salaried chartered accountant and had produced two babies for him in rapid succession, leaving her very willing to let Clive have his children, now ten and eight, whenever he wanted them. He took them as much as he could, suffering painfully from the perception that they had lost both father and much of their mother, occupied as she was with two little ones and a new husband. There were Sundays – and this had been one – when a child was unhappy and difficult and he felt a failure both as a father and a human being.

Mercifully, tomorrow was Monday, and he would be wanted and indispensable somewhere every hour of the day. And Lucy Friern would be back in London. He longed to talk to her but he could not ring her in Dorrington; that was one of the limiting rules she had laid down early in their affair, and he was allowed to ring the London flat only under very strictly regulated circumstances. He went to get another whisky but the phone rang and he picked it up, reluctantly.

'Darling? Have you still got the kids?'

'Lucy! No, they've gone. Where are you?'

'London. Matt's away for a couple of days, so I took the boys back to school then drove down. Do you want some dinner?'

'I've eaten. McDonald's . . . about two hours ago.' He was grinning at the phone, depression banished. 'But I'll come and watch you eat, unless you want to come here? No? I'll be round.'

He collected, hopefully, a suit, clean shirt and tie, a pair of pyjamas and a sponge-bag, stuffed them into a briefcase and went, whistling, to his car, and drove through the London streets. He rang twice on the bell in their agreed signal and Lucy opened the door to him, clasping a towelling bathrobe around her. He closed the door and pulled her to him, feeling the robe fall open as her arms went round him.

'You had supper?'

'I'm not hungry . . . or, not for food.' She undid his belt, and started work on the zip.

'Christ.' He slid a hand between her buttocks and bent his head to suck her left nipple. 'Hang on,' he said, letting go. 'Let's get to bed. My pants are falling off.'

'That's the idea.' She had her hand cupped round his balls and he kicked off his shoes and pulled his jeans and underpants off, one-handed, holding her with the other. She slithered out of his grip and knelt on the floor, taking his penis in her mouth as he pulled his shirt off, then pushed her bathrobe off her shoulders.

'I'll come if you go on,' he said, pulling her hair. 'And I want to be inside you.'

She released him and he knelt down, then pulled her on to the carpet, straddling her, pushing up her legs.

'I want it now,' she said, urgently, flushed and wide-eyed.

He put a hand between her legs, watching her, and she strained against him.

'Oh, you are lovely. All wet.'

He pushed into her gently and she moved easily with him, he pacing himself carefully, watching her until her head went back. He felt her convulse round him and came himself, triumphantly and easily, so that he had tears of pleasure in his eyes when he finished.

'That was nice.' She licked his shoulder.

'And for me. I was really low when you rang.'

'I couldn't ring earlier. The car phone is on the blink, so I had to wait till I got here.'

Clive, who in the best tradition of the civil service

drove a five-year-old Volkswagen and could never have afforded a car phone, grinned at her with tolerant affection. 'I always enjoy having a girlfriend with a car phone.'

'They're very useful,' she began, defensively, then realized she was being teased and pulled his hair. 'Are you doing your simple gamekeeper bit?'

'That's right, my lady.' He kissed her, collected Kleenex from the bathroom and passed her a handful and she watched him as he wrapped one jauntily round his penis, as he always did.

'Sorry. We'll need to clear up the carpet.'

He peered at a wet spot and she laughed, liking the look of the strong springy dark hair above the straight nose. He reached for his glasses which he had discarded at some stage and she observed with affection that he was the only very good-looking man she knew who was totally devoid of affectation; he couldn't see properly without glasses, so he wore them, even if the only other thing he was wearing was a pair of socks. He smiled back at her, questioningly.

'I was thinking how silly I was when I was young,' she said.

He followed her thought effortlessly. 'What, never to give me a go when we were all twenty-two? I was ready and waiting; you only had to ask.'

'Idiot that I was. But then so was Caroline.'

'I fancied her too, but she scared me. *You* could have had me any day, at a glance.' He was briskly collecting up clothes and she reached out a hand to be helped up, watching with pleasure and affection as he found a soda siphon and sprayed the offending patch on the carpet, moving neatly and briskly. He straightened up to kiss her, only an inch taller than she, their eyes almost level, and she put her arms around him, liking the slim, hard feel of him after Matt's soft bulk.

'Now you have had my fair body, can I get something else to eat?' He found his jeans and underpants and pulled them on. 'That Big Mac seems to have vanished without trace. Don't you bother, I'll forage.'

'No, I like feeding you. Omelette do?'

He set the table, knowing her kitchen as well as he did his own, stopping to put his arms around her and feel her breasts as she assembled eggs, salt, pepper and herbs. They both ate ravenously, sharing half a bottle of a very good Chablis.

'I must bring you some drink,' he said, the deep furrow between his eyes very marked as it always was when he was concentrating. 'I always seem to drink yours.' Too much, he thought atavistically, to drink the chap's best Chablis as well as screwing his wife. He knew Lucy would have scorned this thought as being working-class, but none the less he made a mental note that he would bring some drink next time.

'Am I staying the night?'

'Bridget comes tomorrow, but not till nine.'

'I've got an eight-thirty meeting, so I'll be gone. If that's OK?'

'Of course it is. I like it when you are here in the morning.'

He sat, eating his omelette, tired and contented, as she moved quietly round the kitchen. At moments like this he wondered if he could persuade her to give up her husband and move in with him but, realistic and clear-sighted as he had always been, he recognized that she would have real difficulty adjusting to the standard of living enjoyed by an under-secretary in HM Government Service. He had out of curiosity looked up the report and accounts for Friern and been unsurprised to find that one director, and that had to be Sir Matthew Friern, was collecting in excess of £150,000 a year, never mind shares and options. He himself made £30,000 a year, out of which he had to finance child support, a heavily mortgaged flat and a five-year-old Volkswagen. Not a lot left over to support a wife. In fact, viewed calmly, he couldn't really remarry unless he found a woman who could contribute something to the household expenses. He could take one of the job offers available from the private sector, of course, but he was quite sure that even one of those would not meet Lucy's needs. She always complained that Matthew was tight with money, but it was difficult to see wherein any meanness lay. At least in the London flat cupboards opened on racks of expensive bottles which were opened as freely as if they were milk, and a highly paid housekeeper arrived every day. One day, he would try on beautiful, graceful Lucy the proposition that she should throw in her lot with him, but in his bones he was unhopeful of the outcome.

She sat down opposite him, placing a cup of coffee in front of him, and he reached over and stroked her cheek, then realized she was preoccupied.

'Clive. Look. We're going to invite John Winstanley to dinner here. The thing *is* Matt wants to talk to him about Prior Building Systems.'

'Can't he just come and see him in the office?'

'Matt says he wants to do it informally, without the civil servants. I'm *telling* you, darling, so you don't think I'm being underhand.'

He nodded, ruffled, but far too experienced to be particularly surprised. 'What does Matthew want to put across?'

'I don't exactly know.' She gave him the over-candid, wide-eyed look she used when she was telling what she considered a white lie and he looked back sadly.

'Lucy, what he must be trying to do is to suggest he gets an inside track on the sale of Prior Systems in some way. Otherwise he would just write to the Department, same as the other people who think they'd like to buy it do.'

'Oh, are there a lot of them?'

'A few.' He watched her under his eyelashes.

'I expect you're right,' she said, briskly, getting up to refill her coffee cup. 'But that's business after all. I mean, when Daddy bought Autoparts from Allied he went to see the chairman, agreed a price and got a six weeks' exclusive to decide if the deal would fly. It did . . . well, Daddy paid a bit less than the original agreement because he found a few nasties – but Allied were pleased. And so were their shareholders.'

He always forgot, Clive thought grimly, how much this beautiful, sexy creature actually knew about business, as daughter of one and wife to another successful industrialist. 'My minister probably has more difficult shareholders than the chairman of Allied did. He is going to have to be absolutely satisfied that he is getting the best deal for the taxpayer.'

'That means the best price, doesn't it? Well, he'll get a good price from Matt. He's bound to – Matt can get rid of one set of overheads, and he doesn't have to borrow much, he can do it with shares.'

'The NEB will want cash, darling. Apart from anything else, this lot want to cut the PSBR – what Government borrows – so they need cash.'

'*That*'s interesting,' Lucy pounced on the point, and he realized that she was in fact pursuing a well-planned course. 'They can have cash if they'd rather. But the NEB is going to need to sell things pretty quickly?'

'Yes.' He watched her, alert.

'Well, Matt could offer to buy *all* the construction companies, I suppose, if that would help. As a package.'

Clive got up abruptly from the table and found himself face to face with a Pissarro print of a woman in a market, which in normal circumstances he liked. He narrowed his eyes at its gentle lines. 'He couldn't afford to buy them all, could he?'

'Well, he might have to sell off the one he really doesn't have much use for – Carrs.' She was loading plates into the dishwasher and he could not see her face. 'And he says there are two companies there that no one really wants.'

Clive sat on the edge of the table considering his much-loved mistress, as she bent to dispose of a plate. 'Would he be prepared to take them on and sort them out? Close them, or whatever?'

Lucy straightened up. 'He thinks the NEB could close the one that makes kitchens – I can't remember its name.'

'Davecat.'

'Whatever.'

'Mm.' Clive moved off the table to put his glass into the machine. 'Has Matt said anything to my man yet?'

'He only just thought of it. That's why I'm organizing dinner.' She turned to face him, and put her arms around his neck. 'Don't look so cross. I'm telling you so you know before your minister, and he can think you are very clever.'

And so I can soften him up, Clive thought, resignedly, and looked severely at his love. 'Is that why you got me round tonight?'

'Oh, Clive, don't be silly.' She was, he recognized, genuinely angry. 'I wanted to see you. *Will* you stop being so cross?'

'I'm not,' he said, defensively, then native honesty reasserted itself. 'Yes, I am. This lot are far too prone to doing deals with their mates. I know, I know, and the other lot do deals with their mates in the unions. I'm just trying for open government and a fair deal for the taxpayer here.' He moved restlessly out of her embrace to pick up his coffee, which he drank without tasting it.

She came up behind him and put her arms around him, burying her chin in his shoulder, and he stood, letting himself be soothed.

'Why is he getting you to organize the dinner?' he asked, without turning round. 'I mean he's met Winstanley himself. I introduced them.'

'When you were married, who organized all the dinner parties?'

'We didn't quite live that way, Lady Friern.'

'Oh, for God's sake, Mellors. Who invited other members of your humble circle in for a glass of homemade beer?'

'Yes, all right.'

'You *would* rather I had told you?'

'Yes. Yes, I would. And I'll brief my man to resist Matt's blandishments. And yours.'

'I've met him once. I did quite fancy him actually.'

Clive unwound her arms and turning round in one swift movement, backed her against the fridge kissed her. 'You're a bad woman.'

'You like bad women.'

'You're right there. In bed this time?'

'Andy? Matt Friern. Sorry to bother you on a Sunday night. I'm in Dorrington now but I'm flying direct to Düsseldorf tomorrow. I wanted to talk to you about Prior Systems.'

Andy stretched the cord of the wall phone to the maximum, one-handedly fished out a glass from the cupboard and poured himself a generous whisky. He signalled his wife that this call would take time and bent to kiss his five-year-old son, who was being escorted upstairs, thumb in mouth, the other hand clasping an ancient, grubby glove-puppet from which he could not be separated long enough to wash it.

'Yes, Matt,' he said, encouragingly.

'New plan. I've been thinking about what Winstanley said at that conference, about the need to move quickly on the privatization programme. Why don't I offer to buy all five of the NEB construction companies?'

Andy reached for a pad and started to scribble numbers. 'We haven't done a valuation, Matt, because you didn't ask us to, but that has to be . . . what . . . £150m.'

'That sort of figure.'

Andy stared at his pad, Sunday-night lethargy abruptly banished. 'It'll stretch you, Matt. I'd like to have a word with your brokers – it'll have to be a largish rights issue.'

'Not if we get the two duff ones for free, sell or close

them and sell off Carrs and SLG soon as we can. We could borrow it.'

Not very easily, Matt, thought Andy, mind racing. No bank is going to like lending even a good company more money than it should properly be borrowing, on the faith that they will somehow manage to sell off newly acquired assets. All the banks had been there before: lent on the promise of an immediate sale, then found themselves stuck with the loan because the newly acquired company had a concealed nasty in it, or the market turned sour, or both. But Friern was a good company, with a strong cash-flow and a bank – or two – could probably be found to do it. At a price. There would be a nice fee there for Walzheims and they would get the sale mandate. A very nice piece of business. 'Yes,' he said. 'I'll talk to my lending colleagues tomorrow, see what they think. They'll need to syndicate it, of course.'

'Good. Well, you get on with that.'

Andy stared down at the figures that covered his pad and decided reluctantly that there were words that had to be said. 'Matt. I imagine we can get a syndicate together – can't promise till tomorrow – but it's a high-risk strategy for Friern. If it goes sour you're left over-extended with two decent companies you don't want and two real dogs. I suppose it's worth it to get hold of Prior? I know you feel it's an important acquisition and, of course, having seen your Dorrington sites I see what a good fit it would be. But maybe we ought to try to devise a more direct route?'

'If you can, I'll do it, Andy. But Prior's going to be worth a lot to us. More than you can see.'

'There is a gold mine under one of the sites?' Andy asked, hoping he wasn't sounding too doubtful.

'You could say that. I'll need to talk about it properly with you, not on the phone, but let's put it for now that I believe our – Friern's – contacts with the council in Dorrington have to be a lot closer than Peter Burwood's. And it's all down to relationships when most of your work is building council houses, isn't it?'

'Can you put a figure on this, Matt? You got any feeling for the upside?'

'Could easily be £6m a year on the bottom line.'

More like £8m, Andy thought, instantly, from long knowledge of clients who never told their financial advisers the full strength. Or not the first few times, anyway.

But that would double the trading profit for the current year, and do nearly the same in year two. What Matthew was telling him was that Prior could be worth a good deal more than £60m to Friern. Ah, but there were a lot of assumptions in that, of course. And no sensible investor would bank on Friern's council contacts; you couldn't quantify that – it was only hope value. But there was a deal here all right; it was worth while making a real push for Prior, and he felt the adrenalin begin to flow as he started to concentrate rather than just go conscientiously through the motions for a good client.

'Where do the extra profits come from, Matt?' he asked, aware that he had been silent for rather a long time.

'Some from renegotiation of existing contracts. The rest because *we've* got the contacts and we'll get a decent price for the next ones we build.'

Andy shifted in his chair, needing a pee, another sure sign that all his systems had woken up.

'We need to talk when you get back, Matt. Is there

any chance that others – either management or other trade buyers – will be able to perceive the same advantages?'

'I doubt it. They haven't been, let's put it, dealing with the people on the council that I have, for as long as I have.'

There *was* gold in them thar hills then, Andy thought, and it cast a new light on the history of Prior Building Systems. No wonder they had taken on loss-making contracts; they had found it necessary to bid very low indeed to get in, so low that their claims to the work could not be ignored or pushed aside, no matter how many contacts on the local council wanted Friern to have the work. And that gamble had failed; at the prices Prior had bid to get the work, the company could not make money, and had gone into receivership and then to the NEB. But if Friern bought it, those same contacts could help them renegotiate the prices on the old contracts and get good prices on new ones. Open to the management to do the same thing, of course, but those chaps were younger, as he remembered it, and had neither Friern's background nor, well, their resources in the area. His eyes focused on the pad, and he found he had written 'Council, Contacts, CONTRACTS,' in block capitals, one underneath each other. He tore off the top sheet and threw it, accurately, into the wastepaper-basket at the other side of the room. He would have to tread very carefully indeed on this one.

'We're going to have to take your view on a lot of this, Matt,' he began cautiously. 'I mean, it's not quantifiable or verifiable. We'll be very much dependent on your judgement.'

'You will.' Matthew was sounding grimly amused.

'Don't worry, I'll tell you what we can afford without telling you too much about why. You just concentrate on the financing.'

Andy winced; no merchant banker likes being treated as simply a financial technician and moreover that was not the way to make the top fees on which the business and his personal bonus and status depended.

'I ought to be able to help on the political side,' he offered. 'I've kept in touch with Clive Fieldman, as you know, and this is very much his pigeon. Very important for him to get this one right; it's rather a showcase piece of privatization.'

'Lucy knows him too,' Matthew said, briskly. 'I told her I'd rather talk to the organ-grinder than the monkey. We're arranging to get Winstanley round for dinner. He was at school with Lucy's brother.'

'I would suggest it's quite difficult to decide which is the organ-grinder and which the monkey, in this context, Matt,' Andy protested. 'The civil service is very powerful, you know – they can probably sabotage any initiative they don't like. I think we need Clive on our side as well.'

'You talk to him then,' Matt was plainly not convinced, but prepared to accept the offered help, and Andrew wrote 'CLIVE FIELDMAN' in block capitals on the pristine page in front of him.

They chatted for a bit, Matt plainly having nothing better to do in Dorrington on this Sunday night, which caused Andrew to wonder, after he had put down the phone, where the beautiful Lucy was. He poured another whisky and thought about her, as he had often done in the years since she had taken him on for what had turned out to be a one-week fling, not long before she had married Matthew.

That week Lucy had already been engaged to Matthew; in fact the wedding was only about two months away and she had formally terminated her Articles with Smith Butler. He had been working late and hearing a noise on the stairs had got up to see who else was there and met Lucy, pink and not altogether steady on her feet.

'Andy,' she had said, peering at him, and he had realized she was mildly drunk.

'I was at a party near here and I thought I'd collect some of my stuff. I've got the car with me.'

'Have you Matthew with you, too?'

'No. Should I have?'

'I wondered only if you were safe to drive,' he had said, unflustered, used to sisters. 'Was it a good party?'

'No,' she said, tears suddenly standing in her eyes.

'Would you like some coffee? I'll make you some, then I'll help with your kit.'

She had nodded, wordlessly, and when he had returned she was sitting on the stairs, weeping, beautiful and forlorn. He smiled sadly to himself, as he remembered, sixteen years later, how his heart had turned over. He had thought that to be a figure of speech, but it wasn't, it had felt like a physical reality. He had sat down, carefully, about three feet away from her on the stairs and handed her a coffee which she had drunk, still weeping gently.

'Can I do anything?'

'No, nothing. Thank you anyway, Andy.' Lucy had blown her nose and had given him a small apologetic smile, and he had felt himself drawn by an absolutely irresistible force closer towards her. She had watched him wide-eyed, still sniffing and he had reached out for

126

her, overwhelmed, forgetting absolutely that she was engaged and that he had a long-standing girlfriend. He had driven her home in her own car, minus most of the things she had come to collect, and fallen into her bed with her. There had followed a wild week full of guilt-stricken withdrawals by Lucy, followed immediately by passionate reunions, a week in which he had found himself in the office most days with no idea how he had got there or what he had come to do. Even at this distance of time isolated incidents from that week still surfaced in his mind as clear as the day they had happened: Lucy waving him off from her flat, dressed only in a transparent nightdress, giving the postman the treat of his life; Lucy deciding she didn't want him to go to work and pulling him back at the door undoing his zip. And thinking back sixteen years he saw, like a photograph slowly developing, Caroline Henriques and Clive Fieldman converging on him to pick up a contract he had been told to draft, and their expressions of mixed horror and relish as they realized he had not even started. He remembered painfully his shamefaced attempts to find the right precedent, incapacitated as he was by shortage of sleep and anxiety, and the dismissive ease with which Caroline had found a precedent close enough to serve, with some fast alteration by her, as a credible first draft. And Clive, cajoling a typist into staying very late to complete it – no word-processors in those days, of course, it was five carbons to correct every time you made a mistake – and staying to jolly the girl through it. He had been distantly grateful to both of them at the time but nothing had seemed real except Lucy. And when it was all over, eight days later, when Matthew had come back from wherever he had been. and Lucy, having decided without a backward glance that he was after all the right man for her, had danced off to a round of fittings of wedding-dress, thank-you letters and engagement parties, he had never managed to acknowledge their help. He had taken up again with the girl whose existence he had totally forgotten while he had Lucy and had never told her or anyone else about the affair; he was afraid they would all think him a fool, which he had been. Neither he nor Lucy had ever referred to that week again; he had ducked going to her wedding, pleading illness, and by the time he had met Matthew again, ten years later, when he was on his way up at Walzheims, it had seemed more important to bring in a good active client than to avoid contact with Lucy Friern, née Lindfield.

'You're looking very thoughtful. Is it time we went to bed? The children are asleep.'

He looked, momentarily unseeing, at his wife Emma, pretty, slender, blonde and dependable. She would never have ditched him or anyone else after a week of what he had felt to be a most passionate and loving affair, but neither did she make his bones melt in the way that Lucy Lindfield had done, effortlessly, with one sidelong glance.

'What's the matter?'

'Sorry. I was thinking. This Friern deal is getting interesting. And tricky.' He put a hand on her shoulder and kissed her, grateful to her for not being Lucy Friern, and they stopped on the way up to enjoy the sight of their children, both so utterly asleep that only the occasional, almost imperceptible, rise and fall of the quilts that covered them told you they were still alive.

The Minister for Housing let himself into his small, cold

south London flat, hurrying because he could hear the telephone ringing. At this hour on a Sunday it would be a ministerial colleague wanting to talk to him without civil servants conscientiously listening. He picked up the phone. 'John Winstanley.'

'Gerry Willshaw here, John. Sorry, not too late for you, is it?'

'No, no, Gerry,' he assured the telephone, wondering what on earth the rising star at the Department of Transport could want to discuss privately. New road about to be put straight through one of DoE's housing sites? 'I've just got back. I always get the seven-thirty.'

'On Sunday nights I wish my constituency were a bit closer to London,' Gerry said pleasantly. 'Not that I'd want to sit for anywhere else, but it is three and a half hours on the train and it's always late.'

'Well, you ought to be able to fix that, Gerry. What's the point of being in the Department of Transport?'

'I imagine I need not say to *you*, John, that a minister has damn-all power to fix anything if his secretary of state isn't interested in the subject. And we are not, here in the Department of Transport, in the slightest bit interested in railways; it's roads, lots of them, and how to finance the building of same that poor Jim is obsessed with. How are you doing with Housing Construction?'

'Perhaps a bit better than you with railways. My boss is a bit more interested in it – I can see that even after six weeks here.' Winstanley stopped, regretting confiding anything to Gerry Willshaw, who was coming up very fast and was said to be marked for further advancement. Willshaw was a later entrant to the House than he was, having got in against the trend in the second election of 1974, and had made himself indispensable to the Party while they were in opposition; photogenic, naturally sociable, and apparently tireless, he knew everyone, had been everywhere in those five years and had received his reward by going straight to a minister of state job rather than serving his apprenticeship, as Winstanley had had to, in the more junior parliamentary secretary dogsbody role. No need to hand this one any more advantages, whatever he was looking for; if he got a place in the Cabinet that would put him a definitive step ahead of people who had been longer in the House and in the Party than he had. But it might never happen; the Department of Transport had buried better men than Gerry Willshaw and could be relied on to do it again. A bed of nails that one, he reflected complacently, while he wondered again why the man was ringing him.

'Look, John, you're telling the NEB to get on with selling a company called Prior Building Systems, is that right? No, it's not in my constituency, it's just over the boundary, in Albert Dervey's patch. Yes, he's opposed to any sale, or so at least the local papers tell me. I don't spend much time talking to him. My local paper also tells me that you're thinking of floating it?'

'Oh, does it now?' John Winstanley said, alert. 'Well, I haven't talked to the NEB yet, but I understand they are more likely to advise that a trade sale would be the best way of disposal. You got a copy of your local paper there, Gerry? I'd be obliged. I'd guess there'll be a Question down on this. Get your office to send it to mine.'

'I'll do that first thing tomorrow.' Gerry Willshaw agreed, placidly, then hesitated while John Winstanley waited for the other shoe to drop. 'John, I understand from my local sources that management are trying to put together a bid for the company. Might that not be quite a good idea for us? The PM's very keen on employees being shareholders, and of course they aren't very likely to get the chance of shares if the NEB decide to sell to a trade buyer.'

His fellow minister thought about Gerry Willshaw and his 3000-vote majority. 'Are the managers your constituents, Gerry?'

'May well be – I haven't met them yet. A lot of the employees are, and if they get shares *we*'ll acquire a few more votes somewhere and God knows we need them in my part of the world.'

A timely reminder, Winstanley mentally conceded. The further north you went, the more inclined the populace was to stick to Labour, despite its unpromising track record. It would take some new dynamic policies as well as some more charismatic candidates like Gerry Willshaw to make a real dent in the Labour vote up there, the sort of dent that would make seats change hands permanently. At the same time there was no way he was going to hand this jumped-up army-type a political advantage on a plate. All Brownie points were going to go to the Minister who had authorized the deal, and Willshaw could depend on that.

'It's still fairly early days, Gerry,' he said, carefully. 'We also have to be sure of course that we get the best deal for the taxpayer.'

'Which may not mean the highest price, taking a slightly longer view.'

I do not need you to tell me that, Winstanley thought, irritated. 'There is a local firm interested,' he said, pleasantly. 'Friern – a very large family firm, headed by Sir Matthew Friern. Do you know them?'

'Yes. He is a constituent. I hadn't realized they were in for it.'

'Very much so, as I understand it. My advisers tell me that any trade purchaser is likely to be able to pay more than the managers can. And of course, Gerry, we need to consider which is the best home for Prior Systems and, indeed, all five companies. We'd look very silly indeed if we let a management team have it – or any of them – and the whole thing went bust before the next election.'

'Oh, quite.' Gerry Willshaw's agreement was instant and heartfelt and Winstanley grinned, sharklike, at the phone, but Willshaw was not so easily dismissed.

'It would be dreadful for the chaps there too, to have their jobs at risk for the second time in a few years.'

Winstanley agreed, very slightly gritting his teeth. It was exactly this carefully communicated concern for people which had catapulted Willshaw from an unknown ex-army officer, fighting what should have been a reasonably safe Labour seat, into a job with a Conservative Government five years later. 'That is certainly a consideration I have very much in mind,' he said, stiffly. 'I'm glad to hear you've found something to say if we decide it has to go that way, Gerry,' he added, sardonically.

The man at the other end laughed. 'We all have to do *that*, John. Look, it's your patch but bear us poor toilers in the north-east in mind, will you? I think, without knowing enough about it, of course, that we'd all be helped by an employee buy-out, by actually showing chaps up there what our policy is about, on the ground as it were, and it would be a pity to miss the chance. There aren't many handy-sized state-owned companies suitable to be sold to employees, are there?'

'Damn few,' Winstanley conceded. 'This one is quite big, worth £60m they tell me, even with some problem contracts.'

'I know about those. Lot of my people waiting for those flats.'

There would be, Winstanley acknowledged, and in fairness to Willshaw he would know exactly who the people were. It had been as much steady, conscientious, hard labour in the constituency salt mines as Willshaw's charm that had increased a very small majority to something that looked as near safe as anything in that part of the north-east. Much of that was organization of course; Willshaw had used his expensive military training and his own strongly expressive personality to good effect in reconstituting his constituency party and getting in new people – lots of women among them. He was said to operate four surgeries in different parts of the constituency every Saturday; well, you couldn't do that without a lot of efficient volunteer help, unless you had discovered the trick of cutting yourself in four and sending out the bits separately. And, commendably, he had used the years of a Labour administration to sponsor, push, cajole and campaign to get a fair sprinkling of Conservative councillors on to the local city council.

'The more important that we make sure the company ends up with people who will run it efficiently, Gerry.'

'Oh, we need to do that.' The faint emphasis on 'we' rang in Winstanley's ear. 'But I'm told the sites are now rattling along. The present managers must be good. I must try to meet them so I can offer you an independent view. I'll keep in touch, John. Remember, I'm delighted to help if I can do anything useful, locally.'

He rang off, crisply, leaving Winstanley in no doubt that any colleague who ignored Gerry Willshaw's legitimate interests did so at their peril.

7

'Bonjour Madame. Vous n'avez pas reservé?'

'Bonjour Jean Paul, ça marche? Non, on m'a invité. Willshaw. Il n'est pas encore arrivé?'

'He has now. I'm sorry to be late.'

I had forgotten his voice, she thought, turning to smile at him – light and husky.

'I meant to get here first, but I see you are among friends. I was told this place was very smart. I see that my information must have been right.'

'It is fashionable,' she agreed, breathing in carefully, taking in the look of him. Taller than she had remembered and wider-shouldered. 'But that is not the reason I am at home here. I did the legal work when the company that runs this was set up. Aren't you cold?'

He was not wearing an overcoat, apparently unbothered by the biting cold wind outside, shining with health, his crisp brown hair ruffled by the wind.

'I came in a car,' he said, apologetically, and she remembered that he was a minister and would be driven to appointments.

'Of course. Jean Paul!'

The receptionist who was gazing appreciatively at Gerry Willshaw took her tidy tweed coat from her and hung it up without taking his eyes off her companion. She was amused to notice that Gerry was just perceptibly embarrassed; surely with those looks he must be accustomed to that kind of attention from men and women alike. Particularly in London restaurants where

134

some of the nicest and most efficient of the staff were gay.

'Did you really do the legal work?' he asked as they followed the receptionist, who veered at the last moment and deposited them in a corner table.

'That's what I do,' she reminded him, promptly. 'I set up companies, and I draft agreements. One of my partners did the conveyancing – the property work.'

'I'm impressed,' he said, gently, and she decided grimly to stop chattering. She unfolded her napkin, nodded to acquaintances at the next table, and realized that they were all looking with interest at her escort. A partner in a rival firm pushed back his chair and came over to her.

'Caroline. Sorry, but I have been trying to get you on the phone about our mutual friends. Can we make the meeting an hour later on Friday?'

'I've no idea, Peter. My secretary will know.'

She picked up a menu definitively, but he stood his ground and turned to her escort. 'I did enjoy *Question Time*. My mother is a constituent of yours, and she particularly enjoyed it, too. Peter Cairns.'

'Gerry Willshaw,' he said, standing up. 'How very nice of you to come and say so.'

Both men looked sideways at Caroline whose expression was sufficiently forbidding to prevent Peter Cairns from doing more than try one more round of civilities. She watched him return to his table, eyes narrowed.

'Sorry. Couldn't really tell him to piss off.'

'You did tell him, my sweet.' Gerry was struggling not to laugh. 'Just as well you're not in politics.'

'Indeed so,' she said, primly, hearing 'my sweet' echo in her mind. 'Are you always being accosted by perfect strangers?'

He looked deprecating, the expression sitting oddly on those regular confident features. 'Well, the trouble is I do seem to be fairly recognizable.'

'I expect you enjoy it,' she said, consideringly.

'Sometimes. What will you have to drink?'

A passing waiter put a glass of mineral water with lemon in front of Caroline and stood expectantly poised while they both looked disconcerted at the glass.

'Sorry,' she said, embarrassed, 'the thing is I have an account here, so I get the regular patron treatment. I'm sure you can have some lovely water too.'

'I assumed it was gin and tonic,' he said, lightly, 'which is what I will have.'

No nonsense about drinking *kir* or anything else which might be assumed to be appropriate to a consciously French restaurant, she thought, but held her peace, recognizing that she was in danger of being childishly rude.

He was reading the menu carefully. 'What are you going to have?' he asked, feeling her watching him.

'The steak and *frites*,' she said, automatically. 'Please,' she added.

'It's good here, is it?' He read unhurriedly down the menu and ordered duck, leaving her cursing herself. There was something about this man that wrong-footed her and as he looked across at her she acknowledged that she was handling this badly, because she was appallingly attracted to him, and had been when they met; it was an instantaneous flare-up, much more suitable to someone of sixteen than a responsible widowed mother of three, aged thirty-eight. She looked back at him seriously, gravelled for speech.

'You wear your watch on your right hand,' he said, conversationally.

'Yes,' she agreed, gratefully. 'I put my left hand through a window as a child; there's not much of a scar but it itches if I wear a watch on it.' She twisted her left arm to show him and he reached out and traced the scar.

'Very neat job.'

She felt herself go scarlet. 'Yes,' she said, fighting for breath. 'A patient houseman who took hours over it.'

He rubbed his thumb over the fine white marks, and she watched his hand, unable to look at him, as he withdrew it to pick up his drink.

'How old were you?'

'Six. I was having a fight with one of my older brothers, who had been annoying me.'

'How old was he?'

'Nine. And winding me up, as he is still capable of doing.'

'What happened to him?'

'He went through the window too. He has a dented bridge to his nose which is all my own work. Do you have siblings?'

'Yes, three. But I am the eldest. I can't remember any of my sisters trying to put me through a window.'

'I didn't just try, I succeeded,' she pointed out.

The waiter arrived with their food, and he removed his hand, the focused nervous energy directing itself to the business of food.

'Would you like some of my chips?' she asked, for something to say.

'No, thank you, I get far too much to eat anyway, and not enough exercise.'

A big man, of course, she thought, watching the large hands, with fingers that were both long and thick, and the powerful shoulders. Large-boned too, like her Henriques family, and like them he would easily put on a couple of stone if he ate too much. But this one wasn't going to do that, he had himself well in hand, and was not offering any of the Henriques male rationalizations.

'Where *do* you put it all?' he asked, with interest as she speared a forkful of *pommes frites*.

'I've always been able to eat anything I want. It must be genetic, from my mother's side. And then I got rather thin for a year or so, but I'm putting it on now.'

'You're still a little thin,' he said, gently and she ducked her head, incredulously, realizing that tears were not far away.

'It'll pass,' she said, when she could manage to say it briskly. She looked round for a waiter; having refused wine she wanted some more water, then remembered herself and asked her host if she might have some more.

He looked at her, momentarily arrested, then grinned hugely, amusement lighting his face. 'Oh very correct,' he said, laughing at her. He did no more than turn his head and a waiter was at his side and she realized that half the restaurant was watching them, as, more impressively, were both of the waiters looking after their section.

Unnerved, she crumbled a roll, then remembered that actually she knew very little about this man; indeed, how could she, being brought up in the Henriques household, where Conservative politicians were regarded either as villainous enemies or a branch of the light entertainment industry, depending on their abilities.

'Gerry,' she said, abruptly, 'you said you would tell me one day why you had gone into politics.'

'And the day has come, has it?'

She looked up to find him watching her, disconcertingly, with the most tender amusement. 'Yes. In your own words, in not more than four paragraphs. Suitable for absorption by the slowest chap in the back rank.'

'You put the slow ones in the front where you can see them,' he pointed out, promptly, and she saw for a minute the careful confident officer he must once have been. 'I went into politics to make things better, like most people,' he said, easily.

'In what way? Define better. What is your definition of good?' Oh God, she thought, how much I sound like my father, and watched Gerry anxiously, but he was unworried.

'Well, I suppose if I have to summarize, I want everyone to have the best possible chance to do things for themselves, rather than being given what bureaucratic state employers want to give them. As happens under Labour.'

'All right-wing policy starts from a statement of objection,' she said, dismissively, on familiar ground. 'But how do you achieve what you say you want? How do you ensure that people's choice is not hopelessly constrained by where they start from? How much can an illiterate black teenager in Brixton achieve in this society by and for himself?'

'That teenager ought not to be illiterate, and it is a function of Labour education policy that he is. They refused to accept that you have to teach, that education must be rigorous. And they refused to accept the kind of quality control you need to keep teachers – or anyone else for that matter – up to scratch. It's called competition, and if you don't leave room for that, you won't get a decent service in any field. How good would a state legal service be?'

'You have a point. We *know* the answer to that. It's called the judiciary and it is terrible.' She had always been appalled by the operation of the courts; from the highest to the lowest they were as inefficient and self-indulgent as you would expect from a group that powerful.

'I hadn't realized that.' Gerry was, she saw, seriously interested. 'I've been saying things to myself and everyone else about our judicial system being the best in the world. Not true?'

'Absolutely not. Privileged, inefficient, low output, idiosyncratic, a profound barrier to progress. No decent commercial lawyer will let a client near a court, for fear of having him and his affairs brought to a standstill for years.'

'Jarndyce and Jarndyce still lives.' She blinked at him and saw that he was laughing at her. 'I did learn to read.'

'Oh good,' she said, making a fast recovery. 'My family isn't very oriented towards the armed forces, and I thought you did it all in Morse code. Yes, Dickens described it absolutely right, but he did not offer any analysis of why it was like that; it is, I think, because of the privilege embodied in the system. The judiciary, you know, are truly the *nomenklatura* of the United Kingdom.'

'It isn't just slow because of the need to protect the innocent?'

'That isn't what the system does. I used to work for a Neighbourhood Law Centre, as a volunteer, when I was young and had time. The system of criminal law has been bent out of shape by another bit of the *nomenklatura*, namely the police force.' She considered her statement, carefully. 'I'm a little out of date; it is some years since I was in this game, but corruption was certainly running deep in the Met in the mid-seventies. And *that* bites on the poor and the incompetent, and *that* you can't cure by competition.'

'Surely the police are not that bad.'

'*Don't* let anyone tell you this is left-wing paranoia. I too had assumed my father was exaggerating, and he wasn't.'

He nodded, soberly, shaken, and she watched him, anxiously.

'I didn't mean to stop you telling me about Conservative policy.'

'You haven't. I was just mentally adding another area of life in this country that we were going to have to take apart, and free up.'

'I do agree with your lot about the trade unions,' she offered, hastily. 'They had become deeply embedded in privilege. Even Sholto – my father – thinks so.'

'Them I feel very strongly about,' he said, lighting up. '*That*'s where I'd like to start, remove that series of barriers to economic efficiency and training people, and change all those things. But that's going to take legislation. In my own constituency there are people in shipyards who were told they would have jobs for life by the unions, but were unable to work efficiently, because of the unions, so those jobs weren't safe, even under a Labour government, and then we couldn't retrain the people because of the unions. A lot of people made useless as surely as if they had been crippled.'

He looked at her, and at his cooling duck. 'Sorry, talking too much.'

'No, you're not. I wanted to know. So what are you doing at Transport?'

'Well, that's important too. And it's my job. In government, you do what you're asked to.'

'As in the army?'

'As in the army, yes. As well as you can.'

'Without using a thing called "money"? Without which, as anyone can tell you, no progress in transport is possible.' He winced and she saw she had hit a sore point. 'I'm sorry, I'm stopping you eating.'

'I can always eat. No, Transport is difficult, and it isn't what I wanted.'

She looked disaffectedly at her own steak; it was as always delicious, the sauce pink with wine, cream and peppercorns as good as ever, the *pommes frites* both melting and crisp, and she could hardly get any of it down. Gerry was picking at his duck, hiding bits under a fork and shovelling up the green peas which were easier to digest. He pushed the rest decisively to one side and looked thoughtfully at her plate.

'Not nice?'

'Very. I just seem not to be as hungry as I thought I was.'

'Nor am I.'

They looked at each other.

'Wicked waste makes woeful want,' she observed, nervously.

'Ah. And I may live to say, "Oh, how I wish I had that crust".'

'. . . That once I flung away,' she completed the quatrain.

'How do you know that?' they both said, simultaneously, and Caroline recovered first.

'My mother went to a Quaker school. She taught it to me as not quite a joke.'

'I learnt it from my nanny,' he said, amused. 'Tell me about your mother.'

She put her fork down, acknowledging that she was not going to get through her steak, and sighed. 'I'm not sure I can bear to. She was born into one high-minded academic, slightly *silly* Hampstead family and married into another, silly in only a slightly different way. She had a pretty miserable time when we were all young because she was always under pressure and worried about money and it's not that much better now, due to my idiot father still doing prissy, high-minded things for no money, mostly for the Labour Party.' She looked despairingly at him. 'You're never going to understand this.'

'I found my parents pretty difficult too. My father persisted in running a small family textile business which just staggered along financially, thereby, I felt, letting himself and my mother in for a unique combination of boredom interspersed by insecurity. His father – my grandfather – however was a judge and rather a star.'

'So you chose the army as a secure job?'

'I wasn't academic, and I had to do my National Service anyway. So I was commissioned into the county regiment, was sent to Cyprus in the troubles and found I liked the life. So then I went to Sandhurst on a scholarship.'

'I had a scholarship too. To Lady Eleanor's, for all the fees. And to Somerville.'

'Goodness.' He was smiling now with open, amused affection.

'Sorry,' she said, feeling about six years old. 'So then you went into politics, once you didn't need to be quite so safe, to restore the family name, as well as to do good.'

143

His eyes opened in surprise and she saw that this was the first time he had seen it. 'That's right. And you're a lawyer because you still need to be safe, and you hardly need to restore the Henriques name.'

'And I need to earn lots of money.'

She saw that she had hit a nerve again. Ministerial pay was notoriously poor, about a third of what she took home. A man like this would not like the fact that she was so infinitely his superior in the earnings stakes. Indeed he was glancing at his watch and raising a hand for the bill and her heart sank. There can be no need to insist so firmly on your accomplishments and status, she told herself, hopelessly, watching him being charming to the hovering floor manager.

He looked across at her. 'Sorry, I have to go. Transport Questions are third order this afternoon and I have to be there to take over when my secretary of state gets tired of them.' He thought about it. 'If he gets tired of them,' he added, and she saw for a moment how irritated he was by his position.

She said something civil but incoherent, and he recovered to smile at her. 'I meant to say I had a word with John Winstanley about your Prior Building Systems. He tells me the NEB probably aren't going to try to float it on the stock market.'

'I don't think they could,' she agreed. Shut *up*, she thought, horror-stricken, watching him look disappointed.

'But he is thinking in terms of a trade sale, rather than a management buy-out. That's a pity, because it's a politically attractive idea to have employees as shareholders, particularly given our weakness in the north.'

She drew in a breath and steadied herself. 'That is

interesting and that *was* kind of you to tackle him. Well, my client and I will just have to convince him. I must manage to introduce you to the management – who are very good.'

'I have already arranged to go and see them, next weekend. My constituency office fixed it this morning.'

Caroline, accustomed to organizing those around her, considered him, momentarily lost for words. 'Wonderful,' she said, recovering. 'You can see what you think of them.'

'That was the idea,' he said, demurely and she found herself able to laugh with him.

'I must go. Come with me? The car can drop you.'

They walked the length of the restaurant, and heads turned all the way down for Gerry, who seemed perfectly at home and cheerful. He does like it, she observed as her poise returned; he's like a popular boy at school, basking in admiration. They arrived on the windswept pavement and she admired the ministerial car but declined a trip via the House of Commons, realizing unbelievingly that she had ten minutes to get to her next meeting. Thank God one of them had been watching the clock.

'Caroline?'

She turned to him, inquiringly, and he bent to kiss her clumsily on the cheek. 'I'd like to kiss you in a less brotherly way,' he said, unsmiling, looking down at her, head tipped slightly back. 'But I can't here.'

'Oh Gerry,' she said, stupidly, wanting to touch him.

'I'll ring you.' He touched her shoulder in farewell and made for the car, which pulled away as soon as he got in, so that the last she saw of him was his profile as he leant forward to say something to the driver, his

145

attention already concentrated on the next place to which he was going.

In the north the wind was blowing harder than in London, but the two men in the modern office were uncharacteristically ignoring the struggles of the crane gang as revealed in wide-screen clarity through the picture windows.

'She doesn't hang about, Caroline, does she?' Martin Williams said, admiringly, sinking into one of the visitors' armchairs.

'So this Gerry Willshaw's coming to see us at the weekend. What did he say?'

'He didn't. A secretary made the appointment. I asked to talk to him personally so I could find out exactly what he wanted, but she wouldn't put me through, just said that Mr Willshaw would like to look round a site and talk to management if that was convenient.' Peter Burwood was sounding ruffled; it had been some time since he had been unable to extract from anyone seeking an appointment with him the exact nature of their business.

'He's a minister, Peter. He probably wasn't even in the office.'

'So she said when I pushed.' Burwood was unconvinced, and Martin watched him indulgently. He was the older by nearly ten years, forty-eight to Peter's thirty-nine. He had been introduced into the company five years earlier by Peter, then the young production controller. He had been inspired by Peter's certainty and respected his tenacity, accompanied as it was by a substantial and useful dose of caution and a sharp political sense which had enabled him not only to survive but to inherit the managing director's job when Prior Building Systems had run out of road and been swept into the NEB. But he was always uncomfortable, was Peter, in a situation where he did not know exactly who wanted what.

Unlike Graham, who appeared at the door at that moment, looking relaxed as he always did. He also had been brought in by Peter, but more recently; he'd been poached from a supplier to replace the last incumbent of the post, when it had become clear that the sacrifice of the finance director as well as the chairman and MD was going to be required to make the NEB feel comfortable with their investment. Graham folded his 6 ft 4 ins into the other visitors' armchair, tried to tuck away a pair of enormous feet and gave up, deciding apologetically to let the girl bringing them coffee step over him. She was pleased to do it; girls always were pleased to do anything Graham Gough asked because he was a good-looking hunk of a man with pleasant relaxed manners. Beneath the smiling, gentle-giant exterior lay an extremely competent finance director and a ruthless realist; he was never going to get into the same sort of mess as his predecessor, a details man who had failed to grasp the extent of the company's cash needs. Under Graham's deceptively casual leadership cash had been squeezed unremittingly out of every crevice, so that the company had arrived at its year end having paid its considerable interest bill with some reserves of cash tucked away.

Graham, Martin reflected, as he watched him lazily chatting up a secretary, was actually quite as cunning and political an operator as Peter, it was just better concealed. A good team, he thought, and Caroline appeared to be just what they needed, given the impressive speed with which she had analysed their problem and fielded an influential junior minister. The high politics and the legal side of all this were where they were weak and she seemed to be filling that gap.

'Right,' Peter said, watching his secretary out of the room. 'Now. I've had a call from Ron Jenkins at the NEB. He wants to see us about our corporate plan. He wants to show it to the Department of the Environment's merchant bankers.'

'Why?' Graham asked, momentarily bewildered.

'What Ron said was that the DoE's bankers were questioning these forecasts, wanting to know what the risks were, whether there was potential upside, and if so where it was. They want specifically to discuss our assumptions about how much cash we expect to get from renegotiation of the existing contracts.'

'Mm.' Graham reached for the thick pile of documents he had put down on the low coffee-table beside him. 'We assumed we'd be able to get another one per cent – that's £1½m in cash – on Clayhanger, Alleyns and Betts Quay together for this year. About £1½m out of this year's £8m PBIT. That's conservative, but they'll expect that. No one puts all the upside in a forecast. They don't put all the downside in either – you just hope one will balance out the other.'

'Tell me what downside factor we managed to leave out, Graham.' Martin decided it was time this conversation anchored itself in reality.

'Hurricane risk?' Graham said, deadpan, and all three men glanced, involuntarily, towards the window.

'Well, that would be about the only one,' Peter said, drily. 'What about those contract renegotiation figures? Do we tell them?'

There was a cautious silence, while Graham and Martin both decided not to be the next to speak, but Peter was not going to let them get away with it. 'Martin?'

'Well, we don't actually *know* anything different from when we wrote those forecasts, do we?' Martin said, carefully.

'No, we don't. All we have is gossip and hearsay,' Peter agreed.

'And hope,' Graham pointed out, addressing his documents.

'But that's all it is.' Peter was on to him. 'I mean, I wouldn't even like to tell a bank about this one, it's so tenuous.' He spread his hands, treating the other two to a wide honest stare. His colleagues considered him, doubtfully.

'Before we discuss what we're going to say, what do we think the upside potential actually is?' Martin met his chief executive's offended stare. 'The truth's not a bad place to start from, Peter.'

Burwood's basilisk expression vanished, leaving him looking five years younger. 'If we can't think of anything *else*, I suppose.'

'Why not. Just for laughs,' Graham chipped in, catching the prevailing mood and all three relaxed, more comfortable with each other and the discussion.

'If Hughes is right, we can agree in renegotiation a profit level of four per cent on those three,' Martin said. 'Then that's what? £4m this year, give or take a little, Graham.'

'£4m in this year, about £3m next year, £3m in year three,' Graham said, without consulting his papers. 'Instead of PBIT at £12m for this year we'd be at £16m odd. Makes the company worth about £70m on the same assumptions.'

The three of them looked at each other, but it was Martin who was the first to speak. 'And anyone – I mean any investor we might talk to – would value the company like that.'

'Anyone who knew we had a chance at that extra profit would reckon the company was cheap at £60m plus, yes,' Graham confirmed, brutally.

Peter nodded and stared at his hands, while the other two watched him, Graham fidgeting in his chair, not out of nervousness or discomfort, but because he needed to move around: the penalty, Martin thought drily, of being quite so much the classic, tall and powerful meso-morph. He looked at him warningly, not wanting Peter's train of thought interrupted, and Graham man-aged to force himself into uncomfortable stillness. Peter's deliberations always took time, because he liked to think his way round all the angles on a difficult subject right before speaking, even among friends and allies.

'The NEB have treated us fairly,' Peter said, finally, looking at the other two, and Graham shifted his posi-tion with a grunt of relief. 'And we've treated them the same. But it's a different position now. They intend to sell the company and we want to buy it. They own all the shares, and we're not irreplaceable. Or at least Caro-line doesn't think we are.'

'Get another lawyer,' Graham suggested, deadpan. 'You don't pay them to say that sort of thing.'

Peter smiled, reluctantly. 'She's right. She said to re-member that it might suit a trade purchaser down to the ground if we walked out. After all, he'd probably have some spare management he could put in and he'd not have to pay us off.'

'Christ!' Graham, with four children to support, looked appalled.

'None of us can afford that,' Peter said kindly. 'And anyway, it would be stupid. If we can't buy this company, we need to stay on someone's payroll while we find another one to buy, right?'

Martin blinked. He and Peter had always agreed that they wanted to run their own company, but he had not realized that Graham was now included in the plan. Of course, they needed a good finance director, but given Peter's cautious temperament he had not expected the apparently easy-going Graham to have become part of the in-group after less than a year. Graham's look of instant startled gratification made it clear that he had gone through much the same thought-process.

'Yes,' he said, making a rapid recovery. 'I even know one we could move in on.'

Peter flapped a hand. 'Right. But it's this one we want, we know it, we've worked bloody hard to get it pointing in the right direction and I'm not going to give it up to some vulture who has been hovering around waiting for us to fall over again. Now, what do we do about these forecasts?'

'I think we're trying to re-invent the wheel,' Martin said, slowly. 'There are lots of companies where there is a funny about, some variable which could radically change the company's future.'

'There'll be a formula. Why don't we ask Caroline?' Graham heaved himself out of his chair, stretching gratefully and walked the long way round the room to find the biscuits.

Peter pressed a buzzer for a secretary and three minutes later the three of them were grinning, as Caroline's clear voice could be heard on their speaker-phone, issuing instructions to some underling: '. . . and don't let the client anywhere near that meeting, Mark – disaster will follow. OK . . . Peter, hello!'

'One day I'm going to hear you telling them not to let us into a meeting,' he said, grinning at the phone.

'Never.'

'You mean you'll make sure we don't hear,' Martin suggested.

'Yes. What can I do for you?'

Martin smiled to himself, amused by the lack of polite inquiry as to their health and welfare.

'We've got a problem here, Caroline.' Peter paused to gather his thoughts, and the speaker-phone remained impressively silent. 'When we do our corporate plan, we have all sorts of judgements to make; there are a lot of factors to consider and we do the best we can.'

'Yes,' the speaker-phone said, impatiently, and Peter sat up straight and looked at it inimically.

'One of the most difficult areas of judgement has to do with the three loss-making contracts that we are currently working through.'

'Course it does,' the voice said, briskly. 'You've assumed just over £1½m back on the renegotiation in the current year. What's the problem – it's massively more?'

Martin drew in a sharp breath, watching Peter who was notoriously averse to having his thought-processes interrupted, and was staring at the phone as if it had bitten him.

'Yes,' he said, squaring his elbows and Martin breathed again.

'Why?'

'We think we may be making a breakthrough in the price renegotiations. But we don't know for certain.'

'How much more might you get?'

'Some millions, in each of three years.'

'OK. I see.'

Silence fell, with the three men watching the phone expectantly.

'You gave the NEB your corporate plan when?'

'Three months ago, and they want us to go through it with Fredericks, the DoE advisers.'

'That's fair enough. The NEB are your shareholder, you do what they want. That's how company law operates in this country.'

There was a further pause, while papers rustled at Caroline's end. 'Look, Peter they'd be fully within their rights in getting rid of the lot of you if they found out you'd been concealing something material. So you tell them that there is some upside potential but you don't have to be very specific.'

'Will they want more money for the company?' Peter returned to his major preoccupation.

'Probably. It's a bloody nuisance having this renegotiation coming through because it will make everyone restless and greedy, but it can't be helped. What we'll do is offer a deferred purchase deal, say £Xm if the out-turn comes out like the current plan and £Xm plus if it comes out different.'

'Will the NEB be prepared to do a deal like that?' Peter asked, cautiously.

They all heard Caroline sigh. 'When I act for a seller, I try very hard to keep my client out of these deals, because I know I'm letting the poor bugger in for a dreadful hassle in the future. And someone will tell the NEB just that. So it won't be favourite, but what we have to bank on, gentlemen, as I've said before, is that this *isn't* the normal commercial deal, and that there will be other reasons for favouring you over a trade purchaser. And a deferred purchase agreement is also cosmetically useful if we find we can't pay up front what a trade purchaser can.'

'And it's the way of fixing our little problem here – with the renegotiation, I mean.'

'That's right. The paths of righteousness are often the smoothest.'

'This is true.' Graham agreed and blushed slightly as he found the other two gazing at him.

'Thank you, Caroline.' Peter took the reins back, promptly, and Graham went back to his chair and flopped into it, leaving arms and legs distributed where they fell. 'We'll need to think about all this and discuss it between the three of us. But that's most helpful.' He paused. 'How are you?' he asked conscientiously.

'I'm fine. Very good, in fact.'

All three laughed, the tension in the room easing.

'That's what it sounds like,' Peter said, grinning. 'We'll be in touch tomorrow.'

'Look forward to it.'

8

Clive Fieldman, after a week's holiday, was mildly taken aback by the amount in his in-tray. If the under-secretary, the head of a major policy division, is out of the office while Parliament is sitting, the three or four assist-ant secretaries beneath him have necessarily to take over most of the work and dispose of it, since the Parliamen-tary process cannot be impeded, and difficult Questions and briefings for debates cannot wait until the head of division is there to deal with them. But everything that could wait for his return appeared to his jaundiced gaze to have done just that. As he sorted it into piles, he realized that he was doing one at least of his subordin-ates an injustice; the talented, driving James Mather, with the efficiency and confidence of the ex-private secretary, had cheerfully and authoritatively done every-thing that had come to him, including a couple of Parliamentary Questions that could easily have gone elsewhere in the division: his contribution to the in-tray was mostly copies of what he had done to Mr Fieldman, on return, in orthodox civil-service style.

On return after one week I could have done without quite all this, James old son, Clive thought, ungratefully, but on the other hand I do know what has happened in my absence, or at least what has happened on your side. The second pile was small but he eyed it uneasily. Janice O'Brien, another clever one, had finally finished the position paper on the future of the Department's rela-tionship with the major contractors and employers' organization, and *that* would take a lot of reading. The third pile was the largest and simply exasperating: the product of one week of Michael Watson, seventeen years senior to either of the others, promoted beyond his ability or confidence, who referred everything upwards, after long, anxious deliberations, and if told to go back and think about it again, would have two drinks too many at lunch, thereby further reducing an already minimal level of competence. The distinguishing feature of the civil service was that once through the two-year probationary period a chap was there for life. This provision was deeply embedded; its original purpose was to ensure that no politician could sabotage the profession by calling for the removal of a civil servant who opposed him, but the side effects were inevitable and infuriating, and he had been unlucky enough to draw a living example. The only thing to do with Michael Watson now or any time in the last ten years was to retire him, as kindly as possible, but the organization did not provide a method of achieving this end other than the brutal and protracted process involved in getting him declared to be of 'limited efficiency'. There was a scheme, newly introduced, for allowing senior people to retire at fifty-five, voluntarily in most cases, but there was no chance of it working with Watson; unconfident and obsessive at work he was absolutely dependent on his office routine. He would, as anyone could see with half an eye, fight like a cornered mouse to stay. Unless someone senior was prepared to devote a lot of time and energy to getting him out, there he would be, getting in everyone's way till the end came in four years' time, when the advent of his sixtieth birthday meant he would be out of the door, like all civil servants, talented and stupid alike.

Clive, clever, able and hardworking, decided unhesitatingly that, on the evidence of this pile of rubbish on top of everything else, he would get Watson retired, pronto, or as pronto as procedures allowed. And when he had his own Department he would make quite sure that his establishment division understood absolutely that he would tolerate no dead wood; the taxpayer deserved better. Sir Clive Fieldman, KCB, interviewed in retirement, he thought sardonically; what would my old dad have said, given the deadbeats he gave his life to keeping in employment? Not that there was anything else for his dad's customers to work at, whereas Watson could go and drive an employers' federation or a golf club out of their minds. And in the meantime he would encourage the talented impatient young principal, who had recently been shipped in to his division, to work straight to him, bypassing Watson; he didn't want the lad hopelessly discouraged. Which was another good reason for getting Watson out: not only did he infuriate his superiors, but he must have depressed a couple of generations of his confident juniors by now.

Clive settled down to hack his way through Watson's pile, writing acid notes where he felt like it – no sense in not giving the chap warning – then read appreciatively young James's copies. There had been a better way to cope with that particular Question but the overloaded deputy secretary, his own immediate superior, had found it, doing a swift red pen re-draft which combined at one stroke a neat deflection of the Question with polite amazement that the chap should ever have asked. But most of James's stuff was excellent, competent, effective and timely, and he must remember to tell him so. He lifted his head as his secretary appeared with the day's correspondence and eyed the tray; with luck he could get through that lot before his eleven o'clock meeting, then read Janice's paper over lunch.

'Mr Mather won't be in till twelve, Mr Fieldman.' Miss Williams' formality extended itself to younger staff as well. 'You remember he had an appointment; and you are having lunch at Smith Butler, the solicitors, if that's all right? I told them you were away and fixed it on the basis that you might want to cancel since it was your first day back. They seemed quite happy with the arrangement.'

'Mm. No, it's all right, Miss Williams, I will go. I'll probably have had enough by lunchtime. I'd be surprised if their lunches go on half the afternoon – they're busy people, same as us. I've done most of it already. You'll type it in a couple of hours.' With his father's curiosity about people he had established that his admirable secretary, like a surprising number of the older women in the service, had nursed an aged mother for longer than seemed humanly tolerable, sacrificing everything of her own life, except the right to a good senior secretary's job. Mum was still with us and Clive, naturally efficient, kept Miss Williams after hours as rarely as possible, knowing that she would pay a heavy price for being home late.

'I should think you would have had enough,' she said. 'Mr Watson seems to have referred a lot of papers to you.'

'All his incoming post,' he said, bitterly. She was discreet and highly intelligent, and would have made a much better assistant secretary than Michael Watson, and he thought some acknowledgement of all this was fair.

Resolutely, he rang up his colleague in Establishment Division and arranged to start the limited efficiency procedure operating.

'Must you, Clive?' the head of Establishment Division asked, plaintively. 'It's tremendously time-consuming. Couldn't you wait a few months? We are – we must be – going to get a really generous early retirement programme, which will be much easier. This lot seem to be absolutely serious about cutting down numbers in the senior civil service and we've all, in unison, explained that this will cost money in the short term. They understand what we're saying – they've got enough business-men in the Cabinet – but they don't like it because cash is tight this year. No, I don't know why, or even if they've got it right; it's far more likely that the Treasury got in a muddle, deducted the number they first thought of, then added in the date. Oh, well, if you must, you must. I'll get someone to find the Watson file. Of course there is one, dear boy; you don't think you're the first person to have wanted him out, do you? People usually get him transferred, you know. I could probably do that – there's a lot of changes in Planning. No?'

No, Clive said, and rang off, grimly enlightened. Watson had arrived in the division about two months before he had. His own predecessor as head of division had already had three years in the job, and had not bothered to repel an incompetent, indeed had probably thought a spectacularly young successor could with profit be slowed up a bit. Well, they'd picked the wrong man.

Still shaking his head he arrived by appointment to see Winstanley, who was inclined to be sardonic about senior civil servants who felt they could take a week off when Parliament was sitting.

'I don't usually,' Clive said, unruffled. 'But I was here right through Christmas because all my staff wanted to be off, and last week was the kids' half term.'

Since all Members of Parliament leave at breakneck speed the Thursday or Friday before Christmas and do not reappear until at least two weeks later, relying on their Departments to keep the papers passing and the routine business of government operating, he was on sound ground. The fact that the children did not live with him, and had been unavailable over Christmas because Linda had taken them all up to Scotland for two weeks, could usefully remain unsaid.

'You've caught up, then?' Winstanley had asked.

'I have some excellent staff,' Clive had said, part of his mind still occupied with Watson, and Winstanley laughed.

'I know the feeling. I wanted to talk about the NEB construction companies.' He paused. 'It's very important for the whole privatization programme that we get this sale right.'

Clive had not been fifteen years in the civil service without knowing that 'right' in this context was a political rather than a moral imperative, and he mentally sat up. It was inevitable that party political considerations would affect the sale, but the good civil servants had dutifully proceeded as if the present government meant what they said about commercial efficiency and the importance of letting market forces take their course. So the Department of the Environment and the NEB had appointed two sets of experienced financial advisers to tell them about market forces and it might reasonably have been assumed that their advice – which when he went on leave had seemed to be converging – would be taken. What had happened in his absence and why was it unrecorded on any piece of paper he had seen so far? Had one set of these highly paid characters quarrelled with the other and produced different advice, or what? Why had James Mather not warned him?

'Was there a meeting with Fredericks last week?' he asked, as neutrally as possible, because if there had been he had not received a note of it and someone had blundered.

'On Friday,' Winstanley said and the private secretary added hastily that he had dictated the note at once, of course, but feared it might not have got round yet, sorry.

You'll have to do better than that, matey, Clive thought, critically; he himself when in private office had never left without dictating a note of all meetings that day, depositing the result with a night typist, signing the lot off at 8.30 a.m. next morning, and making damn sure that the Department's messenger system got them on to everyone's desks by 10 a.m. That, come to think of it, he had learned at Smith Butler; you worked through the night if need be to get a client a draft or a document and the fact that he did not stop to sleep if there was something urgent to do had given him an edge at every stage over his contemporaries in the civil service.

'What happened, Minister?'

'Oh, nothing tremendously conclusive at that meeting, but we are making progress. Both banks came down absolutely against trying to do a flotation of the companies as a package, but we expected that, didn't we? And both sets of bankers seemed to feel that there was a real problem of valuation around only one of the companies

– Prior. I mean, very much as expected.' He dug irritably at a loose link on his watch strap with one of the Department's biros.

But something's not worth the money, not useful to you, Clive observed, antennae alert. This admirably rational process isn't sexy enough politically. Or is it that there is a favoured purchaser whom this does not suit? He had been unable to talk to Lucy Friern for almost ten days. He could never talk to her at weekends and it had proved very difficult to dump the children in the evenings last week and telephone her; the one time he had managed to get twenty minutes to himself she had been out. Had she, in his absence, achieved the promised dinner party and had Matthew managed to make a persuasive case for a sale to Friern which Winstanley was now trying to accommodate?

'You will need to decide the criteria for any sale,' he said, carefully, and watched Winstanley's head come up.

'I'd assumed that we'd find it very difficult not to take whoever bid the highest for whichever of the companies.'

'Well, there are policy considerations, Minister,' Clive observed, watching his man, wondering how interested he still was in trying to go down the sale as a package route.

'Of course there are.' Winstanley was looking hopeful. 'Returning these companies to the private sector as quickly as possible, for instance.'

'Indeed, Minister. Consonant with getting a decent price and finding them a good home.'

'Oh Lord, yes. We couldn't afford to have the viable ones collapse again.'

'And of course it must be important to preserve employment.' Clive rode over Winstanley's look of instant suspicion at the invocation of this key plank of the last administration's policy. 'I mean, the three decent companies are based in the north and someone is going to build houses there; given the general state of the local economy, it would be a pity if the profit and the employment went outside the area.'

'Oh, that's absolutely right,' Winstanley agreed, relieved. He hesitated. 'And of course there may be other policy considerations; I am thinking specifically of our wish to extend share-ownership.'

'Particularly employee share-ownership.'

'Yes, indeed.'

Well now, that is interesting, Clive thought. The management team at Prior Systems under Peter Burwood must have got to you, although he did not strike me as having much grasp of party politics when I went to see him last year. He bent his head and drew a squiggle; the trouble with Winstanley, he had agreed with senior colleagues, was that he changed his mind in accordance with whomever he had last talked to. This, however, was a situation well within departmental experience and there was a routine for dealing with it.

'Minister, I think we need to get the criteria for this sale right quickly. The bankers – both Gruhners and Fredericks – seem to me to be seeking guidance, and we need to set out the criteria for them. Shall we produce a draft list so you can think about it?'

'Well, now that would be very useful.' Winstanley looked dazed but relieved at the way his problem had resolved itself. He hesitated, cast down by further reflection. 'I suppose we also have to decide which are the most important – I mean rank these criteria in some way.'

'Only in very broad terms. It might well be that you would conclude that three or four were of equal importance and outranked the rest.' And we'll draft it that way, Clive noted, professionally. James can have a crack at it and I'll go over it, but speed of sale, price, good home for company, in random order, come out on top. Account to be taken of need to maintain local employment and extend share-ownership to employees ranking somewhere below. That should, if necessary, enable anyone up to and including the Public Accounts Committee to grasp why we didn't just take the highest bidder – it was the criteria, see. And the bankers, not us, can explain how they picked their way through five more or less equally ranked desiderata, at least two of which were mutually exclusive. He withdrew, leaving Winstanley looking a great deal happier than when he had arrived, collected James and explained to him the outline of his task.

'Neat,' James said, grinning.

'Old, but still good,' Clive agreed. 'I'd like to get that up tomorrow. We need a background piece. I'll do it, I know what I want to say. You get the criteria right. Come and talk if you get stuck – I'll be back about three thirty.'

He arrived outside the Department's frowning tower blocks into Marsham Street, empty as usual of any form of public transport. The civil service does not have most of the ordinary perks of business life; no one below the rank of permanent secretary commands a driver and no one at all is given a private car. The result is that senior civil servants at least from the DoE tend to be late for lunch if they are eating outside the Department. Marsham Street is served intermittently by one bus, the 88, and it has long been an article of DoE faith that there is a drivers' and conductors' card school at either end of the route, this being the only way of explaining why 88s arrive only in twos and at fifteen-minute intervals.

Thanks to the London Underground, he arrived only marginally late at the offices of Smith Butler, reflecting that he had never in fifteen years been back to that pleasant corner of Lincoln's Inn Fields, or the substantial building with its wide flight of stairs up which he had run every day for a year. He hadn't disliked it exactly, but he had known that it was not for him; unlike the DoE where he had found his feet right from the beginning, he had often felt detached and incompetent here. And a bit of that had probably been due to his hostess today. He resolved not to be intimidated this time, dammit, he was nearly the youngest under-secretary in the service, on the high road to the very top jobs, and his mistress was prettier than Caroline Henriques. So concentrated was he that he breezed past a receptionist and had to be courteously recalled and identified. He waited, braced, ready for Caroline to do something annoying, but she appeared almost immediately, smiling and kissed him and he remembered reluctantly that she was always on time, it was just another of the things that had made her such a daunting proposition sixteen years ago.

'How nice of you to come, Clive. Michael Appleton, who is very much looking forward to seeing you again, is at the top of the table today. He is the senior partner now. There are four others apart from me – I'll introduce you as we go in – also five other guests – I hope Susie gave your secretary a list. Good.'

He found himself, flatteringly, at the managing partner's right hand with Caroline on his other side. The other guests were a mixed bag, but senior to him, two chief executives of good-sized companies among them. A carefully chosen group he realized, exchanging civilities with Michael Appleton; two at least of the guests were interested in DoE areas and, having been the principal private secretary to the Secretary of State until a year ago, he was well equipped to talk to them. He realized indeed that he had been talking enough to lag behind, so that everyone else had finished their main course, and he wondered momentarily whether just to stop eating. Caroline, however, introduced another conversation which meant one of the chief executives had to talk, and he was able to finish an excellent chicken dish. He thought about her as he ate; he had not remembered her as being either considerate or socially adroit, just damned bossy, but sixteen years could have changed a lot of things.

'Wake up, Jeremy, circulate the drink,' he heard her say impatiently, just below general audibility, to a negligent colleague, who started guiltily into action, and he grinned, reassured and comfortably conscious that had he been thus addressed he would now have passed her the bottle and told her to get on with it. He jerked to attention as he heard the word Prior and glanced inquiringly at Michael Appleton.

'Sorry, I just couldn't find a minute to tell Clive,' Caroline said, sounding unapologetic, from his right.

'We have just been taken on to act for Prior Building

Systems. Given that the NEB have been asked to sell Prior, it was felt appropriate that the company should have different legal advisers from the NEB themselves. And we are the different advisers, or rather I am. I do know this is in your area and wanted to declare an interest before anyone started talking about privatization.'

Clive, thoroughly familiar with similar situations, remained unflustered. Like most senior civil servants he accepted it as part of his job to be plied with lunch and grilled about policies for which he was responsible. He was conscious, however, both of a feeling of unworthy pleasure that Caroline was now in a position to seek his help and of faint regret that it was not for his brown eyes alone that she had decided to renew old acquaintance. 'That's what you were doing at the conference the other day.'

'In part. I was also there, as one always is, to see what other crumbs I could pick up.'

'Not a very nice way to describe the chairman of the Electricity Council,' Clive said, swiftly, having observed her exchanging kisses with this dignitary at lunch.

Taken unawares, she snorted with laughter and choked on her trifle and he, delighted, patted her on the back, smugly plying her with water. He looked up as she coughed and spluttered to find two partners in Smith Butler watching him from across the table with expressions of stunned admiration, and grinned at them broadly.

'Of course you trained with Caroline, didn't you?' one of them said, wistfully, and Clive looked out of the corner of his eye at Michael Appleton, who had been there too, and was relieved to see he was grinning as broadly as the rest. Caroline recovered herself, indicating minatorily to her partners that they should talk among themselves, and when he next looked at her she was watching him with interest.

'What are you advising them on, Caroline?' he asked quietly, under cover of several conversations.

'How to put together a buy-out. Without numbers other than those publicly available, I hasten to add; one of the first things I did was to tell them that they could not hand over any figures unless and until authorized by the NEB.'

'Very orthodox.'

'Very necessary. Managements have been fired before now for doing just that.' She hesitated. 'In all this we – me and the lads I mean – are assuming that they will be allowed to put together a proper bid for the company providing your chap decides he can't float it.'

'No decision has yet been taken which would preclude a flotation,' he said, stiffly.

The look of hostile exasperation she gave him took him straight back sixteen years, but he found he could stand his ground these days.

'Good prospects for the future in that company. Quite big enough to float,' he pointed out.

'Shitty awful track-record. And you'll never get the merchant wankers to underwrite, unless, I suppose, it's Christmas time at DoE, and you're giving it away gift-wrapped, which, presumably, you can't.'

He gritted his back teeth together to suppress the grin that threatened to spread all over his face at this savagely accurate summary of the bankers' painstaking advice.

'Caroline, my dear.' Michael Appleton sounded disapprovingly. 'We do still have difficulty with her language, Clive, as you can see.'

Yes, but you're all fond of her and you handle her pretty well; she's found a home here, he thought, just as I have in government service.

'I take it you feel you were right to change all those years ago, Clive?' Michael Appleton asked, quietly.

'Absolutely.' He hesitated, seeking a way of describing what he had found without denigrating what Smith Butler had, but Caroline, ruffled by male patronage, spoke first.

'Of course he likes it, Michael. There he is, right in the centre of the web, spinning away.'

'We don't get your kind of money,' Clive shot back, and cursed inwardly, remembering all too clearly the spats they had had as articled clerks.

'No, but you don't have to put up with our kind of hassle. I mean, to put it at its most basic, we are selling all the time while you guys are always buying. And you all get lots of money in your retirement jobs, on the boards of all the nationalized industries.'

Michael Appleton's eyes had closed momentarily as if in prayer, and Caroline had noticed it too. She stopped, drew breath and visibly sought to turn the conversation.

Clive, now enjoying himself, decided to do it for her deliberately, placing a hand on hers. 'So tell me about the lads at Prior. How did you meet them?'

She looked suspiciously at his hand. 'I met Peter Burwood at a party. We got talking. He was then wondering how to approach the NEB, and generally what to do.'

'So you took him over?'

'Well, you've met him. You know he doesn't get taken over.'

'You took each other over?' He would need to warn Winstanley that the management of Prior had acquired this formidable ally.

'More like that.' She smiled at him, amused and, he realized exultantly, respectful. 'Clive. Can you tell me – don't if it's difficult – whether a decision is imminent? I mean a decision on flotation or not. It would just be a lot easier for Peter and us if we knew when the race was likely to start – if it is going to start, that is.'

Clive thought about it and decided that he could not in conscience warn her that his man was considering selling Prior as part of a package deal which might leave the managers stranded. After all they could always try to do a deal with any purchaser. In terms of her specific question no one had yet given thought to an announcement, but if ministers wanted to do that formally in the House, particular caution was needed in dealing with requests for information. To give away anything ahead of a statement would be breach of Parliamentary privilege, resulting in hanging or near offer for all concerned. But timing need not be a state secret.

'We are working towards an announcement of some sort in the next few weeks,' he said, automatically leaving plenty of leeway, and finding himself wondering uneasily whether Caroline had guessed at this margin.

'Thanks. That's useful, not least of all here for planning purposes. They aren't my only client. And if they are going to be allowed to compete, then I must organize some investors.'

'Peter Burwood is not intending to appoint a merchant bank as well?'

'I told him he didn't need one. A combination of me and a good development capital operation to act as lead investor is quite enough. I've done a big one before on that basis and I guess I'll use the same chaps. All a merchant bank would do would be to add confusion, and an extra layer of fees.'

Her unhesitating rational assurance was new, he noted. Caroline Henriques had always been confident, but in the manner of one assuring all comers that parachute jumping was easy, come on, anyone could do it. In her way, the present Caroline was even more daunting than the younger one and he considered her carefully, while trying not to indicate his heartfelt agreement with her views on duplicating advice. Coffee was being served and he sipped it, relaxing.

'Is price going to be the principal determinant in these privatization sales, Clive?'

He might have known that this tenacious woman would still be in action, he thought, burning his tongue. He put the coffee down and took a foil-wrapped chocolate mint to give himself time. 'If you look at the last major sale, I think you can see that considerations other than price were also important.'

'Like what?'

The trouble with talking to Caroline, he remembered, irritably, had always been that she didn't give you time, she didn't waste words and there you were, hustled on to the next hurdle. 'Oh several. The need to return all NEB companies to the private sector as quickly as possible, continued stability of the company, the need to keep up local employment, and the government's general policy of extending share-ownership.'

She would, after all, if the Minister stuck to the course on which he was presently set, see a list of criteria in a couple of weeks that looked very like this. Indeed,

Winstanley was to dine with the Frierns the following week, as he had ascertained from the private secretary, and would have to be briefed to say something much like this to Matthew Friern.

'Ah. So we'd better get ourselves ready to move like greased lightning and not gear the company too highly, or not as highly as the development capital boys will want. Local employment we do anyway and I've already told the lads that I thought employees as well as managers have to buy shares. So that's all right, but how will it wear if a trade buyer offers twenty-five per cent more?'

'That would be difficult. You know about the Public Accounts Committee?'

'Yes. I mean I know what it does. What I don't suppose I understand is how much it matters.'

Clive realized that most of the table was listening more or less openly, and decided he might as well give the Elementary Civics Lecture.

'The PAC is a committee of backbench MPs of both parties, and the Liberals, if one can be found. The government side always outnumber the opposition, but only by one or two. Like all committees of the House it has all the powers and privileges of Parliament itself. It is a standing committee which means it sits permanently.' He paused to allow polite laughter in which Caroline did not seem to find it necessary to join. 'It can look at anything to do with public money it likes. And it can call anyone including senior civil servants and ministers, if it feels like it, to give their answers personally.'

'Does it all happen in public?'

'Not necessarily. But it is serious stuff and to make it worse, half the time you are usually answering for someone else's crimes in the sense that the chap answering the question will be the one who has current responsibility, rather than the one who was there when the problem arose.'

'You get that in partnerships too,' Michael observed, deeply interested. 'But on the whole we use it tactically.'

'As in "It will have been my partner, Snodgrass, who dealt with this case. I wonder why he felt it necessary to have a contract in this form?"'

'That's right. Then you go and get Snodgrass out of the gents where he is in hiding and beat it out of him.' Michael was laughing.

'When I was here we used to blame a lot on the War Damage.'

'Oh, I'd forgotten. We've had to stop doing that now of course. The office was not actually bombed,' Michael explained generally to the table, 'but the square was, in 1942, and a water main fractured which flooded half the basements on this side and we had to throw away a lot of papers. I wasn't here until 1950, but we were still finding deeds inextricably stuck together, beyond all human aid, even then. *Anything* we couldn't find tended to get blamed on the war.'

'Do you remember Lawrence, Clive?' Caroline asked. '*Not* very bright, running a golf club somewhere now. Which of us was it who reminded him that a document dated in the late fifties could not by definition have been lost in the Flood?'

'You,' Clive conceded, grinning. 'It took a long time to get him to understand the point too.'

Michael said repressively to an interested audience that as late as the early sixties the solicitors were still taking young men on as articled clerks who were otherwise unsuitable, but were related to good clients. They had not, of course, been allowed to do any damage. Caroline looked at him so reproachfully that he was forced to ask her if he had got that wrong.

'No, Michael, *that*'s fair. I was thinking you'd automatically used the word "men". Nobody, then or now, takes on the stupid *daughters* of good clients.'

'Oh, I don't know,' Michael said, considering. 'Lucy Lindfield and you were here together, weren't you? We took a view on her.'

'She is not at all stupid. She was just in the wrong place,' Caroline objected. 'And in any case you took her on for quite other reasons. My friend Lucy,' she said, generally to the table, 'was and is a dazzler. Men always took her on for anything she wanted to do. Had she wished to train as a nuclear physicist, I am sure some organization would have obliged.'

Clive, who had been lying low, was interested. 'She wasn't a lawyer, that's certainly right. What should she have done, Caroline?'

'Become a painter. Easily the school's best artist, and we had some good ones,' Caroline reflected. 'Or, she could have run a gallery. Wonderful natural taste, a good eye and everyone would have let her in to buy anything. But her father – who is a dinosaur – didn't want her mixing with the scruffy types at art school, and she thought that the law sounded serious and glamorous.'

'Oh well, at least we taught her something.' Michael Appleton, like the skilled host he was, had noticed signs of restlessness at the far end of the table and drew the lunch to a close, thanking everyone for coming and urging those who could to stay for a second cup of coffee. Clive decided with some reluctance that he had better go back, and Caroline came with him to the steps.

'Thank you for coming, Clive. Can I come and talk to you again after the announcement? An MBO or rather an Employee Buy-out would be politically popular, wouldn't it? I mean I found myself on a train with Gerry Willshaw, whose constituency is next door, and he seemed to feel it would be.'

He considered her, enlightened as to who might have got at his Minister. 'He's a politician, Caro. I expect he would have agreed with whatever you said.'

She looked at him unsmiling and thoughtful. 'You mean they don't know how to say no?'

'They are not in the business of dissenting from any proposition put to them unless they absolutely have to.'

'That must only apply to this lot. No one in the Labour Party appears to mind dissenting from any proposition, including one with which they were in agreement last week.'

'Yes, but that's when they're dealing with each other not with the voters,' he pointed out.

'I suppose I have never seen them other than engaged in internecine warfare.'

'It's still like that in Hampstead, is it? How is your dad?'

'Busy as ever, on idiotic philosophical things. Caspar does most of the practical politics these days, if one can describe adherence to the Hampstead wing of the party in those terms. Felix has had to stop. He was only ever fairly interested and since this lot already think the BBC is a hotbed of pinkos they wouldn't put up with him in Current Affairs if he was in any way active. And

Marcus is in Doncaster. Enough of them, tell me about you.'

'I am divorced. I've got two kids, daughter of ten, boy of eight. I have them every other weekend.'

'Is that difficult?'

'Yes. We sold the house, my flat's a bit small, and it's not easy with kids in London. But we manage.'

'I'm not all that good on my own at weekends either,' Caroline observed, typically stating the real issue. She hesitated. 'Would you like to meet my parents again? We all end up at someone's house for Sunday lunch because that way my three see their cousins and uncles and grandparents regularly, but actually it is much better when we can persuade someone who isn't family to come as well – you know how it is. It's my turn, not this weekend but next, if that happened to be a time when your children were here, or even if it wasn't, it would dilute us a bit.'

'Won't you have far too many people, with an extra three?'

'We're usually not more than ten or twelve. Caspar, who has two a bit older than mine, usually comes, plus the parents. Marcus is out of London. Felix's wife doesn't really like us – well, I do know what she means – so he only comes sometimes. But if everyone comes and we are – what – seventeen strong, I shall just do two sittings, kids first then grown-ups. It works perfectly well.'

It sounded fun, Clive thought, wistfully: lots of other people and other children, rather than a swim and lunch at Garfunkel's. They could still do the swim. And, as he had never dared to say to Caroline, he had conceived a great admiration for Professor Sir Sholto Henriques, whose analysis of the political issues facing a democratic government had changed his entire world view as a student. 'Is that really all right?' he said, assailed by a memory of his own mother, red-faced with anxiety, struggling to put a meal on the table for a visiting cousin and her three children.

'Of course it is. That is 16 February we speak of, yes?' She whipped out a diary and entered it, leaning on the top of the stairs. She looked perfectly at home, he thought, against the grandiose entrance; it would not at all surprise him to see the staff lined up behind her to receive her. He stopped on his way down the steps, checked by a thought. 'You know that Friern are among the contenders for Prior?' he said, looking back.

'The lads told me. Are they serious, do you know?'

He hesitated, wondering uneasily about that lunch Lucy and Caroline had had recently.

'Serious enough to have recorded their interest with the Department,' he said, finding a formula.

'Mm. Thanks. I'll ask Lucy.' She grinned at him, teasingly.

'See you on 16 February,' he said, firmly and made for Holborn tube.

9

'Caroline? Peter Burwood.'

She had rushed to pick up her own phone, finding her secretary not there, and for a moment could not speak for disappointment, so sure had she been that it would be Gerry Willshaw.

'Just the man I wanted,' she said, getting herself together and speaking too fast in case he had sensed her dismay. 'I've just had lunch with the civil servant whose pigeon this is – Clive Fieldman – I told you about him. It's quite clear that they and the NEB have been advised they can't float you. And equally clear that they are willing to count things other than price, like preservation of local employment and extension of share-ownership, and all those good things.'

There was a pause, and she remembered belatedly that Peter thought slowly and carefully, and that he had rung her.

'Sorry, Peter. What was your news?'

His mind had however fastened on what she was saying. 'That's good. Did he say how strongly they would weight employee shareholdings in relation to price?'

Peter was tenacious and thought about only one subject at once, admirable qualities for a chief executive of a difficult business, but a nuisance if you wanted to talk about something else as she now did; Gerry had been to see Peter and the sites at the weekend, as she had momentarily forgotten in her anxiety.

'No, he didn't, Peter,' she said, patiently, reining herself back. 'I'd be surprised if they had worked that out.
Enough surely for the moment that they have accepted
the principle – it's a great help to us.' She paused.
'Sorry, I should have said first that an announcement is
going to come from the Department within the next few
weeks – Clive said.'

'That is useful,' the voice at the other end allowed,
cautiously. 'Now, just let's think this through, Caroline.
What can we do to get a jump on the others? Before
any decision, I mean.'

'I've been thinking about that too.' In the two minutes
since this conversation started anyway, she thought defensively, but after all I have had other things to think
about. 'I suggest that it would be worth getting the
prospective deal leader – the chap who will organize the
equity investment – and his team up to meet you. Can't
give them any numbers, but at least they'll have seen
the sites and got warmed up. And if you hate each other
on sight, I'll have time to find someone else for you.'

'This is going to be a good deal, Caroline. I'd not
want to work with anyone I didn't like. Could we not
have two or three sets of people up and make a choice?'

She sighed inwardly. Typically, at the beginning of
one of these buy-outs, management were touchingly
grateful to anyone who looked as if they might offer to
invest. This phase was succeeded, more or less rapidly,
by the assumption that investors would be falling over
themselves to get in and the demand that several different groups be approached. She hunched herself over the
phone, wishing that this conversation was taking place
face to face.

'The thing is, Peter, that development capital people

are a bit different from merchant bankers, or PR people, or lawyers like me, who work on a fee basis. It's sensible to talk to two or three of those before deciding who to take. They – we – are all selling, so we expect you to pick and choose.' She resolutely ignored the fact that Peter had picked her on sight, feeling it more tactful to assume that he had talked to other people as well. 'But development capital people are buying, not selling. They have something – like cash – that you need, and you have to handle them differently, particularly since we can't give them any numbers. If we take this deal to several people, they'll all think someone else turned it down. And then we are kippered.'

She listened to a long unconvinced silence at the other end of the line. 'Dearest Peter,' she said, putting her full personality into it. 'Trust me. It worked last time. Let me bring up my mate Hamish Brown, who commands a very decent-sized fund, wholly dedicated to buy-outs, *and* who has cause to believe in my clients. If you hate him, of course we have to go elsewhere, because you *have* to like each other at the beginning.' She rested her head on her free hand, trying not to imagine Peter taking the deal round the City, explaining that he was just looking, and all the City smarties sitting on their hands watching him, and ringing each other up the minute he had gone.

'I'll need to talk it through with the other two,' he said, definitively, and she heaved a silent sigh of relief. Martin at least would understand, and she would telephone him quietly, at home, just to go through it with him – no point in leaving that sort of thing to chance.

'Fine, Peter. But we ought to get people up to see you, or you here to see them – whichever – soon. I mean Clive will have stated the maximum time before an announcement. *I* would have, so it may come in two or three weeks. Anyway, I'm sorry. I distracted you. You rang me.' She glanced at her watch, her heart sinking as she decided that Gerry would probably be on his way to the House and hardly able to ring her from a car full of government driver and private secretary. She banished this consideration from her mind and focused on what Peter was saying.

'. . . have Martin and Graham here too now, Caroline. I'll just put you on the speaker – hold on.'

She held on through a set of crackles and curses, amused. She herself had never mastered her own state-of-the-art telephone and was delighted that the infinitely competent Peter Burwood hadn't either.

'We had your friend Gerry Willshaw here on Saturday.'

'Oh good, how did you get on?'

'Well, we took him round Eastleigh – the biggest site, the one you went round. It was a fine day, and everything was going well, then one of the chains on the crane went, so that stopped dead.'

'Oh dear.'

'No, no. He said it was his fault. He said he never went to see anything as a minister without somehow stopping it in its tracks; trains stopped, airports closed down the minute he came anywhere near them, he said. Nice bloke, stopped to talk to everyone, must have lost us hours on site.'

'Grudging whatnot! You just said the crane was stopped, anyway.'

She heard Martin and Graham laugh in the background. 'Very friendly too, he was,' Graham contributed. 'Thinks the world of you, obviously.'

'Well, that was nice. I'm not sure he's met any other women lawyers.' She smiled at the phone, hugely cheered, and amused by the obvious fact that Gerry had made a convert in Peter.

'The girls loved him,' Martin said, drily. 'We had two of them in just to make coffee and answer phones. They haven't stopped talking about him.'

I bet they haven't, she thought, startled by a flash of pure jealousy.

'Caroline?' It was Peter taking back control of the conversation. 'He said he thought the employee shares were very important; it was something the government were trying to encourage, and he personally would strongly support.'

'*That*'s useful. But he's making it more important than Clive implied it was today. We'll have to watch that.'

'Pity it's Winstanley not him at the DoE,' Martin observed.

'Can't have everything,' Caroline said firmly, gazing hypnotized at the winking light on her phone that meant her secretary had a call holding for her and was trying to attract her attention. 'Peter, look, I've been waiting for a call and I think this is it. Can I ring you back? Did he say anything else useful? Yes, please, if you've done a note I would like it. Talk to you later.' She cut him off and her secretary said in her ear, 'Mr Willshaw, Caroline.'

'Thank you, Susie. Hi.'

'God, you are difficult to get hold of. I rang on Sunday night but you were engaged.'

'So I was. One after another of my damned family. I must get another line.'

'Look. I have to go into the chamber. Tonight is OK. I am paired. Are you still all right?'

'Yes.'

'Fine. I've booked a table at Seeleys. Edgington Street. Can you get there for seven thirty?'

'Yes, of course.'

'See you then.'

He rang off, leaving her shaking and amazed at herself, as she had been for the last two weeks, ever since she had met him. She could just remember feeling like this, over her first lover in Oxford. Never about Ben, not this feeling of living on a different planet, unable to sleep properly, hungry but faced with an instant lack of appetite when she actually looked at any meal put before her, alternately snappy and over-indulgent with the children. She sat at her desk, contemplating her best silk suit which was hung on the back of her office door and thinking about Gerry Willshaw. He had left her, breathless, after their lunch together and rung her three hours later to arrange to meet her for a drink later that week. She had been early that time out of sheer anxiety, and had had an excellent view of his arrival, still coatless, his brown hair shorter than she remembered, checked twice by acquaintances, or admirers, as he made his way towards her. He had steered her to a corner table, tucked away so that they could not be overheard, ordered her a gin which she had drunk out of sheer nervousness, and they had sat and looked at each other.

'I'm sorry about that very crude pass,' he had said, briskly and unapologetically, looking at her sideways.

'Not necessary to apologize,' she had said, trying to match his briskness, and turning scarlet in the process. She managed to meet his eyes, finally.

'I haven't felt like this since I cannot remember when,' he had said, looking back at her. 'I cannot believe it.'

'Me neither. I think I was about eighteen last time.'

He laughed taken aback, but genuinely amused. 'Yes, that's it. It's like being a teenager again.' He touched the scar on her left wrist, gently. 'I have to say this would be a very high-risk affair.'

'For you more than me.'

'No, for both of us. You don't want to be all over *Private Eye* either. And the other thing is that I'm not in control of my time – I cannot tell you what evasions I have to go through to get any time to myself.'

'You talked me out of it, Mr Willshaw, that's all right.'

'Oh God. No, that I did not mean to do. It may not be fair and I'm trying to tell you it's difficult, but I very much want you. I've stopped sleeping since I met you.'

She looked back at him, wanting to touch him, but she was painfully aware of the attention being covertly paid to them by the rest of the room. 'I'm not all that easy to have an affair with either,' she said, picking up her glass and just managing not to swallow the slice of lemon floating at the edge. 'Too many children and too much work.'

'Well, we'll just have to be patient. And opportunistic.' He was still watching her with the same incredulous look she had seen in her mirror that morning.

'Have you had much practice?' she asked, sternly.

'At having affairs? I've not led a totally virtuous life but I've not had anything remotely serious ... oh ... for years. And I've been married nearly twenty years.'

'I know. I looked you up.' And established that he was five years her senior and had an address in London, as well as in Dorrington. It was, of course, possible that he shared with another MP, or his wife came up too during the week, in which case she would have a real problem, how to explain to her children that Mummy had a boyfriend, only no one was to know about him. That wasn't even a problem in practice; it was just plain impossible. 'You must have been a child bridegroom.'

'I was twenty-three. Quite old enough. How old were you when you married?'

'Twenty-four. But I had children straight away.'

'Well, so did we, more or less.'

They had sat looking at each other, relieved momentarily to have lowered the emotional temperature, and he looked down at his watch. 'Darling, I have to go, I have to vote. The patience begins here; I need to give you several dozen telephone numbers so you can always find me. I need also to tell you that the rest of this week is absolutely impossible and I am in Paris next week for a shipping conference, then Brussels. But Monday week is clear; can you have dinner with me?'

'Of course I can.' She hesitated, then plunged on. 'My house is full of nannies, housekeepers and children, all excellent observers.'

'I've got a flat. Small, and the neighbours are a bit over-friendly, but it's there.'

He had taken her to the tube and kissed her in the brotherly social fashion appropriate to a minister with an attractive constituent, both of them concentrating so hard on making it look natural that she had been unprepared for the surge of pure desire that left her, classically, weak at the knees.

'I'll ring you,' he had said, shakily touching her hand, and was gone, leaving her looking after him like a child.

She surfaced from these memories, and from those of last week. He had managed to ring her twice, both times from airport departure lounges, once in Paris, once in Brussels, and he had not uttered a word of love or desire but had wanted to know only how she was and what she was doing. He had fended off her inquiries as to his progress, but after all, anyone who could read *The Times* could see what he was doing. It was what she recognized as a crisis in European shipping; each country was trying to protect the existing cartel arrangements, with the UK as the principal voice of reason and liberation, but having in the end to defend its national companies like everyone else. She had come close, during a week in which she had thought of nothing else, to deciding that this would Not Do, the man was married, the whole thing had no future, and she and her children needed either a reliable new husband and stepfather or, if that remained as unavailable as it had so far, they needed a quiet life. Her heart was periodically wrung for her children, all of whom desperately missed Ben, but she still felt they were better off than some of their schoolfriends with divorced parents who had essentially lost both parents, father to another family and mother to the pursuit of another man. There was no way she would allow herself to turn into one of those mothers, fuzzy with drink, arriving late to pick up the children, or arriving at the school play in a state of upset or excitement too great to allow them to look after a nervous child. But equally, she could not pass this one up; no one, including the five men she had gone to bed with in the two years since Ben died, had stirred her more than briefly and she had been beginning to resign herself to a long widowhood, on the model of

186

Queen Victoria. And she had learned, at once, almost from the first moment she had seen Gerry Willshaw, that *that* would Not Do either.

She gazed unseeingly at the thick document in her in-tray, fished it out and started reading, her eye snagged by an infelicity in the preamble. She reached for the red pen, set conveniently at her right hand, and rewrote the paragraph, flipping forward in the contract to see where a consequential amendment might be required, and a minute later she was immersed, fathoms deep, the world shrunk to a desk and the document she was reading.

Lucy Friern let herself into the London flat, and stopped on the threshold, signalling the Filipino cleaner who was hoovering the hall. The woman stopped immediately and clasped the silent Hoover to her.

'Sir Matthew, he here. In living-room.'

Oh blast, Lucy thought, that means no Clive tonight. 'Darling? What are you doing here? I thought you weren't coming down till Wednesday.'

Matthew kissed her absently. 'I'm going back tomorrow, but I have to see someone tonight, in London.' He was scribbling figures on a pad which he covered when he saw her glance at them.

'What a nuisance for you.' Lucy saw that Clive tonight might after all be possible. 'When do you have to be there?'

'It's a dinner. Eight o'clock at the Guildhall. But I'll be very late – I have to go to a club afterwards.'

'I have never understood why men want to go to those clubs. I mean, if you all want a bit of tottie wouldn't it be easier to have one sent round? And safer than what you find there?'

'They have good floor shows there.'

'No, they don't. It's just tits and bum.'

'Well, that's what we all like.' Matthew pulled her to him, hands on her bottom.

'Who are you seeing?' she asked, hoping he wasn't going to start that now.

He hesitated, and she pulled away to look at his face. 'Matthew. *Is* it a girl?'

'No, no. It's Williamson. From Dorrington.'

'Councillor Williamson. And-this-is-my-good-lady Williamson?'

'He's all right. Just doesn't have your advantages.'

'Why are you meeting him here rather than Dorrington, Matt? Is there something else I don't know?' She was laughing, perfectly secure in the knowledge that whatever her other complaints about him, Matthew was comfortably heterosexual.

'Ah, you've noticed. No, he's down here to get away from his good lady, and it's much easier to talk to him when he's on his own and loosened up a bit.'

'What are you talking to him about?'

'Oh. Things.' He pulled her close to him, and moved one hand to her breast. 'What about an insurance policy? If we have a fuck now I won't have the strength to take on anything that shakes her tits at me later.'

'Well, of course, Matt, if it's what you want. But actually, if you remember, you wanted me to fix up that dinner with the Winstanleys. In fact you nagged on at the weekend about it.'

'Yes.' He stopped, irresolute. 'Bugger it. Come to bed first.' He took his wife to bed, but she was annoyed at having her day disrupted and abstracted herself from the proceedings. 'Come on, Lu,' he said sharply, looking

188

down at her. 'I might as well pick something up tonight if this is all the response I'm getting. Where are you?'

'Sorry,' she lied, called to order. 'Planning that dinner-party if you must know.'

'Well, just stop.' He pulled out, swiftly, and turned her over, pulling her hips towards him. 'Better?'

'Yes,' she said, surprised, 'much.'

He laughed and slid a hand round between her legs, moving against her, waiting patiently until she cried out, then he moved his hand to pull her closer to him and she felt him come in a series of long spurts.

'A good one,' she said, amused and admiring, when they had disentangled themselves.

'Yes. That'll keep me off the girls tonight. I'd better get ready in a minute.' He rearranged his balls so that they lay more comfortably and kissed her. 'So what about this party? Did Winstanley's office ring?'

'Yes. He can do the Wednesday of next week, but Mrs Winstanley won't be in London.'

'Mm. Better invite somebody for him to make up numbers, hadn't we? Who else is coming?'

'The Jenners and the Warrens, as you asked. Then I thought Tim and Alison to lighten the whole party a bit. I mean I like Peter Jenner, but he is very heavy going.'

'Not for a Conservative junior minister. Peter Jenner is a constituency chairman up just north of Dorrington. Winstanley's probably met him.'

'That's true. All right, Tim and Alison to cheer *me* up then. And this Winstanley and another woman. That's ten, and this table is a bit crowded with twelve. You complained last time.'

'Yes. Well, what about Caroline Whitehouse? I mean

she's a professional woman; he isn't going to find it embarrassing or think he has to do anything about her.'

The thing about men and one's girlfriends, Lucy thought, was that they resented the years of freedom that these friendships represented and, of course, they knew in their bones that women told each other things no man, and certainly no husband, was going to get to hear. It was a concession on his part to volunteer to invite Caroline to a small dinner-party; it was just, unfortunately, an offer which she dared not accept.

'Well, darling, that is kind of you to suggest her. But I don't think you'd want her there this time. She is acting for the management of Prior Building Systems.'

He had got out of bed and was on his way to the bathroom which opened off the bedroom, and she watched him stop as if he had been shot.

'She's what? Acting for them? But the NEB own them – what do they want lawyers for?'

'No need to shout, Matt. The point is apparently that it was agreed that the company's and the NEB's interests were no longer identical once the NEB had been told to sell. So the company were allowed to hire lawyers and they chose Caroline's firm.'

He had walked back and was sitting on the end of the bed, glaring at her. 'What's she doing for them? Did she tell you?'

'We only spoke for a minute,' she lied, crossing her fingers under the bedclothes and making a mental note to ring up Caroline the minute Matt went out. 'I don't really understand it, darling, but apparently she had Clive Fieldman to lunch today, and he said that if the company couldn't be floated, management would, of course, be allowed to bid in competition with anyone else. So I expect she's organizing that.'

She stopped, hoping that she had explained why Caroline ought not to be handed Winstanley literally on a plate, without betraying the fact that it had been Clive rather than Caroline who had told her what was going on. She watched her husband cautiously; he was plainly furious and she was relieved that she had defused him by a successful fuck.

'Those buggers up there have got themselves organized. And I tell you whose money they're using. Ours. Taxpayers' money, that's what's paying your friend Caroline.' He paced round their room, restless with irritation. 'Ah, never mind, they'll not be able to offer as much as we can; nobody is going to be that interested in putting up money for the people who got the company into this mess.'

'I thought all those people had gone, and that this management were the ones who had pulled the company round.'

He gave her a sharp sideways look. 'Caroline told you that, I suppose.'

She did not answer, unwilling to add any more circumstantial lies. This Prior thing was a frightful nuisance, she thought crossly; every time she opened her mouth either Matthew or Clive jumped down her throat. It was of course exactly why she had so hated her year at Smith Butler; not only was an appalling amount of work expected of her, but somehow you were always having to deal with angry men and she loathed it. Caroline, by contrast, had been enviably unmoved by any amount of furious men. She could still remember a meeting at which both Caroline and she were present where an acrimonious argument had broken out over every piece of wording and the meeting had gone from bad to worse, the other team and their clients being as rude as they dared, and the Smith Butler partner getting pinker and crosser by the minute. She had been exhausted and riven by headache after an hour of this. Caroline, on the other hand, apparently unconscious of her surroundings, had written a shopping list, redrafted a will which had been entrusted to her for practice, then suddenly surfaced in the middle of a savage dispute on the wording of a share option to point out that the clause in dispute was redundant in terms of one three paragraphs back, and that, moreover, it was lunchtime. The meeting had been silenced, unlike Caroline who, receiving a bad-tempered ticking-off afterwards from the partner for speaking out of turn, had told him he should have read the papers properly.

But she wasn't Caroline, and she wasn't going to put up with people snapping her head off over a business thing. 'It's no good being cross with me, Matt. I'm just doing what I'm asked. And I thought I ought to tell you about Prior. But I won't bother if you're just going to get annoyed with me.'

'Sorry,' he said perfunctorily and hunched himself into his bathrobe. 'Look, get what's-her-name, friend of yours from the V. & A., for Winstanley. And I want Andy Eames Lewis and Emma there. If Caroline's playing politics then we'll just remind Winstanley that we've got the money behind us. He'll not find anyone like Walzheims involved with the Prior management.'

She sighed. 'Instead of Tim or Alison, or as well as?'

'Instead. I hate it when the girls can't get round easily to serve. You've booked them, I take it?' His voice was muffled by the roar of water as he turned on his bath.

'Yes, but I must confirm the day,' she called back. 'I'll do that while you get ready.'

'I'm going now, Caroline, unless you want anything else.' The small, dark girl was already dressed for the street, and this question was a ritual. Had Caroline wanted anything else done that evening, her secretary would have been told hours ago. She had been a little hesitant about working for a woman, but in the first two weeks with Caroline Whitehouse she had become reconciled. It might lack the slight sexual *frisson* of working for one of the best-looking of the younger partners, but *that* wore off pretty quickly; they were all heavily married and so hard-worked that in the end you were just a typewriter to them. Caroline was busy too, but she didn't get flustered; she tried to dictate everything she would want done that day by nine in the morning, and if she asked you to stay late, she did it by three o'clock in the afternoon, so that you could make arrangements.

'Thank you, Susie, I'm fine.' Caroline looked up from a document and smiled.

'Going out tonight?' Susie asked, glancing at the suit. 'Yes.'

She was looking very pretty, Susie realized, interested; she had a new haircut and her nails had been done. 'Somewhere nice?'

'I hope so. Just as well you came in – I must change. Thanks, Susie, see you tomorrow.'

The arrangements for changing at Smith Butler were primitive, but Caroline had decided that going home first to spend a fretful hour with the children was impossible when she herself was strung up like a wire at the prospect of seeing Gerry. She had arranged access to the senior partner's shower on the top floor and as she emerged, pink and wet, she peered at herself in the mirror. She looked feverish, she decided, flushed and wide-eyed, and she fixed her mind sternly on details as she put on make-up and combed her hair. As she got back to her own office the phone was ringing to tell her that the taxi ordered earlier by the methodical Susie was here to take her to the restaurant. She looked around the office, automatically checking that no confidential document had been left out, propitiating the familiar god of order and reason.

She was five minutes early at the restaurant and decided that she would feel just less silly being early and over-eager than sitting outside in the taxi. She thanked the driver, turned to make for the restaurant and found Gerry Willshaw at her elbow.

'Hello,' she said, breathlessly. He looked both utterly familiar and quite different: a bit heavier than she remembered him, wearing a dark, tidy, vaguely military raincoat and still with that bursting, restless nervous energy.

'Well, at least I just managed to get here first.'

Correct military behaviour instilled when young, she thought, in recognition. Chap must always arrive before the lady he is escorting at any public place.

'I was early,' she said, in apology. 'The taxi just got here very fast. What have you done with your posh car?'

'It's only mine for official business. I walked; it's not far, and I need the exercise.'

About two miles from his office she thought, as he took her elbow to move her out of the way of a small dinner-jacketed group. He looked at her carefully and she realized that he was nervous too, for all the glowing physical confidence.

'Hungry?'

'No,' she said, boldly, deciding to take a leaf out of Lucy Friern's book. 'Not at all, but I'll toy with a lettuce leaf if you are.'

His hand tightened convulsively on her elbow. 'I'm not either.' He hesitated. 'We could go back to the flat for a drink.'

'I'd like that,' she said, serenely, silently acknowledging her debt to her friend Lucy.

'It's quite close. I'll get a taxi.'

She was about to say they could walk, but a taxi had appeared and he was holding the door for her. He sat beside her on the back seat, tense, leaving a space between them, not touching her, and she understood that, as usual, the taxi-driver had known his face.

'Tell me about your day,' he said, firmly, and she managed to recognize incredulously in this man her own ability to concentrate on an issue even when in a state of acute emotional tension. The taxi slowed and he pulled out money and paid off the driver.

'It's very quiet here,' she said, as they walked up the stairs to the first floor.

'Little bit far from the House, but I can do it in ten minutes in a car,' he said, equally politely, putting a key in the door and turning it, and standing aside to let her in. He shut the door behind them and double-locked it, while she undid the buttons on her coat, suddenly much too hot in the warm, narrow hallway. He turned from the door and she smiled at him, nervous but deeply relieved at finally having got them behind closed doors without half the world watching them.

'Oh God,' he said, without impiety, and dropped the keys and his own raincoat on the floor and put both arms around her, scrubbing his cheek against hers. 'I have missed you so badly, and then I couldn't get through on Sunday and I didn't dare go on ringing after midnight.'

'You could have. I've not slept properly since I met you.'

He turned his head to kiss her on the mouth, putting his hands under her coat and she shrugged it off, still kissing him. Her tidy suit jacket and shoulder bag came off with it, sliding to the floor and freeing her arms so that she could get her hands under his jacket and feel the unexpectedly light ribcage. All the weight must be in the shoulders, she thought, and he isn't wearing a vest in this weather. Or perhaps like me he took it off for the occasion. He eased his grip on her and pulled back to look at her.

'Let's go through.'

'Mm.' She ran her hands over his shoulders and down his arms. Yes, that was where the muscle was, that was what made him look like a really big man. She laid her cheek luxuriously against his. 'You smell of soap.'

'So do you, or of something nice,' he said, tightening his grip, and they both began to laugh.

'I borrowed the senior partners' shower,' she said, in his ear.

'I used the one that I share with two other ministers and the permanent secretary at Transport,' he boasted.

'All at once?'

'What a thought.' She felt his ribcage shake. 'It is so easy to talk to you,' he said, happily. 'Come on, I'll get us a drink. Champagne do?'

'Aha. You knew we were coming here.'

'I knew we'd have to, or I would blow up. I didn't know you were going to get us here quite so early. The champagne isn't cold.'

'I'm not actually thirsty either,' she said, leaning on the edge of the kitchen table and watching in confident expectation the muscles of his back move under the conventional grey and white shirt as he fished in the fridge.

'We'll drink the champagne with ice in it.'

He was easing the wires, not waiting for her to comment, and she decided there were limits to Lucy's technique for bustling a man into bed; this one did things his own way and at his own pace.

'Now,' he said, briskly, handing her a glass. 'Let's go through to the living-room.'

She followed him meekly.

He raised a glass to her. 'Here's to us.'

'To us,' she said, sobered momentarily, but he kissed her gently on the lips.

'Darling. There is an envelope on the floor in the hall, which I somehow didn't pick up as we came in. It's got a speech in it. I have to look at it and get any amendments back to the office before they all go home. It was the price for getting off this evening.'

'You wouldn't have been here yet had the evening gone according to your plans. They'd have had to stay much later.'

His mouth quirked in amusement and he tightened his arm round her. 'If I get rid of it now we have the rest of the evening clear.'

'I am not accustomed to being deferred to a speech, Mr Willshaw.'

'Ah. Well, you'll have to get used to *that*.' He turned her face towards him and kissed her, laughing but immovable, and she leant against him, lulled by his certainty about what he wanted. He stopped to settle her in a comfortable chair with the evening paper; she read, unseeingly. Articles about a revolution in Peru, shifting politics in France and industrial strife in the coalfields of South Wales passed before her eyes, while all her attention was on Gerry, looking much too big for the small desk which had obviously been chosen as the only piece of furniture that would fit into that awkward corner. He was absolutely concentrated, the whole of his attention on the papers in front of him. He finished, after ten minutes' work, and rang his office to get the draft picked up.

'Sorry,' he said, catching her eye, but she was not deceived.

'You don't mean sorry.'

'Yes, I do. The car will be here in ten minutes and then all that is over. Have another drink.'

'Tell me about the Department of Transport,' she said, understanding that she had no option but to wait and not wanting to blur whatever was to come with too much to drink.

He winced, and her earlier impression was confirmed. 'Well, of course, it has always been a political graveyard.'

'Hasn't it,' she agreed. 'Sholto always says that Transport ministers are on a hiding to nothing, because there will always be accidents connected with Transport and it will always, always be the Government's fault.'

'Because "they" hadn't widened the roads. Or spent enough money on new track for the railways. Or built a new five-mile-long ultra-safe runway at Heathrow,' he confirmed, grimly.

'Sholto also says it is like the NHS, in the sense that demand must always exceed any provision that can possibly be afforded.' Caroline looked at him for confirmation and saw that he was looking suddenly tired and despondent. 'Sorry, sorry,' she said. 'Didn't mean to depress, I'm sure you'll make it work.'

'That's more than I am,' he said, soberly. 'I knew it was going to be difficult – I'd rather have had almost anything than Transport; but you take what you're given. I'm stuck with it for a bit too – I'd hoped I'd get Housing when poor Jim Fielder died, but the PM preferred to move John Winstanley up.' He got up, restlessly, from beside her, and looked down at the street. 'There's the car, now. I'll just get rid of this and tell him I'm going out, so we won't get interrupted again.'

He snatched up the papers and put them back in the envelope, and she heard the door to the flat close while she logged somewhere that this man had hit a dry patch in his career and was restlessly looking for a way out of it. He was, of course, that key five years older, and she knew from watching those just senior to her that it was the early forties which divided those who were going right to the top from those who weren't – quite. An anxious moment, she thought, deeply sensitized to him already, and she would be better to stay off the subject of the Department of Transport.

'Right. Done. I'm back.'

He knelt easily beside her low chair and took her glass away and started to undo the buttons of her neat silk shirt, and she held his bent head in both hands as he kissed her, feeling the crisp, short hair.

'You make me so nervous,' he said, stopping to look at her and she saw that it was true.

'You make me nervous, too, but we'll manage.'

He kissed her on the mouth, gently. 'Let's go to bed.'

They went through to the bedroom, arms around each other, and she noticed with affection that the curtains were already drawn and the sheets were clean. Efficient, competent planner he was, she thought, fighting for some detachment, and then he was taking off the rest of her clothes for her while she undid his shirt.

'Stockings. I do like them, much nicer than tights.' He kissed her just above the top of the stocking, sat back on the edge of the bed, fighting with the buckle of his belt, hands shaking.

'This is going to be all right,' she said, suddenly calm and cheerful as she pulled off the rest of her clothes.

'I should wait and see,' he said, standing up to get his trousers off, and she moved to kiss him and he hugged her so tightly she could hardly breathe. 'Come to bed.' He was still wearing his underpants, and for a moment she wondered if he was having trouble but as he peeled them off his penis sprang free and that was all right, evidently. He pushed her back on to the bed and knelt beside her kissing her, sliding a hand between her legs. She could feel his anxiety and remembered in that moment the brother to whom she had always been closest explaining to her that men needed to feel welcomed. Well, darling Gerry was more than welcome. She pushed his hand gently away and slid down in the bed to kiss the admirably flat stomach and then to take him in her mouth.

'Oh God, oh darling.'

She felt him stiffen, then he pulled her back up the

bed so that she was beside him, and was kneeling over her kissing her between her legs. He lifted his head after a bit to look at her, reached across her to the side table and put a condom on efficiently, then came inside her and she came immediately, feeling it all the way up inside her in a way that no solitary masturbation, however pleasurable, could ever achieve.

'Oh, my love,' she heard him say, just before he came, not long afterwards, crying out with pleasure, and she smiled to herself as she held him against her.

'Oh, darling. That felt marvellous.' He rolled off her, strong and quick-moving in this as well, and she watched with love while he neatly tugged off the condom, regarding the contents appreciatively.

'For me too. It felt serious.'

'Ah. I'm glad you felt that. Now talk to me. Tell me everything else about you. The best thing about this is that I can talk to you.'

'The best thing?' She lay back on the pillows, luxuriously.

'One of the best things. Would you like a cup of tea? Yes? I'll make it.'

She heard him moving in the kitchen. Then he appeared, carrying tea, and she took her cup.

He looked at her seriously. 'You still make me nervous, you know. It's something about your confidence, it unmans me.'

'Not so's you'd notice,' she pointed out, surprised and hurt, and he hugged her.

'I did wonder but that was all right, wasn't it?'

She assured him it had been more than all right and rubbed her cheek on his chest.

'Tell me about your family. I know you have three

201

brothers. I looked you up – or rather I looked up your father. Three s. it said, one d.'

'All the s. are older than me. You've met one of them, at *Question Time*, Felix. A stuffed shirt, only a left-wing stuffed shirt, which is a rarer breed and as you know he disapproves, professionally, for the BBC. He has three children. Then there is Marcus, poor love, who also disapproves, but of anything that happened after about 1315. He has three children as well. Then there is Caspar, who is all right really, and only disapproves of monetarism. An economist, member of the Labour Party, divorced and has two sons, older than my Timmy.'

'Would they disapprove of me?'

She looked at him, consideringly. 'As a person? Oh, probably. You're a Conservative, after all, one of the enemy. And you were in the army.'

He frowned. 'But darling, they must all have done some military service.' He caught her sideways look. 'Mustn't they? Your father must have been in the war.'

'He was at Bletchley, of course. You know, place near Oxford where we kept all the intelligence people.'

He nodded, wryly amused. 'I do indeed. Working on Ultra, I assume.'

'So we understand. But he has never told us anything about what he was really doing, and if we ask he talks about *The Times* crossword.'

'And your brothers? They must have done National Service.'

'Sort of. I mean yes, but perhaps not quite as you mean it. They did three months in basic training then went to learn Russian for the next two years.' She laughed. 'I tell you, Gerry, if They invade they'll wish they hadn't. In the front line will be Felix, telling them about the responsibilities of public-service broadcasting, Marcus laying out a schema of medieval agriculture and Caz telling them what's wrong with monetarism – in their own language. Imagine the horror – they'll surrender immediately. I would.'

He was laughing with her, but she observed that he was a little taken aback. 'I take it that they hated basic training, all three of them.'

'Not at all. They took the line that it was a great deal more civilized and less physically demanding than the first years at Winchester.'

They looked at each other, wryly. 'So you're not really quite what they would have chosen for me, no,' she said. 'Even in different circumstances.'

'Mm. Well, I never expected to have a Henriques d. either I suppose.' He moved, restlessly. 'Now are you hungry? I am.'

She thought about it. 'Starving.'

'We could go and have dinner now.'

'I could cook. Omelettes?'

He looked at her, looking amusingly hangdog. 'There won't be anything in the flat. I eat cereal for breakfast and I don't otherwise eat here. I can never be bothered with cooking.'

'Very unreconstructed of you. You'd better not admit that publicly – you'll lose the women's vote instantly.'

'I don't eat much either,' he said, in mitigation, but she was unimpressed.

'What about when your wife is ill? Would she have to starve?'

'I never seem to be there when she is ill,' he acknowledged, ruefully.

A much more conventional marriage than hers and Ben's had been, she thought. This one probably did have his slippers warmed and everything else done for him.

'I'm very tidy. And I can hoover,' he said, defensively, as he slid out of bed. 'Come on, my love, let's get dressed and do something about food. I'll go out to the little shop on the corner if you're really prepared to cook.'

'I'll come with you.'

He stopped, momentarily, fingers stilled on the buttons of his shirt. 'Better not,' he said, regretfully, but definitively.

Of course, she thought, chilled, doing the shopping together was unmistakably domestic, and none of that could be allowed to happen. He looked over at her and bent to kiss her.

'Sorry. I'd like you to come, but we do have to be careful. I don't believe it's paranoia: I'm sure I've been watched before, when we were in Opposition and I was asking questions about steel policy. If you threaten powerful interests – and I have in my time and may have to again – they use everything.'

She gave him a list of what they needed, and watched him go, shaken, but used the time to wash and dress again, feeling distinctly over-formal in the tidy silk suit that had seemed appropriate for dinner in a restaurant. She combed her hair and put some of her make-up back, then heard his key in the door. She went down to meet him and took packages from his hands, and started to organize a meal. He sat contentedly at the table and poured her the rest of the champagne.

'Tell me about Prior,' he ordered, without preamble. 'I went to see them. I liked them.'

'They were charmed too. Particularly the girls.'

'The girls? There weren't any. Oh, the girls in the office. Well, that was nice.'

Took it for granted, she thought, peacefully; well, of course he did. She started to cook while telling him what she was trying to do with Prior.

'Who would get shares?'

'Institutions and managers, and some employees.'

'Not all employees?'

'Institutions, which is who will be financing this lot, aren't that interested in employees.'

'Why aren't they?'

She elbowed him gently out of her way at the stove. 'They don't think in those terms. Workers are just things every business has, and they are either co-operative or not. And if they're not this is always seen as the fault of the unions, having nothing to do with useless incompetent management.'

She felt him stir, restlessly. 'It often has been the unions who destroyed a business. Particularly in the shipyards.'

'Shipyard management in this country has been a byword for complacency, incompetence and corruption,' she said, combatively, and felt him laugh as he put his arms around her from behind. 'Sorry,' she said, luxuriating in the feel of him. 'I digress. We were talking about employee-shareholders. The institutions aren't interested in the idea, they don't see its power. And they probably believe, along with half your lot, darling, that the workers don't have any cash left over to buy shares by the time they've filled the bath with coal and drunk themselves senseless down the pub. But they aren't against the idea either. I mean they aren't going to recoil in horror at the idea of employees as shareholders.

Provided they don't have a lot of shares, anything serious like a twenty-five per cent holding.'

He kissed her ear. 'You know I have never had much to do with the City; it's a new thing for me, all this money and financing. It's a black art.'

'No, no. No more than politics or the law. Can you read a balance sheet?'

'Well, no.'

'You have to be able to. I'll show you. I couldn't either when I was first working as a lawyer, but there is no excuse for that.'

'We didn't need to in the army. But we did need to be able to manage people.'

'Presumably soldiers shoot you in the back if you can't manage.'

'More likely they get themselves killed in some wholly unnecessary way,' he said, grimly, and she remembered that he had been actively deployed in several difficult places, starting with Cyprus.

'And none of it leaves much room for a trade-union structure.'

'No. You don't need one since you are all – or should be – trying to do the same thing. *That* must be the force behind the idea of shares for employees, to make you all involved in the same enterprise and give them some control over what they are doing.'

'Yes,' she said, surprised. 'It's the same thought that inspired the drive to state-ownership.'

'That's too impersonal.'

'It's too *big*,' she said firmly. 'And turns out to be susceptible to corruption. Which is what the lot I was born into have not managed to see, or to accept. God, I get cross with them, particularly my dotty old father.'

'Curiously enough, I didn't remember him as either dotty or old, and it can only be four years ago that I heard him speak.'

'He may be better in public,' she said, darkly, handing him an omelette and watching him eat hungrily.

'Anyway, darling,' he said, through a mouthful, 'listen. Whatever the financial institutions think privately, they'd better be interested in employee shares for Prior's employees in terms of the political realities.'

'Really?'

'Yes, really. The more the better. I'm going to have a much easier time with this – I would have been for it even without you, my sweet – if it can be presented as an employee buy-out rather than the traditional management buy-out. Can that be done?'

'Yes. Some employees are bound to be more equal than others in share-owning terms.'

'Doesn't matter very much provided I can say that employees and managers get a decent percentage. Collectively.'

'I got it.'

They looked at each other, wordlessly, across the table, and she felt herself breathe short.

'Let's get this lot away,' he said, bounding into action and sweeping it all efficiently into the sink and splashing hot water on it. She stood obediently beside him, drying up and occasionally touching him.

'Back to bed,' he said, briskly, piling the last cup away; he was tidy, just as he had said, she observed, and they went through again to the bedroom, entwined. They both fell asleep afterwards, but she woke to the shrill noise of an alarm clock, and found Gerry beside her, instantly awake and fully conscious.

'Darling? It's midnight and I must get you home.'

'Mm,' she said, reluctantly. 'I don't want to go terribly, but I agree I must.'

'We'll manage a night together soon,' he said, reassuringly. 'Well, we must.'

He drove her home, dropping her discreetly at the top of the road, but leaving him seemed suddenly unbearable, and she looked at him to see if he was feeling the same. He was looking harassed and tired. 'This job! I've got no time till next week, but if humanly possible I must see you before then. I'll ring you.' He kissed her quickly and was gone.

Lucy Friern walked round the table, beautifully set with glittering heavy silver and linen napkins, checking it. She held an imaginary salver on her left arm and walked around the top of the table, bending to serve a ghostly guest from the left, and felt her bottom brush against the small chest. This always happened with the extra leaf in the table and she always forgot. It would be wonderful to have a dining-room in London where you could seat ten people without getting in this sort of mess, she thought, crossly, calling to Bridget to help her shift the small awkward chest. The living-room wasn't really big enough either, not even for ten people all needing to sit to drink coffee, and it was ridiculous on Matt's kind of money. Sir Matthew and Lady Friern could well afford a decent London flat. She wouldn't even want one of the big London houses such as her smarter women friends commanded; she had quite enough to manage with the exquisite Friern house outside Dorrington in whose dining-room – once a medieval hall – anything up to twenty people could be seated in spacious magnificence. And where she did a lot of entertaining. But she longed for a decent-sized dining-room and living-room in London and a proper double spare room, so that she could have people to stay in the school holidays without making the boys share, which they hated. She looked around the immaculate dining-room, with its dark Chinese wallpaper and carefully organized lighting, with dislike. Marcia Warren, wife of that major public relations talent, Pat, had called it a charming room, which as anyone knew was the polite way of describing a room too small for its function. The Warrens had a vast flat behind Harrods. Well, of course they did, as Matthew had observed impatiently: it was business for them, wasn't it? But no one quite thought like that in London; they judged you by your surroundings, and gave not a damn that you had one of the soundest businesses in the north-east. If the price of a change was for Matthew to be able to buy Prior Systems, well, then she would contribute in every way she could.

She summoned Bridget to help her make the least unsatisfactory arrangement of the living-room, then decided to go out. The two young women who were to cook and serve tonight had already occupied the kitchen and she had greeted them and made sure they had all they needed. She had a couple of hours before her hair appointment, her clothes were all organized and she could just get to Liberty and choose new curtains for the third guest room in the Dorrington house if she hurried. I can't imagine when I would have time to do a job, she said, defensively, to her friend Caroline, whose voice she sometimes heard at moments like this; I have two houses to run, I sit as a JP on Mondays, not to mention all the entertaining, she explained to that voice.

It may not quite be what we at Lady Eleanor's were educated to do, but the school had always been strong on producing 'good women', who supported husbands, brought up children and ran local affairs without earning a penny from it. Well, she was doing a lot of that. She remembered Shirley Conran's dictum, that it was possible to manage a job and a husband, or a husband

and children or a job and children, but not all three at once, and decided again that Mrs Conran had been right not only for herself but for all women; that was The Truth, and not even the brilliant Caroline had managed to buck it; her household had fallen apart at regular intervals while Ben was alive and it was only now running with such efficiency because she had apparently retired to a nunnery after his death. Better by far to have a husband and a lover and two houses and the time to choose curtains and give dinner-parties, and do a bit for the community she thought smugly, spreading materials expertly round her, hunting a design in dark blue, which she had seen in a rush two days ago, and recognized instantly as a derivative of one in the V. & A.

It would be lovely to have a new flat to decorate, she thought, two hours later, watching her dark hair being blow-dried into shape while a manicurist put polish on her nails with that rapid casual expertise which you could never achieve for yourself. She went home, detouring to buy candles for the table, thinking hard. She rang a familiar number, got Clive Fieldman at once – both of them would have been appalled to know that Miss Williams had understood their relationship within a week of its inception – talked to him for ten minutes and then rang Walzheims, to invite Andrew to turn up a quarter of an hour earlier than the other guests.

Three hours later she was not so sure that this had been a good idea. She had left messages for her husband which had not reached him and he had arrived home with just enough time to bath, change and, as he always did, organize the wine and before-dinner drinks personally. When Andy had arrived, punctual to the minute,

Matthew was trying to fill ice-buckets, fuss over the temperature of the claret and change his mind about the dessert wine simultaneously.

Andy, getting the situation in one, raised his eyebrows at her, indicating willingness to abandon whatever plan she had, but she stood her ground.

'Matthew, darling, can you manage to listen while you're doing that, because I *do* have something to tell you about John Winstanley and Prior. That's why I asked Andy so I can tell you both at once and you can decide how to tackle him.'

Her husband momentarily looked furiously exasperated, but then the speech sank in, and he thrust the original three bottles back in the fridge, told Bridget to sort out ice, cast one single minatory look at the decanted claret and headed for the study. 'Right, Lucy.'

'I've been talking to Clive Fieldman today,' she started, boldly, having rehearsed this opening until she was no longer self-conscious about it. 'Thought we had better keep in touch with him.' She paused to make sure her audience was with her.

It had not been an easy conversation with Clive, who had been displaying what she saw as annoying reticence, though he, she understood, had seen it as ordinary discretion. But she had persevered and was confident that her ambitious Clive was not against her but only trying to achieve everything his minister wanted.

'He thinks,' she said, firmly, 'that Winstanley would much prefer to sell all five companies in a package, but that he is windy about getting the best price.'

'A price he can defend,' Andy said, thoughtfully.

'Yes. And,' she held up a hand to stop her husband taking the point on, 'he says that there is pressure being put on from somewhere on behalf of the management of Prior, who want to do an employee buy-out.'

'That's your good friend Caroline.' Matthew had turned red with anger.

'Is it now important that employees rather than management are involved? Sorry to break the flow, Lucy,' Andy asked, smoothly, apparently unconscious of his client's rage.

'Clive didn't say, specifically, and I didn't ask.' Lucy looked crestfallen.

'I think he did!' Andy said gently. 'A couple of weeks ago, when I spoke to him, he was talking in terms of a management buy-out. The words have changed; that means the thinking has too.'

Andy had been a linguist at Oxford, she remembered – something very difficult like Sanskrit.

'I don't trust these civil servants.' Matthew was fidgeting angrily.

'Do you want me to go on telling you about this or not?' his wife said, coldly.

'Yes, go on.'

Lucy was well able to handle him, evidently, as one might have understood given one's own experience of her, Andy noted drily.

'Anyway,' she continued, 'it seems that it is the chap in the next door constituency, who is also a minister and very much a rising star – Gerry Willshaw – who is very keen on an employee buy-out. And *that* matters, because he is thought to have a line to the PM and to be likely to get a Cabinet job next time round. He's actually been to see the sites, apparently; some of his constituents work there.'

'It's bloody idiotic. What are the buggers going to do

with shares? They don't know anything about buying them; they won't put good money into pieces of paper, not in Dorrington. Or are they going to be given them?' Matthew had gone alarmingly red and his wife and his banker watched him warily.

'I agree it seems a bit silly, darling, but Clive says it's approved policy. It's in the manifesto, and he says that that is always very important for the first eighteen months of a new government.'

'Look Matt,' Andy said, thoughtfully, 'we could devise some ingenious scheme where employees of the companies could get shares in Friern. Very few shares, of course, keep it well under three per cent of your equity. Might be worth it, just to avoid the presentational disadvantage.'

Matthew was struck momentarily dumb by this suggestion, which gave his wife a chance to go on.

'However,' she said, firmly, 'Clive also says that it would be very difficult to take a lower price for this company, or any of the others come to that, be it accompanied by no matter what political frills. So any employee buy-out will have to come up with a fair price.'

'And presumably Mr Winstanley is going to say all these things tonight if asked, and we must have things we can say to counteract the charms of the Prior employees,' Andrew observed, generally, and she sat back deciding to let him get Matthew facing forward, as the headmistress of Lady Eleanor's would have put it.

'I'm certainly going to tell him that workers in Dorrington won't buy enough shares to finance a bloody digger, leave alone a whole company. They're living in cloud-cuckoo-land if they think different.' Matthew was in no mood to compromise and Lucy glanced anxiously at her watch; five minutes past eight, but surely no one would turn up till eight fifteen.

'You could do it rather gently, Matt,' Andrew was lounging, apparently unperturbed. 'You know by wondering aloud how many of the employees – particularly the Prior employees – have any savings at all and whether any of them would be prepared to invest in a local company or companies which went bust once.'

Matthew nodded slowly and Lucy relaxed. He was shrewd, was Matthew, and well capable of playing it very long instead, if he saw this was to his advantage.

'Then, of course, you have your opening to suggest that even with the employee contribution, a management team is unlikely to be able to offer a price that in any way reflects the expenditure of taxpayers' money on this company.'

Matthew nodded, slowly. 'That's good,' he said, seriously. 'I'll have to find my own words, but I've got it. Then maybe I'll remind him that we put up £150,000 for party funds as a company last year, through the books, never mind the other bits and pieces.'

'What bits and pieces, Matthew?' Lucy asked, interested, and Andrew prayed that her husband would ignore her; he absolutely did not want to know about any contributions made to the welfare of the Conservative Party other than those stated in the Reports and Accounts of Friern Construction plc.

The bell rang, taking his hostess from the room in a flurry of dark-blue silk, and leaving him with his client and the wine. 'Most useful chat Lucy had,' he ventured.

'She's a clever girl. And she's always got an admirer somewhere, whom she can get to do things for her.' Matthew had stood up and was checking the glasses, and Andy wondered, as he had before, how much Matthew knew about him and Lucy and their brief fling all those years ago.

'Better go through,' Matthew said, and went first, a big, solid, powerful chap; odd, Andy thought, with real interest, that many of Walzheims' largest clients in financial terms were also the biggest in physical terms. Some important ratio here. Despite the much discussed correlation between small men and success, he could not for the moment think of a chief executive of a major client who could credibly be described as small. Conservative ministers seemed to be sizeable chaps too, he thought, greeting John Winstanley, who had arrived in the official car, and was being charmed by Lucy. He kissed his own wife who was looking ratty; baby-sitter trouble, presumably, her pale blonde elegance outshone by Lucy's dark glittering beauty. He must get Emma some diamonds, some unmistakably real ones such as Lucy was wearing around her neck and in her ears. He moved smoothly sideways to let Peter Jenner, Constituency Chairman somewhere in the north-east open the batting with Winstanley, which he was doing with a series of disjunctive statements about Party policy: what a refreshment to have a local MP after years of those ghastly Labour people, bit of an outpost of course in Dorrington, but grateful for all the help they could get. And very nice having Gerry Willshaw as a minister, made people up there feel they'd not been forgotten.

Not perhaps altogether tactful to go on about Willshaw, Andrew thought, and watched, unmoving, as Matthew neatly cut Winstanley out of the group, introduced him to the pretty woman from the V. & A. and refilled his glass. After a due pause, just long enough for serious drinkers to get in a second round, dinner was announced and Andrew found himself between the V. & A. woman, who was excellent value, and Peter Jenner's wife, who was not. He noted with approval that his own Emma, on the other side of Winstanley, was apparently keeping him very well entertained, if only by listening to political anecdotes when Lucy was otherwise occupied. He rose at the end of an excellent meal, waiting for a lead which was smoothly provided by the Frierns: Lucy sweeping away the ladies of the party and two of the gentlemen, leaving him and Matthew and John Winstanley, mellowed by dinner, to sit over the port and three very good cigars.

'Minister – John – I'm very glad you could come tonight,' Matthew said, easily. 'As you know, we desperately wanted a Conservative government, we are quite sure it's the right thing for the country – I really don't know what we were coming to – and, of course, as a building company we are particularly pleased to see you back.'

Can't say fairer, Andy thought, admiring this eminently straightforward statement.

'I very much enjoyed your speech at the conference – what . . . a few weeks ago now?' Matt went on, steadily, contemplating the end of his cigar. 'And I very much agreed with what you said about getting all these NEB companies, which should never have got there in the first place, out of the public sector.' He paused, to let Winstanley comment.

'The Prime Minister, I know, attaches great importance to that. She was saying only yesterday that we must push on, that there is a great deal of opposition to this policy in all sorts of places.'

'Oh, I'm sure that's right,' Matthew poured some more port. 'Lots of people used to being sheltered in the public sector, terrified of the outside world.' He hesitated momentarily. 'What I wondered, John, is – well, you know that we're very interested in buying Prior Systems – one of the NEB companies. There's another four in that construction group, and I could find something to do for all of them, except Davecat. But I'd take that off your hands and close it – easier for me than you. Is there a chance you would entertain a bid for the whole group?'

Could not have put it better myself, Andy thought, behind a professional deadpan, watching the two heavy faces across the table.

'That could be a very attractive solution,' John Winstanley said, with the air of a man pleasantly surprised, although, as Andy had observed, his political antennae must have told him three sentences ago where this conversation was going. 'I would need, of course, to take the advice of our bankers.'

'Of course you would. Like I take Andy's advice.'

A gesture brought Andy in and he leant forward ready to intervene, but Matt was going on.

'What I suggest, John, is that, if the idea attracts you, we put our bankers together to discuss it. I'm thinking of making you an offer based on an agreed valuation, but to do that I need exclusive access for ... what ... four weeks ... Andy?'

'Four to six weeks, Minister. It's going to cost Friern a bit to get their offer right.'

'Would you have to tell the Stock Exchange?'

'Yes,' Andy said, baldly. 'When we get to the detail. But not, of course, till we had reached provisional agreement.'

'I need to think about this one,' Winstanley said, after another silence. 'But thank you. It's a helpful offer.' He sat up and fidgeted, plainly hoping to be invited to join the ladies, but Matthew, Andy could see, was intent on making all his points and he waited, resigned.

'I gather the management at Prior are trying to get together an offer?' Matthew said, offering nuts.

'So I've been told.' Winstanley sounded relieved to have this on the table. 'And while we'd all like to see a successful sale to employee shareholders, we have to remember there's a lot of taxpayers' money involved. We shall need to be clear that any purchaser pays a fair price and that the end result is stable and not too highly geared for comfort.'

Time to sing for my supper, Andy thought. 'A lot of these buy-outs have been very highly geared, Minister. I do find it a bit hair-raising as a corporate financier.'

'I agree. I was at Schroders for two years.'

'I remember. Excellent people.' He allowed a short interlude while they discussed mutual acquaintances, and received another round of port, then decided to try again.

'The trouble with these buy-outs is that they *have* to be very highly geared in order to give institutions and management the amount they want.'

'I suppose that would be the same if employees were involved as well?'

Andy's hands closed securely round this unexpected catch. 'Oh, even more so, because then the employees are competing with management for the pure equity, so they are asking the investing institutions to yield more equity, keeping the debt package the same. And on that basis the institutions probably wouldn't be able to get the returns they expect.'

'So they wouldn't do it.'

'They would be more inclined to push up the bank so that they wouldn't need to put up so much borrowing capital, thereby making the whole operation more vulnerable.'

'But a lot of these buy-outs do succeed, don't they?' Winstanley asked.

'Oh yes, indeed.' He passed the port. 'One doesn't hear so much about the ones that fail, of course, except at bank board meetings.'

'Wildly embarrassing for the promoters when that happens, I suppose,' Winstanley inquired, hopefully.

'Well, Minister I'm afraid that isn't quite right. We have a development capital arm, so I know that if one of these deals goes right the rewards are enormous for investors. In these circumstances we all tend to accept the occasional total Horlicks in which we lose the company as part of life's rich tapestry.'

Winstanley nodded, slowly, expression professionally blank and Matthew opened his mouth to add to the point, but thought better of it. 'We'd better join the ladies,' he announced. 'Lucy will be furious with me.' He ushered Winstanley out in front of him.

'Nicely, Andy,' he said, quietly, as he passed on his way. Earned my pay tonight, indeed, Andy thought. Winstanley had got it in one; real companies, with names, reputations and the career of the chief executive to protect, didn't take risks; you'd be safe with them. The cowboys in the development capital business on the other hand took huge risks for vast rewards and they were not people to whom to entrust your political career.

His duty was done; unless Winstanley sought him out he could leave Matthew and Peter Jenner to make the rest of the political points and Lucy to charm the man – as she was doing. He resolutely transferred his attention to Mrs Jenner.

At seven thirty the next morning a smaller and less sociable party was also discussing the affairs of Prior Building Systems, four of them at a swaying table, too small to contain them, four British Rail breakfasts and the papers they were trying to consult.

Caroline Whitehouse and her assistant Mark Dwyer were on one side of the table and a large, dark man, older than she, running comfortably to fat, and a silent, slightly younger acolyte were on the other side.

'You haven't read the papers, Hamish, you lazy sod,' Caroline said, coldly, pouring coffee.

'I bloody have. Or enough of them, given that they have no worthwhile numbers in them.'

'You haven't even grasped that these are all the numbers you can have in the absence of the NEB's permission.'

'I have *read* this, Caroline.'

The acolytes looked at each other nervously, but the principal participants ignored them.

'Then you should have grasped that this has to be a deferred purchase deal. It says so, on page one. Pass the salt, please.'

'It's not that I've not *grasped* it, Caroline; I'm just this minute telling you that it'll nae do.' Hamish's voice rose to the rasping pitch that Glaswegians develop under stress, and half the carriage peered round. Hamish came originally from a small village outside Glasgow, second son of a small shopkeeper. The elder boy had got the shop and Hamish had started as a clerk with the Clydesdale Bank, where, using a naturally sociable and expressive temperament combined with the ability to control staff, he had risen very rapidly indeed to manager and then general manager in his mid-thirties, leaving his elder brother and the rest of the family far behind. He had worked with the Scottish arm of a London development capital operation, he as the lead lending banker, on a fashionable buy-out and found a talent for the work. A senior director of the development capital operation had come from London for the completion and offered him a job, ten minutes after the signing when everyone was drinking champagne except Hamish, who maintained his bonhomous approach on a strictly teetotal foundation. He had accepted after a week's deliberation which he had asked for; there was nothing impulsive at all in his temperament. On the plane from Edinburgh he had decided that he would make no change at all to his professional persona, and the etiolated wee gits in London could take him as he was, or not at all. He was now a major personality in the development capital world, a comfortable, smiling thug, an excellent public speaker and a ruthlessly good organizer. He had met Caroline on the other side of a deal, where she had been acting for the seller of the company he was trying to buy. He had started off on a basis of heavy-handed flirtation, as if she were one of the girl clerks at the Clydesdale and, as he said goodtemperedly, had got his balls out of the way just in time.

'She screwed us on the price and on the warranties,' he had reported to his employers. 'It's still a good deal, mind,' he had added in parenthesis, 'but if she hadna had a useless client we'd have had to give a lot more. I'd rather she was on my side, next time.'

Caroline had subsequently been the lawyer for his group on three occasions and, other things being equal, Hamish would have used her whenever she was available. But it was a two-way traffic; lawyers brought business to you, and if you always used the same lawyer, you might be cutting yourself off from another fruitful source of deals. This was the first deal she had brought him, and he regarded her benevolently, unwounded by her comments. He had not, in fact, read anything very much, but his acolyte had; no need for both of them to get through it all at this stage.

'And the price is too high, anyway, even on the useless numbers which are all ye've felt able to let us have,' he said, pleasantly, lowering his voice. 'The company's got no track record, it's a forced sale from what ye tell me – ye know I've no understanding of politics down here.'

'Balls,' Caroline said, sidetracked. She took a breath. 'It is a forced sale, Hamish, but we've got competition. You know, other people who want to buy the same thing – trade purchasers.'

'We'll aye lose out to a trade purchaser, they can afford more cash.'

'*Now* you've got the point. This competition is not entirely about cash, it's about party policy. But the cash has to *look* OK. Therefore a deferred purchase deal.'

'Ye mean ten quid down and another fiver if the sun shines every day for the next three years is the same as fifteen quid now.'

'I knew you were intelligent, really.'

'Will that wash?' Both acolytes had stopped eating, forks poised, recognizing a critical moment in discussion.

'I think so. If it can be made to look all right – if two sets of bankers can convince themselves that the Government has a real chance of getting much the same price by doing something politically popular, we're home. We're the only people who can deliver an employee buy-out.'

'Smiling faces, the wee wifie holding up the certificate bought with the housekeeping.'

'Nearly, Hamish. Crane drivers built like the proverbial brick shit-houses, tearing up union cards, swearing lifelong allegiance to the company and to the Conservative Party what gave them this opportunity.'

'I see it. What is the management team like?'

'You haven't read their CVs either. Where did you stop – the index?'

'They're fairly young, yes?' Hamish persisted.

'Peter Burwood is thirty-nine, the FD Graham Gough is thirty-seven and the *éminence grise*, Martin Williams, is forty-eight. I think they're good, or I'd not have asked you to get on a train, but it's no use me trying to make that judgement for you.'

Hamish nodded. All development capital specialists know how to assess a business and to minimize risk in a deal. But the key variable remains the management team. It is one of the unplumbed mysteries, why one group will make a success of an unpromising business with every man's hand against them, where another, superficially identical, will fall apart, and the company with them.

'Not much business risk left, I thought.' Caroline had been watching him.

'A ripe plum.' Hamish had arrived at the same conclusion from discussion with his acolyte. 'I'm grateful to you for bringing it to us, Caroline. Provided everything is all right when we get the numbers, we'll underwrite and sell down afterwards. We can do that out of our new fund.'

'I don't want them stuck with underwriting fees,' she said swiftly, and got a look under his long eyelashes. 'Hamish, look, these are not stupid people; they know they've got a good deal here, and if you try to stick an underwriting fee into it they may want to go elsewhere. What were you trying for, one per cent? £600,000?'

'Something like that.'

'It'll blow the deal.'

'We'd mebbe not mention it at this stage – leave it till further down the line?'

'I'm acting for the company. We discuss fees up front.'

'Mm. Everyone's going to want a wee bit of underwriting fee.'

'And a wee bit is what we're paying, not £600,000. The equity shouldn't be more than £10m, and I expect the company can fix the lending.'

'I'd have to charge one per cent on the equity.'

'Making £100,000. That I could support, absent too many other frills.'

These preliminaries disposed of, the group finished breakfast in silence, Hamish concentrating on the key features of the deal and a fast read of the careers of the three managers.

'You do any due diligence, Caroline?'

'On the lads, yes. Talked to a mate at Tarmac, where Peter Burwood was before, talked to a chap at Deloitte about Graham Gough, talked to ICL about Martin Williams. Good reports all round. I'll give you the names if you want to do all that again.'

'What about the politics?'

Both of them were speaking very quietly in the interests of discretion, and their subordinates were straining to hear.

'It really is policy to sell this one; no ifs and buts from the NEB will be tolerated. They'd quite like it to go to employees, but all other things have to be equal, or look like being equal. Like I said.'

'Got any support?'

She hesitated. 'Gerry Willshaw, Minister for Transport, MP for the next-door constituency. Lots of his constituents work at Prior.'

'Useful. Do you know him well?'

'Well enough.' He glanced at her quickly but she was looking, startled, across the narrow walkway. 'Matthew!'

Hamish followed her gaze to a large man, who was looking as disconcerted as she.

'Hello. How are you?'

She scrambled to her feet and kissed the chap, blocking him from Hamish's view. Someone she absolutely didn't want to introduce him to, Hamish thought, and leant over the table to ask her assistant a question to which he already knew the answer, managing to watch Caroline's friend out of the tail of his eye. A second man was crowding in, obviously dead keen to be introduced, smiling at her, and equally obviously Matthew – whoever he was – did not want to introduce him. Hamish sat back, sparkling with interest and waited to see what would happen.

It was Caroline who gave way first. 'Matthew, do you know Hamish Brown of Martins? No? Hamish, meet Matthew Friern. Mr Brown. Sir Matthew Friern.'

You didn't often hear the correct formal method of performing an introduction with the proper titles repeated so everyone knew where they were, Hamish, who had trained in a very conventional bank, thought respectfully. Sir Matthew Friern, whose name he had recognized immediately as the chairman of a potential rival for the company, was introducing his fat friend reluctantly and inaudibly. The smaller man gripped Caroline's hand, beaming.

'Councillor Williamson,' he boomed. 'Pleased to meet you.'

Hamish watched Matthew Friern's mouth set tight and his fair skin flush.

'What are you doing here, Caroline?' Friern was asking, his tone just this side of rudeness.

'On my way up to see a client, Matt.'

'Who is that?' Councillor Williamson was plainly determined to get in on this conversation.

'Prior Building Systems,' Caroline's back had tensed and she had put her weight evenly on both feet, like a boxer. Councillor Williamson was ludicrously taken aback, unable to avoid a glance sideways for guidance to Matthew, who had not taken his eyes off Caroline.

'We were just talking about them, as a matter of fact,' he said steadily. 'You know, I'm sure Caroline, that we are interested in buying if the NEB are selling.'

'I'd heard. I am acting for the company, not the NEB.'

'Why does the company need a separate lawyer?' Councillor Williamson had recovered his poise.

'It is felt that their interests and the NEB's do not absolutely coincide,' Caroline said, courteously.

'I would have thought they might employ a local

lawyer,' Williamson said, grumpily, and Hamish watched Caroline's hands twitch in irritation behind her back.

'I take it there must have been conflicts of interest,' she said, carefully. 'I mean, presumably, many of the local firms work for the council. And Prior have contracts with the council.'

It would suit you down to the ground, wouldn't it, laddie, to have Prior advised by a firm who owed most of their business to the council, Hamish thought, on home ground from his days as a bank manager.

'Mustn't keep you, Matt. We're blocking the gangway here,' Caroline was saying, briskly. 'Love to Lucy – I'm having lunch with her next week. Very nice to have met you, Councillor.' She swung back neatly into her seat, and watched them retreat down the train. She turned to Hamish. 'They couldn't have heard us, could they?'

'No, no. Unless they were using bugs. Not very pleased to see you, was he?'

'Not awfully. We've never got on, for all he is married to the girl who was my best friend at school.'

'He'd not wanted you to meet his fat friend.'

'Councillor Williamson. He didn't, did he? I must look the good councillor up.'

'Ye'll likely find he's chairman of the housing committee.'

She looked at him sharply, and he smiled, watching that rat-trap mind close round a new idea.

'*That*'s what I meant by the politics. Never mind the national lot, it's the local boys you'll need.'

'I don't have anyone I know on the council.' You could almost see the wheels turn, he thought with amusement. 'I'll find someone. OK, thanks Hamish. I heard that.'

*

Fifty yards down the train Matthew Friern and Councillor Williamson were seated facing each other, secured against invasion by a litter of cases and coats spread casually over the other two seats.

'She couldn't have heard us, could she?'

'Nothing to hear, Bill. Just a friendly chat.'

'Yes, of course. Who was the bloke with her?'

'He's well-known. Buy-out specialist called Hamish Brown. She'll be taking him up to see Prior's management to see about financing them. They still won't be able to pay what we can. Not that we're going to pay silly prices, for this or anything else.' He rose restlessly and looked along the corridor, then turned back to face the other man.

'Now, are we clear, Bill? You know what you're doing: I want that matter deferred for at least three months. You know how to do that?'

'I've been chairman of this committee for long enough, Matthew.'

'Right. Yes, you have, and a good friend to us. When is it Sharon's getting married?' He made a note. 'All right. OK. That's done. I must pay a call before we get there.'

Ten minutes later the train pulled in, and the parties met again, with constrained smiles, as they moved towards the barrier. Caroline looked round for the Prior driver and blinked as Peter Burwood himself waved to her from the middle of the small group meeting the train. In Hamish's honour, not hers, she thought. Matthew moved in unison with her, making for the same spot and as she kissed Peter, she found Matthew at her elbow, handing a case to his driver. Punctiliously she introduced them, feeling like a minor Shakespearian

229

character. All it needed was a bit of verse dialogue just to explain to the audience who was who, she thought grimly, as she watched Matthew being overbearingly charming. She looked round for Councillor Williamson and just caught a glimpse of him, hurrying off with a small man, his driver maybe, as he was carrying the bags. But he hadn't wanted to be seen with Matthew Friern, or not by Peter Burwood, and she watched his retreating back reflectively.

I I

Clive Fieldman, a child clamped to each hand, stood
hesitantly at the top of the steps, checking the number
of the house, assailed by the sort of shyness he thought
he had lost for ever, years ago.

'I should ring the bell – she'll never hear otherwise,'
an amused authoritative voice said from behind him,
and he turned his head to see a male version of Caroline,
with the same thick blond hair, blue eyes and matt,
slightly sallow skin.

'I'm Caroline's brother, Caspar Henriques,' the man
said. 'We've met before, about a hundred years ago.
And these are my two, Peter and Jeremy.' A wave indicated two rangy teenagers with the Henriques looks,
only marginally differently arranged.

'I remember you. My daughter Samantha and my
son William.'

The children nodded, watching each other carefully,
and the door opened to reveal Caroline.

'Clive, how nice to see you. Hello Caspar, hello darlings.' She kissed both men and her nephews, and shook
hands seriously with Clive's children, bidding them go
through to the kitchen for a drink. They went, cautiously, holding each other's hands for support, looking
very small and dark besides the tall, blond Henriques
boys, and Clive looked after them anxiously.

'My own Susannah and Francis, who are the same
age as yours, are through there. And Felix's Arabella;
she's ten as well.'

'Good God, is Felix here? And Marianne?' Caspar asked.

'Yes, they are. Marianne objects to assembled groups of Henriqueses, Clive; it is the sole point of sympathy between us.'

'What's wrong with her?' Clive asked, cheered by the glass of chilled white wine she had placed in his hand.

'There's nothing wrong with her, Clive,' Caspar assured him. 'The problem is, my sister believes every woman's duty is to be out there doing a man's job for a vast salary, and Marianne believes, on the whole, that mothers should be at home. And she votes Labour. Of course, she and Caro don't get on.' He opened another bottle. 'Are the oldies here yet, darling?'

'Yes. Mum is knee-deep in grandchildren. Sholto has gone to the bottom of the garden with Felix.'

'Poor old man. I'll take Clive with me, and a bottle, and we'll engage in seditious male conversation while you good ladies get the lunch.' He dodged a well-aimed hack at the ankles and retreated, taking Clive, who was anxious to see that his children were all right. At the back of the house, in a huge kitchen-cum-dining-room-cum-conservatory, he found his Samantha drinking lemonade and chattering to two other little girls of about ten years old, one of whom was pure Henriques, and the other a slight, delicately made, red-headed beauty.

'The redhead is mine, Susannah,' Caroline said, from behind him. 'My Francis, also aged eight, is under the table with your William and Felix's son, Michael, who is actually seventeen. I can't think what he's doing there. Mama, do you remember Clive Fieldman from all those years ago? I think you must have met.'

'We have.' Lady Henriques looked very much as he

remembered her, tall and slight, with her daughter's wide smile. And just as much in awe of the fierce cuckoo she had hatched, who was competently switching saucepans around on the stove.

'Has Marianne gone into the garden, too?'

'Yes, darling. She was finding the noise a bit much.'

'I don't blame her. Turn the bloody thing off this minute, Tom.'

A middle-sized Henriques boy turned off a folk-song, and comparative silence fell.

'Rather dispiriting words,' a clear, assured, childish voice observed into the silence. 'Odd, because the tune was quite buoyant.'

Clive tried not to gape at Susannah, while Caspar gave his niece his serious and considered attention. 'That's right, darling. That *is* the archetypal folk-song. Death and disaster covered by a cheery tune, sung by one of those high, uninflected sopranos.'

The child considered him.

'I've murdered Mum and Daddy, too
And Auntie Jill as well,'

she sang, to the tune of 'All Things Bright and Beautiful'.

'I did it with my little axe
And I'll go straight to hell.'

'That's right. They're all like that,' Caspar confirmed, matter-of-factly, as Susannah collapsed with giggles like any other ten-year-old and went back to playing.

'Is she doing very well at school?' Clive asked.

233

'Not particularly.' Caroline was amused. 'She is a lovely child, but like Ben, she won't do things she isn't interested in. So she won't be a prefect or captain of Brownies or pencil monitor – just says "No, thank you" in the most civilized way and goes back to doing what she wanted to. It pisses the school right off. Goodness, I envy her.'

'Did you ever do anything you didn't want to?' Clive asked, startled, and heard Caspar laugh.

'Until she was about sixteen, she was rather conformist,' he said. 'Head of house, captain of boats.'

'It wore off,' Caroline said, grimly. 'Or rather I finally understood that I was wasting time. I only did those things because all the rest of you were *so* peculiar. I thought I'd aim for the conventional.'

Clive accepted another drink and sneaked a look at Caspar, trying to decide wherein his peculiarity lay. He was a full Professor at LSE and, in fact, conventional by most standards if one listened to him argue the case for keeping public spending at its present level, and changing the accounting conventions.

'Caroline.' Another authoritative voice from the garden summoned her. 'There is a minion outside on a motorbike with lots of flashing lights and a portable phone, tendering an urgent bundle covered with red seals. He has come all the way from the City, but I imagine you lot don't worry about the cost of such things.'

'Could you sign for it, Felix, if it is your turn for the BBC biro this weekend?' Caroline raised her voice effortlessly over the general hubbub and slitted her eyes at another large man, bulkier by a couple of stone and with less hair than Caspar, but cast from the same mould.

'I have. He has twelve more of the same to deliver, he tells me. Are any of you going to read whatever is therein contained, or would it have made just as much sense to have it on your desks for Monday? At a cost-saving of hundreds of pounds.'

'I cannot answer for my colleagues in four different organizations, Felix, but personally, the only time I have to look at that document before a further meeting takes place is tonight. I appreciate that the pace at the BBC is somewhat slower.'

Any riposte from Felix was cut off by the entry of Professor Sir Sholto Henriques, looking hardly a day older than he had when lecturing at the LSE eighteen years earlier. 'That young man delivering letters is probably paid more than a research fellow.'

'He probably *is* a research fellow, Dad.' Caroline banged a saucepan down. 'I understand that the staff of these couriers is drawn evenly from the Flying Squad and the more enterprising members of academia, subsidizing esoteric and personal amusements like considering the nature of Good. Caz, would you open the wine, please? I forgot it and I suppose it needs to breathe.'

Caspar placed a hand on her shoulder. 'Calm down, darling, they're winding you up. You haven't introduced Clive to the rest of us yet.'

Caroline, pink, and looking a good deal younger than her working self, took a deep breath. 'Sorry. Dad, Felix, this is Clive Fieldman, who is an under-secretary at Environment. You met him before when we were children. Clive, my father Sholto, and my brother Felix. And his wife Marianne.'

Clive shook hands all round and said something civil to Sir Sholto about his lectures, which plainly gave

235

pleasure. Sholto was even more dominant physically than he had remembered, a huge man, wide-shouldered, with large square hands suited to manual labour, but which so far as Clive knew, had only ever been deployed round a pen. The mind was as good as he remembered; listening to Sholto taking an issue apart for analysis was like watching a first-class surgeon at work. Caroline had the same sort of ability, ungrateful girl that she was to be so rude to her father, but it was more fluent and more graceful in Sholto. And less savage; this was what he enjoyed, this was what he was good at, he was a happy man doing the only thing he had ever wanted to do.

He turned to talk to Marianne, a tall, sardonic woman, who, as he would not have known from Caroline's description of her, was engaged in a monograph on a particularly difficult and limited field of eighteenth-century Turkish ceramics. Felix, about whom Caroline had been equally scathing, turned out to be well-informed, perhaps a bit obsessive, but not at all deserving of censure on the scale his sister was deploying. Clive realized that he was enjoying himself and only slowly understood that he was being very carefully observed by the group.

'You've known Caroline for ever, of course,' Felix said, blandly.

'I'd not seen her at all, for sixteen years until last month, but we all trained together.'

'Do you find her mellowed at all by the years?' Sir Sholto asked, breaking off from a deliberation on where responsibility for dependants should lie, and Clive gave the question careful consideration.

'Yes, I think so. I'm sure she was much fiercer when

we were all young.' He met four disbelieving expressions and Sholto Henriques changed the subject to ask about DoE policy on housing. Clive braced himself, remembering that this was a Labour Party adviser who started from an uncompromising ideological basis, that everyone had the right to a proper home for free. They were deep in considerations of funding housing subsidy when he caught Caroline's sardonic eye on him; she was at the other end of the table talking to Caspar while her mother fended off grandchildren and watched vegetables cooking.

'Ten minutes to lunch, and everyone twelve and under is on the small table,' she called, minatorily, solving the problem he had begun to address, namely how did seventeen people all fit around one table. He offered to help, but she shook her head and went back to her conversation with her brother, who had watched this exchange with interest.

'Your boyfriend seems to be getting on with Dad,' he observed.

'Not a boyfriend.'

'I used the term loosely. An old mate.'

'Much improved by age, but yes, that's right. Oh God, do you suppose Dad will be nursing unwarranted hopes?'

'No. I know you do not rate Dad highly, but he knows you very well. You and Clive don't look like lovers. No spark. But on the other hand, you're looking very pretty, little sister. Do you have a lover tucked away somewhere else?'

Caroline, to her horror, felt herself grow slowly scarlet, and Caspar leant forward to shield her from the other end of the table.

'Why isn't he here, then?'

'Caz, shut up.'

He considered her, much amused. 'I can't remember when I've seen you in such a tizzwozz.' His grin faded. 'Oh, hang on. He's married.'

'Everyone I know is.'

'Except me, and Clive there, and dozens like us; don't give me that rubbish. Caro, you can't *do* that.'

'Why not?'

'You *know* why not. You've always had the strength of ten because your heart is pure, as the old tag goes. You concentrate, you don't get into messy ambivalent situations. I have always envied and admired that.'

'My hair will fall out, you think?'

'You'll take to drink, or the kids will start glue-sniffing. Darling, of course you need a husband, but not someone else's. Even I stay away from other people's marriages these days; grief lies down that road.'

'Dear Caz. Always so kind. I'm not even thinking of marrying this one – he's my lover. Recreational only.'

'You are absolutely not convincing me, little sister.'

'Don't call me that – you sound like one of those awful, doomy Chekhov plays.'

'That's where you'll end up, if you persist. Why are you doing this, Caro?'

'I fancied him rotten from moment one. Or moment two, anyway.'

'Are there not others you fancy?'

'Not since Ben, if you must know. Or not for more than a couple of hours. It's all very well maintaining an uncluttered life when you've got a good husband. I'm sure I resisted all sorts of attractions while I had him. But he's gone.'

'Mm.' Her brother considered her, sadly. 'Who is this chap?'

'I'm not saying. He's married, so it's not my secret alone.'

'You're going to get hurt.'

'How do you *know*? You have the most conventional views of women. Why should I not be able to pluck a flower and pass on, like you three louts?'

'Oh, darling. For a start, none of us in this family are any good at gathering rosebuds. They turn to poison in our hands, they fade and die and we're left clinging on. And you add to that generic family failing the fact that you are a woman. I may know one or two lucky chaps who can flit from blossom to blossom, but I do not know any women who can manage that trick.'

'You may be about to see one.' She rose to prod a pan of vegetables. 'Two minutes,' she said, firmly. 'Will you carve for the kids? Felix can do the grown-ups.'

'How often do you see him?' he asked, refusing to be sidetracked, and watched her back stiffen.

'As often as I can. It's difficult, of course.'

'What, with the kids?'

'No, we use his flat.' She drained broccoli expertly, not looking at him.

'Where's his wife?'

'In the country.'

'You got a captain of industry there?'

'No. Stop fishing, Caz.'

He watched her as she neatly arranged serving-dishes.

'Caro, darling.' He put a hand on her arm. 'Find someone who is at least available to you. I've been there, I know what you're doing, you don't see him much and he's always with his wife when you've got any time, like today.'

239

'Sod off, Caz. I have to do this.' She pulled her arm away, violently. 'When he whistles, I come running. It may not be very dignified, but I might as well admit that that's the bottom line, for the moment. It'll pass, I suppose. Everything does, but right now, this is the news, folks, at 1 p.m., here in London, England.' It was an old joke between them, but she was close to tears, and he was not amused. She pushed past him, calling for their eldest brother to come and carve for her.

'Can I help?' Clive appeared at her elbow, looking compact beside the big Henriques men, and she handed him a pile of plates and got him to organize the twelve-and-under table, which held her three, his two, one of Caspar's boys, and Felix's daughter. That left ten for the big table, seven adults, Felix's two teenagers, and Caspar's eldest, who ranked as grown-ups. Apart from a moment's disruption, caused by Felix remarking on the kind of excessive remuneration it must require to feed them all on two sirloins with the undercuts left in, the meal proceeded smoothly, with the Henriques brothers carving separate joints.

Clive found himself next to Lady Henriques, enjoying himself. His children had mixed smoothly with the others. Caspar's second son was taking a good deal of trouble with Samantha, who was, however, more interested in the formidable Susannah. His William and Caroline's Francis were playing amicably together. As the meal finished the children edged over to join the grown-ups, and Susannah appropriated Caspar's knee and used it as a base from which to consider Clive.

'Caz has fur on his arms,' she said, conversationally. 'Do you, too?'

'If the answer to that question is no, Clive, no need to feel crushed,' Caz said, laughing. 'She has decided that it's an asset in a man, but we tell her there are other characteristics just as important.'

Clive, flown with excellent wine, rolled up his sleeves to reveal forearms satisfactorily furnished with dark hair and the child leaned forward from her perch to examine them, and daringly put out a hand to stroke him.

'It shows more because it's dark, but it's about the same thickness as Caz's,' she said, thoughtfully, and Clive looked up to see Caroline smiling at her daughter, transfigured by love and amusement. She caught his eye, and he grinned at her over the child's head, reminded sharply and painfully of similar moments of shared pleasure in a child.

'I think she's being unfaithful to me,' Caz said, mournfully, and the child, amused, turned and kissed him to reassure him.

Caroline's sons had moved in closer, trying to get into the act, desperate to be near the warmth, and as if they had rehearsed it, Caz cleared one knee for Timmy, while Clive scooped up Francis. He looked round guiltily for his own children, but they had been collected up by Lady Henriques and were totally engrossed in a card game, William leaning easily against her, sucking his thumb as he did when he was tired. Clive sat with the comfortable weight of Timmy on his knee, content, flirting gently with Susannah, who had offered to play the violin to him later, and listening to Sir Sholto and Felix, joining in a disapproving, sharp analysis of current Treasury policy. Good comfortable academic stuff, redeemed by the quality of the discussion. He was holding his own, without too much difficulty, when he found tea was being served. After tea the party started to break up as Felix and his family and the senior Henriqueses, all of whom pressed him with flattering warmth to come to them when it was their turn to hold the family lunch, prepared to leave.

'It'll be mince *chez nous*, you understand, rather than sirloin at God knows how much a pound,' Felix said, with an eye on his sister, 'but I hope you'll feel able.'

'Rising above their habitual dinner of the husks that the swine would not eat,' Caroline said, furiously.

'That's very naughty, darling,' Lady Henriques said, firmly. 'Marianne always gives us a delicious lunch.'

Marianne, unmoved, was thanking Caroline and collecting her children, and in the silence which fell after their departure, Clive decided reluctantly that he ought at least to offer to go.

'Don't leave, Clive,' Caz said, hospitably. 'I always stay till I have to take my kids back, Caro knows that.'

'Don't go,' Susannah said, looking at him under her eyelashes. 'You haven't heard my violin.'

So he stayed and listened to Susannah play and helped Caroline unload the dishwasher, wondering why she had turned out as fierce as she had. Perhaps it was just that the rest of the family was more academic. He tried this theory out quietly on Caz, who scouted it.

'Caro got straight alphas on her jurisprudence and international law papers – I knew her tutor. She just decided to use her brains to be rich and powerful, didn't you, darling?'

'I decided not to be involved with messy people. I think Mum is wasting her time in social work and I hate eating husks.'

'You always let Felix wind you up. Senior chaps in Current Affairs at the Beeb do all right financially.'

'What about Marcus, though?'

'I agree that is a discouraging thought. This is our middle brother who lives in high-minded squalor in Doncaster, Clive, surrounded by children, lecturing for about £600 a year on twelfth-century monasticism, never having been interested in anything else. He got his Professor which helped but he has about two pupils and is embittered by the lack of respect.'

'We all have to send clothes for the children,' Caroline said, casting a look of pride at her own well-clad brood.

'I manage because I am an economist and in demand,' Caz said, to Clive. 'You know, Caro, there's no law that says we all have to earn the top dollar.'

'Anything rather than be like Mum and Dad.'

Caz considered her. 'What you've never understood is that Mum loves our Dad. She may let off steam to you, but she'd not be anywhere else.'

His sister gave him a look of pure disbelief and, catching Clive's interested eye, changed the subject firmly, organizing the remaining children to tidy the place up a bit. She was considerably less formidable in her own background, Clive thought with amusement, much more like anyone's mother. She caught his eye and scowled at him, reading his mind, and at that moment the phone rang and she flew to it.

'Hi,' she said, breathlessly, turning her back on the company. 'Yes, I am here. Mm. Absolutely. Yes, that would be fine. I'll see you there then. Yes. Wonderful.'

She put the phone down slowly and turned back to them, sparkling.

'More visitors, darling?' Caspar asked.

'Not for some time, but I'm going out for a drink after dinner.' She smiled at him, suddenly radiating joy.

'Right, let's get a meal on the table. Clive, what will yours eat? Eggs? Or come to think of it, eggs?'

Clive agreed that eggs would be fine and watched her hum round the kitchen.

'Is Mummy going out?' the beautiful Susannah inquired, anxiously of her back.

'Not until after you've gone to bed, and not for long,' Caroline said, briskly. 'Jean is in – you go to her if you wake and I'm not there.'

Caz put an arm round the child. 'Mummy has to go out sometimes,' he said, firmly, and Clive, catching the look of surprised, guilty gratitude that Caroline bestowed on him, understood immediately that Caroline's bloke must be in some way undesirable. Of course, he was married, wasn't he; that Sunday-night phone call meant that he was on the way back from the weekend somewhere, just like me and Lucy with the sexes reversed. Good luck to her, he thought, regretfully; he had felt at home with the Henriques clan in a way that had not been possible with his own family since he had been about twelve and going to grammar school. Interesting, he reflected, it had been fear of the likes of the Henriques gang that had decided him against trying for Oxford or Cambridge. He had known he could cope with LSE; it was full of clever, working-class lads like himself and blessedly empty of the public-school types. What he had not seen was that the academic public-school families like the Henriques lot would always have chosen their friends for brains rather than background, and it was a pity he had left it rather late to discover that a whole section of society he had been deeply suspicious of was open and matter-of-factly welcoming to him. He watched Caroline, glowing with anticipation,

244

efficiently boiling eggs and producing the Marmite toast soldiers demanded vociferously by Caspar. He wondered who her chap was, realizing that he was more than a little jealous and in what he half recognized as a bid to get her attention back he asked her how the Prior Systems job was going.

'What do you mean, going?' She was looking distinctly suspicious and he blinked.

'Well, I mean how are you doing?'

'Oh, I see.' She sounded relieved. 'The second the NEB blows the whistle we shall be there, panting. The buy-out specialists at Martins are dead keen, at least, in theory. We haven't been able to give them any unpublished figures, of course, but as you must know the published accounts are not at all inspiring and this year's figures and the forecasts show a huge improvement. So I think that's all right – I mean, we'll be able to offer the NEB a decent price.'

Three miles away Andy Eames Lewis parked his blue Jaguar outside the Friern flat and rang the bell. Lucy Friern in jeans and a white sweater, hair smooth and tidy, opened the door to him letting a delicious smell of cooking escape.

'Andy,' she said and kissed him ceremoniously. 'Matt is a beast to make you come round on a Sunday. Poor Emma, I must say. But he's got news for you and he can't wait. Do you mind the kitchen? It's easier there.'

He followed her through to the modern kitchen, luxuriously done in gleaming stainless steel and black wood with what must be a Hockney original hung on the facing wall above a very decent-sized black table, reassuringly featuring a good Sancerre in a wine cooler and three glasses. Matthew Friern was talking into a black telephone. Lucy indicated that he should open the wine for her and pour them all a glass while Matt was finishing, and he did so, alerted by hearing his own name.

'I'll tell him, yes, and ask him how best to play it. But you talk to me alone, Bill, right? Good.' Matthew put the phone down and grinned wolfishly at Andy. 'That'll fix those cocky buggers. Look Andy, that was an old friend of mine on the council. He tells me that they were getting close to agreeing quite a substantial extra payment to Prior on those three contracts they have.'

'On what basis, Matt?'

'Extras, client buggeration, all the things you'd expect. And a completion bonus.'

'Nothing very unusual there.'

'No. But I am now told that agreement on the sums payable is going to be deferred. Or rather, the meeting of the Council Committee, which was going to consider officials' recommendations the week after next, will be deferred.'

'Why?'

'Well, Bill Williamson – my friend – is going to be ill. He's chairman, and it can't go through without him. And when he gets better, which will take a month or so – it's his heart you see, nothing serious, but he'll need to rest it – he and some of his mates on the committee are going to find it very difficult indeed to accept the recommendation. It's going to be too much money, and not necessary, and all that.' He picked up a leg of chicken, and addressed it with relish. 'If there doesn't seem to be any way of getting a bit more back on those contracts, some of the punters behind a buy-out will get cold feet.'

Andrew gratefully accepted a plateful of chicken remembering that Lucy had always been a good cook.

'It'll reduce the value of the company,' he said, cautiously. 'It'll lower the price the NEB can expect to get from any purchaser.'

He chewed methodically, suddenly not tasting what he was eating. 'But I take it that your friend Williamson, once he has fully recovered from his heart trouble, might be disposed, after all, to feel that the original recommendation was reasonable.'

'If we owned the company by then, yes. That's right.' He reached across his wife to refill Andy's glass, the corners of his mouth tucked in in satisfaction.

'I see,' Andy said, taking a hefty mouthful of Sancerre. He decided he had to ask. 'Roughly how much would be involved?'

Matt reached in the pocket of his jacket, got a piece of paper out of his wallet and frowned at it. 'It's £4m odd this year, £3m next and £3m in year three.'

Yes it was, cash or near enough, Andy agreed, silently, since Prior had enough accumulated losses not to pay tax on any extra profit. Even if you discounted it, it was a handy £8m or so, ignoring any expenses involved in securing it. He decided that he would not ask about those; any brown-enveloped payments could be left to his client to deal with; or maybe it wasn't brown envelopes, maybe Friern paid a few bills for people here and there, but it was between him and his auditors – no need for the merchant bank advisers to get involved. You couldn't deal with construction companies, or indeed any major exporter, without recognizing that commission on sales might run rather high and take rather unusual forms. But that extra £8m, added to the economies Friern could make by merging Prior Systems with their own business, gave them a real advantage in a contested sale. He grinned at his client. 'Well, that enables you to go up a bit on the price.'

Lucy, who had been listening, apparently casually, said that Caroline was still a close friend, of course.

'You'd better not tell her anything about this lot,' her husband said, unequivocally.

'No, don't be silly. But she's very, very smart, and she *is* quite close to Clive Fieldman. She had him to lunch with her family today.'

'It doesn't matter what anyone thinks,' Andy said, thoughtfully. 'Even if Prior were to get every penny they hoped for in the end, they haven't got it now and outside investors won't believe that the cash will come through, whereas we know it will. Matt, we'll do the numbers again on that basis – it's all under code, of course, don't worry – and I'll talk to you when you get back from Paris, yes?'

'Thanks, Andy. I'm sorry to cut into your evening, but you see why I didn't want to do this over the phone.'

'Absolutely,' Andy agreed. 'If that's it, Matt, I'd better get back again, keep the peace, you know.'

Lucy took him to the door, gracefully reiterating their thanks. She reached up to kiss him socially, and he caught a whiff of her scent. Diorissimo, he remembered effortlessly. She stepped back and looked at him and he realized that he had not quite got his face back where it belonged.

'Very nice to see you, Andy. Sleep well.'

He got into the car dry-mouthed and sweating, with the memory of a slanted look from her navy-blue eyes.

12

Caroline stared across the desk at her assistant. 'Bloody hell, Mark. Did I really do that? Give it here. Shit!' She stared disbelievingly at the paragraph he had highlighted. 'I have got that precisely the wrong way round, haven't I? Been nice if that had got through.'

'I really only came to check you meant it that way,' he said, apologetically.

'I absolutely didn't.' She read the offending paragraph again. 'I must have been tired when I sorted that draft, but that's shaken me.'

Mark sought for the words to convey that most of the partners at Smith Butler put up a blob far more often than Caroline, and decided it was perhaps better not to embark on this. She was looking tired and strained; the children, he thought vaguely, as she roused herself from her shocked consideration of the document.

'Well, Mark, the client would have been thrilled to find out later that he had no redress under that warranty, it being the one he most needs to rely on. Go over the whole thing for me, would you. *Don't* assume I had good reason for putting in any other lunacies you find, change them or come and ask me. We do not want to push up the premiums on the professional negligence policy any further.'

She attempted a smile, but it wasn't a success. She was obviously shaken and furious with herself, and he thought it best to take the papers and go. She watched him leave the room, a slim, dark, confident, hardworking tough, who would probably end up as managing partner in twenty years' time, then sank her head in her hands. She *was* tired; the organization and planning necessary to spend any time at all with Gerry had disrupted her ordered life and in the weeks since the affair had started they had managed to meet only three times, once for an evening, once late at night after an adjournment debate, following a battery of telephone calls which she had felt would have been sufficient to organize the Normandy landings and once late on Sunday. It was not at first sight reasonable to blame this particular piece of flawed drafting on Gerry; she had actually done it two nights ago when he had rung, desperately apologetic but committed to an appearance on *Newsnight*, which meant that any other chance of meeting had gone. She had thought about going home and explaining to everyone there that the important office dinner she was allegedly attending had been cancelled at the last minute, but decided she couldn't bear to. In any case, she was seriously behind, so she had stayed in the office and worked on a draft in which she had got at least one critical clause seriously wrong. She sat, looking at her hands, hearing a therapist explaining that her clever Timmy's sudden, unprecedented lapses at school came from anger, because his father had deserted him by dying. But Timmy had a point, she argued fiercely with the unseen voice, his dad was gone for ever, *I* had only been, apologetically, lovingly, stood up. Same emotion, she understood wryly, just as strong. She loved Gerry, and he had left her when she was longing to see him, so she'd fucked up a draft. Every time there is a conflict between seeing me and doing something he needs to do to follow his career, he chooses career rather than me. But mistakes like this are not what we expect from our brilliant, thorough Caroline. She would, she reflected, no doubt have done the same thing after Ben's death, but Smith Butler had been ready for her; they had refused to have her in the office for three months and when she insisted on coming back had given her two very good assistants, who probably *had* checked every word she had written. She got up abruptly, unable to sit still, and went to the door, stopping to throw her copy of the faulty draft into the bag for shredding. The phone rang, sharply, and she rushed to it.

'Hi. How are you? I am truly sorry about Wednesday. I had to do it.'

'Gerry, I know people who turn down invitations to appear on *Panorama*. Like my father.'

There was a fractional pause while she decided that she really didn't care if he disliked criticism.

'Your father isn't Minister for Transport, my love.'

Overtired, she laughed, 'I am the Pirate King.'

'What?'

'*Pirates of Penzance*. "For I am the Pirate King, and it is, it is a glorious thing, to be the Pirate King."'

There was a pause while she heard him think his way through this one.

'There are a lot of people depending on me.'

'Then stop apologizing. You don't mean it.'

'I know it upsets you. It makes me miserable too, but it's what I signed up for. Darling, listen, I ought to be in another meeting, but I wanted to tell you that I've managed to sort something out for next week. Can you be away on Saturday for the night? Wonderful. I'll ring you later.'

She looked down at her right hand; she appeared to have dug a hole through six sheets of blotting paper with her pen. She hastily covered it with papers and reached for the phone which had rung again to find Peter Burwood, barely audible at the other end.

'Sorry, Peter, you're on a bad line. Speak up.'

'Hang on, I'm in the car, I'll pull over. Better? Listen, Caroline, we may have a problem: Graham went to see Mike Moody at the Town Hall, to help him put together his paper with the deal on those contracts, but the meeting's off. The chairman of the housing committee's ill – suspected heart trouble. His only coherent words were apparently that the meeting was not to take place without him, and no one likes to push it for fear he'll pop his clogs.'

Caroline thought about it. 'It's only a delay, isn't it? I mean the meeting will be held soon.'

'Yes.' Peter was sounding obsessive. 'I'd like to know *when* though. Thing is, Caroline, Moody was a bit suspicious about this Williamson. He thinks he's close to Friern – they go to the races together apparently.'

'I think that's right,' Caroline said, slowly. 'Oddly enough he was on the train when I came up with Hamish. He was with Matt Friern.'

'Mm.' Peter was far too experienced a contractor to discount the possibility of corruption. Caroline considered the point, then decided she had no useful ideas. 'Look, Peter, it may be nothing to worry about. Let's wait and see for a day or so.'

'I suppose so.' He was sounding paranoid, she thought. 'But if Friern's playing silly buggers, then we'll fix them.'

'Course we will. I'll think of something,' she promised,

hoping he would go away so she could think about Gerry.

In his office half-way up one of the giant Marsham Street towers, Clive Fieldman was working on the submission which Winstanley had asked for on the NEB companies. It was not flowing easily, and at that moment almost every word was heavily scored and cross-hatched with rewriting. It began with the traditional opening: 'Secretary of State' plus a long list of initials to whom the document would be copied, including, in view of the policy issues that were being raised, all other Departmental ministers and the eight top Departmental officials. It continued with the time-honoured opening words: 'The purpose of this submission . . .'

Yes, well, Clive thought, wryly, that was what a decent intellectual training was *for*, to teach you to put the presenting problem and the suggested solution right in the first two paragraphs. And if you couldn't do that, your thinking on the nature of the problem was incomplete or inadequate, and/or your solution was wrong. It felt as if both could be true this morning. He sat back and rang Miss Williams to ask for coffee, and considered the problem again. John Winstanley had summoned him quite unexpectedly two days before to tell him that he had decided that the best way to deal with the NEB's five construction companies was indeed to sell them as a package. Moreover, following Fredericks' advice which had been based on the criteria he had approved, he wanted to do this by way of a negotiated sale on an agreed basis, not by tender. He had, he had said smugly, a prospective purchaser for the lot, one Sir Matthew

Friern. Clive had left the meeting, James Mather at his heels, and had rung Fredericks immediately, invited them in and gone over the ground with them very carefully indeed to make quite sure that they were prepared to stick by their oral advice. And he had waited for the confirming letter he had asked for, which had arrived that morning and which was not quite as unequivocal as he, or, he suspected, Winstanley had hoped; a certain amount of weasel wording surrounded Fredericks' advice that a negotiation with a single purchaser would be the best way to sell these companies. But after all, he reflected, it didn't have to be the *best* way; all the bankers had to sign for was that it was a reasonable and sensible way to proceed. Which the words did do, just about.

Refreshed he crumpled the piece of paper and started again:

The purpose of this submission is to propose that you should authorize the NEB to enter into negotiations for the sale of the five construction and civil engineering companies in their ownership to Friern Construction plc, a major construction company based in Dorrington. A draft letter to the Chancellor of the Exchequer is attached as Annex A, and has been discussed, at official level, with the Treasury.

As indeed it would be, just as soon as it was written. Clive decided to skip forward and do the draft letter next.

I have been considering [he wrote] the best method for returning the five construction companies in the ownership of the NEB to the private sector. I have concluded, on balance, after

254

seeking advice from the Department's merchant bank advisers, Fredericks, that this would be to sell all five companies, as a group. These companies show very mixed performance; two are profitable, two are making substantial losses, while the fifth is currently just profitable, but has, the NEB believe, the potential to be very profitable in later years. Against this background, I have been advised by our merchant bankers that a negotiated sale of all five together offers a better route than separate disposal individually. I have received an outline offer from—

No, damn, better not; *that* needed to be more impersonally put:

A substantial building and civil engineering contractor, Sir Matthew Friern, chairman and chief executive of Friern Construction plc, approached the NEB and has held discussions with the NEB's merchant banking advisers and with Fredericks, which have culminated in an outline offer in the range of £150m–£180m for the five companies.

Winstanley, on Clive's urgent advice, had steered Matthew Friern straight to Fredericks, who had carried him under their wing, as it were, to the NEB and their advisers Gruhners, so that the whole process had been orderly and controlled. Or as much as possible, anyway. Clive reread the first two paragraphs, broodingly. So far so good – that hurdle convincingly passed.

Sir Matthew has told the NEB that he intends to close one of the five, Davecat, a loss-making manufacturer of kitchen and bathroom cabinets, forthwith, and to seek a purchaser at well below asset value for O'Brien Limited, a plant hire company which is also loss-making. The NEB have advised that they, too, would have sought to close or dispose of both companies.

And that was all right too. In fact, put like that, it read perfectly sensibly and the letter could and, indeed, must go on to detail the organizational advantages of getting the other companies into the undoubtedly competent hands of Matthew Friern, rather than having two sets of civil servants and two sets of merchant bankers dealing with this lot on an individual basis. It could take for ever. The problem area was, of course, price. Matthew Friern, as the sole purchaser allowed in, could be getting a sensationally good deal, good enough to attract public censure. Well, in that context surely to God two sets of merchant bankers ought to be able to prevent Friern from getting away with murder, and the fact that they were in place at all provided very considerable protection for the Department and the NEB. He picked up his pen to write something like this down in measured prose, found he couldn't, and stopped again, irritated. He identified reluctantly the worm of doubt that was chomping away at this comforting thesis; the truth was, as he had understood right at the beginning, that merchant banks were used to clients; they made huge efforts to find out what it was the client wanted and to deliver it to him. And sometimes it seemed not to matter that their advice would let a client in for real trouble, he reflected sourly, considering some of the headlines in the *Financial Times* that morning. In this case, Fredericks and Gruhners had grasped that Winstanley desperately wanted a quick, neat, decisive move, such as would raise his stock with the PM. Since it was not actually a silly idea they had gone along with it, no doubt deciding that Winstanley was better placed than they to estimate the political risks of taking a lower price and dealing with only one purchaser. And *that* was true too, of course, except that Winstanley undoubtedly believed that he could defend himself against any political criticism on the basis of the bankers' advice. It was a nasty, uncomfortable circle which he could see no way of squaring; try to put all that lot down on a piece of paper and it would look as if he was trying to get in the way of a sensible commercial decision by his minister. He hesitated, irresolute, then decided that he would have one more go, face to face, with Winstanley to air his worries and would guard his own and as many other backs as possible by quoting, verbatim, in the body of the letter the exact words used by Fredericks, and would put the full text in an annex. Given the cost of this advice to public funds, everyone, including the Chancellor, should have a chance to read it.

These hurdles surmounted, the rest of the submission fell smoothly into place and he called Miss Williams and dictated the whole thing, asking her to give it to James Mather for his comments.

He then stonewalled patiently through a phone call from Lucy, and finally had to remind her, point blank, that he was a government servant and not in the business of betraying official secrets; Matthew's offer was being considered, yes, as he had indeed been told, and any decision would be made soon. He could not tell her how soon or what its terms were. She accepted this with less than her usual grace and went to ask him, pointedly, how he was enjoying working with Caroline again.

'I don't tell Caroline anything either,' he said, irritably, recognizing that he was uneasy about Caroline's reaction when she found out that her buy-out was frustrated, and they had concluded the call on poor terms, with Lucy being irritatingly vague about when she would be available during the week. He had been momentarily cheered by the thought that she might have been made jealous by his renewed association with Caroline, but had recollected that she and Caroline had enjoyed an unbroken friendship on the basis that they had never, ever, fancied the same man, regarding each other's conquests with tolerant amazement. Nor could he believe that Caroline herself thought of him as other than a pleasant male friend; it had been all too clear at lunch that there was an incumbent man, probably married, for whom her real attention was reserved. And Lucy would know that; indeed when and as they managed to see each other again, he would ask her who Caroline's lover was. The trouble with this affair, as he had acknowledged before, was that it was hopelessly one-sided. Lucy had Matthew and her sons, he had no one else. He bent resolutely to the in-tray; to complete a difficult morning he was due to see Michael Watson at noon.

Watson duly appeared five minutes early, looking both anxious and truculent. Invited to sit, he perched on the edge of the chair and looked across at Clive, eyes round and alert, like something caught in the headlights, Clive thought, feeling momentarily squeamish. Reminding himself sternly that the file showed the man opposite him successfully to have resisted two earlier attempts to get rid of him, he hardened his heart and opened uncompromisingly.

'Michael, as you know, the time for your annual report has come round, and I have to tell you that I am not prepared to give you a satisfactory grading. I'm sorry, but your general work has not been up to the standard expected of an assistant secretary and I am recommending you for early retirement. I have told Philip Williams that I am reporting in this sense and, while he is very willing to discuss this report further, he does not dissent from my view. I understand you have been in another division in his command recently, so he is familiar with your work.' He stopped to give Watson a chance to digest what was being said and to gather his forces, such as they were. Not that Watson had much of a place to go; the deputy secretary, Philip Williams, responsible for countersigning and agreeing any annual report, had supported Clive's view unhesitatingly.

'I don't think that's fair.' There were tears in the man's eyes, Clive realized, appalled, and his voice was wobbling.

'I'm sorry you should feel like that,' he said, formally. 'The Department has suffered a great deal of upheaval, of course, and much greater burdens are being laid on the higher administrative levels. I just do not think that you are managing to deal effectively with the work.' He had worked out this formulation as a sop to pride, and possible opening to a gracious exit, but realized as he spoke that he had mistaken his man. Watson, a wild gleam of hope in his eye, seized the olive branch with both hands and was bending it into a new and wrong shape, explaining eagerly how many new duties he had been called upon to undertake, including, he added, hopefully, supervision of the newly formed inspectorate. There was in point of fact not one single inspector requiring supervision, the inspectorate at that point consisting entirely of a committee charged with setting up an appropriate body. The committee had met three times, Clive had chaired all three meetings and the notes had been taken by Watson's best principal, who had given them straight to Clive for approval. Watson's duties had therefore been confined to attendance at two out of three of the meetings. Clive grimly reminded his subordinate of the facts of the case, adding meticulously that he did not particularly want to discuss the detail, and that he was clear about his general view.

'Philip Williams would, I know, want to discuss the report with you as well.'

'But you've made up your mind. And he'll only listen to you.' Watson was twisting his hands.

'Michael, I'm sorry, I'm not going to change my mind. It isn't a public procedure, you get your pension early and you'll be able to get another job if you want one. When you think about it you may feel there are some advantages.'

'I didn't want this job; it's not my field. I asked for one of the local government divisions.'

Clive sighed. 'I shall be reporting that I do not consider your work satisfactory, nor, based on nearly a year's experience, capable of improvement to a satisfactory level.'

Michael Watson stared at him across the table, white-faced. Only the day before the Prime Minister had again said in a speech that the civil service must be reduced in numbers and permanent secretaries were known to be looking at a ten-per-cent cut. The time-honoured method was to cut down first on clerical staff, an option particularly easy for the main policy departments to exercise, since it had for some time been in practice impossible to recruit enough clerical staff in central London. This method had reached a natural limit; well-paid graduates were spending substantial time filing and manning photocopiers and it was clear that administrative posts would have to be the next to go. In this climate, the writing was well and truly on the wall for a senior administrative civil servant graded as unsatisfactory. Watson fought hard, using everything, including, finally and embarrassingly, tears and personal recriminations which Clive endured stolidly for twenty-five minutes, feeling it was the least he could do in terms of the man's long service. It was in some sense not the poor bloke's fault; left as a principal in some gentle backwater, in charge of something like issuing paperclips, he would have been all right, but in a policy division at assistant secretary level his shortcomings were mercilessly exposed, and he was a dead weight, a drag on competent people and a barrier to action. Clive managed to get rid of him only by announcing the imminent arrival of another visitor and, having closed the door, sank limply into his chair. After a few minutes, out of curiosity, he went over to the window and, as he had half expected, saw Watson scurry across the road to the pub. Well, that took care of this afternoon, and he made a note to tell the principals on that side to put anything urgent through to him directly.

At Walzheims, Andy Eames Lewis was suffering from something of a surfeit of Prior Systems, but he had managed to dispatch his client back to Dorrington and was attacking various other accumulated tasks.

'I'm sorry, Andy,' his secretary said, unapologetically, 'but Sir Matthew Friern is on the phone.'

Andy's mouth silently formed an expletive, but he picked up the phone obediently. 'Yes, Matt.'

'I've left some bits and pieces – press cuttings, figures and so on – with Lucy. Ring her up, send a bike for them or whatever, will you? Good.'

He rang off, leaving Andy considering the papers in front of him. Lucy Friern had been on his mind a lot since the conference but he was playing with something worse than fire, more like gelignite, as he well knew. He drew on the pad in front of him, rehearsing the familiar arguments; he was older now and solidly married, he could cope with Lucy Friern, if she would have him, and finish the business she had so deliberately abandoned all those years ago. But her husband was a client, in the middle of an important deal with substantial financial implications for the bank and for him personally. It was a decent-sized deal in itself, of course, lots of fees, but more importantly, he would end up with a good client. With inflation and interest rates screaming up, you nurtured a customer with the balls to do any deal, particularly a good-sized one like this. Still it could do no harm just to have lunch with Lucy, armed as he was with the perfect excuse. He started to dial the number himself, then decided to keep this in the public domain.

'Get me Lady Friern, will you?' he asked, and waited until Lucy had been collected at the other end of the line.

'Lucy? Matthew says you have some papers for us. I've got to come down your way at lunchtime. Emma wants something picked up from Harrods. Have you time to eat with me? San José do? In an hour?'

'Lovely, Andy. Do you really collect things yourself for Emma?'

'No, of course I don't normally,' he said, grinning at the phone. 'I need to buy shirts as well, so I said I'd do it. You could come and help.'

He rang off feeling slightly sick with excitement, and decided that Emma had commissioned him to collect some sort of drink, unobtainable except at Harrods; there must be one, for heaven's sake. Probably something Scottish and unspeakably expensive. Slowly, slowly, he warned himself. Lucy may just be heating you up, because she is cross with Matthew. He forced himself back to his in-tray, trying to pretend he was going to meet a friend of one of his sisters, and had worked himself into the right, slightly avuncular mood by the time he reached San José. This was instantly dispelled by the sight of Lucy, uncharacteristically early, wearing hideous glasses and looking about eighteen, sitting demurely, reading the paper. She looked up and saw him, whipped the glasses off and hid them in her bag, so that by the time he reached her side, grinning all over his face, she was blinking at him short-sightedly.

'I'm sorry to be late,' he said.

'You aren't. I was early, so I've just been sitting here with the paper. Here are the things Matt left for you. For heaven's sake, take them now. He has gone a bit OTT about this deal. I suppose you're just as bad.'

'It's always worse for the chap whose business it is.' He hesitated, then dropped a light social kiss on her cheek. 'How are you, anyway? You're looking very well.'

She gave him a gentle sidelong look and said, demurely, that it was nice to see him, too, and he felt his throat constrict. They talked about their children as Lucy sorted out what she wanted to eat, and he wondered exultantly, being not without experience in these matters, why women always started by talking about their children when they were out with a man they fancied. He pulled himself up sharply, realizing that he was watching her as if she were a particularly delicious dessert, and applied his full attention to the task of ordering the meal.

'Is this all going to work, Andy? I mean, is Matt going to end up with Prior?' she asked him, in exactly the same tones of gentle detached interest in which she had been discussing her elder son's chances of getting into Eton.

'I'm not absolutely sure,' Andy said, startled into truthfulness, and realizing that she was watching him carefully. 'I understand from Richard Watts that it is going to a Cabinet committee, so progress is being made. But your friend Caroline is a bit of a rogue element.'

'She's very clever, she always was. And very political, or at least her family are.'

'Wrong side, though,' Andy observed, thoughtfully.

'I shouldn't think it matters, would you?'

'No. That's probably true.'

'And she knows Clive, of course. But then we all do,' Lucy pointed out.

'That's true,' Andy agreed. 'But I have a feeling that she's been making a bit of an effort there. I know one of her partners, and he said Clive had been to lunch at the office recently.'

'Yes, he was. And to lunch with Caroline's family. And had lunch with Caro by himself the other day.'

He looked at her sharply, and she smiled at him and reminded him that she and Caroline went back yonks.

'That is interesting. I wonder if she is getting a bit of

help there. Still, Matthew managed to get Winstanley to do what he wanted.'

'You were a great help there, Andy, very foxy. You left him really miserable about a buy-out,' Lucy said warmly.

'I enjoyed that.' He smiled at her, delighted that she had absorbed the finer points. 'But it may not be enough.' He watched her, trying to get his approach right. 'Lu, I am a little worried about this business with the council. It would blow the deal if any of that came out. You would tell me if you thought Matt was going seriously OTT, wouldn't you? I mean, between us we might be able to do something sensible to stop him.'

She glanced at him, impatiently. 'This sort of thing goes on all the time in Dorrington, you know, Andy. It's different up there.'

'I'm sure it is more different than I can imagine. But this deal is very high profile – we have to be careful, darling.' He stopped, sharply, taken aback, but she smiled at him, unruffled and assured, completely feminine. 'Oh, I won't let him do anything silly, Andy love, don't you worry.'

He breathed out, incredulous and wary, but she was placidly ordering some more mineral water from an extremely attentive waiter.

'What about Emma's shopping?' she asked, indulgently. 'Hadn't we better go and do that, and not have pudding?'

'Yes, we had,' he agreed. 'And my shirts, if you have time. I need half a dozen. And ties.'

'Won't Emma mind my helping to choose?'

'She'll just think my taste has improved.' He raised his glass of mineral water to her and she lowered her eyelashes modestly, watched admiringly by three waiters, all ignoring attempts from less attractive customers to get their attention.

'I really would like it if Matt could end up with Prior at least,' she said, bringing him smartly to attention. 'But there are other companies he could buy, aren't there? I mean, companies already based down here. Like Harrison, or Cosway.'

Andy blinked at her, startled, then concentrated sharply on what she was saying. 'Yes. They'd cost a bit though.'

'The company can afford it, for something with solid profits.'

'This is true.' He hesitated. 'Do you think Matt would just as soon go after Harrison or Cosway?'

'No. He knows Prior could be a marvellous deal and he's going all out for it. But *I* thought it might be sensible to have something else lined up, while he's in the mood to buy something, in case Prior falls through.'

Andy sat back and considered her admiringly. 'Good thinking. We had of course had a look at all sorts of other things including both of those, but I'll get one of the lads to run the figures again on those two. Not to send them to Matt yet?'

'No, no. I mean, this one may work. But I *am* a bit worried, Andy. I don't want him to get carried away.'

He nodded. 'Tell you what. I'll have a chat with him, say there is a lot of interest in construction companies – that is actually true – and suggest that we have another look at the whole sector, just in case there's a golden opportunity there that we're all ignoring in the scramble. Yes?'

'Yes,' she said, with conviction. 'That *is* clever. But then you always were. Sweet of you to buy me lunch. Now, come on. Poor Emma, we must do the shopping.'

She slid him a sideways glance. 'What *is* it we are buying, Andy?'

'A bottle. It's a whisky she is particularly set on – can't remember its name. I just hope I'll recognize it when I see it,' he lied smoothly, and walked out with her into the blustery March day, feeling twenty-two years old again.

At the DoE, Clive was still working; the draft submission had got into the red box that had gone to Winstanley's London flat to await his return from dinner, but the whole day had been eaten up with this task, and he wanted to clear his in-tray, following a lifelong habit. By 8 p.m. he had finished and walked out of the building, and pushed through the doors of the pub. There are no catering facilities after 5 p.m. in the DoE, or any of the major Departments, and the hard-pressed private offices, who may be working till 10 p.m. every night, keep going on greasy, cooling hamburgers bought at the nearest chain. But the pub opposite had good food, if you had the time to sit down for half an hour, and he was a regular customer. He picked up a substantial plate of chilli con carne and baked potato and, carrying it carefully to avoid slopping pink mince on the faded carpet, settled himself at the corner table, from which he found himself with an unwelcome, grandstand view of Michael Watson. The man was staggering with drink, so sodden with it as to render credible the hypothesis that he had been there since Clive had seen him just before lunch. It was a deeply embarrassing sight, uncomfortable anywhere and particularly in this pub, much frequented by DoE employees. Not an example one wished to see set, Clive thought, grimly, eating fast and without appetite, and as far as he was concerned it was one more nail in this man's coffin. The civil service in general had always been tolerant of near-alcoholics, but those days were fast passing. Out of the corner of his eye he noticed two of his clerical officers, a pretty girl of about nineteen and a slightly older boy, watching Watson, interested. This will not do, he thought. I shall have to go and get the bugger to go home and he's so out of it that it's likely to end in tears all round. I cannot just creep out of here with those kids watching, particularly since it might be said to be my fault that the man is in this state. He sat, gathering his forces, working out how best to get Watson inconspicuously out of the door, when the problem became abruptly urgent. Watson had leant over the bar, loudly ordering another whisky, and the barman had quietly refused to serve him. When Watson refused vociferously to accept this decision, he summoned a colleague and lifted the flap of the bar. Clive got himself to Watson's side with the neat unobtrusive speed he had used on a rugger field, long ago, moving between bigger men, and nodded to the barman who stood back.

'Michael.' The man's eyes focused and widened. 'I'll get you a taxi. Come on.' The man staggered against him as he tucked an arm firmly inside his and the barman made to help, but Clive shook his head warningly and towed the unresisting Watson to the door.

There was, of course, no taxi, but Clive had thought his way through that and towed his subordinate across the street, past a gaping Departmental messenger, and stowed him in the gents' on the ground floor of the north tower, while he organized the Department's cab service. The explanation for an expensive trip to Surbiton, while embarrassing, would help the cause of getting rid of the wretched Watson, he reflected. This task accomplished, he edged cautiously into the gents', hoping not to find Watson passed out; a dreadful noise of retching, followed smartly by running water, coming from a half-open door indicated that he was sufficiently in control to be sick in the right place and to attempt to tidy up after himself. Clive remembered that hardened drinkers had a name for being able to recover and conceal the signs – it was one of the things that made them so difficult to deal with. He waited patiently, leaning against a wash basin, observing that the appalling lighting made even him look sick, and, when the noises stopped, called out instantly so that Watson might compose himself before emerging. It was still a sorry sight; the man was white as a shroud and red-eyed, but more or less in control.

'I've called a taxi, Michael. Will you manage or do you need to sit down for a bit and drink coffee?'

'I need coffee.' It was a bare statement of the practical, without self-pity and Clive was relieved by it.

'I'll get some. You sit in the waiting area.'

Watson drank three cups, black, with sugar, without acknowledgement or thanks, or looking at Clive, who stolidly read an evening paper throughout. Watson got into the taxi when it arrived, still pale, but looking nearer human, and Clive gave the taxi-driver the address and explained, looking him firmly in the eye, that his passenger was not well and would need to be driven carefully. The driver understood exactly what he was being told and looked weary; all this was lost on Watson, who was huddled in a corner of the taxi, a miserable pitiable bundle.

'OK?' Clive inquired, inadequately, and received a grudging nod. He waved the taxi away.

13

'Caroline.'

She looked up from her papers to see Mark Dwyer hesitating at her office door. 'What about Prior? Is there anything to do there? I've got to the bottom of the Capulet pile from last night, and it occurred to me that one of our customers has gone quiet.'

'Yes, isn't it wonderful?' she agreed. 'It must be over a week since I lifted a finger. I'm glad you've done that Capulet stuff – I had Peter Cairns on the phone just now; he's been brought into the Montagu team and wants a meeting later today. I stalled him, so I could find out where we were. I've got the Memorandum and Articles here somewhere.' She nodded towards the usual set of neat piles of paper.

Smith Butler's client was not, of course, really named Capulet any more than Peter Cairns' client was really called Montagu, but merchant bankers are not imaginative when it comes to allotting code names. It had struck the director responsible as particularly fortunate that his real life client's company name began with an M and the company with which it was intended to merge with a C. 'Can't have read the story to the end,' Caroline had observed on being told the codes, 'but that's Eton for you.' The big mergers burned up hours and people, but were enormously profitable and she, Mark Dwyer and two other partners with their assistants had been working all hours to keep up. She stretched, flexing her back unselfconsciously, and Mark thought she looked exhausted but better than last week.

'Ah, well. Thank God it's Friday! Not much we can do over this weekend, and if there is, Mark, the rest of you will have to do it. I'm away for Saturday night, without the children, and there is no way I am unfixing that.' No indeed, she reflected, not after what she had gone through. Gerry, unusually and obviously as a result of considerable manoeuvring, was to be in London this weekend, eating dinner for the Department of Transport on Friday night and for the Conservative Party on Sunday night, which left Saturday free. He had proposed that she come and stay with him. She had leapt at the chance, but then had nearly been defeated by the practical details. She had never in twelve years, since Timmy was born, gone away for the night without leaving a number where she could be reached in an emergency, but there was no way of explaining why she was staying at a London number rather than returning home to her own comfortable London bed. In any case, she had an uneasy feeling that she could not have persuaded Gerry to let his number be used in this way; he was in love with her, she knew, but his self-protective mechanisms were in full working order and their affair was very firmly played by his rules: no letters, only the briefest of phone calls and as little risk as possible, consonant with being able to meet at all. You don't want a scandal either, she told herself firmly, but there was something a little chilling about the care he took to protect himself. And his wife and children, she reminded herself; he *is* married, unlike you. And, for some reason she had never understood, Sholto's observation that Conservative MPs play around sexually much more than Labour

MPs, but pay a much higher price for being found out, was absolutely right. At least two Labour ministers among Sholto's dreadful mates had been open, flagrant adulterers and no one had treated it as other than a minor nuisance, like a tendency to drink too much. A Conservative minister, caught in similar delicto, could find himself asked to resign.

So, finally, after forty-eight hours of deliberation, she had rung her brother Caspar and asked, without explanation, if he would please spend Saturday night at her house, standing fully *in loco parentis*, empowered to deal with all emergencies. She would, she promised, ring him at 11 p.m. on Saturday night and at 10 a.m. on Sunday morning to limit the time in which unforeseen disaster could threaten them all. 'Oh Caro,' he had said, sadly, 'must you?'

'Yes. I'm not going to get many chances.'

'Not at a weekend, no. I remember it well. He won't even let you give me his number?'

'Shut up, Caz. Sorry, I mean *please*.'

He had agreed without making difficulties, so *that* was all right, but given what she had had to ask, the Capulet/Montagu merger could founder, just like the original version had, if it needed action by her between lunchtime Saturday and teatime on Sunday. She shook off her thoughts and invited Mark to sit down and consider some unforeseen features of Montagu's Memorandum and Articles with her, and they were both immersed by the time Susie put her head in, half an hour later.

'Caroline? Could you go and see Mr Appleton?'

'What have I done?' Caroline looked up anxiously. 'Nothing recently, surely,' she said to Mark, and he smiled at her, noticing that she still looked pale and drawn. Not that this made her less attractive; nearly ten years her junior, he had always thought her good-looking, but not particularly sexy. These days he found himself continually wondering what it would be like to go to bed with her, while being just experienced enough to know that the message she was transmitting was not for him.

'I'll be back,' she said, scowling in thought, and automatically, heedless of him, tugged at her skirt as she stood up, hitching up a stocking. She made no other preparation whatsoever to go and see their senior partner, not even glancing at herself in the wall mirror, and Mark reluctantly discarded a promising fantasy of a late-blooming affair raging between Caroline and Michael Appleton.

'Ah, Caroline. Coffee?'

'Mm. What can I do for you, Michael?'

Some improvement on 'What do you want?' which had always been her preferred method of approach, Michael Appleton thought, resignedly, passing her the sugar. 'I've had an approach from John Sanderson-Smith, chairman of all sorts of things.'

'Sir John? I met him the other day, at a lunch.'

'And impressed him, evidently. What did you do, Caro, can you remember?' He watched her scowl at his pen-tray.

'Differentiated criminal from tortious liability, as I remember the conversation. He seemed to feel that British Rail ought to be subject to criminal prosecution for leaving loose chippings on a platform, which had caused his mother-in-law to turn an ankle. I explained you needed to prove intent to get a successful prosecution.'

'At all events, he wanted us to act on a possible purchase of Prior Building Systems.'

'Who for?'

'Friern. He's a non-executive director.'

'It doesn't make sense, Michael. Surely he would have consulted Matthew Friern, and Matt, of all people, knows we are acting for the management team.'

'I was surprised myself. But before giving him a definite answer I thought to check the central files. We do not seem to have had the client letter of agreement returned by Prior Systems, which rather alters things.'

'It's in my in-tray. They have been slow.' She was addressing herself to his pen-tray and he looked reproachfully at the blonde top of her head. She looked up at him, openly rattled. 'Michael, dammit, we've been working for Prior for weeks now, time is logging up like it didn't cost money. We couldn't possibly switch horses – what's the matter with Matt?'

'He wants you to act for him not for his rivals. Presumably he sees the management team as a threat and wants to take it out quickly. A pity he didn't think of it earlier; the Friern business would be very well worth having. There was a strong hint that they might move all their business to us.' He flinched as she sat bolt upright, eyes wide.

'And over all the cities of the plain shall you have dominion also,' she said, furiously, and it took him a minute to get the allusion and then he was angry.

'Caroline, that is uncalled for. I don't have horns and a tail, and I'm not suggesting we abandon a small client in favour of a bigger one. I am, however, questioning whether we actually have a proper client relationship in the sense that the Prior management do not seem yet to have agreed to employ us on our terms.'

'Of course they have.' She had gone scarlet with rage and embarrassment and he was sharply reminded of his teenage daughter.

'Well, I did murmur that I rather thought we were already acting.'

'You *knew* we were, Michael. You and I had discussed it. You said hello to Peter Burwood in the lift last week.'

'I might suggest we could do another piece of business for Friern.'

She sat back, warily. 'Michael, this should have told you – it has certainly told me – that if I win this one, as I intend to, no Friern business will come our way, ever. You can't have them all.'

'Perhaps not. I do however like to know that we are being paid for the ones we *do* have. Perhaps I could have the file today, so I can ring Sir John?'

'Certainly.' She rose, angrily, and stumped out, leaving him furious. Very unlike her to do a lot of work without having the client nailed down. And she had no need to take such a high moral line when she herself was lying through her teeth about that letter of engagement.

Caroline arrived back in her office, equally upset, to find a call from Peter Burwood waiting. Before he could say whatever was in his mind, she pounced.

'The client letter I sent you, Peter. I need it back. We have just been asked to act by one of your competitors and this has caused my senior partner to discover that you are not signed up, as it were. I need it now.'

There was a long silence at the other end, and she gritted her teeth, realizing that she had said this too quickly, without calming down.

'I think we were having a problem with some of the wording, apart from other things, Caroline.' Peter was sounding extremely distant and she took a deep breath.

'I am seriously embarrassed here, Peter. I ought to have sorted this out with you weeks ago. Can we clear it now?'

There was another long pause, and she cast an exasperated look at Mark, who had abandoned all pretence of not listening.

'Of course we can, Caroline. It is we who are out of order here.'

She heaved a sigh of relief for a fair-minded, sensible client, and assured the telephone warmly that no, no, quite the contrary, it was she who had been remiss, and agreed to the small amendments that he wanted.

'Who wanted you to act?'

She opened her mouth to refuse orthodoxly to tell him, then stopped and reconsidered. 'Is that letter on the way?'

'Caroline!'

'I'm not answering your question until I know that you are my client,' she said, grittily. 'Call me when you've posted it.'

She put the phone down, and waited, sorting an in-tray, ignoring Mark until the phone rang again.

'We've posted it.' Peter was sounding grim and hostile, but she was unmoved.

'It was a non-executive director of Friern, whom I had met at a party, who asked my senior partner. When I met him I did not know he was connected to Friern.'

'They were trying to bribe you!'

'Yes. Which means, Peter, that we are getting to them somehow. They're rattled. What have we managed to do to worry them, recently?'

'Shut up will you Caroline? I've got Martin and Graham here. OK, we're on the speaker. Is your line secure?'

'Our phones are regularly swept,' she confirmed, taken aback. 'What's happening?'

'Well, we're not sure. I rang you because the first thing you need to understand is that we have all been told, formally, by the NEB that we are not to talk to anyone at all about the company, including you. Indeed I perhaps should not have signed that client letter.'

Caroline and Mark stared at each other. 'Peter,' she said, urgently, 'whatever is happening, they are your shareholders. You have to do what they say or they can fire you. Remember, I told you.'

'And I heard you, Caroline. But I told Ron Jenkins yesterday that I was not prepared to behave like that; it was disorderly.' Caroline's eyebrows shot up at what she knew to be Peter's strongest term of disapprobation. 'I said that in common courtesy I had to tell you that there was now a pause in negotiations until further notice, imposed by the NEB. He argued and tried to tell me I couldn't but he backed off. Well, I'm not prepared to behave like that with professional people.'

Caroline and Mark looked at each other, bewildered, getting no help from the heavy silence at the other end of the line.

'I got it,' Caroline said at last ungrammatically. 'They're trying to do a quick deal with someone else.'

'Yes,' Peter confirmed, baldly.

'Who with?'

'I'm not allowed to tell you.'

'I see.' Caroline tugged at her fringe as an aid to thought, brain racing. 'Friern or near offer?'

Massive silence at the other end of the line greeted this suggestion and she scowled at the phone. 'The bastards.'

'Caroline,' Peter said, primly.

'It's all very well but I don't understand it. Why let Friern through and not offer you a chance? No, don't comment, I know you can't. Oh, hang on, because Matthew is offering something you can't, not money but *something*.' Her eyes crossed slightly in concentration while Mark watched respectfully. 'I'm being stupid,' she said abruptly, 'but I can't see it. I'll find out, don't you worry, Peter, and I'll work out what to do. I'll teach the bugger to try to bribe my senior partner.'

'Language, Caroline.'

'Look, I can at least find out what's up and why for myself. Be of good heart, don't go anywhere. The cavalry will get there.' She glanced at Mark, and he thought that she was looking momentarily uncomfortable. 'It'll probably be Monday before my spies, who are everywhere, crawl in with the answer. So try to take it easy, all right?'

'You be careful too, Caroline.'

'I will be.'

Later that afternoon, while Caroline and Mark were spending their fourth consecutive hour in a meeting with the Montagu lawyers, Matthew Friern was sitting behind his desk in the small London office of Friern Construction plc, bad-temperedly drinking tea. He glared at the ringing phone but picked it up. 'Yes?'

'Matthew, it's Andy. I just wanted to be sure you knew where I could be reached. The reporting accountants are starting tomorrow, in all five companies. All managers have been told to keep their mouths shut and not gossip.'

'Those chaps at Prior had better do as they're told.'

'I understood all that is all right. Everyone's got my home number, and there's not a lot we can do until next week. They're going to report by Thursday.'

'Why not earlier? We've offered the NEB a damned good price.'

Andy sighed, just sub-audibly. 'It's only five days, Matt. In terms of reporting accountants, that's greased lightning.' He hesitated. 'On Prior, Matt, Gruhners have asked us to give specific consideration to the contract renegotiation – I mean they know there ought to be some extra cash there, and they are going to expect our offer to cover the point. And they want us to make explicit whatever our view is on the likelihood of Prior getting that big contract they are tendering for next month – Marsh Lane.'

'That's easy. They'll not get anything out of the contract renegotiations for some months, if ever. And they'll not get the Marsh Lane contract. We – Friern – have that one.'

'I think the reporting accountants will want some objective evidence on both points,' Andy ventured, but got no response. 'Matt?' he said, cautiously.

'I'm still here. I've got something to ask you, Andy. I want a good experienced detective and I don't want to use my own people. Do you know anyone else?'

Andy looked at the phone as if it had bitten him. 'What for, Matt? I mean, what sort of job?' he asked, carefully.

'I want an insurance policy. I don't trust those buggers at Prior, and I'd like to keep an eye on them. Never mind, Andy – if you don't know anyone, I'll ask around.'

'There is a firm that one of our clients has used, and got good service from.' Andy decided that given the choice between a rock and a hard place, he would rather be involved to the extent of making sure Matthew employed somebody reasonably disciplined. 'I can't offer any references, Matt, since I can't, of course, divulge who the client was but the man's name is James Edwards. An ex-policeman. That's also the name of the firm.' He gave Matthew the phone number. 'You'd need to see him for yourself.' He hesitated. 'I'm not quite sure what you hope to find, Matt.'

'Nor am I. I'll talk to Edwards.' He put the phone down, thoughtfully, and sat, considering the name and number, but the phone rang again sharply.

'Matthew?'

'John. Nice to hear from you.'

'I've had a call from Michael Appleton. At Smith Butler. They can't act for us, they already act for the management of Prior, it seems. Michael was very regretful but didn't feel able to change horses.'

'Mm. Pity.'

'Yes, I thought the young woman I met was very impressive. Not many of them in the City firms.'

'No. No. Well, thank you, John.'

They exchanged good wishes for the weekend and rang off, and after a few more minutes, Matthew dialled the number he had been given and spoke to an exceedingly competent secretary, who promised him calmly that Mr Edwards would call him back inside the hour.

Saturday dawned cold and rainy, and Caroline, tired

from a meeting that had gone on stubbornly – and fruitlessly – until 10 p.m. the night before, found herself facing mutiny.

'I don't want to have Caspar to stay,' Timmy said, crossly, mashing cornflakes into milk and scattering crumbs far and wide.

'I'm sorry, sweet,' she said, guiltily. 'I will be back tomorrow.'

'Why do you have to go away at a weekend? You never came back last night either.' Susannah was also disgruntled.

'Yes, I did,' Caroline said, indignantly. 'I gave you a kiss, you were just awake.'

'Big deal,' Timmy said, rudely, and they glared at each other.

'Kids,' Caroline summoned her best steamroller style. 'I have to go; let's not waste time. Who has not had pocket money and how is all your homework?' She pushed back her chair and checked, appalled by the sight of Francis, silent tears pouring down his cheeks. 'You said I could go to tea with Bill.'

'Oh God. I did.'

The tears dried and he looked at her, ablaze with hope. 'Caspar will get you there,' she said, grimly, deciding that her brother would just somehow have to fit in a forty-minute journey each way to Francis's inconveniently sited best friend. The resultant phone calls, three lots of homework, and Susannah's violin practice, all undertaken with equal bad grace, occupied the next two hours, and by the time she had greeted Caspar and got into the car, she was tense and anxious and broke a fingernail on the car door. A good start, she thought, wearily, to the longed-for twenty-four hours with her lover.

She parked the car in an underground garage, and worked her way through the streets behind the Army and Navy Stores to the small block where Gerry had his flat. Carrying only a briefcase in case she met anyone she knew, she still felt appallingly conspicuous, and momentarily let herself wonder how she had got here and why. Just at that moment she saw Gerry in a mud-coloured sweater, buying a paper, heads turning for him in half-recognition as they always did, and her heart lifted. She waited until he doubled into the flat, moving with his usual briskness, gave him a couple of minutes and followed. He answered the bell at once and she walked into his arms, feeling all the tension evaporate and finding herself suddenly exhausted.

'You're looking tired,' he said, and she reflected that there were very few men who could say that without the implication that you were also looking plain. 'I'm taking you out to lunch.'

'That would be lovely,' she said, meaning it, remembering the rare Saturdays when she and Ben had managed to make other arrangements for the children and sneak off for lunch by themselves, getting quietly a little drunk and catching up with each other's week. I wish I was married, I wish I had that again, she thought, with a sudden sharp pang, watching Gerry lock the flat door and look sharply round to see if he was observed.

It was better at the restaurant where they sat and looked at each other carefully, as they ordered.

'I can't believe we've got a whole day and night,' he said, watching her. 'I'd begun to think we were never going to.'

'Oh, so had I. I was trying to work out who to complain to. And how. By letter, I decided: "Dear Prime Minister . . ." it would begin, very correctly.'

282

'And go on much less correctly.' He was laughing, but she could see he had been momentarily appalled. 'So what have you been doing?'

She considered her week, and decided it would be indiscreet to tell him anything about the Montagu/Capulet deal, even under code names, and tried to remember what else had happened to her. There was, of course, the problem with Prior, but now was neither the time nor the place. She smiled at him ruefully, noticing out of the corner of an eye that the group of young women having lunch together three tables away were all watching him and taking a good look at her too. She straightened her back and tried to look like a successful, professional woman, having lunch with a political friend. 'I've been doing a merger deal which may not come off and which is in what Sholto calls the "burn before reading" category. What about you?'

He told her about his week, making a good story of it, and she considered him with love and wonder. She was herself not short of energy or drive, but this one never stopped and, at the end of a week in which every day had been crammed with engagements, travel, and people, from 8 a.m. to midnight, he still looked fresh and untired and bouncing with suppressed restless energy.

'Not hungry?' he asked, and she realized she had eaten very little of an excellent fish, and addressed herself to it, feeling strength return.

'Too hard a week,' she said, apologetically. 'I needed that.'

'Shall we go back?'

'Mm.'

He looked across at her and she felt her bones melt

and saw that he felt the same. I am lucky none the less, she said to herself fiercely; I thought I might never have this again.

He paid the bill and they walked back to the flat, carefully casual, chatting, not touching each other, until they had shut the door of the flat behind them, and she slid her hands under the mud-coloured sweater and hugged him.

'Bed?' he suggested, holding her. 'We could even just go to sleep.'

She pulled away to look at him. 'Would you rather?'

'No. But you are looking exhausted, and I'd like to make sure you get a sleep. Afterwards.'

They both slept, afterwards, instantly, in each other's arms, and she woke briefly to find him gently disentangling himself.

'You stay there. I'll make tea.' She closed her eyes again and when she woke the light had changed and the flat was silent.

'Gerry?' she called, anxiously, and he appeared in the doorway.

'You *were* worn out. It's nearly six o'clock.'

'I do not believe it.' For a moment she felt appalling disappointment at having wasted in sleep two and a half hours of precious time with him, but he was watching her with the same tender amusement that had so startled her the second time they met and she relaxed and smiled back at him. 'I'm sorry. What a boring guest.'

'I did both boxes,' he said, smugly. 'So I have nothing at all to do until teatime tomorrow.'

'Except me.'

'Except you. Now? I mean again? Wouldn't you like tea instead?'

'I would love tea.'

He returned with a tray and set it beside her, and sat on the end of the bed companionably. He reached over and flicked on the television which was featuring the Chancellor assuring the nation that a turning point had been reached. She watched him, thinking how extraordinarily good-looking he was, even in an old white shirt. He was holding her hand but his attention was entirely focused on his colleague on the TV, all the mobile lines of the face straight in concentration.

'We do need something to go right,' he said, as the Chancellor was replaced by a senior policeman, woodenly explaining the fine detail of a bank robbery. He considered her. 'Tell me about your friends at Prior.'

'Well, I'd like to. But something's gone wrong there.'

'I shouldn't have asked you. You're looking tired again and you looked about sixteen when you woke up. But now I've started we'd better go on. What *has* gone wrong?'

She hesitated. 'It's reasonably clear the NEB are trying to do a quick deal with someone else – someone who isn't management, I mean.'

'Really?' She had his full attention. 'What, a private deal?'

'It's not as wicked as you're making it sound,' she pointed out, coolly, wishing she hadn't told him. 'They own the company and they want to get a quick sale to someone else – that's fair enough. I mean, a real company might do that. It's just hard on my customers.'

'It's politically impossible.' He was alight with interest. 'We can't let the NEB do that.'

'Well, someone must have.'

'The DoE presumably. It's John Winstanley's patch.'

He was sitting on the bed, but momentarily unconscious of her, eyes narrowed in concentration. 'How very interesting,' he said, coming back from wherever he had been. 'When did this happen?'

'Yesterday. Sorry, I was told yesterday.' She considered him. 'It is odd, isn't it? But for the last twenty-four hours I've had no time to think about them, what with one thing and another.'

He put an arm around her but moved it restlessly, giving her shoulder a little pat. 'Darling, I'm going to make a phone call – no, don't worry, it won't take long. Then we'll do what you want. The flicks? A concert . . .' He hesitated, and she felt him wonder whether this was wise and smiled at him, forgivingly.

'We could stay here?'

'We'll talk about it in a minute.'

He went through into the living-room and she understood that she was not meant to follow him. Well, she would have a phone call of her own to make later to see that her household was in order. She dressed quickly, and finished her tea, poured herself another cup and drank that, then took the tray quietly through to the kitchen. She heard the phone go down, then the kitchen door opened.

'Caroline, love,' He was looking, she noticed with interest, just a bit shifty. 'Is it possible that the NEB could be selling all five construction companies as a package?'

She looked at him, poised in the doorway, humming like a dynamo, and forced herself to think. 'Yes.' She let her thoughts go on. 'Yes. Damn.'

'Why damn?'

'Because it isn't at all a stupid idea. I should have

seen it, but those companies are all completely different. And no one, including bloody Clive, even gave me a hint. Damn, damn, damn. It leaves my lads without much of a leg to stand on. Any company, who had a chance of selling five things it didn't want as a package, would take it rather than do them one by one.'

He looked openly disappointed. 'Do they get the best price that way?'

'Not necessarily. A purchaser would expect something off. But it's still not a silly idea: it's quick and it saves hassle. Shit.' She caught his fleeting look of disapproval. 'Sorry. Look, are they putting the group out to tender – did anyone say?'

He hesitated. 'Apparently not. It's one purchaser.'

'Then they probably won't get the best price. But it's still not a bad idea.' She sat down deep in thought, reluctantly realizing that Matt Friern had been very clever. But she had darling Gerry with her, here and now, and everyone and everything else would just have to wait. 'Darling, could we *not* talk about all this – I'm depressed by it.'

'Sorry, sorry.' He pulled her to her feet and wrapped his arms around her. 'What would be fun to do?'

'What's it like outside?' she asked and he peered over her shoulder out of the window.

'Pouring down.'

'What about staying here and eating supper?'

He looked at her and kissed her gently on the lips and she opened her mouth against his. 'Ah,' he said, after a long minute and started to unbutton her shirt.

'Definitely a tits man, in service parlance,' she observed to him, affectionately.

'I'm an everything man with you,' he said, pulling the

cup of her bra down to get at the nipple and rolling it gently. 'But I can't get at the rest of you so easily.' He undid her bra neatly with the other hand and cupped both breasts, watching her face. 'The trouble is,' he said, breathless but conversational, 'that I just want to take all your clothes off the minute I have the chance.' He slid a hand inside the back of her jeans, then, frustrated by the tight fit, used the other hand to undo the zip at the front and got both hands inside her knickers. 'You do feel marvellous.'

'All wet.'

'Yes, come on.' He took his hands out of her jeans and did the top button up for her neatly. An orderly man, she thought with love, following him, you fuck in the bedroom and you don't take any clothes right off till you get there. He was tearing his own clothes off impatiently and her shirt and bra were effectively off anyway, but she decided to amuse him by taking her time about getting out of the rest, removing her left sock particularly slowly and seductively. He made a grab for her as she had known he would and she rolled on to the bed with him.

'Darling. Wait.' He pinned her shoulders effortlessly against the pillows. 'Look, I can come any time – like now if you do that, and that's not what I want. The fun for me lies in giving pleasure. Yes?' He touched her gently, watching her face.

'Oh yes,' she said, feeling tears not far away. 'Oh darling Gerry.'

But something had set up a resistance, and she found concentration and sensation ebbing and started to tense up. He stopped what he was doing and kissed her. 'Not working?'

'Sorry,' she said, trying to look away from him.

'I know why not,' he said, hand on her cheek to make her look at him. 'You don't much like having things done for you, you want to control them.'

She struggled to speak, and realized that she wasn't going to be able to and tried to push him away but he resisted, not angrily but seriously. 'Hey, it's me. I love you.'

'Sorry,' she said, fighting back tears. 'You're right. Couldn't we just try some other way?'

'With you on top?' He was amused. 'It may come to that but not yet.' He kissed her mouth till she relaxed, then moved down, keeping one hand flat on her stomach while he gently moved her legs apart, and she felt his tongue move against her. He went on, holding her steadily, with apparently all the time in the world and she came overwhelmingly without strain, feeling him slip into her as she came to an end and holding him while he came, quickly and easily. He rolled them both gently, so that his full weight was now on top of her, and she felt rather than saw him grinning to himself.

'Yes, I did like it,' she said, firmly, and he laughed aloud. 'I'm sorry it took so long,' she added, and he pulled her hair.

'Darling, I like doing it. So do most chaps, given a chance.' He looked at her carefully.

'I know this to be true,' she said.

'But you always did things for yourself for preference.'

'This is also true.'

'I'm going to have a bath. You can go first,' he added, hastily, catching her eye.

'I'd better, if you want any supper. A complication of

289

this relationship,' she said, luxuriously, on her way to the bathroom, 'is that we have here two natural leaders. It would be interesting to see how we managed if we were married to each other.' She looked back at him, inquiringly, but he was looking wooden and anxious. 'Absolutely appallingly, I should think,' she said, smitten, but trying hard to play it light. 'I shan't be long.'

Keep off the grass, she thought angrily, lying back, trying not to get her hair wet in the bath. You have him now, enjoy what there is. She heard the phone ping and wondered painfully if Gerry was calling base. Well, she must do the same, as she had promised Caspar.

She dried herself and got back into most of her clothes, extracting clean knickers from her briefcase. She went down the corridor to the kitchen; Gerry's phone call seemed to be going on for ever and she would be better occupied assembling supper and establishing what critical ingredient he had failed to buy this time.

'. . . No, Richard, at one level it doesn't matter that much to me, provided the firm and the employment *is* safe. And I can see John Winstanley's got a problem there – and Peter of course – but from the point of view of a northern MP, I'm not very comfortable with it. It's enemy territory, you know.'

Reluctantly but true to her upbringing, Caroline closed the kitchen door and started to explore the fridge. Not that it took very long to establish that both bread and milk seemed to be missing which was going to put scrambled eggs on toast off tonight's menu. She was just considering the nutritional value of a meal consisting of bacon and eggs, topped off with fruit yoghurt, when he appeared in the doorway and she was able to dispatch him to catch the local Indian store before it closed and herself to ring Caspar and the children.

'Thanks, Caz,' she said gratefully, as she heard Gerry come back. 'I'll do the same for you.'

'No, you won't. I know better now.'

'Piss off,' she said, laughing, and put the phone down.

'Was that your brother? Not a nice way to talk to him.'

'He is my brother,' she said, irritated, and added as she had meant not to, 'You were talking about Prior.'

He looked at her thoughtfully as she blushed. 'I was just passing.'

'I don't blame you for being curious. It may be commercially reasonable what John Winstanley is doing, but it's politically idiotic. We'll be accused of doing secret deals with our friends, if it gets out.'

'Well, it must get out in the end,' she pointed out.

'Well, it might be all right by then. But not now, not with us doing so badly. Seven points behind in the polls.'

'Do you take any notice of that?'

'We say we don't, but the truth is we're all glued to them.'

'Presumably,' she said, carefully, 'this was agreed by everyone. I mean in Cabinet.' She glanced at Gerry cautiously and saw him smile to himself.

'Not necessarily,' he said, after a pause, and she watched him, every instinct alert, as he pushed packets into a cupboard.

'So would other people in Cabinet jump up and down, and stop it if they knew?'

'Not necessarily.'

But they would, or they might, if somehow it got around that Friern was being given a private look at all the companies. No wonder the NEB had sworn her lads to secrecy. She considered her lover, watching the big hands that had been holding her down, so effectively, less than an hour ago.

'It would make a good story.'

The hands stopped moving, still clasping a packet of cereal, then moved again. 'It would. Which is why I was talking to a colleague. Are you going to start cooking or do I have to go out again? Have a real drink this time?'

'Gin would be lovely,' she said, accepting that she had asked her last question and thankfully abandoning the subject, and turning her attention to food and drink.

14

It was the telephone, Clive Fieldman realized, that persistent noise, not his alarm clock, and it must be a wrong number. Or something wrong with a child, he thought, fighting clear of the duvet and seizing the handset, observing, dazedly, that it was just 6.45 a.m.

'Clive? Jim Morrison. Sorry to wake you, but I thought you'd better get a start on this particular Monday. *Financial Times*, front page, third column. You don't? All right, I'll read it to you.'

Clive put his glasses on and managed to find a piece of paper, the chief press officer audibly fretting at the other end.

'I'm with you, Jim.' With his glasses on he could see that the bedside table was dusty and ringed with cup marks. Lucy had complained that his flat was depressing and he could certainly see why. A cleaner, that was what he needed.

'"NEB in negotiations to sell five construction companies,"' Jim Morrison recited, dramatically, and Clive drew in a horrified breath.

'Stop there, old son,' he said, briskly. 'I'm on my way.'

'Just let me read you the best bit,' the Yorkshire accent said lugubriously. 'Third paragraph down: "It is understood that NEB officials have given a potential purchaser access to trading figures and other key data for the five companies on an exclusive basis, and that teams from City accountants Fisher Price started work in the companies on Saturday."'

'Jesus. Any editorial?'

'No. Just the story and a bit of speculation about who the lucky purchaser is, with the PR men for Tarmac and Wimpey denying it is them. No one was available to comment at Harrison or Friern, you'll be glad to hear. Can you find Sir Matthew?'

'Yes. I'll do that now. Does the Minister know?'

'The car's picking him up in ten minutes, with the papers. I thought you might like to ring him.'

Clive had managed to get pants and a shirt more or less on, while he was thinking. 'No, I must find Sir Matthew. You do it, Jim, gently; tell the Minister what I'm doing and I'll try to get everyone into the office in an hour, with Friern as well, if I can. Where's the Secretary of State? Thank God for that. It's two in the morning there – no one'll be asking him yet.'

In the event it was nearly nine o'clock by the time any meaningful group had been convened to discuss the emergency, and Matthew Friern was not among their number, since he was still struggling down from Dorrington, having agreed that he, and everyone else at Friern, would go on being unavailable for comment for another couple of hours. Winstanley, jaw set and hair untidy, every ounce of him expressing hostility, was at the head of the table, flanked by Sir Francis Templeton, permanent secretary of the Department – the managing director in anyone's terms – who had been alerted about ten minutes after Clive. The chief press officer who looked, as usual, as if he had just got out of bed in a working-man's hostel was next to Sir Francis, and Clive with James Mather next to him sat on the Minister's right while the principal private secretary perched at the end of the table, with a notebook. Richard Watts of Fredericks was waiting, expensively, in a room along the corridor, in uneasy association with his Gruhners colleagues and the NEB's deputy managing director, but there had been general agreement that the house team had better get its lines right before meeting anyone else.

'The first thing I want to know is how they got this,' Winstanley opened, and four civil servants sighed sub-audibly, while the private secretary gloomily observed the top of an ill-polished shoe. Quite the least important question on the agenda, and a sheer waste of time even to ask it, Clive thought, wearily. But Winstanley was seriously ruffled, and was clearly going to lose points for this in the savage competition between ministers for power and favour. And it didn't pay civil servants to have their man lose influence.

'It is indeed most unfortunate, Minister,' Clive began, pacifically, using the civil service's strongest term of regret and disapprobation, 'but it was not possible for five teams of reporting accountants to start work in total secrecy. The individual managements were told only that these were accountants reporting to the NEB in preparation for a sale. And factually, as you may remember, that *is* the case. Their report will be to the NEB – but Friern have expressed themselves willing to rely on what it says.'

'And the accountants knew they had an audience outside the NEB,' James Mather added.

'So the individual managements were not told that other companies might be included in the sale. As we agreed.' Winstanley obviously felt he was getting the range of the guns.

'Well,' Clive said, cautiously, 'they all knew that the NEB intended a sale, and they all must have understood that this report was part of the preliminaries. But as we also agreed, they were all forbidden to talk about it. When you talk to the NEB people later, Minister, I expect you will want to ask them what form this warning took.' Time to remind the man that the NEB had been in charge of this process.

'But the managers couldn't have known that the NEB was dealing with an actual purchaser for all five,' Winstanley persisted.

Clive hesitated and Sir Francis leant forward. 'Intelligent and suspicious men could have guessed, first, that the other companies in the group were involved and, secondly, that a specific purchaser had reared his head.'

And that very fairly describes the three gentlemen at the top of Prior Systems at least, Clive thought grimly, even if the directorate of the other four were simple chaps. 'But no one mentioned any names, Minister, as agreed,' he pointed out.

'The *FT* doesn't either, or rather it has a list.'

Jim Morrison stirred, releasing a shower of cigarette ash. 'I'm afraid that may be technique, Minister. They'll be protecting a source by wrapping Friern in the middle of a list.'

Winstanley considered him with dislike. 'The only company Friern was known to want was Prior, wasn't it?'

'That is right, Minister,' Clive confirmed promptly.

'So the leak's from there,' Winstanley said, doggedly. 'Can it be your friend, that solicitor – what's her name? – who acts for them?'

'Caroline Whitehouse,' Clive said, trying not to sound

dismayed. 'She shouldn't have known – I mean, if they told her, that was a clear breach of duty.'

Winstanley dug a hole in the Department's blotter. 'She'd have known who to talk to on the *Financial Times*.'

'Oh yes.'

'She's an old acquaintance of yours.' Winstanley was still excavating the blotter. Clive confirmed it, absently, then sat up as the implications of this apparently idle remark hit home, but Sir Francis was ahead of him.

'Minister, I'm afraid in our experience leaks like this tend to be political, in the sense that they come out of Westminster, as it were, rather than Whitehall.'

It was Winstanley's turn to sit up sharply, and he looked at Sir Francis as if he had bitten him. He looked young and inexperienced, measured against Sir Francis's controlled, grey-haired presence. He opened his mouth to ask a further question which died in the face of Sir Francis's courteously inquiring expression and the studious inattention being displayed around the rest of the table.

'Well,' he said, rallying, and looking challengingly down the table, 'it's what to do now that matters, isn't it?' and glared at his audience, who gave this suggestion the welcome usually accorded to a novel but useful idea.

'There's no harm in the NEB pressing on with accountants' reports, Minister.' Clive, who had managed ten minutes with Richard Watts, was on secure ground. 'That's a normal preliminary to any sale, and you can say so. The issue is whether the NEB can continue to negotiate on an exclusive basis with one purchaser.'

'They can't. It would have been all right if they'd got

as far as a provisional deal, but I can't defend it now. Not at this stage.' Winstanley's mouth set in a tight line.

Well, that was clear enough, Clive thought, gratified and surprised, having expected hours of inconclusive argument to have been required before this conclusion was reached. He looked across inquiringly at Sir Francis, who was looking greyer and more eminent than ever.

'I'm afraid that's right, Minister. Painful, but correct. We now have to find the right words.'

The door opened and a junior scurried in and handed a bright orange flat file to the private secretary, who looked at the typewritten note on the front and handed it wordlessly to Sir Francis. 'A Private Notice Question from Alex Neil, Labour, Withlington.'

'Davecat's based there,' Clive said, promptly. 'Well that's that, isn't it?'

Private Notice Questions are not always allowed through by the clerks, but if they are, they have to be answered on the same day.

'I'd like to confirm that the NEB have commissioned accountants' reports and deny everything else,' Winstanley said, bluntly.

'Confirm, and say that no decision has yet been reached on the method of sale, and that these reports are an essential part of the process, and promise a statement asap,' Clive offered, writing a swift note, and seeing out of the corner of his eye Sir Francis nodding agreement.

'That's better,' Winstanley agreed.

'We'll need to square the NEB and Friern,' Clive pointed out. 'Do you want to leave that with us?'

'You should see Matthew Friern yourself, Minister,' Sir Francis said, in tones that broached no dispute, and Clive cursed quietly. Of course that was right; he'd just got carried away, trying to make it all better. Matthew Friern would certainly need some personal soothing, particularly since the Minister had eaten his salt. He cleared his throat and reminded the meeting of the NEB's presence in the waiting-room.

'I'll see them in five minutes,' Winstanley said, irritably. 'Francis, it's been good of you to come, but do you feel you need to see them too? No?'

No, Sir Francis said, and added that he would be in the Department for the rest of the morning if wanted, and left, taking Jim Morrison, who needed to check the level of mayhem in the press office. James Mather and the private secretary were despatched to knock out a draft answer to the Private Notice Question without which the next meeting could not proceed, and to tell the crew in the waiting-room about progress, and Clive was left with his minister.

'I'd really like to find out how this got out,' Winstanley said, looking vengefully out of the window, and Clive, alarmed, sought for a response worthy of Sir Francis.

'Over the last four years, Minister, a process for investigating this sort of problem has been evolved,' he said, carefully. 'It is known as the Prime Minister's leak procedure,' he volunteered, when he felt it to be safe.

'Oh God. Well, I'm not going to do *that*.' Winstanley moved abruptly and glared at a curtain, perhaps deciding whether to punch it, and Clive waited, in unhelpful silence.

'Your friend, Caroline Whitehouse – she comes out of a political family, I think you said?'

'Her father is Professor Sir Sholto Henriques.'

'Oh him. Oh them. Labour.'

'Yes.'

A further unhelpful silence ensued with Clive deeply alarmed by the implications of this line, but not wanting to volunteer.

'Would she have done this for political reasons?' Winstanley was finally forced to ask. 'If her clients had told her what was happening?'

'No,' Clive said, suddenly confident, remembering Caroline sixteen years younger, at the end of a long meeting, laying down the law to a man years her senior. 'No, she wouldn't have been prepared to put her clients, or allow them to put themselves, at risk. She always said it was the least people could expect if they went to a decent firm: to be kept out of trouble.' He looked and saw that Winstanley had recognized something in this statement and decided to go on. 'Besides, the Henriques gang do not believe that the end justifies the means.'

'Good heavens,' Winstanley said, appalled. 'However do they manage – oh, well, the Labour Party, I suppose. No wonder.'

Clive was still choking on his coffee when James Mather and the private secretary appeared, with draft answer and draft notes for supplementaries, every word of which was going to need agreeing with Matthew Friern, the NEB, the merchant-bank advisers, the Secretary of State's office and probably Number 10 as well, and Clive and Winstanley settled down to the rest of the morning.

Caroline Whitehouse had started her morning with two children at the oculist. Ben had been shortsighted;

twelve-year-old Timmy had worn glasses since he was eight and was resigned to them. Susannah, at ten, had finally had to confess that she could see the blackboard only if she was in the front row, and had wept when what they all reluctantly knew had been confirmed: that she, too, was on the six-month appointment treadmill, and would have to wear glasses for most purposes. No, it isn't fair, Caroline had agreed, you should have got my eyes, not Dad's, and he would have said the same, but there it is. And you've got Dad's nice red hair. This had cheered Susannah, who set a great deal of store by her long, red-blonde hair, and Caroline was still feeling mildly pleased with herself as she arrived at work, uncharacteristically, after 9 a.m. Her office seemed to be full of people, but once she focused on the crowd it resolved itself into Michael Appleton, Mark Dwyer and Susie.

'Evidently, you haven't read the *FT*.' Michael Appleton gave her the article and she fell on it. 'Would it have been your Prior chaps?'

Caroline had found ten minutes on Friday to assure him by note that Prior had signed the client letter and to tell him that for some unknown reason said good client was disbarred from talking to its solicitor.

'Prior didn't know that it was a sale of five companies. Oh, wait a minute, perhaps they did – they were being very orthodox with me and I was just too busy to guess what actually seems to have happened. So they were going to sell the lot to Friern, were they? But I don't think this'– she tapped the *FT* – 'is Peter. I really had warned him they must do what the NEB said and he is very orderly. I'd better ring him – he may be under pressure. He rang me, Susie?' She stopped, hand on the telephone. 'I expect you have other things to do, Michael.'

'I do. I just thought you might need some help. I understand that there are calls from several newspapers.'

'Well, we don't comment, do we?'

'No, or if we have to, I do.'

'I'm sure you'd do it better than me,' Caroline said, kindly, and Mark Dwyer closed his eyes momentarily.

'Thank you, Caroline. Let me know.'

Left with Mark, Caroline found herself avoiding his eyes.

'It wasn't them, I'm sure,' she said, to her blotter. She looked up. 'Nor was it me.' She returned to consider the article. 'That does sink that particular bright idea for the NEB, doesn't it?'

'I would have thought so. It's a very critical article.'

'Mm. Stay with me while I talk to Prior.' She did that next, finding them, disconcertingly, exultant, respectful, and totally clear that it had been she who had talked to the *FT*.

'I'd never have put you at risk,' she protested. 'And you now are at risk because the NEB probably think it was you. You'll just have to tell them it wasn't.'

'We've already done that. They're furious but they can't do anything.' It was the clever Martin who had grasped the implications. 'Even if they do think it was us, they can't fire us – think what the *FT* would say.'

'Oh yes,' she said, slowly. 'Yes, that is true, you're safe.'

'Caroline.' It was Peter, obviously bristling. 'It was *not* us. That would have been disorderly and we don't work like that.'

Curious how utterly boring, prissy and censorious a reasonable moral statement could sound, Caroline thought, just like Sholto laying down the law.

'I didn't think it *was* you,' she said, truthfully, wondering just when on Sunday her darling Gerry had found time to talk to the *FT* and throw the plans of a political rival into utter confusion. Well, she hadn't told *him* either, she argued doubtfully with herself; she had merely, in answer to a question, told him that there was a problem and he had found out the rest. It was his constituency, she told the voice in her head; if he'd just stood and bitten his fingernails or taken a high moral line like Peter, the Prior lads might have ended up owned by Friern.

She said goodbye to the Prior team, noting that Peter was still outraged that anyone could have doubted his integrity or ability to behave in an orderly way. God preserve me from having a Henriques clone to work with as well, she thought crossly, waving Mark and a pile of papers out of her office and pulling another pile towards her.

Montagu/Capulet had, luckily, stalled over the weekend on one of the critical questions that always bogged down discussions, namely board membership of the merged entity. It was the usual choice between a board of seventeen people, no offence caused and no real direction of company thereafter possible, or a board of eight or so, which could act effectively on the company's behalf, and massive hard feelings. Caroline, an advocate of getting all the grief over at once, had advised her client to go for the small, functioning board and have all the resultant quarrels conducted by lawyers, leaving managers to manage. This advice, echoed by the

Montagu lawyers, had proved too difficult to take all at once, and the weekend had been occupied with increasingly frantic meetings with individual directors, none of which had moved the merger forward. The whole of Monday had been cleared for Montagu/Capulet and since the only meeting was now postponed to 4 p.m. she had, unusually, not much to do other than contemplate the latest events at Prior. And the man who had been a vital part of them.

She riffled through the phone messages, pausing at one from Hamish Brown, but as she expected there was nothing from Gerry. He had said he would ring on Tuesday, and she did not quite dare ring him. In any case, what would she say? She left it, uneasily, asked for some coffee, fiddled with the in-tray, repudiated, unavailingly, respectful congratulations from Hamish, who appeared to be in no doubt that her empire included the *Financial Times*, and passed, as instructed, an urgent request from the *Evening Standard* to Michael Appleton. That left an hour till lunch and she could no longer shy away from thinking about Gerry.

The longed-for overnight stay had ended badly, in the sense that she had been overcome by desolation on Sunday afternoon, as he had driven her carefully to the end of her road and kissed her quickly and anxiously. She had walked soberly home, taken over the children from Caz, who had, bless him, stayed and fed them all tea just to ease her back into family life. But it had been Gerry she had wanted there, with her children. And his, she had reminded herself, since in the circumstances she envisaged something dreadful but unspecified would have happened to his wife. When Caz went the children had played up, sensing her mood, and Sunday evening had been a battle of wills, leaving her limp, angry and feeling profoundly furtive, conscious that the children were not getting a fair deal. And extremely angry with Gerry, who had never promised her anything, who loved her but insisted on keeping her within a very limited space in his life and with whom there was no space to negotiate. What was on offer was what you got. I have to give up, she thought; the whole thing is Not Me; it's not our star, our mother of three, I-can't-imagine-how-she-does-it-all – Caroline Whitehouse. Ben would have been horrified, she had thought wryly.

She looked restlessly for something, anything to do, and reread the *FT* article, admiring the careful phrasing. It said Gerry to her as clearly as if he had written it; he had given her no clues – sensible, she acknowledged, no embarrassment thereby caused. But a little chilling, given how close they had been. After supper on Saturday, they had watched the late news, peacefully entwined on his sofa; they had each made a phone call to their home base and gone to bed, and slept heavily for three hours when she had woken to find him curled round her, not quite awake himself, but fully erect, and his hands on her breasts. She had moved to help and he woke up.

'It's your turn to decide. Do you like it this way?'

'Any way with you.'

'That's not absolutely true,' he said, amused, stroking her back.

'I did like it in the end.' She turned round to kiss him, then got her knees under her so he could come in. Relaxed with sleep she felt instant pleasure as he pushed in, holding her hips, and came almost immediately, crying out with pleasure, and felt him come too.

'Ah, lovely,' he had said, folding himself over her back. 'Damn,' he had added later. 'I'm falling out.' He sat up and she rolled over, watching him tidily get rid of a condom. He always, always wore one; he knew she was on the pill and that he was the only person she slept with, but it was another of his rules of procedure – sensible, protective of both of them, and a fundamental sign that this affair was to stay within its boundaries without even a remote risk of complications being accepted.

She looked at her hands: they were clenched on the blotter and she flexed them, straightening her back. The phone rang, and she seized it gratefully. The day's lunch guests had arrived – would she go up? Imagine, she thought coldly, pulling a comb through her hair, if I had nothing else to do but long for Gerry. This cannot endure; it is breaking me up. And then suddenly she remembered sharply and clearly his profile as he sat beside her at his kitchen table, poring over the Sunday papers holding her hand, and she understood that there was no way she could give him up. The world was different whenever he was there; the day changed colour. It would be quite beyond her to give up all that restless, dazzling energy and the feel of his hands on her. She drew a deep breath, gaining real relief from accepting that she was in a box and there was no way out. 'Not yet, oh Lord, it would appear,' she said silently, echoing St Augustine, and went up the stairs two at a time, rather than taking the lift as befitted a partner.

It felt like the longest Monday of his life, Clive Fieldman thought, wearily, and it was still only 7 p.m. The story, that the NEB had simply been making efficient preparations to put the companies up for sale, had held, and Winstanley had survived an uncomfortable ten minutes in the House. And an even more uncomfortable ten minutes with a furious Secretary of State on the telephone from New York. Minus several points evidently for DoE ministers, even though the Opposition had not made the most of their opportunities. The Labour MP, in whose constituency the Davecat factory was situated, had managed to sidetrack himself on to a long and badly received dissertation on the necessity for the Government to acquire even more bits of the economy. Against the background of this performance and of an awkward defensive innings by Winstanley, the MP for the next-door constituency to Prior, the Minister for Transport, Gerry Willshaw, had come out particularly well; interviewed immediately after Winstanley on the news Willshaw had been sensibly robust, welcoming the NEB's speedy action and saying that *his* constituents, many of them Prior employees, looked forward to a secure future for themselves and this excellent company in the private sector as soon as possible. 'Very helpful,' Winstanley had observed, between gritted teeth, watching Willshaw with open dislike, and the civil servants had tactfully removed themselves as soon as the item had finished. Clive and James Mather agreed that the Minister for Transport had looked good, as usual, and he had very neatly signalled support for an employee buy-out if that was on offer, without saying a single thing that could have been held to be unhelpful to the hard-pressed DoE.

He looked warily at the phone. He longed to see Lucy – no well, let's get that right, he longed to have a quiet supper and to go to bed with Lucy, but not at the price of discussing any further the day's events. He had also somewhere in the long day supported Winstanley through a trying interview with Matthew Friern, who had finally arrived from Dorrington, around 11 a.m., in a vile temper and full of suggestions for improvement of the road system, involving a six-lane stream of concrete, flattening several major provincial towns in its route. And then it had been extraordinarily difficult to get him to accept that his provisional arrangements with the NEB were off, dead in the water, gone for ever. Winstanley finally had to tell him, point blank, that he was personally not going to take the risk of continuing with a negotiated deal for all five. Matthew, indefatigably, had suggested putting all five out to open tender and had had to be turned down on that proposition too. Winstanley, some time in the early morning meeting, had decided that he was going to take no risks at all with this sale. He had been advised, unequivocally this time in answer to the direct question, that selling all five together meant the NEB might get a lower price which neither he nor they were going to risk.

'We're still learning here what we can and can't do,' Winstanley had said in a rare and wasted burst of honesty. 'And what we have just learned is that everything is going to have to be sold in a way that gets the best price; it isn't just the Opposition, it's your *confrères*, Matthew, who will give us hell if we get that wrong.' This admirably straightforward statement had not been as well received as it deserved and Clive had had to invent a meeting for Winstanley to get Matthew out of the room.

'Just like a gorilla, shaking every tree he comes to,'

the clever James, there to take the note of the meeting, had observed, with fascination.

'I suppose that quite a lot of the time you do get a coconut that way,' Clive had observed, momentarily cheered, but it had been the only amusement of the day; the rest had been wearing, discouraging, and humiliating, and had left all concerned feeling both exhausted and inadequate.

But before all this had happened Lucy and he had agreed to meet that evening. He could now ring her. Matthew had, scowling horribly, told Winstanley he was flying straight back to Dorrington.

'Darling,' she had said, sounding as weary as he felt. 'I'd love to see you but to be absolutely honest *not* if you're going to talk about Prior or the NEB, or Matthew, or the DoE.'

'Oh, I promise. I was wondering how I could ask you not to. I'll be with you in half an hour.'

'Can we eat out? It's been such a bloody day I haven't got anything in. We can come back here afterwards.'

'Don't move. I'm on my way.'

And miraculously he was; an empty taxi came into view as he ran out of the Department and he felt his heart lift as he escaped. He ran lightly up the steps to the Friern flat and seized Lucy firmly in a bear hug as she opened the door to him. She resisted, startled, but relaxed against him after a minute and they stood in the hall wrapped round each other, listening to each other breathe.

'Of course, I'll take you out,' he said, kissing her, 'but I've got an idea.'

'And what is that idea?'

He whispered in her ear and she bit her lip.

'Oh yes, let's do that.'

It was quite one of their best games, he thought, grinning to himself as he tied her hands to the bedposts, and one he could not have imagined playing in the days before Lucy, without suffering agonies of crippling self-consciousness. This was a game that involved Lucy in being a particularly nubile captive who had never had a really good lover before, and she usually came easily. Not this time, and he lifted his head inquiringly to find her looking stressed and cross.

'No good?' he asked, pulling himself up and kissing her in the delightful hollow of her collar bones.

'I'm just tired, I suppose.'

He reached up and untied her hands, then rolled her over, so she was on top of him.

'Yes, perhaps.'

He was tired too, and as she moved herself on him he realized that he wasn't going to last and hastily started to count backwards, as she had taught him, but none of it worked and he came, quickly and without much of either pleasure or release.

'Damn. Sorry.'

'My fault,' she said, sadly.

'Oh darling, don't be silly. I'm way off tonight. Sorry. We'll try again after we've eaten – can't have you going to bed cross, petal.'

They shared a shower, and he watched her anxiously; she was looking withdrawn and tired, although as beautiful as ever.

'I'm putting on weight,' she said, angrily, stepping on to the weighing machine.

'Very heavy towel?' he suggested, but she was not at all amused, and he sighed; the impetus which had swept him here had died and he was feeling exhausted and slightly sick, beyond hunger even.

They both revived with supper, at the small, smart, very expensive Italian restaurant which Lucy favoured. She nodded to various acquaintances and he found himself wondering uncomfortably whether it was sensible to be here, with Matthew Friern's wife, and decided it wasn't. He hurried Lucy out, suggesting coffee at the flat and she complied with only fair grace, agreeing reluctantly that discretion might be the better part. They sat drinking coffee in a prickly silence while Clive wondered if he could raise the *élan* to sweep her off to bed again, and whether he would be any use to her if he did. After a day like today, he thought ruefully, you needed a wife and a cat to kick and all the usual domestic fittings of marriage, not a discontented mistress whom you saw only once a week.

'Sorry,' he said, 'I've just had too thick a day.'

'So have I,' she said, relaxing. 'Look, I know we said we wouldn't talk about Prior and I really don't want to, but I had a dreadful time with Matt. He is furious – I've hardly ever seen him like this. He came back effing and blinding about poor John Winstanley and you, and I managed finally to get through to him that it wasn't your fault the *FT* got hold of it – I mean it must have been very embarrassing for the Department, mustn't it?'

'To say the least.'

'Well, he thinks it's terribly wet of you not to be prepared to go on, and he was talking about going to see the PM.'

'Number 10 won't want to die in a ditch on this one.'

'No, well, *I* can see that. And finally, I think, so can Matt. So, then he started going on about the Prior people. He thinks they told the *FT* and he is threatening all kinds of things.'

Clive sat up. 'What kinds of things?'

'Oh darling, what does it matter. Commercial things, all right? He'll simmer down, but it's just intolerable for the moment. I did tell him I was having a drink with you, by the way; I thought I'd better. He wants me to make sure you understand that he feels he has been let down by the DoE, and the Government. And he can't imagine what he's been contributing so handsomely to Party funds all these years *for*.'

Clive poured himself some more coffee as an alternative to burying his head in his hands. 'Well, thank you for the message.'

'Sorry. But you do see? I had three hours of this before I got him on to a plane.'

Clive contemplated the vision of Matthew Friern stamping round Dorrington, spoiling for trouble. 'Well, darling, we told him. It'll have to go to tender, but he ought to be pretty well placed if he wants to buy Prior.' He thought on, wearied and cross, 'Well, what can he *do* to the Prior lads?'

'*I* don't know. But he's got his whole energies on that; I can't get a civil word out of him.'

Clive, recognizing a cue when he heard one, drew her firmly into his arms. 'Shall we watch the news?' he whispered, huskily, and she burst out laughing.

'You *are* clever. That's just what I want, to sit and watch TV. But not the news – do you mind? There's an old Clint Eastwood I'd like to see again. I'll make more coffee.'

'I'd rather have tea. We working-class lads never quite get used to coffee, you know.'

'I know. Or having a bath without taking the coal out first. What sort of tea?'

'So spoon'll stand up in it, lass, none of this fancy stuff. I'll help you make it – I don't think you know how.' He regarded the contents of the shelf with dismay. 'Neither do I, if I have to start with this fancy rubbish here.'

'We've got some tea bags somewhere for Bridget.'

He started to laugh and she joined him, after a pause while she realized what she had said, and they stood locked in each other's arms. This was what he wanted, he thought, comfortably, a cosy time in front of the telly and a nice fuck thereafter, a long night in a good bed and a decent breakfast to set him on his way. Well, if Matthew Friern didn't seem to appreciate his luck perhaps Lucy would one day, somehow, decide to change and give him a chance to be a better husband than he'd ever been to Linda.

15

It was really very English, Caroline thought, suppressing nervous laughter as she nodded to Matthew and Lucy Friern, and to Andy Eames Lewis, who was sitting next to them, two rows in front of where she, Peter Burwood, Martin Williams and Graham Gough were deployed. Entirely natural, after the feverish two weeks that had elapsed since the *FT* article, that the Friern contingent should have decided to listen to the statement from the public gallery of the House of Commons. She and her team had, after all, made the same decision and all present seemed to be determined to treat it as a routine business occasion. She put on her glasses as a movement at the back of the House, behind the Speaker's chair, caught her eye and she saw Clive filing into what looked exactly like a pew. It was he who had told her that all outsiders are banned from the chamber when the House is in session, but that a convention exists whereby civil servants are allowed in to this box behind the Speaker; formally, they are not there, but their minister's PPS can fetch and carry notes, and a civil servant can slip out unobtrusively to look up a tricky point if no one in the box can remember the answer.

She touched Peter's arm and pointed out Clive, *sotto voce*, as the Secretary of State for the Environment sweated through the replies to questions about planning inquiries, heavily barracked from the Labour side. Peter was alight with interest, wide-eyed at the sight of the lounging row of middle-aged men representing HM Government that afternoon, Winstanley sitting next to his Secretary of State, his carefully combed thick, blond hair looking yellow in the harsh lighting. Caroline looked at him reflectively as he shuffled through papers, wondering if he was nervous or whether this was routine, and then stopped breathing as Gerry Willshaw slid quietly on to the bench, two places away from Winstanley, nodding to him politely. He stretched his long legs, crossed them elegantly at the ankle, and contemplated a set of papers of his own, long fingers splayed behind them, his dark head bent. Caroline sat frozen, winded by his unexpected appearance, then leant back in her seat hastily, as the Prior team indicated to her in various ways that the nice man who had visited their sites was *there*, look. She smiled at them faintly in reassurance, and went on watching Gerry, content just to look at him, comfortable in the knowledge that she really would see him later that night; he had promised and they had confirmed the arrangement two hours ago. They had not discussed the day's business and indeed at the time he had rung she had not been prepared for the descent of her management trio, fresh from the NEB, in a state of high excitement, and demanding to be taken to hear the statement. It had on consideration seemed like a good idea; the lads were plainly going to disrupt her day anyway, and she had shared their superstitious feeling that they ought to be there for the formal declaration that the race had started. She watched Gerry turning pages, shoulders slightly hunched, and understood that he must be speaking later in a debate and that he was nervous about whatever he was going to say. She suddenly remembered guiltily that he had, two weeks ago, absolutely forbidden her to slip in to hear him wind up in an adjournment debate, saying with obvious sincerity that he was nervous enough in the chamber anyway, and would be totally put off his stroke if he knew she was there. She had been regretful, since she had longed to see him perform in the House, but obedient. When Gerry told you not to do something, however charmingly, somehow you ended up not doing it. Authority, that's what it was called, she decided broodingly, and she had not previously realized how useful and how seductive a quality it was – politically as well as personally, she acknowledged. She slid down as far as she could in her seat in case he looked up. She kept her glasses on, hoping that they would act as a disguise; she needed them only for going to the theatre and driving a car, neither of which she had ever done with him. Peter and Graham, flanking her, leant forward in unison, screening her, as Winstanley rose to speak, both listening anxiously, Peter trying to take notes.

'It'll be in Hansard tomorrow, verbatim,' she said, quietly, to his shoulder, knowing this from Clive. 'Just enjoy it.'

He nodded and settled down as Winstanley ploughed steadily through the history and prospects of the five construction companies in the ownership of the NEB and confirmed that two of them would, shortly, be closed by the NEB as having no real prospects of viability. All creditors would, of course, be paid in full. He went on to say that the NEB had now received the reports they had commissioned at the Government's request, and the other three companies would be returned as soon as possible to the safe hands of private enterprise, thereby enabling them to grow and prosper, freed from the depressing shackles of public ownership.

In order to facilitate this return at the earliest possible opportunity, all three would be sold, severally, by tender. The minister, briskly ignoring Labour groans, was confident that all Hon. Members would wish the companies every success.

Nice, Caroline thought approvingly, her attention distracted from Gerry Willshaw, beautifully drafted. Winstanley had remained standing as the Opposition spokesman on Housing got heavily to his feet to ask why the Government was closing prematurely two good companies – he could not have looked at the Davecat accounts, Caroline thought censoriously – and why also were they selling off so hastily companies that had only just been nursed back to health. Were they setting up a private deal with their friends? Caroline watched Gerry, with love and curiosity, but his head was down, apparently not even listening to what was happening two places away from him, where Winstanley was competently rephrasing sections of the statement to deal with the questions. Another man was on his feet, behind Winstanley, to his right, consulting a piece of paper carefully.

'Would the Minister confirm that the sale will be conducted in such a manner as to give the management and employees of Prior Systems – to whose efforts he has paid tribute in his statement – a fair opportunity to bid for their company?'

Caroline sat up sharply then shrank hastily back into her seat, while the Prior management turned to look at her inquiringly. She gave them her best sphinx smile, as Winstanley assured all present that management and employees in all three companies would be given every chance to compete. A supplementary from the Opposition enabled him to say it all over again with the addition of a piece on wider share-ownership, and while he was thus engaged, she watched Gerry fascinated, flattered and charmed. He hadn't told her but he had efficiently fixed up a marker for the management team, doing something for her that she would not have known how to do. It was, she thought, a totally unfamiliar sensation, having someone take charge of a bit of her life without even consulting her. Ben and she had been a true partnership, decisions painfully arrived at and shared, and the workload evenly borne. In fourteen years of marriage, neither of them had taken a major step without consulting the other, and if it had been an efficient and loving partnership it had also been devoid of surprises. This could get addictive, she thought – being told what to do and having things given to you. She smiled warmly on Peter and Martin, who were whispering congratulations and indicated that something else germane to their affairs was going on in the chamber.

'Will the Minister confirm that in considering bids for Prior or the other companies, full account will be taken of the need to secure the maximum return for the taxpayer who has a substantial investment in these companies?' It was a red-faced man in his fifties on the government side of the House, and the Prior team scowled at him unanimously.

'As I said in my statement, the return to the taxpayer will be one of the main criteria by which a purchaser will be selected.'

One for our side, though, overall, Caroline thought exultantly. Got it in the open that management would be welcomed; next stop Hamish Brown where Prior's management could now show him all the numbers and work out what they really thought the company could make if they sweated it.

That seemed to be the end of that, and she had nudged Peter to indicate that they might all move, when she realized that Gerry was on his feet and moving along to the despatch box. The temptation to hear him speak in the House was too great and she whispered to Peter that she just wanted to hear the opening speech here. On behalf of another client, she added mendaciously.

'It was he who fixed that question for us, wasn't it?' It was of course Martin, loving husband and concerned father, to whom people were the breath of life, who was asking.

'Yes,' she said boldly. 'He very kindly said he would help.'

'Beautifully done,' Martin said, approving and unsuspicious.

'It suits his book,' she said quietly, realizing as she spoke that that was true; she loved him and he was certainly in love with her, but he was a talented politician, who had come a long way and had even further to go. She watched him broodingly; he was introducing a debate on the financing of British Rail, and the chamber was filling up; it was evidently important and he had not told her he was doing it. He probably didn't tell his wife either, just got on with it on the basis that men must work and women must weep, even though one of his women was a senior commercial lawyer. He spoke steadily and with feeling, making his subject interesting, but he was not wholly comfortable, forcing a naturally resonant voice, so that she felt a sympathetic strain on her vocal cords. And he loathed being interrupted, letting barracking from the other side distract and put him off. Well, the interruptions were unattractive, but were clearly accepted as par for the course in this place, and you would have expected him to be used to it. A disadvantage of his training as a soldier of course; there would be little tradition of interrupting your commanding officer, as he stood on the top of a tank and told you the odds. Needs training, she thought, professionally; like all modern lawyers, she was herself trained to deliver presentations in order to sell more or less discreetly the services of the partnership. Repetitive in gesture and tone, she thought, disappointed, but then he looked so marvellous, who could mind? And, of course, as she knew, having now seen him do a small piece of a party political broadcast on behalf of the Conservative Party, he was at his best when speaking of an idea; there was much less scope in a description of the function of a clause having to do with the restructuring of British Rail's balance sheet.

'No, I will not give way,' he was saying, voice husky under the strain, and went on to finish, with obvious relief, a workmanlike speech. He glanced towards the civil-service box as he sat down, and she saw that Clive and his lot had gone, and had been replaced by another row of civil servants, doubtless belonging to Gerry's Department. She waited for a minute to see that he was not going to speak again and nudged Martin to move, following him, hunched practically double, to try to keep out of Gerry's sight-line, were he to look up.

'Come on, gents,' she said, briskly, as they emerged blinking into the light of day, past the long shuffling queue waiting to be admitted. 'Hamish is expecting us in about fifteen minutes. Are we ready to go? Graham, have you got the numbers?'

Graham confirmed that, with the NEB's full blessing,

he was carrying the key data that would be sent out to the other prospective purchasers.

'It's all in the car,' he said, as she looked inquiringly at his empty hands. 'Over there, waiting for us.'

They scrambled into the car putting Caroline in the middle of the back seat, dumping her coat and briefcase on her lap with the ease of friendship. This I am good at, she thought in a moment of detachment; I may be not much good at finding another husband, but I can get right into the centre of groups of men and bond with them quicker than any other professional I know – it is, I suppose, the sibling relationship translated. Now let's keep calm while this lot try their teeth again on another group of my sibling substitutes. As the car pulled away, she looked back, alerted by some instinct, to see the Friern contingent waiting for their car.

Andy Eames Lewis sank into the back of the Friern Rolls-Royce, next to Lucy, who had Matthew on her other side. The Rolls, which looked at first sight fairly ostentatious as a chairman's town runabout, made a good deal more sense when all 6 ft 4 ins and fifteen stone of Matthew was in it; the big car then seemed a perfectly ordinary size.

'We'll drop you off, Lucy,' he said, in tones brooking no argument, but she was ready for him. 'At Harvey Nichols, please, darling,' she said, prettily, and turned to Andy to ask after his children, while her husband lunged heavily towards the partition to instruct the driver to conduct a U-turn.

'Goodbye darlings,' she said twenty minutes later, taking it as her due as the driver, sweating, worked his way across two lines of traffic to drop her exactly where she wanted to be, and then wrestled the big car round to make for Friern's London office.

'Come in for a minute – I've got a few things to tell you.' Andy followed meekly, biting back any reference to the work waiting for him at his own office and trying to convey the impression of a man who had nothing else to do but to wait on this client. Matthew shouted at a secretary to produce tea, and shut the door firmly after her as she went out leaving a tray.

'Thank you for the introduction to Edwards,' he said, briskly, and Andy steadied his teacup.

'I hope he is being useful.'

'He's trying all right. Hasn't come up with all that much yet, but it's early days.'

Andy tried for an expression which combined courteous effort to please with an absolute absence of desire to hear more.

'None of the three top chaps at Prior has a mistress or any funny bank accounts – or none that we've found so far. Edwards' people are casting their net a bit wider.'

Andy stirred his tea assiduously, but found he had to look up after a bit, and was relieved to find that his client was gazing out of the window.

'I *know* it was Burwood who leaked the whole thing to the *FT*,' he said, to the window. 'I'll get him for it – bloody cheek.'

This ground had been gone over like something in the First World War over the last two weeks, Andy thought, wearily, and this time, surely, he need not comment. Matthew turned and looked at him and he found himself forced into speech. 'Well, Matt, it's possible of course, but we're never going to be able to prove it. And as you know it does seem more likely that it was someone in London.'

'One of the civil servants who didn't like the policy. I thought Fieldman was looking pretty pleased with himself today – you saw him, did you? In the choir stalls.'

Andy, who had not watched Clive at all, assented, wondering if he was ever going to get away, but to his relief Matthew moved on.

'Well, they're not going to get the company, I can tell you: we are.' He walked round his desk, stopping to rearrange a desk calendar and an ashtray. 'They'll wait a very long time for any negotiations on those old contracts for a start. That'll hobble the management. It's cash they won't have to play with. Matters to them far more than to us. Our borrowings are low enough that no bank is going to worry if we pay a bit over the odds.'

That was true, Andy acknowledged slowly. And it was comforting to find that his client was so confident that the extra £8m was not coming Prior's way or not while the company was under its current management. He just hoped Matthew was right.

'And they aren't going to get the next set of contracts for Marsh Lane, either.' Matthew was addressing the desk this time, as he hunted in the drawers and came up with a packet of cigarettes. 'And that's the biggie – they have to have it or there's a bloody great hole in their order book, year after next.'

'Are you still sure Friern is going to get them?' Andy asked, cautiously.

'Yes.' Matthew dragged on his cigarette, squaring his mouth at the corners to suck the smoke down into his lungs. 'Yes. We are. And we'll have them before the bids for Prior have to be in.'

Andy gazed fixedly at his cup, abandoning firmly all possible questions about why his client was quite so confident he was going to win these contracts? Better not inquire too closely, he told himself; Friern had been operating in the area a long time.

'And those bastards at Prior will fall on their bums trying to explain what they'll be doing to cover their overhead in the second and third year of whatever plan they're touting around.' Matthew was sounding particularly savage and Andy exerted himself to ask a neutral question.

'How much is Marsh Lane worth?'

'£200m, spread over two and a half years.'

'Yes, I see.'

That would be twenty-five per cent of Prior's turnover in each of three years and if they didn't get it, a very nasty hole indeed would appear in the forecasts. Prior wouldn't make much of a profit and certainly not enough to pay the heavy load of interest that a buy-out team would be carrying.

Matthew was giving every sign of a man who was going on to explain, and Andy threw himself into the breach.

'I wonder whether Caroline Whitehouse could have had anything to do with the *FT* article,' he said, at random, hoping only to distract and watched with relief as Matthew, totally sidetracked, considered the point.

'She's a lawyer,' he said, considering. 'Wouldn't put her client at risk.'

'She might, for the deal,' Andy said, happy to keep the argument going, but without any real conviction.

'It's a thought, isn't it?' Matthew's eyes, slightly crossed in concentration, were focused apparently on the door handle, as he hunched forward. 'She'd know the *FT* people too.'

Andy agreed, delighted to have found such a satisfactory diversion, and looked, just ostentatiously enough, at his watch. 'Matt, I'm so sorry but I do have to get back.'

'Of course.' Matthew had lost interest in him, he realized with relief, and he managed to get himself out of the office and into a taxi inside five minutes.

Over at Martins, the meeting had started badly. Hamish Brown had been delayed on his way back from the airport and by the time he came down, slightly out of breath, to fetch them from the bank's reception area, Peter Burwood was picking irritably at the window lining, while Martin Williams was speculating, aloud, on the laid cost of the parquet flooring. Graham Gough, as befitted a finance director, was deep in the notes to the accounts of the bank and, at the moment when Hamish opened the door, was observing, shocked, that no fewer than six of the banks' directors appeared to be earning in excess of £100,000 a year, or more than twice what any of the senior management of Prior Systems were making.

'Aye, well, that'll be the wee boys in corporate finance, not the hardworking lads in development capital,' Hamish said, imperturbably, with a sharp glance at Caroline who was gazing into space, conserving her energies.

'Hamish understands, of course, that your salaries have been artificially held down while the company has been in public ownership,' she said to her team, recovering sharply and rising to follow him through to a conference room. She settled herself firmly in the middle of the team, between Peter and Martin, leaving Graham next to Peter.

'Right, Hamish. The management team now have the formal consent of the NEB to hand you over last year's unaudited accounts, this quarter's management accounts and a forecast for the rest of this year and the next three. I should make it clear that the NEB and their advisers have seen these forecasts as have the DoE and their advisers. So we all start at the same place.'

She nodded to Graham who passed four bound copies across the table. Hamish passed two copies to the acolytes on each side of him, and fell on his own copy, totally concentrated. Figures spoke to him in a way that words did not, and he knew he would be faster to grasp the essence of this company than the young City-trained accountants at his side.

'Ye generate £20m in cash over the next three years, is that right?'

The young accountant, who was still looking at the profit line, blinked, but Graham was ready for him.

'That's right. And there may be some upside on that.'

'Right.' Hamish's head came up and he looked across at Peter. 'Where will it be coming from?'

Peter was looking disorientated and Caroline sighed. The trouble with dear Peter was that he did like things his own way, and he was both angry with Hamish for being late and unhappy at having the meeting run away from him. 'Hamish, I think it would perhaps be worth asking Peter and Graham to sketch out the background to these forecasts for us.' She scowled at Hamish, who was openly, expressively, impatient with this delay and he subsided, reluctant but resigned.

She gave him a swift consoling grin, and sat back,

working out the necessary steps to get herself home, turned round, and out again to meet Gerry at the flat for eight fifteen. She decided that she did need to wash her hair and she did have to find Susannah's games kit, and to remind Francis that he had left his football boots at school, and tell her housekeeper that the laundry went a day earlier this week. She surfaced in time to hear Peter winding down his speech, explaining to Hamish that the secret of his success lay in the efforts they made to involve and motivate employees at every level, which was interesting Hamish not at all.

'And of course,' she said, into a pause, 'thanks to Peter's efforts, all the chaps understand about the importance of keeping very tight control of cash.'

Hamish seized gratefully this efficient *non sequitur*. 'Ye'll not need me to tell you, Peter, that cash is what pays off loans, and finances interest, and in a leveraged deal it matters more than anything else. So any good news you have for us on that front is going to be a help.' He spread his hands, widely, and his audience looked back at him, thoughtfully.

Graham opened his mouth to speak, glanced sideways at Peter and decided to stay quiet.

'We expected to have some good news later this week, in the sense that we had expected to hear that the sums owing to us as a result of the contract negotiations had been agreed. The key meeting has been delayed, so we don't have that yet. But we do know what is being recommended: £4m in this year, £3m in year two, and £3m in year three. Or £10m more cash than we have allowed for in those forecasts.'

'Discounts to what . . . £8m.'

'£8.1m,' Graham agreed.

'But it's not agreed, ye say? The meeting's postponed?' Hamish's Glasgow accent was very distinct.

'The Chairman of the Housing Committee is ill,' Caroline said woodenly.

'What with?' Hamish asked. 'A go of the old trouble – knife sticking out the back?'

'Said to be heart,' Graham contributed.

'One way of putting it, I suppose. Convenient.'

'I don't see why it makes any difference,' Martin protested. 'It's the same for everyone surely – I mean none of us can count on that money.'

Hamish had returned to contemplation of the balance sheet. 'Depends on who's pulling his strings,' he pointed out. 'If it's Friern, he may get more cash out of them than you can. And he's the one who knows what's happening and when.' He looked across at Caroline to see if she had got the point and was unsurprised to find her stony-faced, her mouth set in a straight line. 'Old mate of yours, isn't he, Friern?' he said, helpfully, knowing the answer.

'No. Married to an old mate. He wouldn't hesitate to cross me.'

Hamish looked inquiringly at the management team, who were looking distinctly thoughtful. 'Do you have any friends of your own on the council then, Peter?'

'One or two.' Peter's pale skin had flushed under his red hair. 'But that's disorderly behaviour by the Council. We ought to expose it.'

'How?' Caroline asked sharply, alerted by 'disorderly'. 'What are we going to do, Peter – complain to the newspapers that this Williamson has had heart trouble deliberately to frustrate us? Lose the sympathy vote, that would.'

Peter glared at her. 'We need to make them hold that meeting.'

'Yes,' she agreed. 'That's the end to which we address our efforts. And we won't take up Hamish's time now, we'll think about it afterwards. What else do you want, Hamish?'

Hamish nodded to her, and gave his mind to the detail of the forecasts, working his way carefully through the central assumptions, with both acolytes taking copious notes. The team were acquitting themselves well, Caroline observed; they had thought out all the other assumptions very carefully and were not making the mistake of trying to oversell or to underestimate the possibility of error. They had taken an interest-rate half a point lower than the one she knew Hamish to be using, but their case was well argued and she could see him deciding that Martins were probably being over-conservative.

'Right, then, we've now got the wee assumption about the margin on future contracts,' Hamish was saying, jovially, and she stiffened. A cheerful Hamish deploying the diminutive 'wee' was a clear sign of danger.

'We're assuming a twenty per cent gross margin, because we don't take a contract under that,' Peter said, firmly.

'Not ever?'

'Well, not any more. *That* was what went wrong last time.'

'Aye, so it was. I wonder why your predecessors were so optimistic?'

'Only way they could get the work,' Martin contributed, surprised, and Caroline tried to preserve a professional deadpan. This had always been a tricky bit and she supposed it had better be aired now as later. She sat unmoving, as Martin woke up to the exact nature of the pit he had dug for himself.

'What happens to these forecasts if you can't get a contract at that margin?' One of Hamish's acolytes had leapt into the fray. 'Can you cut back your fixed costs?'

The answer to *that* question was almost certainly no, Caroline decided, on the basis both of general experience and a particular knowledge of Prior Systems' operation. The trouble with any business that started with a factory was that it could usually manufacture at a competitive price only if the factory was fully loaded or nearly so. If you were not prepared to reduce your margins, you might end up with your factory running at, say, two-thirds capacity, in which case all your costs would go sharply up, because you still had the building, the plant and most of the people. It was a bit easier on the sites; one could lay men off – the building trade always had done that – but you would not get your best gangs back when you needed them. And, like the factory, the site carried fixed costs, in craneage and site buildings and senior staff. She waited, unmoving, to see what her men were going to do with this.

Both Martin and Graham were watching Peter, unwilling to embark without him.

'We can only cut back to a limited extent,' he said, coolly. 'But the point is that we are now in a quite different position to what we were three years ago. We've got the systems working. We can get ten to fifteen per cent under any of our competitors and make our margin. And we've got a good name.' He paused and looked across at Hamish's unyielding face and the square-set way he was sitting, immovable as a brick wall. 'We build *better* than anyone in the north-east.

330

And that matters; people understand it. Ours is a better proposition – you get a building that doesn't need constant maintenance.' Nothing in Hamish's face or body stance had changed, Caroline observed.

'The Councillor Huggins building, which does not turn grey and streaky when it rains?' she suggested, helpfully.

'That's right,' Peter agreed, without taking his eyes off Hamish.

'Aye. Mebbe.' Hamish looked at a note. 'But what . . . twenty-five per cent of your turnover is in this contract here, Marsh Lane, in years two, three, four of the forecasts.'

'Oh, that one's ours,' Peter Burwood said, promptly. 'It's exactly the same structures as the Edgington site, only four times as many of them. We know how to do that; we can get twenty per cent under anyone for that contract. It's safe.'

Hamish made a note slowly, while the Prior team watched him impatiently and Caroline thought about Gerry. Then the meeting passed on. Two hours later it wore on to its close and the group straggled to the lift amid discussions of which of the cars was going where.

Caroline, tired by the day, edged near to Hamish. 'Nice to have a straight customer.'

'It's not a straight business, Caroline, as I told you, not with a local authority. Ye'll need to put a fix on yon Williamson.'

'You were right there. I'll work on it. In fact, I must get out of here, or I'll not get that done.'

She kissed her management team, but not Hamish, whom she ranked as a professional colleague, and raced off to get through the difficult routine necessary to get her in and out of the house in time to see Gerry. She found Timmy in trouble with his Latin prep and being slow and recalcitrant about finishing it, and started to snap at him, thereby reducing progress to zero.

'You're always cross these days, Mummy,' her beautiful Susannah said, reproachfully, and she looked, stricken, at the child.

'Nonsense,' she said, hardening her heart. 'Timmy is being slow, but I guess he's tired. Let's do it at breakfast, Tim, OK?' She bent to kiss the boy, who arched crossly away from her and she understood that he was making a typically male statement: if he didn't get enough attention he was going to play up until he did. Sorry everyone, she thought, looking into the sullen face, this I have to do, no matter what ill will I leave behind. She felt tears of resentment not far away, and fled to her bathroom leaving the housekeeper to feed the children.

She arrived at Gerry's flat just after eight and rang the bell; there was a delay while she wondered, panicking, whether she had the time wrong; then she heard footsteps and he opened the door to her.

'Sorry, I was on the phone.' He was looking tired, and ragged, but in charge as he always was, and he pulled her into his arms, pushing the door shut behind her. She clung to him, thankfully, and he held her. They had seen each other briefly, just once, and publicly, since they had spent the night together, and she breathed in the warm smell of him.

'I have *missed* you,' he said on an indrawn breath.

'You haven't had time to,' she said, sharply, rubbing her cheek against his.

'All the time in the world. I sit through meetings

thinking about you. Come through, come and have a drink and then we'll think what to do. I'm paired. I'm off the leash.'

'How did you do it?'

'I told the Whips I needed a night off to catch up with papers.' He fished in the fridge.

'Not being able to say you needed a night off to see me. What do the others say?'

He put down the bottle he had opened and pulled her over to him. 'Which others?'

'Do not other MPs have women who are not their wives?'

'Yes, of course. But mostly it's secretaries or people who work with them.'

'Would be.' Caroline took the offered drink, trying to speak lightly. It would of course be much easier and less risky for Gerry if she were on his staff, or in some way part of the peculiar club that was the House of Commons. She understood, abruptly, with a sinking feeling well below the heart, that the problems of this affair were even greater than she had realized; as an outsider she was inevitably conspicuous.

'I suppose I could be offering advice on new legislation,' she said, thoughtfully, and watched his profile.

'That is what I told the Chief Whip, in fact. He saw us together when we first had a drink and asked who you were.' He glanced at her. 'Well, you're much too beautiful to pass unnoticed, of course he wondered.'

'What would he have done had you replied that, yes, I was your mistress?'

Just for a second the mobile face went still, then he laughed. 'Oh well. Sat me down, bought me a drink, and made flattering noises about my prospects.'

'Told you to give up.' Caroline, wishing she had never started this conversation, found herself unable to stop.

'Or to be very, very careful.'

'Well, you are, aren't you?' she said, and fielded her glass just in time, as he turned restlessly to get himself another drink.

'Sorry. Tell me what you've been doing. How was your lunch? Do I need to be jealous of this Clive?'

She had eaten lunch with Clive Fieldman by himself earlier in the week, just to make sure that the Prior team was properly positioned in the Department's eyes as a promising suitor.

'It was fun. And no, you don't. My daughter fancies him, though.'

'The beautiful redhead? Tell me all about her.' He was of course that rare thing in a man, a good listener, more interested in what she had to say than in telling her about *his* week. Sad, she thought, that for once in her life she would have been entirely content to sit and listen to him, watching the lively, expressive face, throwing off tiredness now, the bright colour coming back. He arranged himself at the end of the uncomfortable sofa and pulled her towards him so she was lying against his chest. She ran out of things to tell him, and turned her head to kiss him. He squinted down at her, chin tucked in.

'We ought to eat.'

'I'm not terribly hungry,' she said, comfortably. 'What about you? I'll boil up or fry whatever's in the fridge, if we have to live off the land as usual.'

'It isn't quite as bad as that,' he protested. 'I bought eggs and bread and things.'

'Shall we go to bed first?'

'Women are so unromantic. Yes, absolutely.'

It was unfailing, she thought with pleasure, the sheer physical attraction between them; he seemed to her the perfect man for her as he took her bra off and bent to kiss her. They ended up as usual with clothes all over the small bedroom.

'Wait,' she said as he pushed inside her and he laughed and rolled them over so she was on top.

'Easier to wait this way,' he said. 'You tell me when. God, this is nice.'

She looked down at him with love, arms braced. 'Isn't it? I wish we had more time together.'

'So do I. I must organize. This life is intolerable – I am just rushed from place to place.'

'You like it,' she said, sharply, moving on him.

'I like this better.' He altered position, watching her face. 'If I just keep doing that?'

'Oh, yes . . .'

'*I*'ll make the tea this time.'

'No, I'll do it. In a minute.'

'I didn't want to move but I thought I ought to volunteer.' She was lying against his shoulder, contented and not at all sleepy, liking the feel of the muscles round his shoulder. 'I'm hungry now.'

'What, again?'

'For food, you cuckoo.' She stroked his cheek, noticing the deep lines round the eyes. 'I wonder if you'd be such a success if you weren't so good-looking?'

He smiled, pleased and unembarrassed, and she was both amused and apprehensive. She knew that smile, she had seen it on her friend Lucy, who felt entitled to every bit of the admiration and help her looks brought her.

'Come on then,' he said, briskly, throwing off the duvet. 'Let's get some food.'

That was his other charm for her, she thought, that they were so alike: he was as quick-moving and fast in reaction and as expressive as she. She started on supper with him setting a table beside her, working together as if they had done it half their lives.

'We would probably quarrel dreadfully,' he said, suddenly.

'I was thinking something like that,' she said, soberly. 'We are actually very like each other – we both push more into a day than will go.' She cracked eggs, carefully. 'And I cannot imagine a moment when we could have married, even if we had known each other before.'

'You wouldn't have liked being an army wife,' he agreed.

'I couldn't imagine it. And I'm not used to being towed at people's chariot wheels, as I'm sure your wife has always been.' She realized that he was looking wooden. 'This isn't a criticism; it's a comment.'

'I was thinking that one of the things I found so appallingly attractive about you is that you're always there or just ahead of me. Difficult to lead you.'

'We'd wear each other out,' she suggested, as lightly as she could, thinking horror-struck of the ineffable, unspeakable pleasure of being told, unequivocally, what to do, instead of making the many large and small lonely decisions that made up her life. She thrust the vision firmly from her.

'Perhaps,' he said, restlessly, opening the fridge.

She turned his omelette out. 'Bit overdone, sorry,' she

said, watching him wolf it. 'Did I ever tell you about the domestic bursar at my old college, who had been a soldier like you? I once managed to congratulate him on a college feast and he said, in a melancholy way, that congratulations were due not to him but the cook; he himself had never been interested in any food you could not eat out of a mess tin, standing up.'

Gerry swallowed his last mouthful, just, and burst out laughing. 'Oh, how I agree with the chap! One of us he must have been. Sorry, darling, I know I eat too fast. I'll make the coffee.'

He put the kettle on, standing beside her, and she leant her head against his side, letting her omelette cool, as he stroked her hair. The phone rang and she felt the shock go right through him. 'Don't answer it.' He waited, tense, as it went on, then stopped, then started again.

'I have to,' he said, and moved unhesitatingly to pick it up. 'Yes. No, that's all right. Oh Christ! How many casualties? No. I've got my own car here. I'll be in in ten minutes. Tell the PM you've found me. Yes.' He banged the phone down and turned to her, fizzing with nervous energy. 'Darling, I have to go. There's been a disaster – a tanker came off a bend on the M1 and caught fire, and they don't even know how many dead. I must get to the Department. David's in Portugal for a conference, so it's down to me.'

She looked at him, sick with disappointment. 'Of course you must,' she said, discipline reasserting itself. 'You get organized, I'll wash up.'

He disappeared and she bolted her omelette, not tasting it, and tidied up, leaving the dishes in the rack. He came back, moving like a dervish but quietly, not barging about as her own family would have done. He cast a comprehensive glance around the kitchen and was at her side, putting dishes and glasses away, removing any trace of a second person in the flat, she realized, painfully.

'OK?' he said. 'Got all your things?'

She nodded, unable to speak. You would have been safe in a war with this one, she thought, suppressing a desire to sit down and weep, not allowed to forget your socks or ammunition or anything else you needed.

He looked at her and saw her for the first time since the phone-call. 'I am sorry. God, I am sorry.'

'Can't be helped.' She put her coat on stolidly, he helping automatically with the sleeves, and she followed him out into his car. 'Drop me at your shop. I'll get a taxi.'

'I was going to drive you home.'

'Well, you can't, can you? I'll be OK.'

He shut her door for her and got into the driver's seat, and she leant back stifling tears.

'I heard you in the House today,' she said, when she had control of her voice. 'I went to hear Winstanley's statement.'

'God, that seems like last week.' He was flinging the car round corners, watching his speed.

'To me too. Did you organize that chap to ask the questions about a buy-out?'

He hesitated, momentarily, and she wished she hadn't asked; the *FT* article had never been mentioned between them and it might have been better to play this the same way. 'Yes. I couldn't do it myself, you see.'

'So I suddenly understood. We were all most grateful.'

'Don't look like that. I don't want to do this either.' She

338

was unable to reply but managed to touch him in acknowledgement. 'I like your chaps, I think they'd run the business well. And a successful privatization with lots of employee shareholders would do us a lot of good up there.'

'And help you in your constituency.'

'That too. Darling, we're there. Will you be all right if I drop you on the corner?' He hesitated, then leant over and kissed her on the cheek. 'I'll ring you. Later tonight, if I can.'

She watched the tail lights vanish through the gates, then leant momentarily against a lamppost, blind with tears, shivering in the wind. She saw a taxi and flagged it, too miserable to care that the driver took one look at her and refrained from addressing a single word to her all the way home. She paid him, counting out change, holding herself in against the moment when she could get to her own bed and cry.

'Thanks, Mrs Whitehouse,' she heard him say, and she looked up, startled.

'I'm sorry, I didn't recognize you.'

'It's a cold night.'

'That must be it,' she said, steadily and managed a smile, feeling his eyes on her back as she turned for her door and found her keys. Seeing him waiting to see her in, she waved, warmed by the small human gesture.

'There's been a crash on the M1.' The young housekeeper, a bright, plump girl from Lancashire, sounded pleasurably excited and Caroline took a long, deep breath, and pulled her shoulders back. 'Oh dear, where?'

'Just south of Birmingham. It's on the news.'

Caroline stood at the door of the living-room, taking in the comfortable scene. Jean and her friend Sheila had been companionably eating chocolates, and papers and sewing were spread all over the big sofa. Then, suddenly, Gerry was on the screen looking serious and tired, saying that it was obviously a disaster, no, he could not confirm any reports, he was just now going to be briefed by his officials. Nothing about him, she thought incredulously, would have told anyone that less than an hour ago he had been half dressed, laughing with her in his own kitchen. His short dark hair was tidy, all the buttons on his shirt were done up and his tie was straight while her clothes, as she became sharply aware, had been thrown on anyhow. She watched, chilled to the bone, as he dealt seriously and courteously with inquiries before turning away into a group of anxious and untidy-looking men.

'He's so good-looking,' Jean said, admiringly.

'Isn't he,' Caroline said, discarding the momentary insane impulse to confide in her. 'I must go to bed. I came home a bit early, because I'm feeling rotten – no, don't get up, I'll make a cuppa for myself.'

16

By the third week of March the weather had reverted to something more suitable for midwinter. Clive Fieldman stared out of the windows of Winstanley's outer office, watching a snow flurry batter dispiritingly at the towers.

'Would you like to go in?'

He nodded to the young assistant private secretary, collected James Mather and walked into Winstanley's office.

'I thought we'd have a word before I get the Fredericks people to come in. Given that we now have so many inquiries for Prior Systems, ought I really to see the management team?'

Clive had suggested to Caroline that the management team might like to make their number with Winstanley, moved to this by the feeling that it was only fair that they should have the same opportunity as Matthew Friern, or various other interested parties who had surfaced. Three days later he had found a crisply drafted three-paragraph letter to the Secretary of State, signed by Peter Burwood, on his desk for advice. He had laughed to himself; the hand might be that of Peter Burwood, but the voice was that of Caroline Whitehouse, and he had advised, amused, that Winstanley should see the team.

'Yes, Minister. It gives you an opportunity to say all the necessary things to them, so that they know they aren't getting any favours. I think it's extremely useful for you to see them.'

'Right.' Winstanley, endearingly, knew how to stop

agonizing over decisions. 'Should I have Fredericks with me for that meeting?'

'Yes, you should.'

'Well, remind me to tell them they'll be wanted. Jenny, go and get Mr Watts, will you, he's in the waiting-room.' He watched her out of the door. 'On what we're paying these chaps I don't like to keep them hanging around. Will your friend Mrs Whitehouse be coming in with the Prior lot?'

'I imagine so, Minister. She is masterminding their campaign. The letter asking for the meeting is very much in her style.'

'Of course, you are old colleagues,' Winstanley said, with a sidelong look, but Clive stood his ground. 'That's one of the reasons it is useful that you should see them, Minister. So that they hear the ground rules from you personally, in case I have not managed to lay them down with sufficient force.'

'I can't quite imagine you being unable to make yourself clear, Clive, but it's always difficult with old mates. Ah, come in, Richard, Tim.' He rose punctiliously to greet his merchant-bank advisers, both of whom were looking haggard. 'I gather you are just off a plane – good of you to come.'

Richard Watts was heard to indicate that at the moment he always went to New York on Sunday night and returned on Wednesday – tiresome but a very inter-esting deal, Minister. They did work hard, these over-paid smoothies, Clive conceded, grudgingly.

'The memoranda of sale on Carr and SLG went out yesterday, Minister, about 70 on Carr and 40 on SLG. All the usual suspects applied, apparently, and the NEB are hopeful of two quick sales there.'

'Mm. What about Prior?'

'We have had thirty-five requests for the memoranda, Minister. Twenty are from banks allegedly on behalf of clients. Some of these will be real clients, others will be seeking copies for their libraries. Five are from overseas banks. The remaining ten are from construction companies, eight UK based, one in France, one in Germany.'

'I don't want Prior to go to a foreign buyer,' Winstanley said, alarmed. 'I've had enough flack over this sale as it is.'

'Cross that one when we come to it, Minister?' Clive suggested. 'These are of course our EEC partners.'

'The French would find a way of stopping any of our companies buying one of theirs. So would the bloody Germans,' Winstanley snapped.

Richard Watts looked professionally blank while Clive found a formula to suggest that if push came to shove the Department and Fredericks between them could be fully as obstructionist as any foreign government.

'Well, anyway, Minister.' Richard Watts sensibly decided to plough on. 'All the inquirers have three weeks to say who they are and indicate a target price, plans for the company and their attitude to the key aspects of this sale – continuity of local employment, participation by management and employees, and so on. At the end of that Gruhners draw up a short list for discussion. The management team, of course, have also put themselves forward.'

'They're coming to see me. I'll need you there.'

'Yes, of course, Minister.'

Winstanley considered his advisers. 'Any surprises on the list, Richard?'

'Waltons have surprised us by being apparently very keen to bid. They've been lobbying Gruhners and the NEB. It's not really their sort of building. It would be a departure for them.'

'Well, they're a very large and respectable outfit, aren't they?'

'Large, certainly.' Not a Fredericks client, Clive thought. He caught sight of the clock and winced; he had an hour to clear his desk and get over to lunch with Lucy. She had made it clear that she only had just over an hour, and he longed to see her. Matthew had been in London almost continuously for the last three weeks and the only free evening Lucy had found had been the evening on which he, like Matthew, was committed to attending the Housebuilding Federation's annual dinner, so he had spent the evening with the wrong Friern.

Winstanley, who was both uneasy and fed-up with the sale, was pressing Fredericks for an opinion which Richard Watts was sensibly declining to offer, reminding him gently that in three weeks' time, when everyone's intentions had been to some extent probed, all would be much clearer. Winstanley, not at all a stupid minister, as Clive reflected, gratefully, let them go after another few minutes, recognizing aloud that he was engaged in an exercise equivalent to extracting sustenance from a blade of grass.

Clive got back to his office to find that the principal establishment officer was on the phone. 'Clive? You've started something, you know. I put yours and Philip's report on Watson up to the Secretary and it came back inside twenty-four hours saying, Yes, get on with it, operate limited efficiency procedure asap all in that minuscule handwriting, so that as per usual I had to get the magnifying glass out to check what it was he wanted. And two hours after that he rang me himself to say that he thinks I should put out a minute reminding all under-secretaries that the limited efficiency procedure exists. Not *quite* as simple as that, you understand; I am to wrap this statement up in an *aide-mémoire* on annual reporting.'

'Really? Crumbs.'

'It would, of course, be entirely cynical to make any connection between this and our masters' wish to cut ten per cent of all administrative grade staff.'

'Fair enough, though. Better to cut out the duff ones.'

'Indeed so. I am only a little taken aback, dear boy, because, as you well know, the usual practice has been to encourage our best and most useful people to take jobs in the private sector at double the money. Cutting out the duff ones, as you so gracefully put it, is a whole new concept for us.'

It'll be standard practice when I get to be Permanent Secretary, Clive thought, grittily. 'So we may actually be going to get rid of Watson fairly quickly?'

'Oh, I wouldn't put it as highly as *that*. But the procedure may take months rather than years if the Secretary maintains his present stance. He has said that he will see Watson himself, by the way, which is really an unexpectedly useful contribution.'

'Marvellous. Well, you can start finding me a replacement, right now. I'll tell you who I want.'

'No, you won't. You have two first-class assistant secretaries in James Mather and Janice O'Brien, and you'll get what I have as your number three. That is, if we don't decide to eliminate Watson's post altogether as part of the ten per cent savings required of us.'

Clive opened his mouth to speak, then decided to take it slowly. 'I'd be glad to be able to say that, given an extra principal, I could just load Watson's job on the other two assistant secretaries,' he said, carefully. 'They are very able, as you suggest. The trouble is that this division covers a policy area in which the PM is said to be personally interested – indeed, that was the main reason why I didn't feel it safe to try to soldier on with Watson.' He raised his eyes to heaven, hoping that lightning was not going to strike him now.

'Very nice, Clive,' the telephone said, appreciatively. 'I like that. I was having you on, as the children say. You *shall* go to the ball. Watson will be replaced. But you just let us find you someone, hm?'

'Sir.'

'*That*'s better.'

Clive left his office, still grinning, at a run and took a taxi from under the nose of a fellow under-secretary to arrive only two minutes late at the Friern flat. He would willingly have skipped lunch in favour of taking Lucy to bed, but realized that this was not on the programme. She was immaculately dressed and made-up on the basis that she was going to a fashion show, and lunch was laid for the two of them in the dining-room rather than in the kitchen.

'I could have bought you lunch at Harrods,' he said, apologetically, still shivering slightly from the snow-storm outside.

'No, darling, it's such awful weather.' She kissed him, warmly and he held her, feeling suddenly much, much better. 'I'm sorry I'm in a rush, but I am. Tell me what's going on.' She handed him a glass of wine and poured him some soup.

'I've just come from seeing Winstanley and the bankers. We've got over thirty lots of people wanting the particulars of Prior Systems, not counting the management team. Matt is one of them, of course.'

'I'm sick and tired of that company. Matt's very keen, you know – he means to see Caroline's lot off. It's jolly awkward for me, I must say. He's furious about the management bid.' She finished her soup and removed both their plates, and returned with a soufflé carefully wrapped in a towel. She divided it neatly between them and he ate it hungrily; he had got to the office at seven o'clock that morning to catch up on various bits of work which were not getting done on Michael Watson's side. It would be foolishly optimistic to expect serious attention to the job from a man under imminent threat of classification as limitedly efficient.

'Actually, I haven't dared tell Matt I'm having lunch with you, darling. He's off you; he thinks you're fraternizing with the enemy, because you lunch with Caroline.' She caught his eye. 'I'm afraid I told him you'd had lunch with the family too.'

'Much better not to conceal that sort of thing. Caro doesn't get any special favours from me, any more than you do for Friern. She is coming in to see Winstanley, with her lads, but that's in the normal course of business. He'd always see the management team in these circumstances.'

'But you advised it?'

'Well, yes.'

'You always fancied Caro, didn't you?'

He stopped in mid-mouthful and blinked at her, then swallowed.

'Lucy. What is this? I always fancied *you* more. And it's you I go to bed with. When you have time.'

He realized that the proviso would have been better left unsaid; it sounded both accusing and bitter, and Lucy stiffened. 'I am married, after all. You know that.'

'Of course I do. If I thought there was any chance – look, for God's sake, you know I'd marry you if you wanted to divorce Matt. But you don't, do you?'

She scowled, distorting the admirable features, plainly in a mood to quarrel, but aware that she wasn't on the right ground.

'Well, you could marry Caro.'

He decided the best course was to try to distract her. 'Caro's got a chap. I rather think *he*'s married, but she isn't interested in anyone else. You should have seen her when he rang up; she grew a couple of inches and started to put out sparks.' He felt mildly disloyal but realized that he had succeeded admirably in persuading his love out of her unexplained bad temper; she was sitting up, bright-eyed.

'She *hasn't*. She never told me – she always gives me the impression she lives like a nun.'

'She didn't actually tell me either – I was just there when a phone call came through.'

'How do you know he's married?'

'Well, he'd have been at Sunday lunch, wouldn't he, instead of me? And Caspar, her brother – you must know him – was looking very disapproving.'

'*Caz* can't talk. He went off with a Labour MP's wife – and there was a frightful row and a stand-up fight in the Hampstead headquarters. Caro told me all about it, very censoriously. Then the girl left Caz and went back to her husband.'

'Well, that's maybe why he was disapproving. Because it ended in tears for him.' He watched Lucy hungrily, noticing small details that had escaped him when he first arrived. She was wearing a very bright red lipstick which he disliked, feeling it detracted from her classic, dark blue eyes and black hair, her nails were immaculate and she was wearing higher heels than usual. He pulled his chair closer to hers and put a hand on her knee, pushing up her skirt.

'Go on telling me about Caroline's man,' she said, pushing his hand away and getting up to fetch coffee.

'That's all I know. And that's mostly guesswork. But I was sure he was married and that he came back from somewhere on a Sunday night, but not always, since she hadn't been certain to expect him. Bit like me with you.'

She was putting coffee in the jug and he watched her back stiffen.

'I've often thought it can't be that much fun for you,' she said, distantly, and the sense of discomfort he had felt all morning intensified.

'I love you, you know,' he said, moving to stand behind her and put his arms around her, sniffing uneasily at a new perfume, one he did not recognize, rather than the familiar Diorissimo.

'Don't, Clive, you'll make me drop the cups.'

He moved his hands, offended, and stood back. She turned, carrying a small tray, not meeting his eyes, and his nerve ends prickled.

'What's the matter, Lu?'

'Nothing. I'm just a bit tired.'

'Of me?'

'I don't know. I'm just in a muddle.' She sank elegantly into a chair on the other side of the table, well out of his reach, and he watched her, utterly dismayed.

'What's happened? Have you got someone else? We always promised we'd tell each other if that happened.'

'No, it's not that. Look, Clive, I think I'd like not to see each other for a bit, just till I can work out what I want.'

'Is it Matthew? Is he really suspicious?'

'No.'

'You *can't* be jealous of Caro?'

She hesitated, then met his eyes. 'No, I'm not. We've never fancied the same men and they've never fancied us. And I bet you she's in love with someone *impossible* – you should have seen the ghastly actor she had before Ben.'

'What happened to him?' Clive asked, willing to be diverted from an increasingly painful conversation.

'He's directing plays for children's TV. When he's not being dried out. I know his wife.' She looked at him in appeal and he stared helplessly back.

'I must go to this thing. Look, ring me tomorrow, Clive. Please.' There was no mistaking the note of appeal and he held her in his arms.

'Tell you what,' he said in her ear. 'You need a break; all this Prior stuff is too much. Let's go away for a couple of nights – I'll fix it. We could stay at the Garden House – you could be with your mate who teaches at St Hilda's.'

He held her, anxiously, then felt her relax. 'Yes, I could. Let's do that. Sorry, you're probably right, it's just too much Prior. I can't tell you how bloody Matt is being, always on the phone, or out fixing things up. I wish he'd never heard of that company.'

He should take her straight to bed, he thought, irreso-lute, but he was running out of time before his three-thirty meeting, and she was combing her hair, ready to go out. He would put the time into clearing his desk, so he could take a couple of days' leave and take her to the hotel, twenty miles from Oxford, which she had liked so much. All they needed was some time together in a place of his choosing rather than hers, and it would be all right again.

They left the flat together and he put her into a taxi. He was standing looking for a second taxi for himself, when he saw Caspar Henriques standing at a bus stop, head bent over a newspaper. He hesitated, and Caz, drawn by some telepathic transmission, looked up and saw him.

'Clive,' he said, sounding endearingly pleased, folding his newspaper and stuffing it into the pocket of his fashionable leather jacket, 'just the man I wanted to see. I told Caro to ask you, but she's a bit scatty these days – very busy, of course. I'm doing Sunday lunch on the first Sunday in May – not in my own flat, which is tiny, but in the parents' house. You've been there surely? Caro's coming and she did say she'd ask you. What are you doing in these parts?'

'I'd love to come,' Clive said, firmly ignoring the last question. He fished out his diary. 'I've got the kids, though, since I shan't have them for Easter. What can I bring?'

'Some booze,' Caz said, promptly. 'That would be very nice. About twelve thirty? Tremendous. There's my bus.'

Michael Watson was sitting at a corner table in the pub across the road from the Department, trying to get himself together and go back for the afternoon. He had treated himself to a proper lunch, steak and three vegetables, to anchor the bottle he had known he was going to get through. He was supposed to be taking a meeting in half an hour, but he had taken the precaution of telling the principal that it was possible he would be back late from lunch and that she should start if he had not arrived. He didn't want to go back to the Department; he didn't want to go home to his cheerless flat; in fact, he could not think of a single thing he did want to do. He stared drearily out at the snow flurries and decided that he would have a quiet brandy and finish the crossword, then see how he felt. He walked a little unsteadily to the bar, heaved himself on to a stool and nodded carefully to the nondescript man further down the bar who was watching him.

'Afternoon,' the stranger said, courteously. 'Beastly day, isn't it? I can't quite face going out in it either.'

Michael Watson, who felt that no one had spoken a kind word to him for several years, looked across at a man a little older than himself, but grey-haired and undemanding, not one of the bustling, decisive, rude young men who surrounded him at the Department.

'I was going to have a brandy to keep the cold out,' he said, hopefully.

'What a good idea. I'll do that too.' The stranger peered at his newspaper. 'Did you get thirteen down, if I may ask?'

Watson turned over the page and checked it. 'RECESSION,' he said.

'Oh, of course. Wonderful; that means I can finish later. Look, let *me* get you that brandy – I was absolutely stuck.'

They took their drinks over to a corner table, and

Michael Watson, with the residue of the caution engendered by nearly forty years in the civil service, asked his new acquaintance what he did.

'I've just retired,' the man said, apologetically. 'I'm still coming in three mornings a week to the office – it's an insurance agency – in the Horseferry Road. This is one of the mornings. Where do you work? Oh, for the DoE? But that must be very interesting.'

Watson, gratified, told him wherein it was interesting, enlarging his own contribution to the point where a detached observer would have found it difficult to decide what had been left for successive Secretaries of State for the Environment to do with their time, but his new friend was gently encouraging.

'I envy you,' the man said. 'I thought I was going to like being retired, but I don't. You don't go for a bit, I assume?'

'Well,' Michael Watson, his sore heart eased by the first sympathetic person he had seen for weeks, hesitated. 'Well, there is pressure to get rid of some of us old hands early – it's the Government, you know, testing their virility.' He had heard the permanent secretary, normally the soul of discretion, use this phrase in exasperation at recent cuts in the housing programmes.

'Oh, that's very bad luck.' The man hesitated and glanced towards the bar. 'Have you time for another?'

'I'll get them,' Watson said, punctiliously, and swayed as he tried to rise, but his new friend had managed to get two more brandies by lifting his hand.

'Is your part of the Department likely to be involved?' the man asked, carefully, when the barman had gone.

'Yes, it looks like it.' He felt a dreadful, tired relief at being able to acknowledge that this awful thing was

353

actually going to happen. 'I'm one of the old hands. I'll get an early pension, of course; they have to bribe us to go. But still, it hurts, you know, I've been in for thirty-six – no, I tell a lie – thirty-seven years, and a new government comes along and suddenly your face has to fit or you're out.'

'Which bit of the DoE are you in?'

'Housing division. I'm an assistant secretary there.'

'That's pretty senior, isn't it?'

'Yes, and I started as a clerical officer, in the old Board of Trade, not even with A-levels, never mind a degree.'

'That's impressive.'

The bell rang for time, and Michael Watson looked round, blearily. 'I ought to go back.'

'Must be very hard to go on when you can see that things you mind about are going wrong.'

Watson looked at him with gratitude. 'It is.'

The stranger rose without haste and nodded to the barman.

'Tomorrow's another day when I'm in for the morning. I usually eat lunch here about one – it's convenient. Perhaps I'll see you then? I'm very much obliged for the help with the crossword. Look at that!' He steadied Watson, tactfully, looking out at the driving snow flurries, and they left together, Watson greying and nondescript, plunging across the road to the towers, heedless of traffic, huddled into his raincoat, feeling happier than he had been for weeks. The stranger, equally unmemorable, small, and balding, watched him across the road, then turned left for the Horseferry Road.

17

'Right, Peter, I agree we have a problem.' Caroline stopped, conscious that she was being abrupt and impatient, but the day seemed to have been going on for hours, although it was only ten o'clock in the morning. She and Mark Dwyer were having a preliminary meeting with the Prior team before they advanced on Hamish Brown again. Another morning gone.

She seemed to have lived and breathed Prior Systems since the statement. The team were going to get a nasty shock when they saw her interim bill; she scowled at her blotter, remembering that it should have been sent last week. She made a note, mentally shaking her head; it was second nature to any partner to make sure they sent regular bills, particularly for the sort of time she was logging up. What was the matter with her? Well, the answer to *that* question was obvious; Gerry Willshaw was, and no one else must be allowed to guess. He had been massively occupied with the aftermath of the crash, and it seemed to her that she could not switch on her television set without seeing him, concerned and driving, pushing the crash investigation on, surrounded by victims' families, being interviewed everywhere. She had seen him just once, for a couple of hours in the last three weeks, and was missing him painfully. She realized that Martin was speaking, trying to ease the generally fractious atmosphere.

'It is a bit difficult to deal with. Williamson is chairman of that committee, and the latest news is that he should be back in two weeks' time. But that was what they said two weeks ago. And there is a lot going on behind the scenes – people lobbying against our getting anything on those contracts.'

'It is difficult,' Caroline agreed, trying to make amends. 'I don't know what to do either.' She met squarely three reproachful expressions. 'I don't have many bent councillors among my clients, gentlemen – sorry. What would you do? I mean if I weren't here, and we weren't doing a buy-out.'

'Have a word with the local paper,' Peter said, promptly. 'They're always happy to print stuff about council corruption.'

'Mm.' Caroline sounded doubtful.

'Have a word with someone else on the council,' Martin, older and more patient than either of them, suggested, hastily.

'Like who?' Caroline concentrated on him.

'There's a largish Conservative minority in Dorrington. Strong enough to give the ruling group a bit of trouble. They had to withdraw that road scheme last year, remember, Peter? That chap Malvern. Hang on, hang on, he's very close to Gerry Willshaw. It's all coming back to me. Willshaw was involved in getting the scheme recalled.'

Everyone looked hopefully at Caroline, who poured herself some more coffee, looking professionally deadpan. 'Mm,' she said, looking up to find them all still watching her, and realized that some response was required.

'I could ask him, I suppose,' Peter said, when he could see she had made her contribution. 'I mean he came round the sites.'

'Is it absolutely necessary to go through him? I mean, could you ask this Malvern directly, yourself?' She looked back at them. 'I have this feeling that we ought to keep our big guns in reserve.' She watched with relief as the three men round her slowly nodded in agreement; nothing, she knew in her bones, would more surely undermine her affair with Gerry or, for that matter, his support for this buy-out than asking him to do something that might be difficult.

'I slightly know Malvern,' Martin volunteered. 'I'm active in the constituency next door. I can certainly talk to him.'

'Don't go in too heavy,' Caroline advised briskly. 'Just tell him your worst fears, wondering gently whether you are not being paranoid, then ask him what he would do.'

'I thought of doing something along those lines,' Martin said gently, and she realized that her relief at having deflected them from Gerry was blurring her judgement. 'Sorry, Martin, sorry. Suck eggs? Here's how you do it, Granny.' She touched his hand, apologetically, and he burst out laughing, pleased with her.

'We've got another problem,' Peter said, obsessively frowning at them both. 'We talked to the NEB this morning and the sale memorandum has gone to twenty-eight lots of people.'

'Not to be worrying, Peter,' Caroline said firmly. 'Really not to worry about that one. Every bank in the City will have asked for one for reference. Most of those inquiries won't be for real.'

Things which could have been better put, Mark Dwyer thought, delighted, as he watched Peter's face.

'By that I mean that they will be from or on behalf of

groups who are too small, too broke, or too far removed from your business to be able to offer for Prior.' Caroline had also seen Peter's expression and she distracted them by pointing out that they had to leave now, and they arrived without further incident at the vast modern block that housed Hamish Brown and his team.

They were shown up immediately, into a conference room rather than into Hamish's office, where they had met before.

'Serious stuff,' Caroline said, dumping her briefcase on the nearest chair. 'Means that Hamish has got a full team on. Probably not just number crunchers either; brace yourselves, gentlemen. Let's huddle together here, with our backs to the light. Mark next to me.'

'Where do you want me to be?' Peter asked, mildly offended.

'Right in the middle of course. Put Graham next to you, and you'd better have me on your other side. We're into the nitty-gritty this afternoon.'

The door opened to admit Hamish Brown, jovial and friendly, followed by a small army of grey-suited men. He surged across the room to greet Peter, and Caroline watched, interested by the total contrast in type being presented to her: Hamish the dark, plump, comfortable, infinitely crafty Gael, and Peter, the thin, light, finely drawn, red-headed, fiery Viking. She pulled herself together to concentrate on the rest of the cast: three of Hamish's acolytes, all Scots, accents ranging from Glasgow to Aberdeen – and she really must this time sort out who was called what; two older men, holding themselves a little distant from the party. There was also one familiar face, Peter Cairns the partner in Andrews Johnston, who had interrupted her first lunch with Gerry, and last but far more important than the rest, a tall, bulky, grey-haired man, waiting patiently at the back of the queue. His eyes met hers, and he edged round towards her, as she took Peter firmly by the hand.

'Very nice to see you again. I understand we have you to thank for this introduction.'

'William, this is Peter Burwood. Mr Burwood, Sir William Eyre. As I'm sure you know, Peter, Sir William is Chairman of Martins. I take it you're not staying for the meeting, William?'

'Other duties call, alas. But I did want to come and meet the management team. We're very glad to be involved; it's a most exciting opportunity.'

The Prior team, not quite sure how to respond, murmured various civilities under Caroline's minatory eye, and Sir William took himself away after a further five minutes.

'Is he always polite to management?' Martin asked Caroline, *sotto voce*.

'Yes. Or he is at this stage,' she said, grinning broadly. She glanced around to see where everyone was placed and drew the team together by the window. 'The fact that they fielded him at all tells us Hamish has decided to go all the way with you. Doesn't mean he won't fight every detail, but he's on.'

'So he bloody should be,' Peter said, belligerently.

'Yes. But it's nice to know he is. Right. They'll want to take the price of the deal first, then management share. They'll be bidding low, like I said. Not to get cross. Follow the plan. Here we go.'

Everyone sat down and from that position solemnly introduced themselves, Caroline professionally drawing a sketch plan which she passed over to Peter.

'Why have they got other lawyers here?' he asked, quietly, putting his thumb on Peter Cairns' name.

'He acts for Hamish's lot. He is here to make sure I'm not ripping them off. I'm on your side, remember.'

'Do they pay them?'

'No. We do, directly or indirectly. Wait. This, too, will be discussed today. The other two are their industrial advisers – chaps who know the trade.' She looked across the wide table to where Hamish's side were arranging their papers, blinking in the sun.

'We've had the opportunity to do a good deal of work, both on the company and the industry,' Hamish said, pleasantly, spreading his hands wide in front of him. 'And, of course, to talk with your good selves about the company's prospects. And very fair prospects they are. Aye. But there are also some quite serious downside risks: ye have a dominant customer in Dorrington council and sustained, difficult competition for that customer's business. All this reduces the prices ye can expect. I know ye have plans to expand your work for other customers, but this will take time. I'd like ye in this context to hear what Andrew and Michael have to say about the industry.'

Peter shifted in his seat, lips compressed, the colour coming up in his pale skin and Caroline pressed her knee against his, in warning. 'Let them wear themselves out,' she said, lips hardly moving, and he nodded, relaxing, and sat in imitation of her, gazing unsmiling across the table as the two industry experts, using flip charts and coloured crayons, described trends in interest rates, orders, population.

'So that's the way we see it,' Hamish said, with undiminished heartiness, a quarter of an hour later. 'Nice company, excellent management, but a difficult industry and in your particular situation a limited customer base which must necessarily restrict the margin ye can hope for on future work.'

He says 'wukk' with no 'r' in it – why have I never noticed, Caroline thought, preparing herself for battle, as Peter went into action smoothly, with a gathered and coherent response, instancing the big contract they had for a council a hundred miles away, and reminding them of the huge reduction in costs they had achieved. He ran down after ten minutes and glanced at Caroline.

'Where does all this leave you on price, Hamish?' she asked, and the other side of the table sat up.

'We'll come to that in a wee while,' Hamish was just perceptibly flustered, but she was adamant.

'Riveting though this discussion has been, Hamish, it has not left us the opportunity to tell you that some twenty-eight groups have received the outline memorandum of sale, as of this morning. Of these, some eight or nine, in management's judgement, are for real.'

Management, who had not considered the components of the list in detail, tried not to register anything other than complete conviction.

'We know also – and this I did pass on yesterday, Hamish, to one of your staff – that Friern have offered £65m informally. We have no reason to suppose that they are in the business of exaggerating the company's prospects. So I hope all this,' a flick of the left hand dismissed a fifteen-minute presentation, 'does not mean that you are much below £65m on price.'

'Aye, we are.' Hamish, thrown out of stride, came back fast.

'Where are you then?'

Hamish took a deep breath, and consulted a piece of paper, Caroline and the team watching him like a pack of cats at a mousehole. 'We feel a range of £45–£50m is the right one.'

Peter turned slowly scarlet, while Caroline sighed. 'Wouldn't it be nice? Dead easy to finance; we'd all make a bloody fortune. The only problem is, Hamish, we won't even be in the running. We'll be taken out by Friern straight away.'

'It's bloody ridiculous. If that's what you people think, we'll need to talk to someone else.' Peter could contain himself no longer.

'Well, of course we will, Peter,' Caroline said, reassuringly. 'But look, we're all here, we may as well spend five minutes finding out why Hamish, who after all has done deals before, thinks we can get this one at anything up to twenty per cent less than anyone else will pay.'

The four of them swung in unison to face the other side of the table, with expressions of pleasant academic inquiry, and a senior acolyte took over the bowling.

'We assumed, Caroline, that there were special political factors that would enable your group to get this company at a sensible price.'

McMaster, McAndrew, McMurray? she wondered, squinting at her plan.

'So there are, Iain,' she said, cheerfully. 'Like I've always said, the political advantages of Peter and his team should enable us to do a deferred deal, and should save us maybe £10m in cash up front. But, to get that, we have to yield some of the upside potential – we have to agree to share any windfall profits. *And* our bid on a deferred basis has to look as if it is a very close-run thing. And £45m–£50m just is not close enough.'

'So the political advantages aren't really worth all that much?' Iain McMurray suggested, clearly feeling he had scored.

'I don't know how your development capital people value up to £10m deferred, of course,' Caroline said sharply. 'Assuming a price of £55m plus £10m deferred, and that we manage a flotation on a not very demanding price/earnings ratio of seven in three years, your internal rate of return would be over 100 per cent.'

'110 per cent on our assumptions,' put in Graham.

'Seems worth it to me,' Peter said, grittily. 'I read that most development capital houses look for forty per cent a year and are lucky to make twenty per cent.'

The other side of the table considered him in a silence thick enough to cut. Peter Cairns had his head down – working on another case, Caroline decided from long experience – but Prior had the full attention of the industrial advisers and Hamish's internal team.

'Ye'll have made some demanding assumptions about gearing, nae doubt?' Hamish said, reluctantly, breaking the silence.

'Not particularly,' Caroline said, briskly. 'We have, as you suggested, postulated a likely structure for NewCo – the vehicle for the purchase. Graham will pass it round.' She smiled across Peter at Graham, who proceeded to distribute the small pile of papers in front of him. The Martins side fell on them.

'There's something very familiar about this structure, Caroline,' Hamish said, heavily, five minutes later.

'It does draw on our recent, joint experience, yes, Hamish. No point in working with leading development capital firms if you do not use that expertise.'

'In the case we're both thinking of, Caroline, we'd

more confidence in both cash and profit margin projections,' Hamish objected. 'That company had multiple customers and no doubtful bits in their cash projections.'

'That is presumably why you valued that group on a much higher price/earnings ratio than anyone is considering for this company.'

Hamish grunted and the senior acolyte, McMurray, came to the rescue. 'Aye, well, there's no point discussing a different company with which many of us are not familiar. But, Peter, do you not feel the debt/equity ratio is too demanding?'

Peter – briefed by Caroline that any concession at this stage on the amount the company planned to borrow meant yielding a point or so of the management equity – responded smoothly, reciting the likely upside in the forecast and reiterating his confidence in the cash coming from the contract renegotiation, occasionally calling on Graham for supporting figures. An hour later, the position was much the same but the smoke had cleared from the battle lines. Martins had tacitly conceded that they might have to bid £55m plus £10m deferred and were dug in trying to reduce the proposed bank borrowing by ten per cent, to get the amount of equity available for management and employees from twenty per cent down to fifteen per cent, and reduce the amount in preference shares from £15m to £10m. The Prior team was not going to move at all on the equity available for management or the amount of preference shares. By mutual consent both sides backed off in favour of negotiating the nuts and bolts of the deal: who was drafting what, and what expenses would be paid by whom. The Prior team won the first discussion hands down, by passing across the table draft heads of agreement between Martins and the management team and draft Memorandum and Articles for NewCo, putatively christened PBS plc, initials being felt to be more modern and in tone with the 1990s. Peter Cairns, as Hamish's lawyer, looked considerably taken aback to receive this lot, Caroline observed smugly, but she and her acolytes had always been faster and more efficient than most of her male contemporaries. She gave Mark a sidelong look of congratulation and plunged, with relish, into a discussion of costs, more than effectively supported by the Prior team who were genuinely horrified at the fee that Martins were suggesting.

She and Hamish finally acted jointly to call off an increasingly acrimonious negotiation, agreeing tacitly that they would try for a compromise outside the meeting. People rose stiffly from their places, and made efforts to approach their opposite numbers courteously, though Peter Burwood was ruffled, and Peter Cairns, as lawyer to Martins, was plainly feeling it necessary to even up the score. Caroline, trying to take her group home in order to agree the next set of actions, found him at her elbow.

'I'll be in touch with you about the drafts tomorrow,' he began, busily. 'Though, of course, there is a lot of time yet.'

'Not really.' She was not feeling inclined to help him. 'We have asked to see the Minister for Housing, and the team will not want to do that without reasonably well-documented support from a development capital house and the senior lenders.'

Peter Cairns' cheekbones pinkened. 'When I saw you having an intimate lunch with Gerry Willshaw,

Caroline, I assumed you would have all this completely under control.'

'The Government's still going to want *paying* for this company, Peter, in their quaint, old-fashioned way. We're going to have to be able to say we have the cash – guaranteed by either Martins or another.' She was rattled, she realized, and conscious of the Prior team gathering protectively around her. It was Martin, of course, who put an arm around her and told her to come on, Caro, they had to get a train, but they'd buy her a drink after all that hard drafting, and she left with them, feeling Peter Cairns' eyes on her back.

Four hours later, at five o'clock, she and Mark Dwyer were deep in consideration of a pile of documents, which had arrived by special messenger just before lunch, deciding that they were not going to be able to do anything sensible without some proper help, when the phone rang and she picked it up without looking away from the documents.

'Mr Burwood for you, Caroline. Sorry to interrupt, but he says he must speak.'

Caroline looked inimically at the phone. 'Hang on, Peter, I've got Mark here, I'm going to put you on the speaker.' She scowled authoritatively at the array of buttons. Mark, who had worked with her for over a year and knew she had no idea how to work the phone, leant over and pressed the right two, so that Peter was suddenly in the room with them, sounding frantic.

'. . . We got back to find the whole factory stopped. The paint-shop is critical, as you know.'

'But what happened, Peter?'

'We don't know yet. They're taking it apart on site, but everything that came out of Saturday's run is defective – no coverage, and it's flaking off. We'll have to clean those panels and start over.'

Mark considered Caroline doubtfully; most Smith Butler clients did not feel it necessary to ring partners up with a blow-by-blow account of some piece of buggeration in their factories.

'You've lost, or will lose, several days' production, then, Peter. But look, don't these things just happen in paint-shops? I mean what could anyone have *done* to it in the time? How *does* one sabotage a paint-shop?'

'There are lots of different ways. And you can get at most of ours – it's designed that way.'

'Put sugar in the mixing process, for instance?'

There was an arrested silence and Peter observed, grudgingly, that it might well be something along those lines, and if it was, God help them, the whole thing would have to be stripped and every pipe cleaned by hand. 'But the only outsiders in the factory on Friday were Macleans, who supply Friern as well, and whom we're getting rid of,' he said, grimly.

'Let's assume you're right,' she said, briskly, as he wound down. 'You'll get it fixed some time, but you'll be even later on the Deighton Hall contract. So you may run into a penalty clause; it's not the end of the world. But you can't try to excuse it by saying you were sabotaged.'

Yes, well, there you had it, Mark thought. No one was going to believe that, were they?

'It's going to sound like those excuses kids make for being late with their homework, isn't it?' Caroline pressed on ruthlessly. 'My dog ate it. My mother hid it.'

They both listened to the furious silence at the other end.

'Yes,' Peter said, finally. 'But Friern's buggered up my paint-shop.' It was a cry of pain and Caroline's mouth quirked in sympathy.

'But why, Peter? Why now? To what end? And does it have to be Friern?'

'Hang on, Caroline, Graham's just come in.' There was a pause, full of muffled voices and Caroline signalled wordlessly for more coffee.

'Caroline? Graham here. Frierns are putting it all around the district that we've got trouble in the paint-shop. That's not yet public knowledge so they were involved all right. You know the biggie we are bidding for – it comes up in a couple of weeks – the Marsh Lane site?'

'I'd forgotten the timing.'

'Well, Friern are up against us. If they can say we're not reliable, it doesn't help, does it? We'll come in lower than them, we know that, but this way they can say we're not competent. Which, given the history of that factory is a bit easy to say. We didn't *need* a failure in the paint-shop.'

No indeed, Mark thought, soberly.

'Anything you can do, Caroline, would be very useful.' Peter had come back into the conversation.

'I was wondering what any of us could do,' she countered, swiftly. 'Are you likely to be able to prove it – I mean, if you actually found something in the works that really could not have got there anyway short of some evil person putting it there?'

'I've just come from there,' Graham said. 'Martin thinks it's something chemical – I mean not sand or grit. Be hard to prove.'

Caroline considered the point, frowning absently at

Mark, who was sufficiently used to her to know that he was currently invisible and was unmoved by the scowl. 'Look,' she said, abruptly, eyes focusing: 'it's no good. Accusations of foul play – unless provable in every detail – just won't do at this stage of the game. But the effect on the new contract *is* a worry. I think what we need to do is to arrive at some very simple explanation of what went wrong in the paint-shop. A nut worked loose, if there are any to do that – so that it was a one-off, an insignificant accident that won't happen again, and we all feed *that* explanation into the next council meeting. OK?'

'Caroline. You do believe us, don't you?'

'Oh yes,' she said, slowly, 'I believe you. I believe in Prior Systems, its most senior managers, the bulk of its corporate plan and the existence of its enemies. These are bad men.' She heard rustlings in the background and then Martin's voice.

'Caroline? About the contract renegotiations. I talked to Ted Malvern, the Conservative councillor, as we agreed. He'll do what he can, but he says the other two on that committee aren't much support. It has to be time to rally our top political support. Particularly after what happened in the factory. That's *outrageous*.'

'It has shaken me too,' Caroline said, soberly, and Mark thought how tired she was looking. 'I agree, we need to brief our friends. I'll do that as soon as I can. No, I understand the urgency. 'You three watch your-selves going home; don't speak to any strange men.' She smiled at the various mocking responses, but when she switched off the speaker phone she was still looking very thoughtful.

'Stirring times, Mark. Can you finish that for me

somewhere else? I must now make a phone call for which I need to be on my own.'

Mark, thus abjured, gathered up papers and went, reluctantly. Caroline, equally reluctantly, looked at the telephone. She really did not want to ask Gerry for help; she knew in her bones that he would hate being more closely involved, but she had to do her best for the hard-working, beleaguered management of Prior Systems. She gritted her teeth and picked up the phone. She hated leaving messages with Gerry's office, but it was nearly impossible to get through to him directly, despite the variety of different phone numbers she had for him. He was only ever alone at his flat and then only first thing in the morning or late at night. She had plucked up courage to complain about the difficulties and he had provided her with a copy of his schedule which gave her some guide to what he might be doing. She ran down the pages and decided he might just conceivably be in his room at the House of Commons by himself, and rang, thumb on the bar to cut it off after five rings, before it tripped over to his private office. She breathed again as he answered on the third ring.

'It's Caroline. Have you the odd half hour? I've got a work problem on which I need advice.'

'I'm due out to dinner.'

He was sounding edgy as he always did on the phone. She winced but persisted. 'I know. I mean you told me. It's on your schedule. But my problem is Prior and I don't know where to start.'

'Doesn't sound like you.' He was sounding cold and flustered and for a second she wanted to bang the phone down but the thought of the Prior team steadied her.

'So, can we meet at the Cardinal?'

'No. Come here. I'll meet you in the central lobby.'

'Done. I'll be with you in twenty minutes.'

She was two minutes early, and glad of it as she found herself going through the whole process of having her bag searched and waiting patiently to go through a machine guaranteed to disclose whether she was carrying a bomb. She walked up the stairs, along the wide corridor, full, even at this hour, of chattering tourists, and arrived at the central lobby, a vast circular hall, high-ceilinged with benches round the sides. She went up to the small desk as she had been told to do and asked for Gerry, waiting while the policeman telephoned. She was gazing reflectively at the panel depicting St Andrew, tastefully done in five colours and chips of stone, when Gerry touched her elbow. She turned to kiss him, but he had his public face on, the greeting to importunate constituent expression, as she thought of it, and she rallied and shook his hand solemnly, grimly admiring her own performance. He had had his hair cut, she thought despairingly, and his hair had been too short already; fourteen years in the army had a lot to answer for. He led her through half-lit corridors and up darkened stairs, nodding to acquaintances, and into a small office.

'What an awful place this is,' she said, nervously. 'Not your office, but the rest of it.'

'Oh, ghastly. A hell hole. We need to change the whole thing.' It was an automatic response and she waited for him to settle down. He busied himself pouring her a drink when what she wanted was a kiss; it was odd, she reflected, that with Gerry, whom she loved, she could not use her normal brisk approach. For as long as she could remember, her first reaction to a man in a difficult frame of mind had been to kick him out of it, but with Gerry she was helpless: she just seemed to have to wait and let him make the running. She was, she understood, a little afraid of him. He swallowed half a glass at a gulp and then put his drink down.

'Hi.' He touched her cheek.

'Hi, darling. I'm sorry I had to invade you.'

He took her drink away from her, and put his arms around her and she rubbed her cheek against his, deeply relieved. 'It's lovely to see you, even for half an hour.' He kissed her, sliding his hands under her jacket, and she kissed him back in a daze of pleasure.

'Oh God, Gerry.' She kicked her shoes off to be able to get closer to him.

'Typical that we aren't allowed beds here. Tell me about Prior. Come and sit down.'

He pulled up an uncomfortable armchair and she sat in it, feeling bereft, and trying not to look it. She explained the Prior problem to him as succinctly as possible, complete with Councillor Williamson's putative heart attack, and the unexpectedly limp behaviour of Gerry's fellow Conservative, Ted Malvern.

'But why is Williamson doing this? To save a Labour Council money?'

Caroline blinked. 'Well, no, darling. One assumes he is being paid off. By Friern or others – it's not proven.'

'You mean he has been bribed?'

Caroline considered her lover anxiously, wondering fleetingly if with the eye of passion she had grossly overestimated his intelligence.

'Sorry, darling, I'm obviously being slow,' he said, irritably rearranging his desk. 'This is corruption in local government, then.'

'That's why people go into local government.'

He stopped in mid-fidget and gazed at her. 'It can't be. I mean it's not why people go into the House of Commons.'

'No, because MPs don't have any real power.' She saw his expression and hurried on. 'I mean you cannot individually influence things that involve mates of yours getting cash or contracts. If you want a new road-building programme, darling, you've got to persuade an awful lot of people – like most of the Cabinet – and even if you manage *that*, you can't direct the work to particular contractors. But if you're in local government, you're likely to be in charge. Like this Williamson who chairs the committee which decides whether to agree my customers get another £8m, and which also decides who gets the next contract. That's what takes a lot of people into local government – the power.'

He was looking appalled, but interested. 'You mean that even as we speak local councillors are accepting bribes? Yes? What sort of bribes?'

'Traditionally a brown envelope full of cash in untrace-able notes. I've never done it – lawyers don't. But the expression "a brown envelope job" implies an arrange-ment which has involved an irregular payment of cash.'

'Why a *brown* envelope?'

'*Larger* than a white one. Cash, in notes, takes up a lot of space.' She watched him as he finished his drink, thoughtfully.

'Darling, are you asking me to stop Councillor Williamson from accepting bribes, and if so how?'

'I thought, see, that the Conservative minority on Dorrington council might be willing to help, but they don't seem to be. Why aren't they? Wouldn't finding corruption among Labour councillors do a lot for your side? Tell me what to do Gerry, and I'll do it.'

He looked immediately wary, all the lines in the mobile face set straight, and she sighed.

'Is there a political way through or do we adopt my client's sledge-hammer approach of giving the whole thing to the local newspaper? I've a feeling that's the atom-bomb solution and there ought to be something short of it.' She considered reinforcing the story by telling him about the sabotage at the factory, but decided against it. In her bones she knew he would shy away from any hint of melodrama. Her advice to the Prior team had been right: we just bite on that bullet.

Gerry's expression was somewhere between admiration and apprehension, and she decided to distract him. 'I wouldn't mind another drink.'

'Sorry.' He shot to his feet, took her glass away and organized a drink. 'There has to be a political solution to this one, I agree,' he said, contemplating the bottle. 'Look, leave it with me, can you, until next week? I'll talk to a few people. Can it wait till then?'

He looked surreptitiously at his watch, and she guiltily swallowed half the second drink which she had not really wanted.

'Oh yes. Thank you, darling. I must go so that you can get organized.' She finished her drink, in another gulp, and stood, feeling the room sway slightly. She had been at work since seven that day and lunch had been a sandwich. He was by her side instantly, steadying her and she smiled at him apologetically. 'Sorry. Long day.'

'I'd like to take you back to the flat and get into bed with you and watch you go to sleep,' he said suddenly agonized, holding her. 'But I can't let people down; I have to go.'

374

'Of course, you do,' she agreed. 'People like us don't cut out of carefully organized parties at the last minute.' No, but wouldn't it be marvellous, she thought dully, if we were both just a little less sure of who we are and where our duty lies.

'I'll come and get you a taxi.' He put her coat on for her and took her down to wait in the draughty area of the Members' entrance for a cab to arrive in response to the blinking light at the gate.

A tall, heavy, grey-haired man, whom she half recognized, passed them, going into the House, nodded to Gerry and gave her a single, comprehensive look. 'Who was that, Gerry?' she asked, watching the man's back.

'My Chief Whip. I shall have to explain it was a particularly interesting legal point.' He was looking harassed, and she smiled at him sadly.

A cab drew up beside them and he opened the door. 'Goodnight.' He kissed her briefly, and waved, turning to go back into the building.

18

It was Maundy Thursday, and, Andy Eames Lewis thought savagely, a typically bloody Easter stretched before him. Last week's snow had given way to this week's bucketing rain, and the prospect of five days with Emma's parents in Hampshire, with a baby and a five-year-old and without the nanny, frankly appalled him. He had spent the last week hoping, furtively, that something somewhere in corporate finance would go sufficiently wrong to require his attendance. In a department boasting ninety-five corporate clients and ninety professional staff, a job somewhere ought to be demanding senior time, but this was Easter and even the normally reliable predators seemed to be taking a holiday. He pressed the buttons hopefully, hunting through the list on the screen for the department's bigger clients. The market seemed to have gone to sleep: only movements of pennies each way, presumably people balancing the books before the end of the account. He sighed and decided that he could not feel worse if he tackled the quarterly accounts, which would be needed in the week after Easter, and he might conceivably feel better. He put a thumb on the buzzer to summon the director responsible, a position traditionally held for a year by the most recently appointed young man, or young woman, if there had ever been such a thing as a woman director at Walzheims. There were still enough really clever men fighting to get into Walzheims for the employment of women to be something no one bothered to do, unlike wretched solicitors who were having to recruit women. Caroline Whitehouse had been a lone forerunner, but in the years behind her there was a massed army of women, some of whom would soon be partners in hitherto respectable, all-male hierarchies. He scowled at the thought of Caroline and at that moment the phone rang.

'Mr Edwards for you,' his secretary said, and Andy picked his phone up warily.

'Yes. Hello. How are you?'

'Well enough, thank you, Mr Eames Lewis.' The Edinburgh accent was familiar, and reassuring. 'And grateful to you for the introduction to Friern. I thought I would just let you know – though I don't doubt you've heard already – that we are doing some work there. Very much at the preliminary stages of course.'

Impossible not to feel uneasy about talking to Edwards on the phone, Andy thought, even though his phone, like the whole system in Walzheims, was routinely swept for bugs, by another firm of consultants on industrial security. There are certain activities a merchant bank would prefer not to know about, such as payments of unusual commissions on construction contracts, and *prima facie* there was a case for not knowing anything about Matthew Friern's methods of doing down a competitor. It was a nice judgement, but ultimately this Pilatian attitude was unsafe in the sense that any mud that stuck to Friern would also, in this highly political case, adhere to their bankers.

'I'd be glad to talk with you at intervals, James,' he said, briskly. 'I don't want to bother you for details, but equally I don't want to find that you and I are getting in each other's way. This is a difficult one.'

The voice at the other end of the line warmed. 'The political ones always are. The short way might be for us to copy our reports to Sir Matthew to you, if that would be agreeable to him.'

The suggestion hung in the air while Andy thought his way through it. Convenient though it would be, every instinct was against it. For a start he would have to hold a conversation with Matt he did not want to hold and, secondly, in the event of trouble, he absolutely did not want to have received any of those reports.

'I'd rather not do that, James,' he said, deciding that the truth had its own ring. 'Look, can we leave it that from time to time you will tell me what's going on.' He decided to remind the man who it was that buttered a substantial proportion of his bread. 'You know enough about the sort of things Walzheims do to have a pretty good idea where our activities overlap. What are you doing at the moment, for instance?'

'Oh, well. I've got one of my best people sniffing round the DoE just to pick up what he can – any hint that the principal opposition are getting any help they ought not to be having. He's looking for any unusual contacts between them and the Department, that sort of thing. He's found a good source in the right part of the Department – an older man, who's getting the chop.'

'I didn't know civil servants ever got fired.'

'It isn't common. This one's got an alcohol problem, apparently. Then I've got another person digging around in Dorrington.'

'Pairson', as he pronounced it, presumably meant a woman, Andy thought, sidetracked. 'You are briefed, I take it, on Friern's contacts with the council?' he said hastily.

'Oh yes, don't you worry about that. It's a weak spot, though, as well as being useful, so we're just looking to see whether there is anything on the other side, as it were. There are five Conservatives and four Liberals on that council, you know.'

'I didn't,' Andy acknowledged. 'Anything useful yet?'

'No, but I'm seeing Sir Matthew next week, after the holiday. I'll keep you informed.'

Unleash the dogs of war with the Edinburgh accents, Andy thought, in a rare flight of fancy as he put the phone down and stared into space, deciding not to tell the junior director on the Friern job anything about all this. Let him just get on with the nuts and bolts of the financing and not worry his pretty head with anything else.

Three miles away, in the rainswept wastes of Marsham Street, the Prior Systems team was huddled in a Jaguar. Peter, as befitted his status was in the front seat, Martin and Graham were in the back with their lawyer squashed between them, feet companionably and necessarily intertwined with Graham's.

'You all look very nice,' she said, firmly, and the three men looked at her, inimically.

'My ears are cold,' Graham complained. 'Is the Minister really going to care that we had haircuts, or even notice?'

'It is the principle of the thing. We are here to look competent, professional and able to produce £60m out of our back pockets, if need be.' Caroline was extremely nervous but intent on not showing it.

'And reliable,' she added, warming to her task. 'Safe. Sort of people who won't go embarrassingly bust just before the next election. Sort of people who have haircuts. Now, are you with it? I'll introduce you, because I've met the man and I know the senior civil servant, then Peter comes in. As we agreed, I don't speak thereafter, just nod and smile.'

'That'll be the day,' Peter said, in affectionate warning.

'Well, I *mustn't* speak. Or not much,' she added, thinking her way through the various hurdles, and her clients burst out laughing. 'All right, all right. Look, we may as well go in. I guess we'll be out again in an hour, Brian – I should get some coffee.'

Peter's driver thanked her woodenly, looking sideways at his boss who was looking mildly taken aback at having his staff taken over, but Caroline was unconscious of the by-play, urging Graham to open his door and get his big feet out of the way, for heaven's sake.

They waited ten minutes in the Department's shabby visitors' waiting space, all four of them depressed by their surroundings, Caroline wondering aloud why it had been felt necessary or desirable to match pale mustard walls with a deeper mustard nylon carpet. A private secretary entered, upon this reflection, and led the party into Winstanley's office, where the Minister, Clive Fieldman, James Mather and Richard Watts were gathered, all smiling hospitably. In the confusion of introductions, handshakes and civil offers of coffee, Caroline intercepted a single look of reproach from Martin, and realized that not only had Winstanley and his chief adviser not had their hair cut for this meeting, but they hadn't bothered for several months, by the look of them. Winstanley's thick blond hair was curling over his collar, and Richard Watts was having to push his dark forelock out of his eyes. She took a huge gulp of coffee in order not to giggle and found herself momentarily unable to speak as it scalded its way down. Peter, however, had the baton securely.

'It is good of you to see us, Minister,' he began, as they had rehearsed it, and went on to introduce his colleagues again and explain the background to their decision to bid for the company. The Minister nodded, amicably, so Caroline concentrated her attention on Richard Watts, who was taking notes in very small handwriting. Winstanley let Peter get to the end of his re-hearsed speech, then launched into what was clearly his own, well-practised piece, explaining that of course it was the responsibility of the NEB to make the decisions on the sale of Prior Systems, or indeed on anything else they owned, but equally it was he, Winstanley, as the Departmental Minister, who would have to explain to Parliament why the NEB had done whatever they de-cided. So it was particularly useful to him to see the management of Prior Systems, and to emphasize to them how important it was that the taxpayer got a proper return for the substantial sums invested in the company.

'We expect to be able to offer a fair price, Minister.' Peter had been holding himself back with difficulty, mindful, Caroline trusted, of her urgent instruction to *let* the Minister make his speech, because he had to get it into the record. But for Gerry, she thought, I would not know these things. I would not have seen quickly enough how the machine worked.

'We have support from a major development capital group,' Peter said, firmly.

'At what level?' Richard Watts pushed his hair out of his eyes and leant forward.

'At a level that could reach £60m plus.' Peter was ready for this after two hours' rehearsal during which Caroline had fired every difficult question she could think up at the team, ruthlessly interrupting them and not letting them settle into their stride. 'No minister is going to be as difficult as me,' she had assured an increasingly irritable Peter, 'but train hard, fight easy.' The Prior team, professionals all, had gritted their teeth and gone on until all were satisfied that nothing short of war being declared in mid-meeting would distract Peter.

'In cash?' Richard Watts' eyebrows had gone right up.

'We would be offering some element of the price on a deferred basis. It seemed to us the most fair and transparent way to bid in a case like this where the company's profits could vary substantially from the forecast over the next three years.'

Winstanley was looking impressed, Caroline noted with pride, and looked cautiously towards Clive at the other end of the table. Endearingly, he was grinning and, catching her eye, winked at her.

'You didn't bring a representative of the development capital house with you.' Richard Watts was not charmed by Peter, but after all, as Caroline reflected, he was paid not to be.

'It didn't seem necessary,' Peter said, with exactly the right air of mild surprise. 'They offered to write in support, of course.'

Winstanley looked inquiringly towards Richard Watts who said, somewhat huffily, that Gruhners would presumably require this sort of assurance as part of the process of selecting the short list. In the pause that followed, Peter, with a defiant glance sideways at Caroline, said that he hoped the Minister and the NEB would bear in mind that all businesses had commercial processes which they would not want to expose to a competitor. If he were made to show the factory to every Tom, Dick and Harry who wanted to have a look, it would lower the value of the company. Caroline, who had told him that this speech, while no doubt valid in content, particularly given an act of industrial sabotage, sounded like an attempt to stifle competitive bids, decided with a sinking heart that she had been absolutely right. This lot was going down like a lead balloon. Clive was sedulously not looking at her. Winstanley was fidgeting while Richard Watts was watching Peter as if he were a particularly promising piece of food. And if she didn't stop him he would probably start explaining about the damage to the paint-shop.

'Peter,' she interrupted, minatorily, 'I think the Minister would be very interested in some details of your plans for employees to take shares in the new company.'

Peter, taken out of his stride, turned his head to frown at her; she slitted her eyes at him, so that he checked himself and asked Martin to describe the prospective employee share scheme, which he led into very well, Caroline thought. Glancing over at Clive, she was disconcerted to see him choking with laughter.

'Most interesting,' Winstanley was saying reluctantly, and she turned her head cautiously to listen to Martin, who was sketching in the arrangement for actually explaining to Prior employees what a share was, and what you did with it, which was planned to involve a massive presentation and extensive use of video.

'It is of course rather new ground for a labour force in Dorrington,' he said, apologetically, in conclusion, 'but we know the dimensions of the problem, we all know how much effort we will have to put in and we are all confident we can succeed.'

'Very exciting,' Winstanley said, and indeed meant it, she thought exultantly. This had got to him – you could see him being turned on by it. How right Gerry had been; Brownie points would be scored, evidently. Of course Gerry grasped anything that might get him a political Brownie point quicker than anything else – it went with the territory – even if he didn't really understand business and finance any more than Prior's heavy-duty labour force did. She listened with pleasure to Graham making the solid financial points, and re-emphasizing the volatile nature of the forecasts which he did competently and pleasantly; rehearsed to the hilt, he was relaxed and impressive. As they had also agreed, he was making light of the problems with renegotiating the contracts, saying easily that they were a bit delayed but he would hope to be able to report progress before the sale process had got very much further.

Winstanley thanked him and went briskly down the ranks of his own advisers, asking if anyone had any questions. Richard Watts, obviously feeling he ought to earn his money, asked about sensitivity analyses on the forecasts and got four pieces of paper handed instantly across the table from Graham for his pains. Clive, who never spoke merely to add to the ambient noise level, waved his turn away, which left Winstanley to deliver the Department's agreed closing speech which wished the team luck and left them with the warning that they would have to be as good as the competitors on price.

Winstanley had, however, departed significantly from his script in one respect by expressing particular interest in the plans for employee shares, and the Prior team were looking quietly pleased with themselves as the routine of handshakes and civilities repeated itself in reverse.

'Very nicely done, Caro,' Clive said to her, grinning, under cover of the general farewells, and passed her on to Winstanley, who considered her carefully as he shook her hand. The Prior team contained themselves till they got to the car, then exploded in mutual backslapping, and congratulations to Caroline for having thought of it.

'You were all marvellous,' she said, laughing, 'and I'm *very* sorry about the haircuts. We'll not bother next time. I'll ring up Hamish and tell him how good we were, then you lot can get home and I can clear my desk for Easter.'

'We got the paint-shop running again this morning,' Peter said.

'Jolly good.'

'Five days' production lost, though.'

'Peter,' she said, warningly. 'I'm doing my best. Have faith.' She kissed them all and waved them off, thankfully, into their car, refusing a lift back to her office.

'Lucy? Are you ready? We need to go *now*.'

In fact, Lucy Friern thought furiously, they should have left a good hour ago; the journey to their sons' school and then to Dorrington would be hell. She had been ready herself for the last hour and a half and had just rung the housemaster to warn him that they were running late. She stormed out of the kitchen to say all of this to her husband, but one look at him decided her against. He was in a towering temper such as he very rarely indulged in, and moreover he had obviously had a couple of stiff drinks somewhere.

'Darling.' She went to kiss him. 'Did you have lunch? I am ready, but I can make you a sandwich.'

'I had a sandwich. Two sandwiches. We need to get off.' He returned her kiss and she felt his stiff shoulders ease. 'Sorry I'm a bit late,' he said, grudgingly, to a point about a foot away from her right ear. 'I'm afraid it means we'll have a slow journey.' He *had* been drinking – she could smell brandy.

'I assumed you'd got held up somewhere.'

'I did, I did. I need a pee.' He pushed clumsily past her, shedding his coat. 'That bloody Williamson,' he shouted, against a background of sustained high-pressure splashing.

'Councillor Williamson?'

'Him, yes. Stupid bugger.'

'What's he done?' Lucy hoped her husband wasn't going to specify.

'It's more what he hasn't done. He was told to stay home and keep quiet, so what does he do? Plasters his basement, and greets his wife's nephew carrying all the kit.'

She decided it would be nice if Matthew stopped telling her anything about this mercifully incomprehensible saga, but realized that her luck was out as he walked, a little unsteadily, into the living-room, zipping up his flies. He was at least looking less like a volcano.

'We were managing to delay any renegotiation on those Prior contracts,' he was saying, as if she were totally familiar with the whole situation. 'We'd got the meeting put off because Williamson's heart was playing him up. So he opens the door to his wife's nephew, who just happens to be a factory engineer for Prior, carrying a bloody great board and a plastering trowel. Stupid bugger. I told him to lie low.'

'Well, if he's better . . .' Lucy began, hopefully, then understood what she was being told. Lips compressed, she slapped Nescafé and sugar into a mug, poured boiling water on them and handed the mug to her husband, who sipped it cautiously, observing that he'd only need another piss when they got to the school.

'Matt, aren't you taking rather a risk with all this business?' She was furious, but watching him carefully in case he was going to blow up. He went on sipping his coffee, looking no worse than thunderous, and she decided to persevere.

'I mean, darling, is it worth it if you have to do this kind of thing? I know business is business, but obviously this Williamson isn't even very competent. He'll get you into trouble if you don't watch out.'

His eyes slid round over the rim of the cup to look at her and she realized with relief that she was getting through, and wisely decided not to push her luck.

'You look cold. Are you sure you wouldn't like something else to eat?'

'I'd love some soup, actually.'

'Well, you shouldn't miss lunch.' Well organized in all domestic matters, she had found tinned lobster bisque and was preparing a stylish bowl and saucer, and buttering brown bread to go with it. She set a place for Matt, giving him mineral water to drink, not making a point of it, and sat down companionably with him. He wolfed the soup hungrily then looked up, belched and patted her hand.

'Sorry. I needed that. You're right, Lu, that bloody fool Williamson is dangerous. But he's chair of housing. I have to use him, even if he does seem to be too stupid to be safe.'

'Or under too much pressure. Why was he doing his own plastering?'

Matthew's eyes widened and he looked at her with real respect. 'Why indeed. He's feeling poor, I suppose.'

'Isn't his daughter getting married?'

'Yes.' Matt considered the table. 'He shouldn't be too worried about that, anyway.'

'Should he not?'

Matthew laughed, shortly, unamused. 'You're right. He hasn't had much from us for some time. You'd think he'd be more sensible, if he wasn't under financial pressure right now.'

'Most people are.' She got up to clear his plate, and waited confidently at the sink for him to follow and put his arms around her.

'I should have talked to you before.'

'I'd rather not know some things.' There were areas where they never lied to themselves or each other.

'I know that,' he said to her hair. 'And usually you don't need to but I have been making a bit of a Horlicks of this one. We'll see him comfortable and we'll use him sparingly.'

'Don't you do it all, Matt.'

'No, no. Someone else can do that. Give us a kiss.' He turned her round and kissed her gratefully.

'No, we don't have time, Matt. The school will kill me.' She was laughing and he agreed reluctantly, so they left to pick up their sons, who from long experience had settled by a fire in their housemaster's living-room with two books each.

*

388

In Lincoln's Inn Fields, by three o'clock, the offices of Smith Butler were visibly running down ahead of the Easter holiday. Half the firm had already managed to leave, including virtually all the secretaries and the articled clerks. In an office high above the square, two girls, specifically employed to work unsocial hours, were typing long drafts, while as usual a motor-bike messenger, in leathers, was sprawled in reception, his helmet beside him taking up a second chair, radio chattering companionably, but ignored as he bent his attention on the *Daily Express*. Some of the partners had managed to leave, to join traffic jams on the circumference of London, but Caroline Whitehouse was in her office, working like a demon. The Prior team were making good speed back to Dorrington – she knew because they had phoned her twice – and she was engaged in bringing as much order as possible into her work by 5 p.m. when she was covenanted to get home and take over the children so that her living-in help could get a train. She was working without inspiration, and without any particular desire to get it finished. The Easter holiday stretched in front of her. Gerry had already left for his constituency without ringing her up, and his car phone, which she had tried, was solidly engaged. She looked at her own silent phone balefully and bent her attention to the papers in front of her, sorting out outdated drafts on a difficult agreement, and starting the weary process of checking that the current draft did do what it was supposed to.

She had got sufficiently engrossed to jump when the phone rang in her ear and to pick it up without her mind being engaged.

'Caroline Whitehouse.'

'Hi. Look, love, I've found someone for you to talk to. My constituency agent. Salt of the earth. I explained to him that you were having difficulty and that you needed the subatomic solution. He got it in one. Blast, sorry, a lorry cut in on me.'

She shook herself free of the drafting, noticing that, delighted as she was to hear Gerry, her right hand was still engaged in logging a point which she did not think could be squared with an earlier sub-section. 'Where is he? In Dorrington?'

'No. On his way to London as we speak. He is having a weekend away with his family. He has promised to ring you this afternoon. You'll need to meet him. I wouldn't do all this on the telephone.'

'Not with the Forces of Darkness all listening in, no.'

He laughed, reluctantly. 'Sarn't Major Bailey – his name is Tim – knows what you are trying to do. I have said that we had met by chance and you came to me for help, knowing it was close to my constituency.'

'Good line. I shall stick to it.' It was stupid and undisciplined, she told herself, savagely, to be wounded by Gerry trying to distance himself publicly; he was married, he had never in any way indicated he didn't want to go on being so, and he had a political career to protect.

'What are you doing?' he asked, sounding as usual truly interested, and she cast a disaffected look around her desk, unable to find anything amusing to tell him.

'Just work, I guess. Sorting out an agreement. Full of technical problems.' It was, it occurred to her uneasily, the sort of thing men traditionally said to girls, who were trying to 'take an interest'. 'What are *you* doing?' she asked, hastily.

'Driving along a motorway, catching up with phone calls. I've got a reception tonight, then I'm going to sleep in tomorrow. And think about you.'

She smiled, softened, calculating wryly her own chances of a long sleep in, with Timmy who still had nightmares one night in three and Francis who woke up at 5 a.m. and by 7 a.m. had usually managed to wake everyone else.

'What are you doing the rest of the time? Are you seeing my rival?'

He was not, as she knew, at all jealous of Clive; in fact, it probably made him feel less guilty to know that she had someone else around. 'Not this time. We're off to the Borders tomorrow. It'll be lovely,' she lied, bravely, there being no way she was going to admit that none of it looked very inviting when the man she really wanted was miles away in the bosom of his family. *All* the clichés about being in love with married men were absolutely true, she thought, grimly. It was not worth it even if, like her, you had one who was just much better value and more fun than anyone else.

'My love, I must go. I'm coming to a turn-off and I need to concentrate. I'm seeing you in ten days, on Monday, yes? I think that vote is going to go away and we shall have the whole evening.'

'Have you heard anything new about it?' She knew him well enough by now to understand that he did not like delivering bad news and tended to find a way of doing it by stages.

'The Whip's office were saying they weren't quite sure what was happening yet.'

'We could meet earlier then.'

'Good idea. If I can get out of the office, let's do that. Must go. Look after yourself.'

I'll have to, won't I, she thought, in a flash of unwanted perception. Well, he can't look after me can he, she argued with the voice in her head and bent grimly to the draft. The phone rang again before she could get the thread back and she picked it up crossly.

'It's Tim Bailey here, Mrs Whitehouse. Gerry Willshaw suggested I might ring you.'

'Oh, you are kind.' Caroline pushed the draft firmly out of eyeshot and reached for a pad. 'He told me he would do that. Where are you?'

'In a call-box near Holborn tube. Can we meet? There seems to be a café just here where we could have tea. Luigi's.'

'Be with you in five minutes. I know you must be wanting to get back to your family.'

She had locked her office and was going out of Smith Butler's massive front doors before it occurred to her that she had no idea what Tim Bailey looked like. When she arrived at Luigi's, however, a man rose instantly from his seat at the sight of her. She shook his hand, seeing a man fifteen years older than she, solidly built, high colour in the cheeks, thinning hair, short and immaculately tidy, wearing a sports jacket and grey flannels, with highly polished brown shoes, looking out of place among the grey suits of the lawyers and the jeans and long hair of the passing trade. She knew he had left an infantry regiment as a sergeant major ten years before and was a tough, a local man, extremely familiar with his district. But not quite comfortable with his mission, uneasy with her, so she exerted herself to charm, wanting him to carry a good report of her to Gerry. She made him laugh with her account of the morning's meeting between Prior and the Department and they were soon chatting easily enough for her to ask him what exactly Gerry had told him and to expand on it.

'My customer thinks he just tells the local paper and justice will be done,' she confided.

'There was always one like that in the regiment,' Tim Bailey said, comfortably. 'No, no, that's not the way, or not yet. Williamson will hold the meeting, Mrs Whitehouse, don't worry about it.'

'And am I not to ask how you are going to do it?' Caroline was ruffled as always by paternal reassurance.

He looked at her, thoughtfully, considering her. 'I'm going to have a word with my Labour opposite number. We don't want to wash any dirty linen in public.'

She nodded, comprehending. 'Neither do I.'

'You just want to get the results, yes?' He sat back in his chair, watching her, bright-eyed.

'That's right.'

'And why not? Look, Mrs Whitehouse, anything else funny goes wrong, any little thing, you get in touch with me. I'll give you my card. Our Gerry's a very good Member, but he's got a lot on his plate.'

'And he isn't on the spot,' Caroline agreed, comfortably. 'And he's dead busy as all ministers are. Thank you. I hope I don't have to apply for help again, but I have an uneasy feeling we may need to. Would you call me Caroline – I'd be more comfortable?'

'And my name's Tim. Gerry still calls me Sarn't Major, but that's a habit.'

'Were you in the same regiment?' she asked, knowing he had not been, but wanting to talk about Gerry.

'No, but it's all the same in a way. Can I get you another cuppa?'

'If you have another few minutes. I'm afraid I'm keeping you from your family.'

'You've a family too, have you not?'

'Oh yes. Three children.'

'But you lost your husband?'

'Yes. In an air crash.'

'So Gerry was saying. That's very hard. You're only a young woman.'

'Thirty-eight,' she said, bristling. 'Not *that* young.'

'It seems young to me, but I'm fifty-four. Of course you all seem young – Gerry too. Have you met Susan, his wife?'

'No. She is mostly in Dorrington, I believe, and I only seem to be there for a few hours and to be locked in meetings when I am.' She stopped, conscious that she was overexplaining.

'A very nice person. Very good in the constituency. Are you politically inclined yourself?'

'It will seem an awful thing to say to you, but I'm never sure I could stand constituents all whingeing at once.'

'There's a lot of that,' Tim Bailey was openly amused, slightly flushed from the hot tea. 'Gerry feels like that sometimes. But Susan now, she never loses patience and she keeps all the constituency organizations going as they should. The army is very good training for being an MP's wife.'

'I see that,' Caroline said, in reluctant recognition. 'Army wives have to be very adaptable.'

'That's right, and of course the officers' wives are expected to look after all the women's problems. Plenty of those in Germany, lots of little girls of seventeen who've never been outside Dorrington, trying to manage with a baby in a foreign country where they don't speak the language and their men can be on manoeuvres for weeks. Susan's had a lot of experience with all that.'

Caroline sat still in her chair, reluctantly thinking about the woman who had been married to Gerry Willshaw for twenty years. She and Susan Willshaw could surely not be more different; she had spent the last twenty years forcing the world – which meant the male world – to adapt to her, using brainpower and a lot of raw natural energy. Susan Willshaw had deployed whatever qualities she had been born with into following wherever Gerry had gone, and making the best of wherever she had found herself, supporting him by looking after the teenage wives of his men or entertaining constituency associations as required, and watching his back in local politics. Of course, Caroline reflected, she and Ben had also been a team, but a very different one, both of them with highly successful careers, and both jointly responsible for the management of household and children. Gerry, it came to her slowly and uncomfortably, had been much indulged in his marriage: the hearth kept warm for him, his children, his men, his constituency nursed for him, so that he was free to go straight for the top in both his chosen careers, and to hog any limelight that was going. And Susan Willshaw must be an extremely capable woman, as well as by all accounts a very nice one.

'Penny for them?' Tim Bailey was watching her and she met his eyes, suddenly aware that he had known exactly what he was doing, and that he too was guarding Gerry's back. She stiffened and went on the attack.

'Uphill stuff being a Conservative agent in your part of the world?' she suggested, briskly.

'Yes. But getting easier with candidates of Gerry's quality around. We're beginning to get some good people into local government too.'

'Like Ted Malvern of whom the Prior lot speak well. Not that he was useful in the present emergency; he didn't seem quite to know what to do.'

'Ah well, he's a chartered surveyor. What do you expect, Caroline? Hardly knows enough to come in out of the rain.' Bailey had realized that she was having a go and was prepared to stand his ground.

'Knows enough to have got himself on to the housing committee,' she said, sharply, and watched with pleasure as Bailey became abruptly serious.

'What are you suggesting?'

'I just had this vision of them all being in it together, for money, regardless of political persuasion. Whatever it is, it'd just better not be against my customer's interests.'

'I don't think you're right.' He was taking her entirely seriously, she was pleased to see, the note of avuncular patronage completely gone. 'No, I really don't think so. But I'll look around me, don't you worry.' He nodded to her, and reached in his pocket for money.

Perhaps she had rattled him enough that he was going to make a phone-call right now, she thought, with malicious pleasure, then remembered that she needed him, and put out a restraining hand. 'I've heard nothing against Malvern at all. I was just a bit surprised that he was being so helpless. Perhaps it is only that they all depend on you to sort things?'

He smiled at her, flattered but undeceived. 'There's a

bit of that. You can depend on me too, Caroline; I usually know where to start in my patch.'

'I can see you do.' They were both standing and he looked at her sideways.

'You should think about politics. You'd be a good candidate for us. Could do with you in the north, but you probably want to be in London.'

'I was brought up on the other side from you and Gerry.'

'None of us can help where we were brought up.' He extended a strong, chunky hand, elbow rigidly crooked. 'It's been a pleasure. And ring me, any time – I'm easier to find than Gerry.'

19

Two weeks later, the sun came out and spring arrived belatedly but suddenly, all in one day. Rain and cold winds had persisted steadily over the whole of Easter and the week following, causing Andrew Eames Lewis to come close to an open quarrel with his parents-in-law as they all tried to cope with a teething, fretful baby and a noisy five-year-old in a country house underendowed with central heating and overprovided with small perishable objects.

Caroline Whitehouse had fared better, if only because her children were older and past the age of teething. They had all had a good ten days with her parents-in-law in the Border cottage that had come with Ben and which he had loved. The children also loved it, relaxing in an environment they had known since they were babies. Caroline, for whom it was a little too reminiscent of the drafty Henriques country cottages of her childhood, had found herself unexpectedly soothed by the whole atmosphere, and the undemanding but genuine concern of farm neighbours, who had known Ben. The children were happy there and she was guilty of having neglected them and Ben's parents, in thought if not in deed, ever since Gerry had come into her life. After these two weeks she felt she had made it up to them a bit.

Clive Fieldman and the Frierns had not had to concern themselves with the English weather; the Frierns were skiing as they always did at Easter, and Clive, faced with the prospect of not seeing Lucy at all for ten days, had taken his own precautions and had gone to Florida to see an old friend from LSE on an extremely cheap charter flight that left Luton at 3 a.m. The Prior Systems team had, reluctantly, taken four days off, only because they knew it would be desperately expensive and counter-productive to try to keep the factory or any of the sites running over the Bank Holiday, but had put in a hard week's work since Easter.

Up in Winstanley's private office, a mood of optimism prevailed. The House had risen on Maundy Thursday and would not resume business until the next Monday. Winstanley had taken a holiday and the private office, running with a skeleton staff, had managed to get through the whole Easter period with no more than a minimum ration of oil-spills, structural faults appearing in new housing estates and other hazards for which the Department of the Environment could be held responsible. For once, the principal private secretary had not had to be called back and the parliamentary secretary left in charge had coped without recourse to his senior ministers. Wives had been reintroduced to husbands, and children to fathers, and about two thirds of the private office was now back and gearing itself for a fresh start on Monday.

John Winstanley, looking fresh and relaxed, hair tidy and visibly shorter, was considering a single sheet of paper. He read it twice, then looked to Richard Watts, who looked washed-out and was beating off a heavy cold.

'So this is it. This is the short list for Prior Systems. All six of it.'

'It is fair to say, Minister, that this is the long short list. What you have here is in our view the only possible six candidates, but we cannot be confident that two of them will actually be prepared to bid. Those two, Minister, Greys and John Hegarty. They are perfectly credible purchasers, in the sense that they have the resources to buy Prior Systems. It's just that, for both of them, Prior is a bit out of their usual line of business, which means they won't want to pay top whack. They'll pick it up if it is a good enough deal and make a sensible job of it, I don't doubt, but they don't want it enough to make a real effort.'

'So there are four in hot pursuit, as it were?'

'That may be putting it a little too highly, Minister. The management team certainly wants to buy and they have got their finances in order – we have met their backers. Sir Matthew Friern is extremely keen to buy and of course he speaks for his board. Of the remaining two, Waltons could buy it out of their petty cash, but they aren't famous for paying decent prices. And Shaw, who seem keen . . . well, I don't really quite know why they want it. They are clients of Gruhners, who advise the NEB, and I'd have to say my feeling is that they have been talked into it.'

'Are Gruhners allowed to act on both sides?'

'As I understand it, Minister, they feel they have removed any possibility of conflict by putting two different directors on.' He considered the point. 'But I think we would have taken a different view, yes,' he said, definitively and smugly.

Winstanley glanced down the table at Clive. 'Only two customers then.'

Clive wordlessly raised an eyebrow at Richard Watts,

who confirmed that this was his best view, and Winstanley looked cast down.

'Minister, we have a short list of six perfectly respectable candidates. Presentationally, this should be more than adequate,' Clive said, firmly, in his best speech-to-the-troops-before-Agincourt tones.

'That's quite true.' Winstanley cheered up. 'What are the NEB doing – are they going to announce?'

'Yes, Minister, on the assumption that you approve the list, they'll announce it on Wednesday next week, by press notice. Sir Matthew Friern only got back yesterday and it was felt appropriate that he should be in the country.'

And not a word from Lucy, Clive thought, alerted. Not a message, not a phone call. He would ring the flat after this meeting. He could always put the phone down if Matthew was there – he had had to do that before. He considered the table, thoughtfully; he was not particularly tense physically, he had had a very pleasant week with a friend of his friend in Florida, a good-looking recent divorcée, who taught English Literature. But it was Lucy he wanted, he recognized, and after two undiluted weeks of Matt she ought to be ready for a change. At any rate he hoped that Matt would be in Dorrington tomorrow and, provided Lu was not still getting the children back to school, they could have a bit of time together. Lunch, he thought, hopefully, and surfaced to hear Winstanley professionally checking that no one else had anything to say or ask before he let Richard here go back to his bank. He looked towards James Mather, who would with any luck have been concentrating enough to know the answer to that question, and indicated to Winstanley that he had nothing to add.

He left as quickly as he decently could, in Richard Watts' wake, rang the Friern flat, and got Lucy, who was in a hurry to get out to lunch 'with your friend Caroline' she said, pointedly, but agreed to meet him the next day. Cheered, he looked at the in-tray, which he had mostly cleared. On the top was a note from establishment division, telling him formally that Michael Watson had now been deemed by the board concerned to be suitable for early retirement on grounds of limited efficiency. Watson had, as one might well have assumed, given notice that he intended to exercise his right to appeal to the relevant second permanent secretary at the Treasury. The note added, in courteous explanation, that said second permanent secretary was the last stop; from his decision lay no further appeal. Clive, one of whose gifts was neither to resile from, nor to worry about, decisions once arrived at, put the note in his in-tray, relying on Miss Williams to bury it somewhere safe, and decided not to risk ringing up E Division to ask about a replacement; better to leave it for a week or so. He would get some snack himself, and not go into the canteen; he would have a quick snack at the pub opposite and a walk in the park, since it was a beautiful day. He had arrived at the counter and had bought his meal before he remembered what had happened last time he had been there, and he looked cautiously down the bar as he ordered a lager to go with the meal. He had just decided his luck was in when he caught sight of Michael Watson at a corner table talking earnestly to a man a little older than he, who was nodding in what could be read across the pub as sympathetic interest. Clive looked away hastily, both irritated and reluctantly concerned. The only thing to do was to behave as if he had not seen Watson, but what was the silly cuckoo doing? Several glasses littered the small table over which he was hunched, he was red in the face and his gestures looked both expansive and clumsy; indeed, as Clive buried his face in the evening paper, an empty glass hit the carpet, propelled by an emphatic sweep of Watson's arm. Clive decided that he was going to eat his lunch as quickly as possible and get himself out of there before he had another embarrassing scene to cope with. This design was frustrated; a woman asked if she could get past him, to the other side of the table, and the resultant flurry of movement drew Watson's eye. Clive studiously ignored him, looking away, hoping that the man would think he had not noticed him, but as he sank back into his chair he was uneasily conscious that Watson had seen him and indeed was covertly pointing him out to his friend. Presumably, he featured as the villain in this particular drama, he thought wearily, giving himself indigestion by polishing off the chilli con carne inside five minutes. He gulped his lager, looking as stern and purposeful as he knew how, and headed for the street, angry with himself, and thinking grimly that the sooner the second permanent secretary at the Treasury could be pushed into turning down Watson's appeal the better, if he was going to be unable to have lunch in peace on his own doorstep.

Lucy Friern rushed through the door of the restaurant, putting on her glasses, guiltily aware that she was late for lunch. She gazed around and stopped in her tracks, suddenly arrested by the sight of her friend Caroline, who was sitting quietly at a corner table, gazing into space, looking sad and young and vulnerable, her blonde hair lying flat, her hands empty of papers. A bad moment perhaps, Lucy thought, taking off her glasses and stuffing them into her handbag, and reminding herself to calm down a bit as she picked her way over to the table, apologizing sweetly to anyone or anything she fell over.

'Darling.' She bent to kiss her friend, and was relieved to see Caro shake off whatever had been preoccupying her. 'I'm sorry I'm late.'

'Barely ten minutes, Lu.' Her friend was unimpressed but not, she was relieved to see, really cross. 'Did you get the boys off?'

'On the school train just this morning with, as usual, no help from Matt. He'd promised to take them, absolutely promised, then some bloody man rang up about Bartholomews. Something wrong in the interim accounts, so Matthew, without even telling me, took the car and rushed off there.' She caught Caroline's eye. 'Then I was late having my legs waxed and the girl was slow.'

'Not something one can stop in the middle of,' Caroline agreed. 'Ah. Why were you having your legs waxed?'

Lucy looked at her, disconcerted, then laughed. 'Yes, well, darling, you're absolutely right, that's why.'

'Lucky old Clive.' Caroline was uneasily aware that she was sounding edgy; she had rushed to open the post hoping for something from Gerry and found only a postcard in terms that could with propriety have been received by her grandmother.

'Should we order?' Lucy asked, and as usual a waiter materialized at her side; she and Gerry were alike in that, Caroline observed. The waiter retreated, backwards, still watching Lucy, who was looking particularly pretty, her violet-blue eyes very bright against her sunburn.

'Lovely shirt,' Caroline said, admiringly, taking in her friend's pale-blue silk blouse and the gold necklace worn casually just inside the neck.

'Nice, isn't it? I bought it this morning.'

'Even luckier Clive.'

'*He* says *you*'ve got someone too, darling.'

'How did he know?'

'He said a chap rang up when he was there for lunch, and you lit up like a Christmas tree. Who is he?' She looked at her friend, bright-eyed with interest. 'Is he married? Clive thought he must be or he would have been at Sunday lunch.'

Caroline, she was interested to see, was appalled. 'Clive was always too clever by half,' she said, bitterly, after a pause. 'Yes, darling, he *is* married and it is hell, since you ask.'

'I thought I'd better,' Lucy was unperturbed. 'You were looking about six and lost when I arrived. Honestly, Caro, couldn't you find someone unmarried?'

'Not while selfish women like you are soaking up the unmarried ones.'

'Darling, you don't want Clive, do you?'

'No. I want the one I've got. I was just having a go at you.'

'*Because*, if you did, I think we're going off each other.'

Caroline looked up, sharply, across her glass of Perrier. 'Oh, Lu. You mean *you*'re going off him. They never go off you.'

'Well, I expect they would, but I tend to go off them first,' Lucy said, matter-of-factly.

405

'Poor Clive.' Caroline spoke soberly. 'Oh God, I suppose in the end married people do go off you.'

'Well, they have to, sweet, if they're going to stay married.' Lucy was watching her friend anxiously. 'Caro, what about your chap – I mean, is this serious? Do you want to marry him? Who is he, anyway?'

The question hung in the air while the waiter brought the salads they had both ordered, and Caroline gazed at the smoked salmon she normally loved, wondering if she would ever feel like food again.

'Yes, it is serious. I love him. No, I do not expect to marry him. And I can't tell you who he is; it wouldn't be fair.'

'Do I know him?'

'No.'

Lucy digested this, salad unregarded in front of her. 'You mean he's someone famous. Caro! Do tell. You are mean.'

Lucy sounded so like her eighteen-year-old self that Caroline managed to laugh, rather than cry. Her good friend Lucy, she noted wryly, was actually piqued that she had apparently been outgunned in the status stakes.

'I can't, Lu. And it's not at all an advantage having an easily recognizable lover, let me tell you.'

'You have to creep about in disguise? It was a bit like that with William.'

'Well, it would have been. Yes, we have to be extremely careful. And we can't get much time together.' She picked at her smoked salmon, feeling wretched, and looked up to find Lucy's wide eyes fixed on her in real concern.

'But, darling, why are you doing it?'

'I can't believe I'm hearing *you* ask me this,' Caroline riposted as briskly as she could.

Lucy waved a fork impatiently. 'Oh, Caro. It's quite different for me. I'm married, it's a sideline for me. Anyway, I was never as . . . well . . . serious, as you are. You're exactly the wrong person to be having an affair with someone heavily married. If you want to do that, you have to be able to take it as it comes.'

'I do. I do.'

'What a common girl. I mean, be a bit relaxed about it. No? Well, why can't you marry him? I mean, does he love you too?'

'He has a wife and children. And, yes, I think he does, but people don't divorce for that sort of reason, do they? I mean, *you* don't.'

'I'm not unhappy with Matt. He drives me mad a lot of the time, but we quite like each other,' Lucy said. 'Waiter. Could we have a couple of glasses of the house white? No, shut up, Caro, you need a drink.'

'I do after that statement. I have no reason to believe my man is unhappy with his wife either.'

'He doesn't say he's unhappy? No, well, then he isn't, you're right. The chaps who are seriously uncomfortable at home always go on about it.'

'I defer to your superior experience.'

'Caro! This really has got to you, hasn't it?'

'Yes. Yes, it has. I am miserable when I'm not with him, fuck it. Oh, blast, and damn.' With true Henriques disdain for the conventions, she scrubbed her eyes with the restaurant's napkin, then used it to mop up the Perrier she had spilt.

Lucy leant back in her chair and within a minute a floor manager was producing clean napkins, tablecloth and the wine she had ordered, while Caro scuffled in her bag for a handkerchief.

'Sorry, Lu. It is all clearly a bad idea but I cannot stop. He is very much what I want in a man, that's the trouble.'

'Is he like Ben?'

Her friend put her fork down and stared into space. 'No,' she said, reluctantly. 'Much bossier, much more selfish, much clearer about what he wants to do.'

'Much more difficult to live with,' Lucy said, authoritatively. 'Darling, it would never do. I cannot imagine you with one of those, when you're so decisive and clear what you want to do yourself. You'd quarrel all the time. Ben used to steer you, not tell you. Well, he had to.'

'This is true. I cannot tell you, Lu, how horrified I am to find at my age that I seem to fancy one of those selfish, dominant men. Just like all those Georgette Heyer heroines.' Caroline was somewhere between laughter and tears, but deeply, wholeheartedly, relieved to be able to tell someone about her situation.

'Is he good in bed?'

'Yes.'

'Just yes?'

'Yes, very.' Caroline had gone bright pink, and Lucy looked at her bent head indulgently. 'Oh, well. You needed a man, Caro, and if this doesn't work out, at least it will get you going again. There really are plenty of them out there, you know.'

Caroline stopped eating, realizing that none of this conversation came anywhere near the truth. 'But, Lu,' she said, in despair, 'I am in a truly terrible mess. I can't marry this one. He is already married. He has never suggested he might not be. And I cannot imagine wanting to live with anyone else.' She looked helplessly at her friend. 'I don't even approve of breaking up marriages. This isn't a moral judgement or anything embarrassing like that,' she added, hastily. 'I just cannot imagine what it would take – or how I would feel – to create that amount of havoc and destroy a family. I think I would be frightened that the effort would leave both parties with the most awful regrets.'

'I think it does,' Lucy said, soberly. 'It's why I've never been tempted to try it, now I've got children, even though I often wish I'd married Jim – you remember him? – rather than Matt.'

'Might you have?' Caroline was momentarily distracted from her own grief by the memory of the older, sardonic American professor of . . . what was it? . . . something none of them understood at all. Cybernetics?

'Oh, yes. The love of my life. But he had a wife and children in Los Angeles.' Lucy's blue eyes were suddenly very bright.

'I'd forgotten,' Caroline acknowledged. 'And you couldn't go on?'

'Oh, I would have. I knew no better – I was twenty-two, remember. *He* couldn't.'

'Do you think that happens?' Caroline said, blowing her nose. 'That you find the real love of your life and can't marry them? It can't, can it? I mean, there must be others around. You wouldn't really want to trade Matt in, would you?'

'Quite a lot of the time,' Matt's wife assured her, calmly. 'But taking all in all I suppose not – I mean, I would have already, if I was going to, wouldn't I?'

'I suppose so.'

Her friend looked anxiously across at her. 'Darling, if you can feel this deeply for a chap again, it's a good sign. You can find another. Try to enjoy it while you've got it, if it can't last.' Lucy reached over and took her friend's hand. 'Don't look so stricken.'

Caroline nodded, wordlessly, feeling pressure behind her eyes again. 'I never cry,' she said, wonderingly.

'Do you good. Can't you go home, not to the office?'

'Home is full of children and housekeepers. At least I have an office to myself. I'll be OK, Lu. I wish Matt and I weren't so absolutely head to head on Prior Systems, but I can't stop. The lads are absolutely determined.'

'So is Matt. I'm trying to find him something else to distract him.' They looked at each other. 'But he really wants that company.'

'Oh dear. So do I.'

'Yes, that's what you're like,' Lucy said, interested and irritated. 'However would you manage with a man who was as single-minded as you?'

'What, like Matt? We'd be a disaster.' Caroline was laughing, restored by the thought. 'What are you doing this afternoon, Lu?'

'Shopping. I'm seeing Clive tomorrow.'

'I thought you were going off him. Oh, I see, you still like him in bed, poor chap.'

'I still like him,' Lucy said, with dignity, paying the bill. 'I just think it's time he found a wife.' She looked defiantly at her friend and, after a few seconds, they smiled at each other, wryly amused.

'Sir Matthew Friern for you, Andy.'

'Matt? Hello. I didn't expect to hear from you today.'

Andy Eames Lewis, recognizing a crisis when he heard one, pulled a pad towards him. 'The committee recommended a settlement on the outstanding claims – at what, sorry? That is a bit less than you predicted, isn't it? No possibility of delay in the end.'

'It's got very political, Andy. The three Conservatives and the two Liberals on the committee pressed for a settlement, and more or less openly threatened to make a fuss. Bastards.'

Reflecting that the biter had been comprehensively bitten, Andy decided he would be wasting his time in attempting any consolation. 'Oh well, doesn't help the management team specifically. Everyone will be expected to pay a bit more for the company.'

'Bugger that. Someone put those chaps up to this. Neither of the Libs on that committee know enough to come in out of the rain. My man says they were briefed and in cahoots with Malvern – that's the Conservative. Someone's playing politics.'

Andy heroically refrained from comment, not wishing to attract the fury of a political operator who had just been comprehensively outgunned in his own territory, and wondered aloud how Caroline and her team had managed it. 'Of course the team are local men and have their own political contacts, do they not?' he added cautiously.

'Yes, they do. Some. But they would never have got organized like this by themselves. That's Caroline White-house.'

Yes, it probably was, Andy silently agreed, remembering, sharply, Caroline at twenty-two faced with a rival firm trying a piece of sharp practice on a Smith Butler client. The rival had retired, not so much hurt as mauled, and had then had to face a formal complaint to his senior partner. No one at Smith Butler had been prepared to gainsay Caroline in her best avenging-angel style.

'I want that company, Andy. I was talking to someone at Bluett, who had an idea about getting a bit closer.'

'Their people are very enthusiastic, of course,' Andy said, coldly, hoping that he was managing to convey that Bluett was a consortium of dangerously rash and probably crooked bankers, only loosely disguised as a member of the accepting houses committee.

'A bit of enthusiasm is what I need, Andy. That bloody woman is right on my tits.' Matthew was plainly beyond the point where it was worth suggesting that there were worse fates to befall a chap, and Andy bent his mind to the problem.

'Well, you're already using James Edwards,' he began, cautiously.

'Yes. Yes, he's been useful. One of his people has found out that the civil servant – Fieldman – is closer to Caroline than I'd realized. Might be something there. I mean, she is a widow, she could easily be putting herself about a bit. They have to be very careful those chaps, don't they?'

'He's divorced, I believe.'

'Yes, but he still shouldn't be fucking her, if she's acting for Prior, should he?'

'If he is. Fucking her, I mean.'

'Worth finding out. Andy? You still there? Or am I upsetting you?'

'I'm sure James Edwards will advise you.'

'But you don't want to get your hands dirty. What *are* you doing for us?'

This I do not have to take, Andy thought; this isn't the chairman of ICI I've got here. On the other hand, it is a big client, and we've sunk a lot of time into this one. He lifted the edge of the phone off a computer print-out, which recorded £90,000 in costs run up on Matt Friern's account so far. And the agreed success fee was £500,000. He drew in a careful breath.

'Oh, organizing the lending, talking to the brokers, things like that. And briefing my chairman on the position at Prior, so that he can mention it at lunch with the Chancellor.'

'That would be useful.' Matt was still loaded for bear, but the mention of the Chancellor had given him pause, and Andy followed up his advantage.

'You know, Matt, I think we may be in danger of going overboard here. When it comes to real cash and the question of who can actually manage this company, then Friern is going to look awfully attractive.'

'Mm.' Matt, while not convinced, was sounding calmer. 'All right, Andy. Ring me when you've got an idea. I'll be waiting.' He banged the phone down.

Andy, balefully, replaced his receiver. He sat, calming down, trying to decide whether to ring Edwards, then concluded that Matt would be blocking the line at this moment. And he would prefer to wait till Edwards called him. But he really was not prepared to have clients speak to him like that. He looked thoughtfully at the phone and dialled another number, finger on the button to cut off the tone if necessary.

'Lucy.' He let out his breath. 'Andy here. How are you? I'd love to hear about your skiing. Emma and I thought we might go there later. Have you time for a drink this evening, you and Matt? Oh, he's in Dorrington, is he? What about you? Or lunch tomorrow, if that works better?'

413

'You are sweet, Andy.' The slightly husky voice sent a message straight down his spine and he shifted on his chair. 'I can't do lunch tomorrow, but I'd love to have a drink today – I'm meeting a girlfriend at the theatre later.'

'Caroline?' he said, edgy with disappointment, having hoped for a moment that she was free for the evening.

'No. I had lunch with Caro.' She sounded innocently surprised and he pulled himself together and arranged where they would meet.

'It's your constituency agent, Minister.'

The bloody civil servants always contrived to make it sound like a call from your favourite cocaine dealer, Gerry Willshaw thought, in exasperation, signalling that he would take the call. For God's sake, how did they think you became an MP? Of course they didn't think, did they, with their self-conscious political neutrality and index-linked pensions.

'How are you, Sarn't Major?'

'Well, thank you. We did the business for Prior. Contract terms agreed this afternoon. We owe the Libs one.'

'Jesus.'

'I know.' Bailey was sounding amused and self-righteous. 'Thought that was what you wanted, though.'

'It was. Thank you, Tim.' He put the phone down and got restlessly to his feet, wanting to ring Caroline, but realizing that he had no time before the next meeting. And bless her, she never rang him without a cast-iron excuse, so that his office had accepted her as one of the many political friends and advisers he occasionally saw. More disciplined, more careful than anyone he'd

414

had before, he thought; he hadn't had to explain very much there at all. Just for a moment he wanted her fiercely, but the phone rang and he put all that out of his mind, smoothing his short-cropped hair with both hands, as he crossed the room to greet his next visitor.

'John. Good to see you.'

John Macdonald, one of the junior whips, with whom he had worked in opposition, shook his hand and accepted a drink, settling himself in a corner of the office.

'Very nice of you to come to the Department. I'm stuck here, waiting for a late meeting.'

'So your office said. I felt I hadn't seen you for a bit, and I thought I'd like to find out how everything was going.'

Gerry took a long pull of his whisky and leant back, nerves alert. It was like being in the jungle, he thought, and hearing a rustle in the leaves which could be the wind, but probably wasn't.

'Susan well?'

'Yes. In good form. Very busy with the constituency, of course. Now I've got this job, I do not know how I would keep them happy, if she hadn't taken over a lot from me.'

'Be nice to see her down here again,' the older man said, gently, and Gerry sat still.

'Yes. She'll be here the week after next.'

'Oh, that's good.' Macdonald nursed his drink, and looked around the office. 'You're looking well, Gerry – good holiday, was it?'

'I was glad of a break. We went away for a week – it's no good trying to take a holiday in the constituency, we find.'

'Oh, certainly not,' Macdonald agreed. 'People want

you to come round for drinks, and you can't really say, no, I'm home and I just want to fuck the wife and snarl at the children.'

Gerry choked on his drink, laughing. This was all right; it was no more than a feeler, and Macdonald had accepted the reassurance he had been offered. But it was more than flattering that this inquiry had been undertaken at all, he thought, nerves prickling, remembering sharply what the whip's office was like. And Macdonald had come round to see him; there must be something up. He got to his feet, knowing that if he sat still, he would rush into speech, and offered another drink.

'Just a small one, thank you, Gerry. Everyone was very pleased with the way you handled that Engelfield disaster, by the way.'

'That was awful.' For a moment he was back with bereaved, bewildered families. He had done it well, a part of his mind acknowledged, but the army trained you to that, consoling weeping women, embracing desperate children, rallying the chaps' friends – it came as part of the job. It was no use being frightened of grief – these things happened and there was a routine for them: the coffin had to be properly seen off and interred, the survivors organized, rehoused, helped to put their lives back together, all in due order. But something *was* up; the Engelfield disaster was some weeks old, and colleagues in the House had congratulated him either sincerely, or, even better, enviously, on his performance at the time, and the whip's office had indicated then that he had done well. Macdonald had not come today to renew these plaudits. Macdonald's sphere covered Employment as well as that notorious ministerial graveyard,

Trade and Industry. It couldn't be Peter Fleming – the PM's Golden Wonder – who was coming unstuck at the seams, could it? He decided he did not dare ask, even indirectly, and sought around for a way of further assuring Macdonald that he was here and ready. Macdonald, however, seemed to require no reassurance; he was placidly finishing his drink and gossiping gently about the Opposition, so Gerry sat tight, as he had learned to do long ago. Finally, he escorted his visitor personally to the lift and stood chatting civilly, in full view of his own Secretary of State, who had gratifyingly checked his stride on seeing them together. He watched the lift doors close and went back to his own office to sign off the rest of the day's post, which he managed with barely contained impatience.

20

Spring had finally got here, Clive thought, approvingly, looking at the blazing yellow of the forsythia that grew beside the gate to the Henriques parents' establishment. He considered the gate, finding himself transported back sixteen years; it had an awkward, rusty catch which had grown no easier with the passing years. He took a firm line with it, which left him with the catch in his hand, together with some rotting wood.

'Oh, Daddy,' both his children said, horror-stricken, and at that moment Sholto Henriques emerged, hospitably, to greet them.

'What have you done, Clive? Oh, that. I screw it back every week. I suppose it has reached the stage where we really need a new gatepost.' He pushed at the gate which fell disobligingly off one hinge, wedging itself across the path.

'Oh, for God's sake, Dad. Haven't you had that gate fixed yet?' Clive turned to see Caroline peering out of the window of a Volvo estate, Timmy by her side in the front seat. She looked at her father in familiar exasperation.

'It really doesn't matter very much, Caroline. People can still get through, and I'll fix it when I have time.'

Caroline's lips compressed, as she visibly decided not to fight this particular battle but started to unload children and books from the big car, shouting irritably at the boys. Clive noticed suddenly that the beautiful Susannah was standing beside her, gently stroking her sleeve, and just then Caroline turned her head and saw her and smiled, relaxing visibly. The child beamed back at her, and Clive smiled involuntarily too, as he went over to help unload. Caroline was wearing jeans and flat shoes and he still had half an inch on her, he noticed with pleasure.

'Hello.'

'Hello to you too. Are your children with you?'

'They are. They've vanished with your dad.'

'He'd better get some of them to mend the gate. Any of them including Francis would do it better than he does.'

'Your dad isn't here to mend gates, Caro. I'll have a go at it, if he'll let me. My Dad was a foreman chippie, so I do know how to do it.'

She considered him carefully, thinking about what he had said, and he grinned back; a lot more sound than fury about Caroline, if you took her right, and these days he knew how to do that.

'Life is about mending bloody gates,' she said, firmly, reaching the end of her thought. 'That's what men *do*.'

'No, it's not. People like your dad – and there aren't many – are there to think and make other people think.'

'Are you two staying out there, in which case I won't interrupt again?' They looked up, startled to see Caz looking enormous in the doorway. 'How about a drink, whatever you're doing?'

His sister went over to kiss him. 'We are engaging in philosophic disputation about the Role of Men. Clive appears to be an adopted Henriques man in this matter, believing that there is no need at all for anyone to mend gates.'

'Not what I said,' Clive said, equably, handing Caz his offering of a couple of bottles of wine.

'I bet it wasn't. The wretched girl exaggerates. Thank

419

you very much for this, Clive. Now let us go and drink before lunch the champagne she has so flashily provided. Why champagne, Caro?'

They followed him down the shabby passage to the kitchen.

'My lads at Prior Systems and I have got Martins – the chaps who are providing the cash for this purchase, idiot, I did *tell* you – to underwrite a price which enables us to compete with anyone. We got it done on Friday.'

'How do you know? I mean, that it's enough to beat the competition.' Caz handed her a knife and she prodded a boiling pan of carrots.

'My spies are everywhere.' She avoided Clive's eye. 'These are done, Caz. I should take them off and shove them in the oven.'

'How much are you bidding?' Clive asked, deciding it would do no harm to be ahead of this game.

'£50m cash and £10m deferred, depending on profits. Matthew Friern has bid £65m, but he'll shave a bit off in negotiation.'

Clive kept his face straight, while he wondered which of her spies had reported this.

They were interrupted by the sound of devotional music from the living-room, and Sholto Henriques erupted into the kitchen.

> 'And beastly little children
> Shall raise their paws to thee,'

he sang, obviously furiously irritated, in a fluting falsetto. Caz and Clive stared at him and Caroline said coldly that the children had learnt it at Sunday school and were rather pleased with it.

'Why ever are you making them go to Sunday school?' the country's foremost moral philosopher asked furiously and his daughter said evilly that she felt it a useful stabilizing influence in a one-parent family. Her father considered her, then gave up the battle, apologized for interrupting the conversation and was brought up to date on her deal by Caz.

'What about the other chaps, though?' Since Professor Henriques had focused sharply and was asking the questions he would as soon not ask, Clive decided he could safely just stick around and listen to the answers.

'We and Friern are serious, and Shaw are at least fairly serious,' Caroline said, with a sidelong look at Clive. 'Of the other three, one is known to have indicated to the NEB that they would take Prior off their hands as a favour, with several pounds of tea, so we can forget them, given the presence of two real bids. The other two are interested, but it's well outside their real field. £60m cash down is actually a very decent price, so we assume they won't pay it for something peripheral to their interests.'

A much, much clearer and more incisive summary than that offered by the Department's expensive advisers, Clive thought, as he watched Caroline's father think about the answer, a very big man, sitting impressively still at the kitchen table. 'Not necessarily a valid judgement,' he said, the blue eyes bright, 'but a sensible working assumption. Do you have the ability to change your strategy if this assumption – or any other – should turn out to be wrong?'

A sound structural question as one might expect, Clive thought, and no reason at all for Caroline to look exasperated, impatient and about fourteen years old.

'Can you raise the price, for instance?' Clive asked, abandoning discretion in the urgent need to prevent Caroline making a fool of herself with her father, and was relieved to see her take the question properly.

'No, no, that is top whack. It is an agreed policy – I certainly shouldn't be telling you this, Clive – to offer our best price up front and stand pat. The lads can hardly bear it, trained as they are always to keep a bit in hand, but I persuaded them that we'd be better off telling the truth.'

'I take it this is unusual as a strategy?' Professor Henriques asked, gently, and she met his eyes.

'Yes, it is. In the real world out there, people expect you to have kept a bit in hand. I felt, however, we would be better served by behaving as if this were an open-book deal, thereby differentiating ourselves from all other purchasers. It works quite well, politically.'

'The truth having its own validity.' Professor Henriques was angry but patient, and Clive realized that Caspar was watching this fight as carefully as he.

'Something like that,' Caroline said, reluctantly.

'So you don't have much of an alternative strategy?' Caz said, cheerfully, into the charged silence. 'You've got your price and if anyone offers a lot more, you're kippered, presumably. If they offer around the same you depend on being the most attractive purchaser, politically, given that employees get shares.'

'Tell me how employees get shares,' Professor Henriques asked. 'Have they agreed already to buy them?'

'The financial institutions have underwritten the deal in the sense that they will put up all the money whether chaps buy shares or not. However, they have also agreed that fifteen per cent of the equity is reserved for employees and management.'

'Is it, in fact, intended that the employees get these shares?' Professor Henriques pressed on.

Oh dear, oh dear, Clive thought, these two really do fight, don't they? What a way to hold a conversation.

'Amazingly enough, Dad, yes. My lads truly believe in employee share-ownership, and as we sit here, they are closeted with the key personnel of a theatrical company, working out how to communicate most effectively with their labour force. They mean to make sure that their employees take up their full entitlement.'

'I am glad to hear it.' Professor Henriques was tight-lipped but unbowed, and Clive watched wonderingly the two faces, so like each other in expression if not in detail: both pale skins pink with aggravation.

'Tell me about the theatricals, Caro,' he said, hoping to distract the combatants.

'It's driving me insane.' She turned to him with relief. 'I can't get any sense out of Peter Burwood at all, he is knee-deep in scripts and dancing girls. It is a musical drama, called "How We Bought Our Company". It sounded like a cross between a medieval passion play and the *Ten O'Clock News*, when I last heard about it.' She was laughing. 'He plans to invite everyone, including your man, Clive, and the PM. No, don't worry, I told him she wouldn't be free to come.'

'Is it an entertainment directed to persuading employees to buy shares?' her father asked, doggedly, while Clive noted that whoever else might have doubts, Peter Burwood was quite, quite clear he was going to get his company.

'It will have all the right cautionary words in it, Dad – I am quite a good lawyer.'

'I know that.' The two of them looked at each other,

unsmiling and unyielding, and Clive and Caz broke severally and disjunctively into speech.

'It's ready,' Caz said, firmly, as Clive stopped awkwardly. 'Call the kids, Clive – they're with Mum.'

Clive went off to find the children, all seven sprawled on sofas in the big living-room, which did not seem to have been repainted since he had last seen it, sixteen years ago. Lady Henriques greeted him warmly, and he found himself feeling very much at home as he led the troops back, more so, he realized, than the furious blonde cuckoo, sitting scowling at the far end of the dining-room table, as far from her father as she could get, ostentatiously examining a fork which was in serious need of polishing. Caz passed him a bottle and he came up on her left side, pouring it deferentially to make her laugh.

'Relax,' he said, quietly. 'No need to be such a thug – you're making the kids anxious.'

She sent him a reluctant, acknowledging look and exerted herself to place the children and see that they all had what they wanted. Clive sat down by her father and disappeared easily into a conversation about Cambodia, just letting himself acknowledge how infinitely more comfortable he was here than in the family into which he had been born.

They were drinking coffee in the living-room, watching the boys play in the garden while Clive's Samantha and Caroline's Susannah played an elaborate game with small plastic animals on the floor, when Sholto snapped the TV on, murmuring that he really had to see what was happening in Cambodia. The screen image, in black and white, resolved itself into a depressing seascape featuring two trawlers, both listing at peculiar angles. 'Collision in the Channel,' Sholto observed, as the BBC reporter was heard to say that Gerry Willshaw, Minister for Transport, was in our Dorrington studios.

Caroline, who had been looking for a book, determined not to be interested in Cambodia, stopped, and sank into a chair. The camera moved from an earnest, self-righteous BBC face, directing the question whether this latest crash was not the clearest possible indication that some new form of licensing was required immediately, to Gerry, looking tired and defensive, badly lit, in a tidy but ancient sports jacket that contrasted too sharply with his clear pale skin. He was steadily and patiently sticking to the line that a foreign registered trawler had not logged its intentions and had arrived wholly unexpectedly in a crowded shipping lane, and there was no regime which could deal with this kind of folly. But, yes, he would be instituting an inquiry, and had indeed already set it in motion. And, yes, the substantial loss of life was to be deeply regretted, whatever nationality was involved.

Caroline watched him with a sinking heart, understanding that she would not now see him that week, as they had arranged, nor would he telephone her later that evening, because he would be absorbed with this disaster. She watched him, longingly, arms wrapped around her knees, cold with disappointment.

'Very good-looking man,' her mother was observing, thoughtfully. 'Lovely face. Wonderful angle of the jaw.'

Caroline sensed rather than saw her father look quizzically at her mother, who laughed and tucked her hand into his arm. She felt someone tap her shoulder and looked up to see Susannah, indicating wordlessly that she wanted to sit on her knee, and she opened her arms, reluctantly, peering round the child in order not to miss any of Gerry.

'Thank you, Minister,' the BBC person said, giving an uneasy impression of baffled rage. Gerry faded from the screen, and Susannah put her face against her mother's. She hugged the warm child to her, and after a few minutes she put her daughter gently off her knee, saying she must get some more coffee, and slid quietly out of the door into the blessed solitude of the hall, where she stood looking at the patches of colour made by the sun streaming in through the elaborate stained-glass panels of the door, fighting for control. She heard a door click behind her, but did not turn.

'What is it, Caro?'

'Nothing, Caz. I just needed some air.'

'Not much of that in the hall.' Her brother walked round her and looked at her carefully. 'What happened? Susannah saw it too – you suddenly looked absolutely heartbroken.'

She looked back at him, unable to think what to say, and he stared back, eyes widening. 'Oh, no. Is *that* who it is?' A burst of sound from the living-room made them both jump. 'Come upstairs.' He bustled his sister into the small square bedroom that had been hers as a child, and she sank on to the bed, leaning back against the headboard, noticing as usual the smudges on the wallpaper and the faded, dirty paint. He stood menacingly at the other end of the bed, watching her. 'Is it Gerry Willshaw with whom you are having an affair?'

'Yes.' She found a handkerchief at last and blew her nose, profoundly relieved to be able to talk to someone.

'But Caro, why? I mean, he's not nearly as clever as Ben. Or as you, for that matter.'

'Oh Caz,' she said furiously. 'The last thing I care about – have ever cared about – is brains *per se*. What use are they? Gerry knows what he wants, he goes for it, he does not agonize about it, and oh, God, Caz, it is so restful. And stop standing there like the Archangel Michael.'

Caz subsided on to the other end of the bed. 'What are you going to do? I mean, he is married, and it isn't – it doesn't seem to be making you happy.'

'I don't know what I'm going to do,' she said, coldly. 'We never talk about it, but he has never even suggested he might leave his wife.' She stared at the wallpaper. 'And now I won't even see him for days, because of this collision. Oh, yes, that's all I could think about. Sod the twelve dead and six dying – Caz, to what have I come?' She started to cry.

'Don't feel too bad,' he said, reaching out awkwardly to her. 'That's what it's like, I do remember.' He held her, patting her shoulder until she had cried herself out, then reached over to the battered washstand and wrung out a flannel for her. She pressed it to her face, then looked at him.

'You'd better do it again, several times.' He looked at her, doubtfully. 'Why don't you stay here? I'll explain you're having a sleep.'

'I'm not sure I can bear to be alone with my thoughts,' she said, wearily. 'I never cry or I never did, but I might just weep all afternoon if left.'

He sighed and wrung out the flannel again, and sat watching her as she breathed deep into it.

'You ought to consider why you got into this,' he said, thoughtfully. 'Do you know?'

'Not really,' she said, bleakly. 'I just found him irresistible. I still do.'

'He must have hit a nerve somewhere,' Caz said, thoughtfully, and she ground her teeth.

'I have spent far too much of my life listening to Dad or one of you louts seeking a complicated meaning for some quite simple action. Why can't you all just shut up and *do* something for a change?'

Her brother was stung. 'I suppose in those terms, given what you think of us, Gerry Willshaw has absolutely everything going for him; a Conservative junior minister with, what, fourteen years in the Army, while we are all mildly pacifist Labour Party supporters and academics. You would have had to invent him, if he didn't conveniently exist, wouldn't you?'

Caroline stared back at him, choking with rage. 'He lives in the real world,' she said, furiously. 'He deals with people, he uses power. He is elected to do things, rather than being a self-selected theoretician like Dad. Yes, it is what I want.'

'Darling, wake up, open your eyes!' Caz was scarlet with anger. 'He's a politician, for God's sake. You get between him and the top of the greasy pole and you'll be out. Those people want the power and the status, and they don't much care about individual people. It's true, of even the active politicos in our – well – my lot. And it goes in spades for your Conservative chums.'

They glared at each other, and Caroline felt sheer rage clearing her head. 'You'd better go back to the lunch party,' she said, coldly. 'I would be grateful if you would say I was resting.'

They stared at each other, bleakly, and suddenly she remembered from the depths of her own misery what had happened to him.

'I know you've been there too,' she said, awkwardly,

and reached out, cautiously, to touch his hand, and he winced. 'Gerry is actually rather like us. An idealist, like Sholto, in a way I couldn't define.'

'What you've never seen is that Dad is not only an idealist, he knows what he wants and goes for it.'

She considered that, reluctantly, sniffing to clear her head. 'And Mum gets swept aside.'

'Oh, Caro, open your eyes. I don't know why she moans to you, but you should by now understand that it's nonsense.'

Caroline looked past him at the wallpaper, hearing her mother complain that there was never any money and things got so dirty, and remembering her heart being wrung. But if you looked at it carefully, as after all she was trained to do, a six-bedroom house in the heart of Hampstead was worth a lot, and they could have lived somewhere less grand and had new wallpaper. Her father would not have cared; he notoriously didn't mind where or how he lived. She looked back at her brother, feeling sick and angry and trapped.

'He loves you, the poor man,' Caz said, wearily. 'And you kick him in the teeth every time, unfailingly. You needn't worry about me gossiping about your lover. If you want to deliver that particular blow to Dad, you have to do it personally. Come down when you're ready. I'll invent something.'

In the immaculate Georgian house outside Dorrington, Lucy and Matthew Friern were also having coffee and watching the television, but without their children.

Matthew heaved himself out of a deep armchair and turned the TV firmly off. He sat down by his wife on the sofa.

'Come upstairs.'

Anything, Lucy thought, putting her coffee down, that would make Matt less tense and difficult should be welcomed. He had been walking around all weekend, exuding mixed anxiety and excitement. It had to be Prior Systems; he'd been jumpy ever since he had come back on Friday.

'The boys will be back in an hour, darling – don't forget. I'm driving them back to school,' she warned as they reached the bedroom.

'I know it doesn't leave you worn out.'

'Depends what it's like,' she said, provocatively, starting to take her clothes off.

'No, wait.' He walked over to her and started to undo the buttons on her blouse. 'Don't,' he said sharply, as her hands moved to help. 'Just keep still.' He took off her blouse and skirt, leisurely, then inspected her, touching her breasts as she reached out for him. 'Stop it. Just stand still.' He undid the suspenders, touching her gently, and rolled down her stockings, telling her sharply not to fidget.

'I'm all wet.'

'I'm not going to hurry.' He slid a hand inside her pants. 'You are, aren't you?' He took his hand away and reached to undo her bra, gently rolling her nipples in his fingers. He inspected his handiwork with pleasure, as she shivered slightly in the spring air.

'Matt, I'll come just standing here, if you don't hurry.'

'No, you won't,' he said, holding her and pulling her pants off. 'You can stand there and wait till I'm ready.' He stood back, stripping off his clothes and watching her as she backed against the wall – wide-eyed. He pulled his shorts off and moved towards her.

'Like this. Standing up?'

'Oh, yes. You'll have to help. Oh, God.' He felt her clench round him as he came inside her and he hung on as long as he could, until she came, explosively. 'That's what two weeks' skiing does for you,' he said, boastfully, in her ear, as he reluctantly disengaged.

'Of course it is,' Lucy said, pleased. 'You can keep your knees bent long enough. We must go more often. Actually that's silly. I could stand on something rather than test your knees.'

'You could, couldn't you?'

They both stared round the bedroom critically.

'A pillow wouldn't be firm enough,' Lucy observed.

'Be a bit slippery too. Couple of books? Anyway, we won't get lucky again today, skiing or no skiing. Come here, I want to lie down for a bit.'

'Ten minutes. Then I must get up – the boys will be back. You can stay here, you need a sleep.' She tucked herself in beside him. 'Why were you wandering about last night?'

'I did some work.'

'Why? What on?'

'On Prior Systems. How we'd organize it.'

She sighed. 'You seem very sure it's going to come our way.'

'I reckon we've got a pretty good chance.'

She considered him warily. 'You're depending on Councillor Williamson?'

'Only partly. We may have lost round one there, but Prior isn't going to get the next one, Marsh Lane. We're ready this time, we have that committee tied down. We've got one of the Conservatives with us now.'

'When is the next contract due to be placed?' she asked, wearily.

'A week come Monday. We'll go under their price.'
He was relaxed and easy, and settling himself comfortably against her, but she was alarmed.

'Matt, is that sensible? You told me that they can bid fifteen per cent under our price, anyway, on that particular system, because of their cost structure. Won't we lose money?'

'It isn't going to work like that. We'll get the contract for Friern, then when we get Prior we'll use their factory to do it. And we'll get the price up a bit again in negotiation as we go along. Just like that bugger Burwood did.'

'But I thought the council gave them extra because they really had changed their minds in several different ways, and messed up the contract.'

He stiffened. 'You've been talking to Caroline.'

'I always talk to Caro, but not about this, since you two have decided to fight to the death. I got *that* from the local paper. Jenny Michaelis's article.'

'Stupid cow listened to Burwood, didn't she?' He rolled away from her, and she sighed.

'Perhaps we had better not talk about it, but *I'm* worried that you're making yourself ill. I don't want to be a young widow, you know.'

She stroked his back and after a minute he curved himself into her. 'You'd have plenty of offers.'

'Yes, wouldn't I?' she said, smugly. 'But just the same, I don't want you having a heart attack or a stroke over this. There are other bigger companies.'

'I don't like losing. And I'm not going to lose this one. Just wait till tomorrow or Tuesday, you'll see.'

'Why?' She pulled herself up in bed and peered over at him, suspiciously, as he lay buried in the pillows.

'Never you mind. Christ, look at the time. You'd better get dressed.'

'Oh God.' She was distracted immediately. 'And I need a shower.' She fled towards the bathroom, and he closed his eyes firmly, and managed to be sound asleep by the time she emerged, hair washed and ready to dress.

In Hampstead, Caroline had also restored herself to a state fit for company, so that she looked no worse than pale and puffy round the eyes, which would have, she thought grimly, to be postulated as being the result of a sleep in the afternoon. She came down cautiously to a silent house, and put the kettle on to the decrepit gas-stove, exasperated, as always, by the lack of an electric kettle. She had given her mother one, once, but she would not use it on the basis that either there was no room or if there was, it was just as convenient to heat water on the top of the stove. She recalled suddenly that when she had attacked this argument on the grounds that factually it took twice as long and required twice as much energy to heat a comparable amount of water, it had been her mother, not Sholto, who had wriggled away from the logic by stating that it was better to have a method of heating water that did not require electricity, because where would you be in a power-cut? There was, she recognized wearily, a lot in what Caz had said about her mother, and it might well be that she had been spending energy fighting on the wrong ground for someone who did not want her support.

The children were all in the garden and she peered guiltily out at Clive who was patiently bowling to her Timmy, with his William and her Francis as joint wicket keepers. A decent medium-pace bowler, too, she observed, and broke into a smile as she saw her Susannah posted at slip, chatting across the wicket to Clive's daughter, who was equally *dégagée* from her part in the operations. Timmy caught an edge of the ball at that moment and it flew past Susannah, who turned to watch it with interest while all the masculine participants roared at her. Caroline laughed aloud, delighted.

'Tea!' she shouted, deciding to distract the parties. Her boys and Clive's scowled at her, but Susannah came running, relieved to see her back in the land of the living. She put an arm around the child and looked over to Clive, who was retrieving the ball from the herbaceous border. He grinned at her, his face lighting up, and she smiled back at him, soothed.

'You OK?' he said, quietly, under cover of tea.

'Yes. Yes, I'm sorry to rat, I just needed a sleep.'

'You're looking tired.' He was watching her carefully, and she could think of no response, so she just looked back at him, observing the pleasing way his dark brown eyes were set, and the strong crease between his dark eyebrows. 'Your lass'll never make a cricketer,' he said, firmly, and she blinked at him, then realized that Sholto was watching them.

'No, I'm sorry, Clive,' she said meekly. 'To be honest, I haven't encouraged her very much in that direction.'

'She'll never find a good husband,' he said, darkly, and the moment passed, with Susannah, confident and disbelieving, asking him whether she really, really had to be a cricketer in order to persuade men to take any notice of her.

'Sarn't Major? Gerry here. You saw the TV? I'm not going to make our meeting. Even as we speak I am being driven to London. I must get David to do something about the train service, but that's for another day. Any problems that can't wait?'

Tim Bailey organized himself into a chair and reached for the papers in front of him.

'If you can't keep next weekend's engagements, we maybe have a problem, but we can worry about that later in the week. I'll have a word with Susan then.'

'Any council business?'

'There is a difficult item but not till Monday week. But I was going to raise it with you, because it'll be too late by next weekend to do very much. It's the contract for the new estate over at Marsh Lane: 103 flats in 20 blocks, three years to build.'

'I remember. What's the problem?'

'Do you have anyone with you?'

'A driver.'

'Well, I'll go carefully then. There are three bidders: Maceys, and you don't need to think about them, Friern and your friends.'

'Ah. Trouble?'

Tim Bailey considered a scribbled note on the edge of his papers, straightened it up and wrote 'S' at the top of it to remind himself to feed it into the shredder when he had dealt with the issues it raised.

'Your friends are said to be the lowest bid, by about fifteen per cent.'

'They ought to get it, then.'

'Friern have managed to find a loophole which means they can have a second bite at the cherry. I understand they are going to come in lower yet this time.'

There was a pause, while he wondered if the line had gone dead. 'Gerry?'

'Yes. Is this usual? The procedure, I mean.'

'No. But it's difficult to argue with anything that gets the council the best price.' He listened to the silence, but he decided he had to plough on. 'Your friends are going to want to argue, aren't they?'

'Yes. Yes, they are.' Another thick silence ensued, which Bailey decided to sit out. 'We don't control that committee, of course,' he said, cautiously, when the silence had stretched for a full minute. 'Not a lot we can do. Maybe we leave them to fight their own battles on this one.'

'Mm.'

Oh, that isn't going to work, is it, Bailey noted, interested. 'I'll have a word with Ted Malvern,' he volunteered, suppressing a tiny flicker of unease which he traced instantly to Mrs Whitehouse and her comments about chartered surveyors.

'Would you do that?' Gerry was sounding relieved. 'I could talk to him myself, but I know this week isn't going to have any time in it.'

'Better you don't do it, anyway,' Bailey said, bluntly.

'This is true.' There was a hesitation and a crackle on the line and Bailey listened, alert. 'And particularly not at this moment, Sarn't Major – there's something up. I don't know quite what.'

'Watch your step, then,' Bailey said, alarmed into directness.

'I will, don't worry. But look, Tim, if the people we speak of get done out of that contract, they won't take it quietly. There will be a frightful row, in which I may have to be involved, and it would be nice not to have that happen. Not now.'

'I've got a few people I can talk to, Gerry. I hear what you say.'

'Hear from you later in the week?'

21

Clive Fieldman was not at his best on the Wednesday morning, three days after he had lunched *chez* Henriques and knew it. He had endured an hour of Michael Watson's farewell party the night before and, deciding that honour demanded no more, had gone home to his flat, had three brandies in two hours of mindless TV-watching, and then fallen asleep heavily in the chair, waking chilled and cross at 1 a.m. He had dragged himself to bed, but slept only fitfully thereafter, between tiredness and alcoholic dehydration. It was only 10 a.m., but he wanted nothing more than to curl up and go to sleep under his desk if necessary, on the departmental carpet. He compromised by folding his arms on the desk and resting his cheek on this inadequate pillow, let himself go off into momentary oblivion.

'Mr Fieldman.'

He woke and opened one eye at his secretary. 'Just having a bit of a kip,' he said, redundantly, and she smiled at him constrainedly in what he recognized, with surprise, as real affection.

'I am sorry to disturb you. The Secretary wishes to see you.'

Not many civil servants used that form correctly, he thought, sitting up in surprise, pulling his tie together and buttoning his collar. 'The Secretary' was Sir Francis, the permanent secretary, so called to distinguish him from all the impermanent, ministerial secretaries.

'Why? Did he say?'

'His office did not know, Mr Fieldman. They asked if you would be free at 10.30.' She looked at him and hesitated, and he glanced at his watch.

'I'll go and have a wash. And I need a coffee. Tell them I'll be there – I've got ten minutes, after all.'

He got there, washed, suitably braced by a cup of coffee and alert for danger, by 10.30. He had been in his post for only just over a year, so the possibility of some distinguishing career move could probably be discounted. It had to be trouble of some unspecified variety.

'Clive. Sit down.' Sir Francis Templeton KCB gave him a quick glance before returning to the three closely written sheets in front of him, and Clive sat on the edge of the visitor's chair, nerves jangling.

'I think you'd better read this. Addressed, as you see, to Peter Wilson, at the Civil Service Department.'

He knew the handwriting, he realized, as his eyes focused, the immaculately legible small writing of a man who had entered the service as a clerical assistant and taken a long time to rise to a position where he had anyone to type for him. Michael Watson's writing, pages of it, for the man's mind was too woolly to make a point concisely. He blinked as Caroline Whitehouse's name leapt out of the cramped lines and started again. It was a terrible letter; Watson had poured out his accumulated grief, rage, disappointment and sense of rejection, and the result was both pitiable and poisonous.

... did not expect to find an under-secretary so forgetful of the duty of a civil servant to remain neutral ... perverting what should be objective advice to serve Ministers' political ends ... favouring a woman friend by telling her how to shape their proposals to match the wishes of politicians ... abandoning objectivity in advising that a financially insecure grouping should be preferred on the basis of a fashionable shareholding arrangement ... doctrine of accountability subverted in order that greedy managers should be able to secure public assets at too low a price ... public should be informed.

'Of course, if he *does* try to inform the public, he puts his pension at risk,' the Secretary said, briskly. 'And no one is going to answer that part of the letter in other than that sense. However, I do have to produce a note for the CSD dealing in some way with the points he raises.'

Clive, who was feeling as if he had been dropped down a mine shaft, took a deep breath and announced that he would just read the letter again. It was infinitely better the second time, he realized, as his heart stopped thumping and the taste of bile at the back of his throat receded. What the bloody man was saying was that undue favours in terms of encouragement, access to minister and information had been given to Caroline Whitehouse and the Prior Systems team, this patronage being extended by him, Clive Fieldman, in the faith that he was furthering his minister's wicked dogmatic party political ends. No mention at all of Friern.

'You will remember, Secretary,' he began cautiously, using the code that meant his chief executive knew perfectly well the facts he was about to recite, 'that Prior Systems is the system-building group which the NEB are selling.'

'Indeed. And Mrs Whitehouse?'

'Is the solicitor acting for the management of the

group, who are one of the rival bidders for the company.'

'And ministers would naturally be keen to see a management/employee buy-out succeed, given their manifesto commitments,' Sir Francis said, helpfully.

'Yes.'

'So what did you do, Clive? Against that background?'

'Advised the Minister to see the Prior Systems team when they asked to come. I did talk to Mrs Whitehouse – with whom I trained as an articled clerk sixteen years ago, and whom I have not seen at all since that time – on what ministers would like to see as a feature of any buy-out. *And* told her that it would have to be a fair price. I have otherwise done nothing other than make encouraging noises to all comers.'

'It is in any case the NEB who are responsible for the sale.'

'Indeed,' Clive said, gratefully observing the structure of a strongly worded defensive argument beginning to rise from the muddy ground.

Sir Francis considered him carefully. 'How well do you know Mrs Whitehouse? I remember her as very attractive – I know her father.'

'I never knew her that well – I mean we worked together when we were young. She's very able. Then I met her again ... what ... three months ago, at the privatization conference. I've been to lunch with her and about ten of her family twice, and to her firm once, and I've taken her out to lunch once. And she hasn't had any inside information from me about what her rivals are up to – not that she needs it. She seems to have her own methods.'

'Might others be able to claim that Prior Systems had had anything of an inside track because of this relationship?'

'Well, Secretary, there are six groups bidding, three of whom never approached me or the Department, or not to my knowledge. But by coincidence, not only Mrs Whitehouse but also the wife of the chief executive of Friern Construction plc, who are one of the management team's principal rivals, trained with me at Smith Butler. Lady Friern did not finish the course, Mrs Whitehouse did.' He paused and cleared his throat, wishing he could manage not to sound husky. 'I actually know Lucy Friern – Lady Friern – better than I know Caroline Whitehouse. Indeed, if I have to add it up, I think I've seen Lucy more often than I've seen Caroline in the last three months.'

Sir Francis looked at him thoughtfully, his round pale blue eyes looking particularly bulbous. 'Not altogether helpful. I suppose it is just better that you are on terms of friendship with two groups rather than one.'

'It was not designed to be helpful, Secretary; these are the facts. I suppose I might have refused to meet Mrs Whitehouse or Lady Friern at all, had I thought about it, but, particularly since we are not directly responsible for the conduct of the sale, I saw no reason to go out of my way to offend old friends.'

Sir Francis was unimpressed. 'Had *my* old friends been two women of my own age, each involved with one of the main contenders, Clive, I think I might have denied myself the luxury of their company for the duration. Awkward.'

Clive sat, seething, but recognized that the Secretary was not understating the case. The trouble was that he had not been willing to do that kind of thinking because of his – not his, never his and certainly no longer his – Lucy. And it had for some time been clear to him that he was not Caroline's only source of political advice, but he wasn't going to say *that* either.

'I'm sorry, Secretary. I do not believe that I have given anyone any information or preference they should not have had. I see, however, that it would be possible to place another construction on the matter and I'm very sorry that poor Watson – whose case this isn't, and who actually doesn't know much about it – has done so.'

Sir Francis nodded, briskly. 'Yes. Well, that's the sort of thing I'm going to say. No, I'll draft it but I will, of course, show you it before I send it. I don't think the CSD is going to fuss unduly, given the source of the letter. I understand that Peter Wilson found the appeal interview particularly tiresome.' He paused, and waited until he had Clive's full attention. 'Clive. Remember, it's a very sharp pyramid. Doesn't take much, given the competition, to leave you stranded just below the top. And that would be a pity.'

Clive, furious and embarrassed, managed to mumble a further apology, but his superior waved it away. 'Let's just hope he doesn't give a copy to *Private Eye*,' he said, briskly. 'I'll send you the draft some time tomorrow.'

Clive walked back to his own office, feeling as if he was walking on eggs, or marbles, and sank into his chair, shaken to his bones. Thank God Watson had attacked on the wrong front, in an area where he felt secure in his own behaviour. The Secretary was right, and just how right he did not know and was never going to. Unforgivably, and meanly, he found himself hoping that Friern, or anyone who wasn't the management of Prior Systems, would turn out to be the winning purchaser. But if Friern won, as he had been sharply reminded, he could also have problems, even without Michael Watson. And it wasn't quite worth it. He loved Lu, but she had never been going to leave Matthew for him. I must stop this, he thought, seriously. Either marry or burn, he thought, walking restlessly from door to window to steady himself against the realization that the office he had just left, at the top of the tower, was where he was meant to be, and that he was putting his career at risk for a woman who had never cared enough for him even to consider risking her own marriage.

He sat down, elbows on the desk, looking down at his hands, his brain churning, and he slowly remembered that Caroline was in this, and should be warned. He wondered fleetingly why it had taken him a good twenty minutes to think about her and realized, wryly, that his own guilt had made him behave like a rat on a treadmill, and pushed him into worrying obsessively about a woman not even hinted at in Watson's letter. Because he truly had nothing to blush for, other than the most trivial indiscretion in relation to Caroline Whitehouse, he had not even considered whether she ought to be put on warning. Well, she ought, and officially as it were, in fairness to her. In any case, he realized, brain belatedly beginning to work again, Sir Francis would assume he would communicate with Caroline; very well, he would consult Sir Francis about the form any communication would take, so that from here on he would have cover from his Department, and the proprieties would be rigidly observed. He called to Miss Williams to get him another ten minutes with Sir Francis and found himself in the Secretary's office almost at once. He waited, quietly, while Sir Francis signed a letter and rose formidably to his feet.

'That letter, Secretary,' he said, formally. 'I'd like to tell Mrs Whitehouse at least the gist of it. It seems to me that she ought to know it's around.'

Sir Francis considered him, levelly. 'Sit down, Clive.' He waved him to one of the big armchairs. 'I thought,' he said, conversationally, sinking into a chair, 'that we should inform the Minister as well.'

Clive looked back at him, trying to keep his jaw in place. What was the matter with him? Anxiety and guilt were making him totally inefficient. 'Sorry, I had assumed we would,' he said, making as fast a recovery as he could. 'I remembered, however,' he said, thankfully, 'that the Minister is away till tonight. Do we want to trouble him with this in Manchester, on the phone?'

Sir Francis was still watching him very thoughtfully. 'No. It shouldn't be necessary. Tonight will do. But he must be told, in case this surfaces somewhere else.' He paused. 'I have asked the principal establishment officer to ensure that Watson is interviewed, and warned against repeating these allegations.'

'Ah,' Clive said, feeling slightly dotty. 'Yes.' He just stopped himself from adding hopelessly that it seemed like a good idea.

'About Mrs Whitehouse,' Sir Francis said, having waited courteously to see if Clive had anything else to say. 'The senior partner of Smith Butler and I are old friends. I will talk to him. I think that would be better.'

'Oh, absolutely,' Clive said, hastily. 'Yes.' One more idiotic noise out of me and he'll ask me if I ought to go home for a rest, he thought, despairingly. 'Thank you,

Secretary.' He got himself out of the office somehow, and crept back into his own, barricading himself behind Miss Williams and a loaded in-tray.

Two hours later, Michael Appleton stood irresolute in Caroline's outer office, scowling at a closed door with the 'Do not disturb' light on, noticing irritably that the dust on the processor screen showed up in the bright morning light. In addition to his other problems, it looked as if the partners' complaints about the variable standard of cleaning were justified and he would have to do something about it. He knew Caroline was in; he could hear papers rustling and he did need a word, but he was not relishing the prospect. I am senior partner, he reminded himself, responsible for forty other partners as well as this stormy petrel, and emboldened by the thought he knocked on her door, to be greeted by a wordless snarl, then a shouted order to go away and come back later. He opened the door decisively on the full force of Caroline's best people-repelling glare, which changed to sheer surprise as she recognized him.

'Michael. Come in. There isn't any more coffee, but I suppose I could make some.'

He considered the big meeting table at which she was working, which was entirely covered with neat piles of paper, each with a covering sheet on top. He read the one nearest to him; it was a sharp summary of the problems of the particular draft and a courteous suggestion that the articled clerk responsible should address them forthwith. He looked at eight similar piles, with respect; this particular bit of his ship was back under command.

'I'd got behind,' she said, unapologetically, 'but I

445

think I've caught all the balls before they hit the carpet. Just.'

'I didn't come to complain about your work. How long have you been here?'

'Since dawn. Six o'clock, to be precise. I have no meetings today, so I can work. What *have* you come to complain about?'

That one didn't miss much – never had, he thought, reluctantly forced to the point. 'I've had a chat with an old friend in the Department of the Environment. There's been a complaint which implies that we – you – are using undue political influence to get Prior for its management.'

He was not quite looking at her, out of embarrassment, but she made a little suppressed noise that drew his attention. She was gripping the table and had gone a greenish white, and, as he moved instinctively to reach for her, she lifted a hand to fend him off and knocked over her coffee cup, soaking the draft she had been annotating. Both lawyers, as one person, reached for the Kleenex and worked in unison to arrest this disaster.

'That's for my ten o'clock meeting tomorrow,' she said, huskily, clearing her throat. 'Who complained? And what about?'

He explained, giving her the gist of the letter, and watched her anxiously as she drew a deep breath, the colour coming back to her face.

'Oh, well. Oh, *that*'s all right. Poor Clive.'

'What were you expecting?' he asked the top of her head.

'I suppose that for a lawyer being told that there is a complaint is the modern equivalent of "Fly, all is discov-

446

ered".' She was not prepared to look at him and he knew she had been up to something. She put her hands flat on the table and breathed out, carefully, then smiled at him. 'However, this is pretty vague and has very little substance.' She considered the position again, turning slowly pink with relief. 'In fact, Michael, all it says is that I really *am* doing my best for a customer.'

'This is not the kind of letter we want flying around, Caroline.'

She nodded. 'I do agree. I'd apologize, if it was my fault but it isn't this time. I really have done nothing untoward in this context and neither has Clive. He'll be in trouble with his shop, I don't doubt. But one can't worry too much about letters from people you've just fired, for heaven's sake.'

There speaks Sholto Henriques' daughter, Michael Appleton thought, wearily. 'The Department is naturally worried about any of this getting into the newspapers. We need to have some words ready, in case.'

'Well, if it happens, the Department will have to bat first. And if anyone asks us, all we say is that of course our client has sought guidance from the sponsoring Department, and has had meetings with both the Minister responsible, Mr Winstanley, and the senior civil servant, Mr Fieldman. We assume anyone in their senses who wants to buy Prior Systems has done the same. Because they *have*. You see, Michael, I know Matt Friern actually had Winstanley to dinner, and Clive knows Lucy better than he knows me – I mean in the sense that those two kept in touch more than Clive and I did.'

Michael Appleton was writing, carefully. 'Yes, that works. We don't speak unless we are spoken to either. And any commenting gets done by me, Caroline, not by you.'

She looked across at him with affection as he sat, four-square, finishing a sentence. He passed her the draft and she made, unhesitatingly, two minor amendments. 'Do we disclose that Clive trained here?'

'If I am asked. And I shall emphasize it was sixteen years ago.'

'And he had to train somewhere, after all.'

'Thank you, Caroline.' He rose to go, but stopped at the door. 'You said it wasn't your fault, this time?'

She looked up at him and he understood she wasn't going to tell him. 'I have been known, Michael, to make the odd mistake in my long career.'

'Good heavens, Caroline. Are you feeling all right?' She stuck her tongue out at him, looking about seven years old, and he was grinning as he closed the door, but he went to his office a worried man.

Left behind, Caroline found she could not carry on working. It was just after noon and she still had a vast pile to get through before her first meeting at nine o'clock the next day, but she was, she realized, too distracted. She looked at the phone, hesitated, then decided to go ahead and talk to Clive. The poor chap – he was pretty rattled, she decided, but as she pointed out to him they were both innocent. She heard him laugh, reluctantly.

'They think I'm pretty silly, here.'

'I suppose it was thoughtless to go on having lunch with me. But what we were going to get up to in the presence of ten of my family I cannot imagine. Are you really in the shit, Clive?'

He hesitated. 'It'll blow over. These things do. We're telling Winstanley about it, so he's on warning. And the chap who wrote the letter has been told it is more than

448

his pension's worth if he does that again. Or tries to say the same thing anywhere else. That'll shut him up.'

'It would any of us,' Caroline said, reproachfully. 'Rather a heavy-duty threat for the poor old boy.'

There speaks a Henriques, Clive thought, in pure exasperation; that poor old boy was an idle drinker who was threatening a distinguished civil service career, and all the years he had put into it.

'Sorry,' she said. 'Much worse for you than me. I'm merely being accused of being pushy while you are accused of dereliction of duty. Sorry. Why did he do it?'

'Well, now, that's the odd thing.' Clive, melted by the sharp analysis of the problem and the apology, decided to share his difficulties. 'Our security people rang him up and he says he was urged on to do it by a chap he used to meet in the pub opposite the Department. I think I actually saw the chap one day, that's what's even odder, but I couldn't describe him in any detail. Anyway, Watson had this chap's business card with an address, but no one had ever heard of the chap. I mean, the firm was there all right, it's just they'd never employed anyone of that name.'

Caroline stared at the phone. 'But that's *very* odd, Clive. An *agent provocateur*. There can't be any security implications, can there?'

'Not possibly. I mean it's a construction company we're talking about here, not a rocket-building outfit. I understand that the right people have been consulted, but we're all baffled.' He hesitated. 'I'm sure they didn't expect me to tell you all this, Caro – keep it quiet.'

'Oh, I will. But I'm in this too.' She was sounding serious. 'Because you see it's actually directed at us – not you. Someone is trying to sabotage the management bid for Prior by discrediting us. It's industrial sabotage.'

'Now, that is right,' Clive said, slowly, his heart lifting, guiltily. 'Or that's the effect of it. I just assumed Watson was trying to drop me as deep in the dung as he could. But the chap who put him up to it was concerned to make trouble for the Prior team.'

They both fell silent as they worked their way through this, Clive deciding that it would be extremely helpful to put this theory to Sir Francis.

'Bloody Matthew Friern,' Caroline said, slowly.

'Surely not?' Clive said, taken aback, his own thoughts interrupted.

'It was he who was going to buy the whole lot of them, just to get his hands on Prior. No, don't comment, Clive, I know you can't, but I did hear tell. And it's he who's doing all the other funny things up in Dorrington, like sabotaging my lads' paint-shop, and getting in the way of the contract negotiations. No, I'm not going to bore you with it.'

She was sounding, he realized, alarmed, just as she had in the old days when another firm of solicitors was trying to cross her. 'Caroline! Do simmer down.'

'I'm sorry you're having a bad time, Clive.' She was sounding brisk and sociable. 'I'll quite understand if we can't even lunch together for a bit, but when it's all over I'd love to see you. Must rush.'

She put the phone down firmly, and moved restlessly towards the window, nerves jangling. The difficulty was that all the big guns were on the other side; Friern really did have more purchasing power than the Prior team who were tied in to the very tight rates of return required by the institutions. They weren't, of course, totally inflexible; there was a dearth of good deals and it was clear that the economy was moving into recession, which gave a supplier to a local authority a real advantage. No Labour-controlled authority was going to stop building flats for their voters. But there was a darker side to all this. Matthew Friern was playing really dirty and if he wanted Prior enough to do that, then he also had the financial resource and backing to bid high – like fifty per cent above the Prior team's finely calculated offer. And no amount of political help she could realistically muster would enable a new government to sell a public sector company to its management when there was a bid that much higher from a sound public company. I would be pretty critical myself, she thought, grimly, contemplating sadly the hard-working, patient, quick learners up in Dorrington, who rested such confidence in her. She fished out the *Financial Times* from under a pile of papers and found the listing for Friern. The share price was just below the year's high, and their interim results were due in two weeks, thought by the analysts to be an advance, if not much of one, on last year's results. No help there, she thought, and then remembered a bit of a conversation she had had in the last two weeks. She sat down abruptly, shocked at herself, and then thought of Peter and the lads struggling with a wrecked paint-shop, of Councillor Williamson, plump and pleased with himself, and of Clive's wretched subordinate, pushed and manoeuvred into writing a letter that could have put his pension in jeopardy.

'All right, Matthew,' she said, to the silent room, and sat down with a note pad for ten minutes before picking up the phone.

By four thirty Andy Eames Lewis felt he had had enough; he had been out to lunch on a sales pitch – not that a senior director in Walzheims' corporate finance department quite put it that way – and he had felt it necessary to drink two glasses of wine rather than the one which was normally his absolute maximum. He pressed the buttons on his console; the market would close in half an hour and he flipped through the department's major clients – nothing particularly exciting happening to any of them. Friern was down a bit, but it was close to the end of the account. He decided to have some more coffee to wake himself up. He was due to meet Emma at a dinner party at which Matthew and Lucy Friern would also be, but he needed to look at the merger analysis that the troops had done for another client before then. He worked through the analysis and was interrupted by the phone after twenty minutes.

'Jeremy Winnick, Andy.' It was a familiar drawl, but Andy sat up, sharply. He usually spoke to this man's assistant.

'Nice to hear from you. Quiet day in the market, I see.'

'Up to a point. Something's going on with Friern's shares. What's happening, do you know?'

'No. How much down?'

'They're 20p off and going south smartly. Not a pretty sight.'

No, indeed, and quite enough to alarm the third most senior partner in Marquands, brokers to most of the prestigious names in the market and to Friern.

'To the best of my knowledge, Jeremy, everything is going fine, just as I told William when we talked about doing the rights to pay for Prior Systems.'

'The word is that they have trouble in the civil-engineering subsidiary, what's it called, Bartholomews?'

The voice was languid, but Andy was not deceived; this was a crisis and if by any chance there was a nasty which Matthew had not disclosed, Marquands would not be relaxed about it. They were grand enough – and arrogant enough – to be able to do without Friern's business any day of the week. And if Matt's share price went down sharply, not only could you kiss goodbye to getting a rights issue off at a decent price to pay for Prior Systems, but consequential damage to Friern's status and standing in the market would follow. Blast and damn. Tiredness forgotten, he said a hasty goodbye to his caller and told his secretary to find him Matthew Friern, forthwith.

'I know he'll be at the same dinner as me later this evening, but I must talk to him before then. Try the London office, then the London flat.'

'Caroline? Hamish here. I've just been having a wee chat with the other side of the house. He tells me your friend Matthew Friern's share price is bombing down. What's the word?'

'Good heavens, Hamish, is it? By how much? Oh dear, I am sorry.' She grinned into the phone.

'If it goes on, he could be out of contention for our friends in Dorrington. Could we bid a bittie less, do you think?'

'*No*, dearest Hamish. (a) Friern aren't the only sharks in the pond, (b) their share price may recover and (c) we could blow the whole thing if we start backing and filling. Our whole political stance depends on being ostentatiously truthful about the value of the company. For better or worse.'

'Mm. Well, you're the political guru.' As pronounced

453

by Hamish, the word had two long u's and about six r's. 'A problem in Friern's civils side, they say. Would you know about that?'

'No,' she said, with as much disinterest as she could muster, 'but civil engineers are always in trouble. They tend to overvalue the work in progress. Either that or there's a fraud they didn't find – that's very possible.'

'Aye. Well, I hear our friends in Dorrington have had trouble too.'

'Someone dropped a spanner in the paint-shop, a couple of weeks ago, as I understand it, and they lost a few days' production. Damn nuisance.' She succeeded in sounding merely irritable. 'I could do without being told every time any little thing goes wrong up there. Since they insist on keeping me informed, I told them to tell your lads, so you could worry too.'

'Very good of you, Caroline. I'll think of you next time.' Hamish sounded relaxed, and she breathed out, noiselessly. She said goodbye to him, pausing only to tell him the latest joke which she had picked up at lunchtime, as a contribution to his carefully collated collection of jokes suitable for after-dinner speeches.

The phone rang again sharply and she picked it up.

'Hi.'

'Oh, Gerry,' she said, letting out her breath. 'How are you?'

'I'm sorry I haven't rung all week, but you saw what happened?'

'Yes. I realized we wouldn't be able to meet tonight.'

'I've got an hour. I've got to vote, then I've got a meeting with the inspectors later. But I've said I must get home and have a bath and change. At eight thirty? Is it any good? I'm sorry I couldn't let you know.'

'Yes,' she said, mind racing. 'I *am* still theoretically going out to dinner. I'll meet you at the flat?'

'Oh good, I do want to see you. I'm sorry, my love; I'm just being buggered about this week.'

As always, she thought, momentarily, as she put the phone down, but there was nothing to be done. When he was free, she would scramble across London to see him. Well, that settled the evening, and she started to pile up papers; she was more or less ready for the next day and that would have to do, if Gerry was around.

The phone rang again and this time it was Peter Burwood, sounding rattled. 'Anything new your end?' The question was deceptively casual and she understood she was being asked for reassurance, as usual.

'Just that the Friern share price appears to be dropping rather fast,' she said, smugly, sitting back.

'What does that mean?'

'Panic,' she said, succinctly. 'It means Friern would have to issue a lot more shares in order to buy you. At best if their share price really drops, they may not be able to do that at all. And anyway a falling share price scares shitless – sorry, I mean really worries – the board of a public company, and makes them concentrate on their own business rather than anyone else's. It makes them vulnerable to takeover, for example.'

'Why is their price falling, Caroline?' Martin cut in.

'It links, apparently, to a rumour of trouble in Bartholomews' accounts. There's always trouble in civil-engineering subsidiaries.' She beamed smugly at the phone. 'People are very jumpy at the moment in the market, or so my *FT* said yesterday. Tell me about the show, Peter. You will remember, won't you, that I need

455

to see the script? We don't want you running the company from a prison cell.'

'It's got to be clear and punchy,' Peter was sidetracked immediately, as she had hoped.

'And it has to be true, and a bit better than that in the sense that it must also not mislead,' she said, sharply, and listened to the stubborn silence. 'Peter? I'll leave you,' she warned.

'Oh, you can't do that, Caroline.' It was Martin, laughing. 'What would we do without you? Can we tell people here that Friern's share price is on the skids?'

'Better not. Wait till the morning; it'll be in the papers. But an expression as of men who have escaped the Pit when the word "Friern" is mentioned would not come amiss.'

Andy Eames Lewis, his wife recognized immediately, was in a filthy temper. He moved smoothly across the room to where she was sitting with a fellow guest and kissed her, but he was rigid with tension.

'What is it, darling? Something gone wrong?'

'Mm. Are the Frierns here yet?'

'Just Lucy. Matthew is apparently running late and we are not to wait.' Perhaps he was just hungry, she thought, hopefully, as he hailed Lucy Friern, a vision of elegance in a black velvet suit, who had returned with their hostess from a trip to view some new acquisition of the household.

'Andy, how nice. We thought all the men were going to be late, like my wretched Matt.' She kissed him gently and, tense though he was, he felt himself relax insensibly. 'You won't wait, will you, Susie? He is naughty, he just left a site too late, even if he isn't quite saying so. He'll get here.' She looked under her eyelashes at Andy, who understood immediately that Matt had explained the full strength to her and sent her on ahead to keep the Friern flag flying, and to conceal the frenzied backstage activity. He waited his chance and managed to extract her from the group.

'What's Matt doing?'

'He's with Bartholomews' MD. There *is* a worry there – we fired the last finance director, but Matt's always said that the new bloke wasn't turning up anything terrible.'

'He never bloody told *me*. When did the FD get fired?'

'About three months ago.'

'Christ! And the new man's been in – how long?'

'Six weeks. Don't look like that, Andy, six weeks is quite long enough for a good FD to find out if there is anything dreadful happening.'

That was probably true, Andy thought, in the sense that a competent man ought to know by now whether there was a mass grave rather than a few bodies individually buried. But Bartholomews were responsible for thirty-five per cent of Friern's turnover, and rather more of its profits, and trouble there could be serious. Nor had his second conversation with Marquands' Jeremy Winnick, just before he left the office, been at all comforting. Friern's price had dropped another 5p after hours and it was expected to fall further the next morning. In fact, the presence of Jeremy Winnick still in the office at 7 p.m. was, of itself, deeply unreassuring. The trouble was that the market had heard this particular story of 'trouble with a subsidiary, nothing to worry about, got a new man in there' many times. And in too many cases the story ended in tears, revelations of real horror, resignations and the share price dropping like the proverbial stone. Still, he decided, finishing an excellent glass of champagne in celebration of his hostess's birthday, Lucy was here, looking beautiful and apparently content to stay at his side; sufficient unto the day would be the evil thereof. And just at that moment the bell rang and his host could be heard greeting Matthew with the hearty relief of a man who was not now going to have to pick the hostess off the ceiling. Matt appeared, seconds later, red-faced but immaculate in his dinner-jacket, a big man who made his host look slight and insignificant. He looked around the room and made purposefully for his wife.

'Sorry, darling,' he said, and kissed her perfunctorily, without looking at her. 'Andy. Must have a quick word.'

Several, indeed, Andy thought, vengefully, and they edged towards the window, leaving Lucy to divert or distract anyone who thought they might want to talk to either of them.

'My chap swears there isn't a real mess. He wants, his being new and all, to take some provisions which would knock Bartholomews' profits back to about ten per cent below last year. But he doesn't *have* to. If we give him cover – and alter his bonus system for next year – he can live with getting the profits out at just about the same as last year.'

'Is he sure? We'd do better to take a few days and get it right.'

'It's not your fucking share price.' The response was swift and furious. 'Yes. I'm sure. The MD's a cunning bugger. He didn't think anything was seriously adrift, he just didn't quite trust the last bloke, thought he wasn't thorough enough in a difficult year. Nor was he, but it'll only make ten per cent difference and that need not show.'

'Good.'

'So what do we do tomorrow? An announcement?'

'Not necessarily. Not if we can help it. Not if the share price steadies. Can you get your board together if you have to?'

Matthew thought, putting down his empty glass which he had drained as if it were water.

'It's always the non-execs that are the trouble.' He scowled at Andy to remind him that it was Walzheims who had insisted that he appoint two powerful non-executive directors in place of the dim, local solicitor and the even dimmer chairman of the local farming co-operative in Dorrington. 'The buggers are always off at another board meeting.'

'Oh, I think you'll find they will get there, if they're needed,' Andy said, confident in the knowledge that both of them owed their places on this and several other boards to Walzheims. He gazed at the curtains, working methodically through the steps necessary to protect a client and decided he had taken them, or as many as he could. But your defence was always, in the last analysis, only as good as the facts, and a lot now turned on whether the difficulty in the civil engineering subsidiary really was only minor.

'I expect your people at Bartholomews are working tonight?' he ventured.

'They are,' Matt said, grimly. 'They'll ring me at midnight – I'll have to get home for then. Oh, Christ, that's Frank Lewis over there. I'd better have a word – you keep Lucy company.' He picked up his glass and detoured via his host to pick up some more champagne before advancing on the most recent arrival at the party, the chief executive of a cement company who was a major supplier to Friern. And would make a good customer for Walzheims, if they could be seduced from Fredericks, but right now Andy thought, he had had enough. He looked quickly across the room to see that Emma was all right, decided that she could usefully go on talking to her hostess, and turned with relief to Lucy.

'Was Matt expecting all this?' he asked.

'Absolutely not. He was tremendously pleased with himself yesterday. He wouldn't tell me why, but he thought he was winning. The battle for Prior Systems, I mean. They've got trouble in the factory and Matt was tremendously chuffed this morning. Then this. I'm furious; I wanted to sell a few shares to buy something, and now I can't. Not at 205p.'

Of course, Lucy Friern was a substantial shareholder; indeed she had two per cent of the company, some settled on her by Matt, the rest given to her by a doting father. 'You will remember, Lu, to tell us if you want to sell, won't you? Married to the chief executive as you are.'

'Of course, Andy, I know that.'

He considered her; she was more seriously ruffled by this latest turn of events than he had ever seen her; interesting that – truly her father's daughter beneath that flowerlike exterior. A drop in the share price really got to her.

'So what are Walzheims going to do, Andy?' she said, asking the question that her husband had not yet formulated.

'Sit tight, and make quite sure of the extent of the trouble in Bartholomews. Matt says it is trivial?'

'He really does think it is,' she confirmed. 'He's likely to be right,' she added, detachedly. 'He's perfectly sensible about that sort of thing and he's had years of experience.'

Andy wondered fleetingly if this was the level of tribute he could expect from his own wife and hoped she cherished a few more illusions.

'Should I know more about this trouble at the Prior factory?'

She considered for a moment, broodingly watching her husband. 'No,' she said abruptly. 'I'd like never to have heard of bloody Prior; it's been nothing but trouble. Look, Andy, did your people look up Harrison? Yes? Well, I'll talk to Matt and let you know when I have.' She gave him a sidelong look. 'You could buy me lunch.'

'Any day. Tomorrow? I could explain Harrison a bit if that would help.' He watched her profile, and the familiar sweep of black hair, stylishly piled on top of her head. 'You're looking very striking tonight.' He got a slow look from the violet eyes that left him short of breath, as he followed her into dinner, in obedience to their hostess's signal.

Just across the river, Caroline stopped her taxi short of Gerry's flat, in deference to his views on discretion.

'Darling, come in – I'm on the phone and must finish. Sorry.'

Then hurry, she thought, nerves twanging, if we only have an hour. She took her jacket off, crossly, and hung it up.

461

'Hi,' he said, appearing beside her and taking her in his arms, and she melted, as always. He was in shirt-sleeves, his collar rumpled, undone at the neck, his tie pulled loose as it always was the moment he was out of the public eye. Unlike partners in big solicitors' offices with their tailored suits and shirts made for them, his suits did not fit particularly well, his shoulders were too muscular and his bones too big for off-the-peg tailoring, and the collars of his shirts did not sit properly. But the physical exuberance of the man and the planes of the face overrode all, she thought, as he kissed her urgently. Interesting that her mother should so instantly have noticed his looks, though, come to think of it, Sholto, too, had distinguished good looks, and wore frightful suits and badly fitting shirts and, like Gerry, did not care.

'My love,' Gerry had not noticed her attention was wandering. 'Do you want the bad news now?'

'Do you know,' she said, in a flash of revelation, 'that when you start a sentence with "my love" it always contains bad news?' Does he do that with his wife as well, she wondered, with a momentary chill while she watched him, disconcerted, consider the point.

'I must watch that. Sorry. But look, I have actually to be back at the madhouse in an hour. I didn't try to tell you because I wanted to see you. Come and have a drink at least, and tell me what you have been doing. Are you busy?' He wasn't looking at her and she felt sudden childish rage overcome her; he was just going through the routine for dealing with yet another duty in his life.

'Very. Friern sabotaged the Prior factory and I've been retaliating as best I know how.'

462

'What?' He turned, a glass in his hands, looking anxious, and she looked back at him soberly.

'Never mind, Gerry. We'll manage – I am managing – but it's a remarkably dirty battle. I had not realized what an unscrupulous fighter Matt Friern was going to be.'

Not doing too badly myself, come to that, she thought, watching Gerry pour them both drinks.

'Tell me,' he said, authoritatively, and she told him about the paint-shop and the suspected sabotage.

'I couldn't prove it, no,' she concluded. 'But what Friern are really at is undermining our – Prior's – ability to get the next contract.'

He considered her, seriously. 'Do all lawyers get this much involved with their clients?'

'No, they don't,' she said, defensively, feeling that she was being criticized. 'But my lot are not up to the weight of Friern, who turn out to be very big and bad indeed. The lads need me.'

'You be careful,' he warned. 'What have you been doing to Friern?'

'Nothing much,' she lied, deciding that he really didn't have time to hear all this, particularly since he didn't have much feeling for finance, and she had other things to tell him. 'But I'll think of something.'

He looked at her searchingly, and she leant forward to kiss him, realizing, as she had before, that he might not be academically clever, but he had very finely honed instincts and, if his attention was truly on her, he was not easy to fool.

'Don't worry.'

'You promise me, Caro, to watch yourself? You will talk to Tim Bailey if you need more help, won't you?'

'Yes, darling. I'm sorry I even mentioned it. Particularly not when we only have such a short time.'

'I'm sorry. God, I'm sorry.' He was sidetracked into an apology as she knew he would be, and pulled her towards him.

'You need to eat,' she said, regretfully.

'No, I don't.' He sounded smug. 'I thought of that, I got my office to give me sandwiches in between meetings.' He tucked his chin in and looked at her, bright-eyed, watching her to see what she wanted and she laughed.

'Just time for a quickie.'

'God, you are unromantic.'

'You've gone off me.'

'Never. It's a bit much to get you round here and fall on you. But I wanted to see you.'

Probably that was all he did want, she thought, momentarily, but I need him. She untucked his shirt at the back and slid her hands up his shoulder blades, as he kissed her hard, reaching under her blouse for the catch on her bra.

'Bed,' he said, sliding a hand over her breasts. He let go of her, picked up her jacket, discarded on the floor, tidy as always, and chivvied her into the bedroom, unable to avoid an anxious glance at his watch.

'Stop doing that,' she said, furiously, peeling off her blouse. 'We've got twenty minutes at least. Historically, that has been enough.'

He stopped, arrested, with his shirt half off, and for a moment they looked at each other as strangers. 'This isn't fair on you. I ought to take you away somewhere.'

'Oh Gerry,' she said, in sudden pain. 'It's a fantasy. Your face is so well known, we can't go away anywhere where the TV gets – which is *everywhere*.'

He pulled off his shirt and walked around the bed to hold her.

'I need you,' she said, baldly, near tears. 'And now.'

'Me too. Come on. Last one in bed makes tea.' He was first, because he pulled trousers, underpants and socks off in one movement, while she was delayed by the need to undo stockings, so she was still struggling by the time he was lying on his back, hands behind his head, smugly displaying an enormous erection.

'Oh, very good,' she said, laughing, touched by the easy expressive masculine complacency. 'Oh, Gerry, I do love you.'

'And I love you. And all this is awful, but we just have to make the best of it. Come here. Aha. No. I'm going to wait until you absolutely can't stand it any more.' He kissed her stomach gently and moved down, feeling with his tongue, and she relaxed in the pure pleasure of it.

'Come here, so I can do you,' she said, reaching out, but he pulled away and she understood he meant her to come first, which she did in an excess of pure sharp pleasure. He made sure she was finished, then as she arched against him, he worked his way up to kiss her on the lips. She reached for him, but he was leaning across her for a condom. Condom or no condom, she thought, catching her breath, it might be that, unusually, she was going to come again, and she concentrated, failing to get there again, but not minding, as he came suddenly, surprised by himself, with a sharp cry of pleasure.

They lay, entangled, for a few minutes, but she could feel him fidgeting, and under the terms of their agreement, got up and made the tea, dressing before she left the bedroom. When she came back with the tea, he was dressed and was tidying the bedroom, and she stood in the doorway watching him between love and exasperation.

'Are you expecting your Secretary of State to carry out a kit inspection?'

He looked at her, arrested by the thought, and laughed. 'The training does stay with you for life. The trouble is that there are lots of us living near here, and people drop in if they think I'm around. Let's have tea in the kitchen.'

He glanced at his watch as they sat down, and winced.

'You're already late,' she said, smugly.

'Well, I did warn the whips. They can manage on this vote, but I must be there for the next one.' He looked at her soberly and swallowed his tea. 'My love – do you know you are absolutely right about that, I must watch it – the bad news is that I can see no way of seeing you for the next couple of weeks. I'm spending this week here but I'm doing a tour of Wales, trying to convince them that we're still here and still love them, and next week I'm in Brussels. I'm sorry, this is awful.'

'It is,' she said, sadly and he got up, restlessly.

'And you're right, it's a fantasy that we could go away together. We can't do any of the things that lovers do: wake up together, go away together, even spend a lot of time together.' He was looking out of the window into the dusk of a spring evening, all the lines of the mobile face straight. She watched him, reminded sharply of the Greek verse-speaking competition she had entered, as a fifteen-year-old schoolgirl, presumably to annoy Sholto, who had thought she ought to be doing physics. How had it gone, that passage from Homer? 'And there will come a day when Sacred Troy will fall,

and Priam and the people of Priam of the ashen spear.'
There had not been a dry eye in the house, she recalled,
with pride; even through the archaic language she had
been able to communicate the emotion and the sense of
bleak terror as the long-dead speaker stared clear-eyed
into the future.

'Gerry,' she said, sharply, frightened, and he turned
to look at her.

'We'll manage. I'll think of something.' He kissed
her, then started to tidy up, bustling as he always did,
and the moment passed as they worked as a team to get
the flat straight.

'The car's there,' he said, looking out. 'I'll go, then
give me five minutes and just bang the door after you.
OK?'

'I can manage that.'

'I'll ring you.' He kissed her, and was gone, leaving
her leaning against the wall in the hall, waiting out five
minutes.

22

Friern Construction plc
Interim Results:

Despite the rumours which recently chopped 60p off the share price (currently down to 200p from the year's high of 246p) Friern Construction plc's interim results compare well with last year, and the company should be on course for full-year profits of £34m, a million above last year. At the half-year, they were showing profits of £14.2m, an increase of £700,000 over the same period last year, and expect to increase the profits in the second half above last year's £19m.

Chairman Sir Matthew Friern agreed that accounting problems had been encountered in the civil-engineering subsidiary, Bartholomews, but says that these will not affect the full-year results. If Friern are successful in their bid for government-owned Prior Building Systems, they have already said it will be financed by way of a rights issue. Given the recent alarms and excursions, any issue will have to be at a substantial discount to the share price. SELL, if you are in for the short term, but the company is sound and the price could go up substantially in the medium term.

Andy Eames Lewis read the *Investors Weekly* piece again, despondently, and decided he had better bite the bullet and ring Marquands before they rang him.

'Not a pretty sight,' his usual contact said, with that ineffable critical confidence which all Marquands' directors inhaled with the air in that building. 'But he's right,

Andy, we're talking about a discount of at least fifteen per cent here.'

Andy decided to make sure he understood exactly what he was being told. 'Assuming today's price . . . what have you got there? 202p, OK, then new shares would be . . . say 170p – I'll come back to you, William.'

'Don't reckon on the price holding up, either. Andy, is your client absolutely sure he wants Prior? These high-profile political things are buggers; there's always a fuss and his share price does not need it. What? Yes, of course, we can get a rights issue away, I told you.'

'Glad to hear, William. Thank you for your support, and I'm sure Matthew will be grateful too, when I tell him.'

'We're still hearing that there may be more of a mess in Bartholomews than anyone's owning up to.'

'I do assure you, William, we've pressed Matthew and the subsidiary management very hard on this. They really are confident the accounts are right.'

'Mm. Well, we'll talk to a few people, and try to get the market to share your confidence.'

'Our confidence, I hope, William.'

'Sorry.' It was the most perfunctory of apologies and Andy ground his teeth, but managed not to be distracted from his question.

'Do you know where the rumour is coming from, William?'

'I heard it again yesterday from a chap I talk to in Fallons. Peter Lyms. Do you know him?'

'Any relation to Frank Lyms at Martins?' Andy asked, sharply.

'Brother. Why?'

'Martins – the development capital side – are funding the MBO for Prior,' Andy said, evenly.

'You mean you think it may be inspired?' William was on to it at once.

'Not necessarily. Martins act for a couple of the civil-engineering biggies as well and they might well have got the gossip from them.'

'Mm. Sorry, Andy, are we done? I'm being summoned. Keep in touch, won't you?'

Well, that will provide something to fuel the gossip mill this morning, Andy thought, savagely, and considered the problem carefully. A persisting rumour, and reappearing today, when the market was settling down a bit. Looked a bit neat to be a coincidence. But it wasn't really Hamish Brown's style; cock of the walk in the development capital field, he frequently boasted that he didn't understand the stock market. And even aiming off for legitimate exaggeration, that was probably true. His eyes narrowed as he thought about the other key player in the team advising Prior, the experienced corporate lawyer, who, professionally, did understand the stock market. Caroline was not one to let an underhand injury pass unrevenged, as he would have warned Matthew had his client had the grace to consult him. It was a neat and damaging blow that had been dealt to Friern, and not traceable unless the perpetrator overplayed their hand. And she didn't need to do any more; too much damage had been done to the market's view of Friern's shares for them to stage a solid recovery and give Matthew and his board the elbow room to put in a knock-out bid. He sat, doodling on the pad, eyes narrowed, and his secretary, silently opening the door, considered his absorbed profile and closed it again, equally quietly.

*

In the DoE, Clive was watching his minister absorb the short brief which was meant to update him on the sale of Prior Systems. Winstanley had been looking pleased with himself when he arrived. He and James Mather had spent the morning in committee with the Housing Bill and had made more progress than they had hoped – indeed a squint at James's meticulously noted copy told Clive that they were doing particularly well. But the Friern news was acting as a depressant.

'Time we got this one sold,' Winstanley said, crossly. 'You're not telling me, I hope, that Friern are in trouble?' He looked sideways at Richard Watts who, as usual, had arrived straight from Heathrow.

'No, Minister. Merely that their share price is substantially down which places a limit on their ability to make a huge offer for Prior.'

'They wouldn't drop out?' Winstanley looked alarmed.

'They have not apparently indicated any such intention, Minister. Quite the contrary; according to Gruhners, Friern's bankers – Walzheims – apparently made a special trip to assure the NEB of their continuing interest, and their confidence that a rights issue could be placed without difficulty.'

'So who else is left in the running? Apart from the management.' Winstanley was looking anxious.

'Formally, there are three more candidates. Of these I am told that only Shaw are talking about a price in the right bracket. £60m, I mean. But don't discount Friern, Minister; it's just that it's going to cost them more than they thought.'

'And perhaps more than they want to pay,' Winstanley said, reluctantly.

'One of my chaps did the numbers this morning, Minister, and met me with them at the airport. Even with a fifteen per cent discount on the share price at its current level, it still works for Friern at £57m–£58m. Doesn't reduce earnings per share, which is a key number.'

Clive took the offered paper and considered it. 'But at anything over £58m the current earnings per share *do* get reduced.'

'Yes. It's a matrix, of course, Clive; if the share price goes up, or you can squeeze the discount back, then you can pay a bit more than £58m. But not otherwise.'

The point is, Minister – as I hope you have absorbed, Clive thought putting the paper away carefully – that Friern's lead has been eliminated, and if the management's offer of £50m down plus £10m deferred holds, then it is quite as good as Friern's and there are all sorts of good reasons for preferring the MBO if the price is only marginally worse. And plenty of flexibility has been left to you to exercise that preference. He watched his minister, who was fidgeting impatiently, obviously wishing the whole problem would go away.

'Anything I've forgotten?' Winstanley asked, looking over to his advisers, and Clive shook his head, being himself desirous of getting to his own lunch-date. He was profoundly uneasy, when he let himself think about it, about the situation between him and Lucy; he loved her and hated the thought of losing her but it was indiscreet, to put it at its lowest, to be so involved with the wife of one of the only two realistic bidders for Prior, particularly after his recent experience with Watson's letter.

He sped down in the lift with Richard Watts, envying

him his waiting car and driver, while he undertook the usual hunt for a taxi. To his relief one drew up and he sat in it studiously going through the bill clauses the committee had managed to get through that morning, to avoid thinking about the coming encounter.

He rang the bell at the Friern flat and had to wait a few minutes until Lucy arrived, harassed but unapologetic, explaining crossly that she was on the phone. He sat down at the kitchen table, in the bright spring sunshine, watching her as she dealt at length with some difficulty with a new set of curtains. She was very smartly dressed in shades of faded navy, carefully made-up, and wearing a lot of costume jewellery. Not the sort of outfit that anyone was going to get to tear off in a flurry of passion and he understood, painfully, that she was pulling away from him, as she had been when they last met. He put his hands gently on her shoulders, but she tensed rather than leant back against him. He held her as the conversation ended and turned her to face him.

'What is it, Lu? Do we both have to say that it's all got too difficult?'

The round eyes widened and she looked at him properly for the first time since he had arrived, and he felt his throat constrict. She was so beautiful and so familiar, and whatever caveats he had applied intellectually to the affair, the truth was he still wanted her very much.

'Oh, Clive.' There were tears in the beautiful eyes and he understood that he was putting her under too much of a strain by asking for an answer. He kissed her, tasting the salt on her cheeks and, feeling her move against him, started to burrow under the silky layers at her waist.

473

'Clive, I'm supposed to go out in an hour.'

'Too bad.'

She pushed him away from her and he resisted, angry and miserable.

'Clive, we must talk.'

'All right. You talk.' He held her, firmly.

'I need to sit down. I'm squeezed against this table.'

He let go of her, crossly, and she sat elegantly down, on the sofa, pinning back a wisp of hair. He sat down close to her.

'Tell me.'

The violet eyes flickered and he realized that he had lost the initiative and waited grimly to see what she was going to do.

'I'm having a very difficult time with Matt. He's got very wound up about Prior Systems, and, of course, the last week has been dreadful with our share price going down. He really does need me. And he's got very suspicious; he's never really liked Caro and now, of course, she's up against him and he knows you're a friend of hers. I think he thinks you two are conspiring against him.'

'Then he's mad,' he said, flatly.

'*Anyway*,' she said, with a sidelong look, 'it really is very difficult to see you at the moment – I had to tell the most fearful lies to manage today at all. It's all a strain and I just think we ought to stop, at least until the Prior sale is over.' She looked at her hands and then at him, cautiously, to see how he was receiving this.

Clive, who knew that he ought to have been relieved that she was saying it for him, felt wretched. 'We could go away,' he said, heavy-hearted.

'Oh, darling. How? I don't think you understand what

it's like at the moment. Matt's around all the time, in a bad temper, dragging me up to Dorrington to be civil to bloody people on the council, or insisting we have dinner here with some boring stockbrokers. I don't have any time just now.'

Clive looked back at her, beautiful, distressed, trying very hard to convince him. Bugger this for a game of soldiers, he thought, in the idiom of his childhood, and reached out for her.

'You're right. We ought not to be doing this, the way things are!' He took the key hairpin out of the back of her hair, ignoring protests, and kissed her until she relaxed and started kissing back. He stopped and looked at her.

'I *do* love you,' she said, ruefully.

'Let's go to bed, come on.' He ignored her hesitation and marched her into the bedroom, stopping to kiss her, then hauling off the familiar counterpane with a practised movement. 'It had better be good if it has to keep me going,' he warned, sadly sitting down and pulling off his tie, and she smiled at him, admiringly.

'Oh, it'll be good.' She pulled off the various layers without any apparent difficulty, and he, having managed to undress even faster, helped her out of a very small pair of knickers.

'I'm not having you on top,' he warned, sharply, and rolled her over.

'You know I like it this way too. Wait, I'm not ready. I can see you are.'

'Reliable, that's me,' he said, smugly, then felt a desolate sense of loss and sheer rage.

She was watching his face and caught her breath as he pushed into her. He moved in the familiar warm place and as she arched her back against him he found himself inspired by anger, and felt her respond sharply. She came quite quickly and would normally have taken him with her, but nothing was working and he could only go on, getting increasingly far away from any release. He stopped, resting on his arms, and started uncontrollably to weep.

'Clive,' she said, crying too, and pulling him down on her. 'Oh, God, Clive, darling. Wait for a minute.' She rolled sideways and held him to her.

'Sorry,' he said, helplessly. 'It's not just me, is it? You want to stop. Have you got someone else?'

'No. I would have said so.'

Yes, of course she would, he thought, being in her way as direct as Caroline. When did either of these bloody women ever do other than tell their chaps the odds, in words of one syllable? Comes of giving them the vote, he thought, suddenly remembering his father, who always produced this in response to difficult female behaviour.

'Well, it was very good for me,' she said gently. 'Shall we try the other way up?'

'No.' Released by the recognition that there was not another bloke in the frame and cheered by the realization that a recovery seemed to be taking place, he kissed her and slid into her again, and with a huge effort of concentration he managed to come.

'Oof.'

'Very flattering, darling. Delighted it was such a success.'

'All you up-market women are the same. Want it wrapped up in pretty paper. Where I come from, we just get on with it.'

'I *know*, darling; it's absolutely why I have always been so glad not to live there.' She was looking marvellous, he thought, with a pang, stretched out luxuriously, her narrow waist emphasized by the curve of her hip. Like most women she thought her hips were too wide, and he had never been able to convince her that they were just what he – and most other men – wanted, particularly in bed.

He looked at his watch; he had managed to keep all meetings off to 4 p.m., and he still had half an hour. He squinted at Lucy who was showing no signs of leaping out of bed to keep her date, and decided not to remind her.

'So tell me why Matthew is being so difficult?'

'It's the share price. If it falls, it's more difficult to buy Prior.'

'I've just had that explained to me.'

'By Caro?'

He sat up and put on his glasses, seriously startled. 'No, of course not. By the Department's overpaid merchant bankers. I wouldn't discuss this with Caro – more than my job's worth. Does Matthew think I do?'

'I don't know what he thinks. Except that he thinks Caro sabotaged his share price.'

'How did she do that?' He peered down at her to find that she was looking irritable and uncomfortable.

'He thinks she spread the talk about trouble in Bartholomews in the market.'

'How would she have known?'

'She's got civil-engineering clients. She could have picked it up there. She's very clever.'

Clive contemplated his loved, beautiful mistress and realized, again, that there was a dimension of her he always managed to ignore. This was her father's daughter, and she would guard her interests – that was what she was telling him; in the end everything would be sacrificed to the prosperity of the Friern business, which was the financial base on which she operated. It was not lack of ability but lack of motivation that had kept her out of the business world, and she knew, now and always, exactly what she was doing.

'Have you seen Caroline recently?' he asked, wondering if that friendship, too, was going to be abandoned for the moment.

'We had lunch together last week, and I haven't dared tell Matthew *that*. He'd spit feathers.'

'It is dirty pool to attack his share price. *If* Caroline had anything to do with that.'

She sighed. 'Matthew's not playing by Queensberry rules either.'

'What's he doing?' he asked reluctantly, understanding that Caroline's reference to the paint-shop had not been merely conversational.

She rolled over, away from him to sit on the edge of the bed. 'Forget it, Clive, I don't want to talk about it. He is my husband after all, but he's just gone a bit OTT about all this. I wish he'd give up the idea, concentrate on the rest of the business and buy something else later. Prior Systems just isn't big enough for all this grief.'

She leant forward to settle her breasts in her bra and straightened up, so that he could do it up for her. He looked at the narrow, elegant, familiar back and put his hands flat on her shoulder blades. 'Are we ever going to do this again, or are we really saying goodbye?'

'Oh, Clive. It had to come some time.'

He turned her so that he could see her face. 'I'd like to go on, though, when this bid is over.'

'I need time to think.'

He looked at her, sadly, taking pleasure even through grief at the perfect line of her jaw. 'When I was a lad, that meant that the girl had got fed up with you.' He did not wait for her to reply but turned away to finish dressing.

'Darling, do you want tea?'

She was in a silk dressing-gown, standing in a patch of afternoon sun by the kitchen counter, her black hair stark against the bright white of the kitchen, and he hesitated.

'No. I've got to get back. I'll ring you.'

She was crying, gently. 'I'm sorry.'

'For Christ's sake, stop apologizing.' He kissed her gently on the mouth and went sadly out into the bright day.

The late afternoon sun was slanting across the board-room table of Prior Building Systems, which was all but invisible under piles of papers and drawings. Caroline, who had arrived half an hour ago on a crowded train devoid of any buffet facilities, and was nursing a splitting headache, surreptitiously took three Anadins.

'Peter. Don't bother my pretty head with the fucking details. Sorry. Just let me get the essentials and I'll go and see what I can do. Friern have come in just under your bid for Marsh Lane, right? That's the contract that accounts for about a third of the workload in year two and three on the projections, and on which we thought we had a fifteen per cent price advantage. OK. What if we don't get it?' She sat, waiting for the mounting pain over her right eye to subside, while two board members of Prior assured her, variously, that there was no question of not getting this contract, it was *theirs* and the buggers at Friern should never have been allowed to rebid, and that if by some black mischance Friern did get it, they had not a cat's chance in hell of doing other than making a thumping loss on the contract, the way they were planning to do it.

'*We*'re the only people who can make money at our price,' Peter Burwood reiterated. 'We've got the system and the factory.'

The headache had made Caroline less than tactful. 'Friern could be reckoning that they will own your factory and the system by the time they have to deliver on this contract.'

'That's right.' It was Martin who hadn't been working himself into a fury, who was ready for the point, while the other two gaped at her like landed fish.

'But they couldn't risk that,' Peter said, appalled. 'If they can't buy us – and by God they're not going to – they could lose a fortune.'

Caroline looked at Martin, who was sitting very still. 'What would you do, Martin, if you had a contract on which you couldn't make money, but one of your rivals could?'

'I'd subcontract it. And take a management fee.'

'We'd never bail those buggers out and let them take a fee.' Peter exploded, fair skin abruptly scarlet.

'Would it not be worth it to you to have that load in the factory in years two and three?' Caroline decided that the outside messenger would have to bring in the bad news, and waited out the ensuing furious silence stoically.

'Could be.' Graham's mind was working again.

'Friern are not going to get their hands on this company, or on that contract. It's ours.' Peter was in a tearing rage and she and his two board colleagues eyed him warily. He glared at them inimically. 'I've not spent all this time with Hamish Brown and his merry men without understanding that if we don't get that contract, they'll drop their valuation of the company. They won't support a £60m bid – we had enough trouble getting them there.'

'This is true,' Caroline said, into the pause. 'It does bugger up your bid. And, if Friern gets it, then he *knows* he can do it at a profit, if he gets his hands on Prior. And there isn't much downside risk to him, because if he doesn't get his hands on you, he can turn the contract over to someone else – or to you – for a fee.'

'And if Friern gets it, we can't maintain our bid but he can still top us. Even with his share price down where it is.' Peter banged the point home.

'OK. Then Friern don't get it.' Caroline dug out another two Anadins. I shall rattle if I take any more, she thought, but needs must.

'Can we go and see Winstanley again?' All three men were watching her hopefully, and she felt momentarily paralysed by responsibility.

'No,' she said, rallying. 'No point. Chap is not responsible for local government corruption, and it would take far too long to explain to him. No, we've got to attack at source. Take me through it again. Why are Friern allowed to rebid?'

Martin sighed. 'They are claiming they added up five pages twice.'

'But all anyone has to do is to check the original tender document.'

'It will have different pages in by now, so that the number adds up to near enough ours,' Peter said, wearily.

Caroline considered him, wishing her head would ease. 'It ought to, I agree. Can we check? Never ignore the obvious; they might not have got round to changing the pages.'

'They'll have substituted a whole new tender, Caroline – I would have. You don't want to be caught in a council office fiddling around with binders,' Graham objected.

'Lots of new copies, I suppose. How many did you have to provide? Six? You'd have needed a suitcase. And another one to take the old copies away. Bit suspicious, I would have thought.' She looked around at them. 'Or am I being naïve? People probably walk in and out of council offices with suitcases all the time.'

Martin shook his head. 'No, they don't. Not when there is a tender about. Even Dorrington council's not totally stupid.'

'Councillors have briefcases. Pass me that.' Headache momentarily forgotten, she reached for a copy of the Prior Systems tender and an empty briefcase. 'You could get two in here, and that's all,' she decided. 'And when did all this happen? Today. Well, maybe they didn't manage all of them. Worth checking, now.'

The four of them looked at each other, wide-eyed.

'I don't believe I'm thinking this,' Graham said, and Caroline looked at him, seriously.

'Nor do I. Nothing as difficult as this happens in top London solicitors, believe me. So, who is going to burgle the council offices? No, all right. Well, who can we get in there?'

'A councillor?' Graham wondered aloud.

'Well, there is Ted Malvern,' Martin said, doubtfully.

'Bloody unhelpful last time – I mean he was pushed into being any use at all by Caroline's mate.'

'That's the answer,' Caroline said, abruptly. 'Can I have an office? I'd rather not have an audience, but don't go home, I may need you.' Amid assurances that no one at Prior Systems ever went home at 5 p.m., unless it was a half day, she was escorted to an office, solicitously plied with tea and biscuits and given two telephones. Well, Gerry had said to call on Tim Bailey if she needed some local help, she reminded herself, and help was certainly needed – fast. She dialled his office number and breathed out in relief when she found him, and told him that she was on her way round. She finished her tea before shouting for someone to drive her to the station hotel where they had agreed to meet.

'This is a one-to-one conversation,' she said, apologetically, to Peter, who had elected to drive her himself and had parked discreetly away from the lights of the hotel.

'I know.' He gripped her arm. 'Good luck. You know how important it is.'

Indeed I do, she thought as she walked into the hotel, and here I am, with the father and mother of a bad head. She saw Tim Bailey immediately. He was sitting quietly at a table, back to the wall, where he could watch the door. To her surprise he kissed her and put a heavy arm around her, and she looked at him doubtfully.

'You're up on wires, girl. What's the problem?'

483

She told him, refusing alcohol in favour of more tea, and he listened, asking only a couple of questions.

'So I wondered, Tim, if you could wheel in your man, Malvern. We didn't manage to get him going last time, although we know him.'

'What if there's nothing there? If we find only an orthodox six copies with the right numbers?'

'Then we'll think of something else. Private detective perhaps, because that's what *happened*, Tim, and it'll have left a trace somewhere. But your man isn't being asked to risk his neck: he is a councillor, he can ask to look.'

'Oh yes, he can do that. I just wanted to know what your next plan was. Does Gerry know about all this?'

'No, he's busy and I didn't bother him. He told me anyway to ask you if I needed local help.'

'You stick to that, girl. This is my patch.'

She was instantly enraged, but remembered who she was and what she was trying to do and managed a simper. 'Of course, Sarn't Major. Goodness, you are kind.'

'Less of that and all.' He looked at her carefully. 'Got a headache?'

'A splitter. I missed lunch and I'm absolutely full of tea and Anadins.'

'Sit here quietly and wait. I'll make a couple of calls and see you're fed.' He got up, light on his feet for so stocky a man, and she closed her eyes, exhausted, and fell straight into sleep.

'Caroline, where're you staying? Here?'

She opened her eyes, completely disorientated, to see Tim Bailey's face sideways on, as he bent to speak to her.

'No,' she said, when she could speak. 'Have to go home. Got a meeting tomorrow, first thing.'

He made a disapproving noise, but did not try to dissuade her, simply checked which train and that she had no reserved seat. He vanished again and she closed her eyes, gratefully, managing only to drowse until he came back. 'God, I'm sorry, Tim,' she said, with an effort. 'I don't seem able to stay awake. I must ring the lads at Prior.'

'Don't promise anything.'

'No. I just want to tell them I'm doing my best and that I'll get the train tonight.'

'We'll do that. My girl will pass a message. She's organizing a seat on the train for you. Come and eat.'

She followed him, dazed, but comforted, and attempted to thank him, but he passed it off. 'Gerry told me I was to help. He's a great admirer of yours.'

'So am I. Of his, I mean.' She considered this hopelessly ungrammatical statement and gave it up, as a steaming plateful of soup arrived. She ate it fast and without attempting to talk, feeling life flow back and her brain starting to function.

She pushed the plate back and looked up to find Tim Bailey watching her with an expression which disconcertingly combined affection and disapproval. 'I've seen Gerry do that after a bad week,' he said, unexpectedly.

'He has a dreadful schedule,' she agreed and found she had to look away from his inquiring eye.

'It's likely to get worse, not better.'

'Oh?' she said, politely. 'Why?'

'Word is he'll get a step-up in the next reshuffle.'

She could feel him watching her.

'Really?'

'Yes. Yes, people up here will be pleased, I think, though he's very much needed in the constituency.'

She kept her head bent over the steak which had appeared in front of her, and helped herself carefully to mustard. She looked up and met Tim Bailey's look squarely. 'He'll be very good. He'll do it well, whatever it is.'

He nodded and took the mustard, ladling a huge quantity straight on to his steak. 'What's the next step for you, Caroline? I mean, do you get a step-up if you bring this deal off?'

'Yes and no. Top of my tree is senior partner, and I'm some way from that. Below that the main differentiation is money, I mean salary. I might get a marginally bigger share next year and a lot of Brownie points. Which is not the point. Tim, I want this company to go to its management four-square and I'm quite prepared to break any of these bent wankers who are trying to get in our way.'

'Caroline! Language!'

'I meant it.'

'I know that. If it can be done, I'll do it – oh yes, I believe you. I'm sure it happened as you say, but you get things like this all the time.'

'It will not do. It is wrong, and like much that is wrong, it's also inefficient and distorting,' she said, just understanding that she was speaking faithfully in her father's voice.

'I don't like things messy,' Tim Bailey said, methodically finishing his steak.

She recognized the statement as being directed at her and decided to take it straight. 'Don't worry, Tim. I know what I'm doing.'

'In business perhaps.' She blinked at him and he smiled tightly. 'I know. I don't know you well enough to say things like that to you. Sorry.'

'You don't mean "sorry".'

'No.' He sat back and considered her. 'You deal very directly with men, don't you? No concessions, just treat them absolutely as equals, like Gerry says. Oh yes, he talks about you.'

'But it won't work?'

'Caroline, he's been happily married for twenty years. And he loves her.'

'I never assumed otherwise.' She sat hunched in her chair, and he sat silently with her for a minute.

'Time for your train.'

'Thank you for everything. I'll call you.' She walked off, slightly round-shouldered under the weight of her briefcase, and he watched her out of the door.

23

'Andy? Jeremy Winnick. Just wanted to let you know it will be me not William at the meeting this morning. Hope you have good news for us.'

'Indeed we do, Jeremy, in the sense that Matt Friern really is confident about his results. But he'll tell you himself.'

'Good, good. See you then.'

Andy replaced his phone, soberly, and prayed that Matthew Friern was going to be at his most convincing. The share price, after dropping like a stone, had steadied at about fifteen per cent down, but the presence of one of Marquands' senior partners could only indicate profound unease about the rights issue on the part of Friern's brokers. And Marquands expressing unease was a sight to turn strong men queasy. Still, he had done all he could. The phone rang again and he picked it up hastily, grateful for the interruption.

'It's James Edwards here, Mr Eames Lewis. I wonder if I could take ten minutes of your time to discuss our mutual friend. Now? It's not a matter I'd like to discuss on the telephone.'

Andy felt his blood chill. 'Is it anything to do with our mutual friend's civil-engineering group?' he asked, urgently. 'We have a meeting this morning, you see.'

'Nothing to do with the company's figures. Indeed, it concerns the company only indirectly, but it is of importance.'

Andy indicated hastily that he would be delighted to

receive Mr Edwards and shouted to his secretary to book a room while he cleared the in-tray. The buzzer went to tell him that Edwards had arrived, and he rushed for the lift to the meeting rooms on the seventh floor; for security reasons outsiders are never allowed in any corporate finance department. By the time he arrived, his visitor was demurely seated, drinking coffee, a thick envelope at his elbow.

'It's good of you to see me,' the man said, civilly rising. 'I have a problem on which I would welcome your advice.'

Andy opened his mouth to enter a bankerly caveat on the kind of advice he might properly be able to offer, and shut it again. It would be wasted on this tough experienced customer, who would not be here unless there was something quite out of the ordinary to talk about.

'By way of introduction,' Edwards was saying, taking off his spectacles and cleaning them painstakingly with a very small piece of yellow cloth, 'Sir Matthew Friern asked us to look at the Prior management which we did for five weeks without finding anything useful. He then commissioned us to look at the possibility that the civil servants concerned with advising ministers on the sale of Prior Systems might perhaps be too closely connected with one of Friern's main competitors in this projected purchase. In this regard, after investigations, one of my partners received information that the most senior civil servant involved, a Mr Clive Fieldman, might be developing a relationship with the solicitor for Prior Systems, a very attractive widow, Mrs Caroline Whitehouse.' He paused and put his glasses back on. 'My partner persuaded the informant to tell senior officials but they just closed ranks.' He glanced at Andy. 'In discussion with Sir Matthew it was then agreed that a watch would be kept both on Mr Fieldman and Mrs Whitehouse for a couple of weeks.' Andy tried to keep his face unmoving, wondering what on earth was coming next. 'During that period,' Edwards went on, imperturbably, 'Mr Fieldman visited a flat in Knightsbridge once and also a house in Hampstead, which belongs to Mrs Whitehouse's parents, at which Mrs Whitehouse was present. He also had lunch with a lady at San José.' He stopped, perhaps for breath, and reached for his coffee.

'Now, this is where it gets silly,' he said, refreshed and abruptly dropping the police court style of recital. 'I was away, and my partner, who was looking after the work with my agreement, you understand, sought authority from Sir Matthew for another week of surveillance, which was carried out and during which Mr Fieldman again visited the Knightsbridge flat. Then I got back yesterday, read their reports, and I thought I recognized – and I hope you can help me here – the picture of the lady who opened the door to Mr Fieldman, and who waved him off again about two and a half hours later on the first occasion. It is as you see the same lady he lunched with at San José.' He reached for his brown envelope and extracted two photographs which he dropped on the table. Andy looked at them and for a moment felt his ears ring and the room go dark.

'That is Lady Friern.'

'Ah. Thank you. Now there's nothing untoward in her lunching with a male friend or greeting him with a kiss – indeed, I understand this is a well-established social custom – or even entertaining him in her flat. But my partner, who is well experienced, you understand, was doubtful about the relationship. And all his doubts were removed when Mr Fieldman visited the flat a second time. There were also a couple of telephone calls.'

'My God, Edwards, you didn't tap Matt Friern's phone.'

'No, it seems, mercifully, that my partner's conscientiousness faltered at this point. But we were able to listen to Mr Fieldman's calls at the Department – to no great result, and don't you worry Mr Eames Lewis, that device has now been removed.'

'What *else* did your partner do?'

'Well, he secured a photograph of the two of them in the bedroom at the back of the flat.' He fished again in the brown envelope, while Andy watched in fascinated horror, and produced another photograph.

'Again, there's nothing very dramatic going on: both parties are fully clothed, but they are in the bedroom, and they are embracing.'

It was a blurred photograph, but Andy felt his guts twist at the sight of Lucy's profile and her arms around Clive Fieldman's neck.

'What stopped him? I mean, why didn't he go on and get a better picture?'

Edwards gave him an offended, sidelong look. 'I imagine that the parties then moved further into the room so that they were no longer visible,' he said, primly, his Edinburgh accent sounding more pinched than ever.

That would be right, Andy thought, savagely. If he had had Lucy Friern in his arms, in a bedroom, he would have wasted no time at all in putting her in a position where neither of them would have been visible from outside the flat. Like on the bed. Or on the floor. He drew in a deep, steadying breath, and pushed the photographs away.

'Didn't your partner check the address?'

'Oh yes, he checked. The flat is registered in the name of Lumina Properties and the company is registered in Jersey. *I* would, I think, have realized that it belonged to a rich individual, who kept some of his cash overseas, as we're all allowed to nowadays. All bills go to the Friern office, and my partner looked only at the Jersey address. Not a mistake he'll make again.'

'Well, I see your problem.' Andy reached for a cigarette and lit it at the third attempt, then belatedly offered Edwards one, who refused, pointedly.

'The other problem I have,' he said, abruptly coming clean, 'is that we didn't have much joy from watching Mrs Whitehouse either. We couldn't monitor her telephone calls; that office is looked after by competitors of ours and it would have been too much of a risk. It is swept regularly – and on a random basis as well. We did keep her under personal surveillance and, for the first two weeks, I have to say she seemed to do nothing but work and go home to her children, and there was no further contact at all with Mr Fieldman.'

That would be right too, Andy thought; if the bugger had Lucy Friern to play with, he hardly needed Caroline Whitehouse as well.

'One evening, however, she did make a call on her way home from the office. She went by taxi and, rather strangely, she took a wee walk around the district before she went into a small block of flats – just four in the building. My man was not able to see which of the two first-floor flats she went into, but about an hour later an official car arrived – with one of the number plates reserved for the Government car service – and a man whom he recognized as Mr Gerry Willshaw, the Minister for Transport, came out of the block and got in the car. About five minutes later Mrs Whitehouse emerged and made her way to the main road. She got a taxi. One of the two flats on the top floor belongs to the gentleman in question.' He waited while Andy digested this.

'She could have gone to the other flat.'

'Oh yes, of course she could. It is registered to a Mr Al Khafi. It seemed to us more likely that a lady like Mrs Whitehouse would know Mr Willshaw socially, unless Mr Al Khafi could be a client.'

'She does know Willshaw,' Andy said slowly. 'Someone told me the other night she'd been seen having lunch with him. I didn't give it a thought.'

'No. No, well she's a senior lawyer, isn't she, and doubtless lunches with a wide variety of people.'

They sat and looked at each other. 'Worth pursuing,' Andy said.

'Indeed.' The silence stretched between them. 'Well,' Edwards said, thoughtfully, 'I'm wondering what I shall be able to report to Sir Matthew.'

'He's going to be very pleased with the bit about Mrs Whitehouse and Willshaw. I would guess he'll authorize you to keep watching her. And you can also report Mr Fieldman's lunch with Mrs Whitehouse. No reason why Mr Fieldman should not be leading a rather hard-working life with very few women in it, after all.'

'No, no, indeed. Well, I am grateful, Mr Eames Lewis, you've cleared my mind and I must let you get on with your morning.' He reached for the photographs but Andy kept a thumb on them.

'You've solved your problem,' he said.

James Edwards' gaze flicked over him, momentarily, and then dropped. 'Right. Right, well, I'll be off.'

Andy saw him to the lift, gravely courteous as was the Walzheims' house style, then went back down the corridor to his own office and locked the envelope containing the photographs into his top right-hand drawer. He looked at his shaking hands and made for the palatial seventh-floor gentlemen's cloakroom. It was mercifully empty and he went into one of the cubicles, sat down on the seat and put his head in his hands, letting himself reflect for a passing moment on a twentieth-century life in which, if you wanted privacy, a lavatory at the office might be the only place to find it. After a few minutes he got up, wearily, and decided he might as well have a pee while he was there.

He was washing his hands, mechanically, guts still churning in reaction to the interview with Edwards, trying to calm down sufficiently to function at the next meeting, when John Michaels, the second director on the Friern job, came in.

'Sorry to pursue you, Andy. Sir Matthew Friern has arrived and Jeremy Winnick from Marquands. We've kept Winnick in the reception area and put Sir Matthew upstairs.'

'Well done.' Andy drew down the curtain on bitter jealousy, disappointment and rage; the next crisis was here and needed all his attention. 'Got the projections? Fine. We must have five minutes with Matt – just get someone to go down and see Winnick and explain I'm coming back from somewhere. See he has coffee and a paper.'

He dried his hands and ran a comb through his hair,

494

looking carefully into the mirror, expecting to find himself looking quite different after the shocks he had sustained that morning, but the familiar dark blond hair and square face looked back at him, plumper now than when he had been in Articles, and more determined. Well, he knew a lot more than he had in those days and he was close to the top of the engine room of London's most important merchant bank, and he was not going to be bounced up and down again by the likes of Lucy Friern. What did the silly bitch think she was doing, conducting an affair with that jumped-up northerner on the make, particularly when he was involved in selling a company to her husband? Where did Fieldman think he was, for that matter, in the middle of the moon, to be taking a risk like that? He allowed sanity to penetrate rage; he of all people had cause to understand why people took risks in order to have Lucy Friern, but in a situation where Lucy's husband had become sufficiently obsessed to be prepared to go well outside normal business practice to get his way, it was madness. What if Caroline Whitehouse and her gang got on to it? He stared into the mirror, his stomach clenching. Christ, he was being slow. Caroline almost certainly knew already; she and Lucy had kept up their friendship and women told each other things that any sane man would go to the stake before disclosing. And Caroline had not sought to use her knowledge, hopefully because her own position *vis-à-vis* Clive was equivocal. But if Matthew succeeded in striking another body-blow to Prior Systems, that unfeminine, ambitious, talented, combative thug could decide to sacrifice a friend. From every possible point of view, Lucy's affair with Clive had to stop, now, and it would be nice – no, it could be absolutely essential

– to have something dirty on Caroline Whitehouse, which, please God, James Edwards was going to find. He took a deep breath, nodded to himself in the mirror and made his way up to the meeting-room.

Caroline, that morning, neither looked nor felt like a threat to anyone. She had slept uneasily on the train back from Dorrington, and thrown up most of the meal that Tim Bailey had fed her, as soon as she got home, the stress, the travelling and far too many Anadins taking their toll. Work on other cases was piled up around her, and but for Mark Dwyer, who had arrived in her office and was sitting containedly opposite her, she knew she would have been six feet under the water rather than holding her chin just above the waves. She said as much, riffling through the neat piles of drafting.

'You'll be glad when the Prior Systems case is out of the way,' he said, pointedly, thinking he had rarely seen her look so worn, her hair flattened, unbecomingly, to her head.

'Don't hope,' she advised. 'It's one of those. It is going to be trouble every inch of the way and it really is not the fault of our clients. It's bloody Friern – well, you can see it is. And the lads are right; Hamish won't go on the line for £60m if we don't get the Marsh Lane contract. They want me to go and ask him for his views, but I don't think it's politic.'

'No. Much better not stir him up until you have to.'

'God send that all his other deals have gone wobbly, so that he really needs this one.'

Mark Dwyer agreed that this was their best hope, and they bent their attention to the papers for the meeting they were due to attend in the next ten minutes.

Caroline emptied her mind of everything else to concentrate, and was relieved to find a minor problem on page four and a major, but reparable, one on page twenty-five. Age and experience must, thank God, count somewhere, she thought, surfacing from the papers and catching sight of her assistant's expression.

'Mark, the whole thing is a bloody good piece of drafting. But I've been round that corner before; if you do it your way, it works but it leads to unnecessary hassle, if you do get a dispute on the warranties. You have the wrong people doing the work from our client's point of view. See?'

'Yes, I do. Sorry, I was up all night with it.'

She grinned at him, amused by the male way in which he automatically hit back, getting his points in. She had imbibed this particular skill with the cornflakes, in a family with three quarrelsome, dominant elder brothers, and rather than being harassed or bored by it, found it familiar and comforting.

'To battle,' she said, and hoping she wasn't going to feel sick all morning, she picked up her papers and headed off with all thoughts of Prior well below her level of consciousness. She stayed in the meeting for two hours, until it stalled on drafting points in the eight pages of warranties. Knowing that Mark Dwyer and the assistant on the other side could produce the next draft more quickly if the numbers at the meeting were reduced, she left, taking the opposing partner with her. She was still feeling like a wet rag; the one cup of coffee she had essayed had nearly been disastrous and she had stuck thereafter to mineral water. She sat down gratefully behind her own desk and focused on her messages. Three from Prior Systems, nothing from Tim Bailey, and one, alas, from Hamish Brown, the man himself, which came complete with details of his timetable for the rest of the day, so he really did mean that she should ring him back.

She rang Prior Systems first; they had no news and had plainly been ringing her only to discharge anxiety, a familiar client activity in times of trouble, but one she could have done without that morning. She hesitated, looked at her watch and tried Tim Bailey, who was conclusively unavailable, and resignedly rang Hamish.

'Caroline, nice to hear from you. I understand things are not going so well with our friends in Dorrington.'

Reflecting that 'I understand things are not going so well' was a particularly sinister understatement, she kept her head, expressed interest and surprise, and asked him what it was that he had heard.

'That there is some doubt about whether they are going to land the – what is it, Iain – the Marsh Lane contract. We'd be concerned if that were so, Caroline, given its importance in relation to the year two and year three forecasts.'

'I couldn't be more delighted to hear that you have yourself focused on the projections, Hamish,' she said, nastily.

'Aye, well, the moment does always come.' Hamish was not intimidated. 'But what about this wee contract?'

'Well, Hamish, they never expected just to be handed it. It's the usual routine competitive tender, but so far as I know they remain confident.'

She heard him sigh at the other end of the line. 'What I'm hearing, Caroline, is that Friern are coming in under the Prior price. Now, I can see why they might want to do that, if they reckoned to own Prior in short order, but I assumed ye'd be ready for them.'

Bloody Hamish, she thought, dourly; no one had a better eye for a complex negotiation, and he was capable of imagining any level of depravity, as low-church Scots so often were. 'So we are, Hamish,' she said, with a confidence she did not feel. 'That's why we decided not to trouble you with the details.'

'You've got some political help?'

'Yes.'

'The thing is, Caroline, that if Prior did not get this contract, it would call into question our commitment to a figure of £60m which, as ye well know, we already think is toppish.'

'Lord bless us, Hamish, are customers walking in through your doors carrying gold for you these days? £60m toppish for those assets and these projections? Must be the best deal in the City by some way. Or so some of the other development-capital outfits would feel, judging by the keenness with which they are seeking to seduce my customers away from you.' There was a thoughtful pause and she sat, tense.

'It's not a bad deal at all,' Hamish allowed, carefully, 'but we did construct all our estimates on the basis of getting this contract. It leaves them with not a lot in the factory next year, if it doesna come through.'

'It would be a bloody nuisance to have to go out looking for work, we all agree, Hamish, and we are all putting our best feet forward, like always. How's trade with you? A bit slow, I imagine, or you'd not be ringing me up to worry about all this.'

She listened, grimly, as Hamish disquisited indignantly on the number of deals Martins Development Capital was currently considering.

'I'm very glad to hear all this. But I'm keeping you back?' she suggested solicitously, using the courteous West Highland circumlocution, and heard him laugh, reluctantly.

'I've plenty of time today, Caroline. But I know when I'm getting a poke in the eye with a sharp stick. Just you go and fix that contract, and remember that there's an awful lot of contribution to profit in it.'

And we're going to knock at least £10m off our offer of finance, caveated backwards, forwards and sideways, she understood, as she thanked him politely for his interest. At this stage, despite the shortage of deals doing the rounds, it would be very unwise indeed to gamble on getting another development-capital house in to improve on the Martins' offer. Other houses were using fair words in plenty to such of Prior Systems' management as were accessible, but Martins had done the work, understood the figures and were ready to go. Quite apart from the presentational disadvantages of changing financiers mid-stream, it would take at least ten days to get another outfit up to speed and through their various authorization procedures. She compressed her lips and rang Tim Bailey again; he was sounding hurried and distant, and her heart sank.

'No luck. We've looked at two copies and they're all right. I mean, they're not all right, they add up to the lower number. I can't risk going to get the other four.'

She felt her jaw muscles clench, as when she was a small girl working herself up to take on three older brothers. 'We need that contract, Tim, and it ought to be ours. If we can't do it this way, I'll put the whole thing to *Private Eye*. I know the proprietor. That ought to create enough of a row to get Friern backed off. My lot can rebid, if that's the game we're in.'

'We don't want a row.' The response was instant.

'Why not? It's not your lot who controls the council.' She listened to the silence. 'Tim? Sarn't Major?'

'You don't know what you're stirring up.'

'I didn't start this. All shit-stirring was being done by the other side, and I've just realized that we'll have to join in. When are you going to check the other four copies?'

'There's a problem about that.'

'Gerry told me to come to you but I'll call him if I have to. You were very good and kind and useful last time. Why can't you go and find the other four?'

'Because I can't.'

'Then what is wrong with my idea about *Private Eye*?'

'They won't do it. There are libel laws, you know.'

'Truth is a good defence to any action for libel, I distinctly remember from law school. Look, Tim, *Private Eye* don't give a monkey's about writs from members of Dorrington county council. Of course they'll run a story. Mind you, the timing's a bugger. They print on Friday, so I only have tomorrow to talk to them.'

There was a long considering pause and she waited, left hand clenched round the telephone and shoulders hunched.

'Caroline, I do think that would be counterproductive. If you can just hold your horses and leave it with me, and not make waves, I think it will all sort itself out.'

'My father says that when people start suggesting

that you should take it easy and leave it all to them, that is a clear signal that they are working out a way to bury you.'

'I thought your father was a teacher.'

'He is. And also a philosopher, and we quarrel all the time and he drives me mad. But he is right, isn't he, Tim?' She found she was on her feet, still clutching the phone. 'Right,' she said, breathing in, 'here is the news, and this is me bringing it to you; come six o'clock tomorrow I'll ring up Gerry and my good contact at *Private Eye*, and we take it from there. What is going on in Dorrington, Tim, is corruption in local government, and it is wrong and you aren't trying hard enough. I don't know whether you are in it or condoning it, but either way it is a disgrace and I have to look after my clients.'

She winced and moved the phone from her ear, as Tim Bailey hung up on her, resoundingly. She replaced her own phone and stood, considering her trembling hands, as Mark Dwyer appeared in the doorway, holding down the top of a pile of documents with his chin. 'I'm so sorry, Mark, I'm just going to be sick again,' she said, civilly, and fled past him.

A mile away, Andy Eames Lewis decided that any food at all would make him sick. He considered, steadily, the photographs that Edwards had given him that morning, wiped them carefully and put all three of them into a new envelope. He checked that his secretary had gone to lunch and typed a label. He put a stamp on the envelope, just remembering to avoid the office franking-machine, wiped the whole over carefully with his handkerchief and posted it, five hundred yards away from the building. It was a perfect May day, he noticed reluctantly, warm with a soft wind just rippling the Thames at high water, and the new leaves on the sparse trees were the unreal bright, pale green of spring that lasts only a few days before exposure darkens them to a more familiar colour. Well, one of the darling buds of May was about to be shaken by a very rough wind indeed; where did she get *off*, making gentle seductive advances to him while running an obviously thriving affair with bloody Clive Fieldman, of all people? He let himself wonder, just briefly, whether Clive, too, had been honoured in the old days when they were all young, and stopped, heartsick, with tears stinging behind his eyelids, looking blindly out over the glittering, swollen river.

'Andy!' It was an authoritative, distant call, and he whipped out a handkerchief and held it protectively over his nose as if he were blowing it.

'Peter.' It was his head of corporate finance, a man five years older than he with an infinite range of contacts everywhere and a sharp, disconcerting intelligence.

'Look.' Peter glanced around to see that they were not overheard. 'I've just had a drink with Jeremy Winnick. He seemed to feel that he'd been bringing us unwelcome news this morning. About Friern.'

'He was.' Andy blew his nose and stuffed the handkerchief away, tears vanquished, as he turned to walk with the older man. 'What he was saying was that at their present share price, Friern would be pushed to bid anything over about £55m for a very good acquisition they're trying to make, in the teeth of opposition from incumbent management.'

'Prior Systems?'

'Yes.'

'He's right, isn't he?'

'Oh, yes. But we may lose the deal.'

'Mm. I've forgotten what the drop-dead fee is?'

'£25,000.' And you knew the answer to *that*, Andy thought, savagely.

'That is a pity. I would have hoped we would have been able to negotiate a rather more substantial fee than that?'

Andy ground his teeth. 'There was a lot of competition for the job,' he said, stolidly. 'I pushed it to what I thought we could get without losing it. And I felt that the negotiation on the success fee had gone particularly well.'

'Well, it would be a very nice success fee,' his senior agreed, courteously. 'Will you manage to get the company?'

'We're still hopeful. It would have been good to be able to go to £65m, if we needed to, but on the other hand, we understand that the management team has got financing problems too.'

'Martins are doing it, aren't they? Hamish Brown's not famous for paying top prices. Do you need any help, Andy? I know the NEB people, of course. And a few of the present Cabinet.'

Andy considered him, remembering that this man was probably understating the range of his contacts. 'Do you know a junior minister called Willshaw?'

'Gerry? Oh yes. Going places that one, they tell me. Why?'

'He's the Member for the next-door constituency to Prior. And there's just a thought that he may be connected to the lawyer for Prior.'

'The lovely Caroline Whitehouse? Wouldn't blame him at all if so. Come to think on it, Andy, I have seen them together. At the House, in the central lobby. Not doing anything unsuitable; she could easily just have been there for a drink. I could ask around a bit. Would it help?'

'Yes it would. Prior are getting a lot of political help from somewhere, and it would help if we could prove it.'

'We don't want to get into that sort of thing, though.'

'No, no. We want to put Caroline in baulk, no worse.'

'I'll make a few calls. Are you going to the cricket tomorrow?'

Andy said, bitterly, that he had forgotten what a cricket field looked like, and the other man laughed, observing sunnily that it had been exactly the same with him a few years ago, old boy, and that everything passed. May you fall in the river and drown, Andy thought, courteously concurring with these sentiments.

24

The next day, Caroline Whitehouse, who had been up late talking to Prior's management and been immersed in a drafting meeting since 8 a.m., realized thankfully that it was now time to leave for lunch. She nodded to her opposite number, rested a hand for a second on Mark Dwyer's shoulder and left, stopping off at her office to check on her messages.

'Mr Willshaw just rang, Caroline.'

'Oh damn. Did he say where he was?'

'No. But he will ring you after four this afternoon.'

'Thanks, Susie. If he rings when I am in the Smythson meeting, get me out for a minute. I'd like to see him, and if you don't fit in with those chaps' schedules you never see them.' With Susie she had adopted the hypothesis that she and Gerry Willshaw were two busy people, who liked each other and met for the odd drink or meal when they could, and that this involved her being willing to make the effort. She rushed into the ladies' cloakroom to tidy up, her face lifting involuntarily into a smile at the thought of seeing darling Gerry, perhaps tonight. He had only got back from Brussels that morning and he must have rung her straight away. She had talked to him only once in the last week, the conversation kept short and not too personal in deference to his anxieties about telephone calls, and she longed for him fiercely. But lunch with Lucy would nicely occupy some of the time before he could ring her again. She shot out of the massive front door, just keeping her footing on the steps, and into the square, bright with sun and the sharp acid green of the new leaves. Lucy had rung up that morning, sounding rattled, and, finding Caroline pressed for time with only an hour between meetings, had agreed to brave the trip from Knightsbridge, which must mean that she really needed someone to talk to. It would be some difficulty with a man, of course, Caroline thought, serenely, armoured by the knowledge that Gerry was back. Probably some delicious, forbidden chap had very kindly offered, and Lucy needed some help in deciding to say yes. She bounced into the restaurant and stopped, arrested by the sight of her friend, shrouded in a Hermes headscarf and dark glasses, seated at a corner table.

'You have wiz you ze secret plans?' she hissed, bending to plant a kiss on a silken sunflower.

'Oh, Caro. It isn't funny.'

Caroline sank into the chair opposite and peered across the table. 'What *is* it, Lu? Why the glasses?'

'I've been crying all morning.'

'Speak to me. Are the kids all right? Yes? And dreaded Matthew? Pity. Then what?'

'I got this awful thing in the post.'

'A chain letter? Give it to me and I'll throw it away.'

'It's photographs.' Tears escaped round the edge of the dark glasses and spilled down her cheeks.

'Lu, darling. Have a hankie . . . I know I've got one. What photographs? Show me. Or are they too dreadful?'

Lucy gulped and mopped up her tears with Caro's none-too-clean handkerchief. 'No, they're not terrible. They're not indecent – it was just such a shock.'

Caroline poured her some water and shook her head

507

at the hovering waiter, watching her friend anxiously. 'Darling, can you show me? I would then be more use.'

Lucy nodded, sniffed inelegantly and reached into her handbag for a plain brown envelope. 'Careful,' she warned, 'take them out carefully.'

Caroline slid the prints out one by one, carefully, sheltering them with her own bag, and considered them.

'How did they take them, Caro?' Lucy asked, sniffing. 'I mean, someone must have been watching us.'

'Oh, yes. Someone must. It's a telescopic lens. The last time I saw anything like this I was doing my four months in litigation as an articled clerk with old Reg Lytton. Do you remember him?' She clasped her hands together to stop them trembling and hoped she was not going to be sick. 'Very good of you *and* Clive,' she said, trying for a light touch. 'And as you say not at all indecent. Just utterly revealing.'

Tears welled down Lucy's cheeks again and Caroline apologized. 'Was there any message with them?' she asked.

'No. They just came in an envelope. No message at all.'

'Darling, did Matt also get an envelope like this addressed to him?'

Lucy took off her dark glasses to make a better job of her eyes. 'I thought of that. I opened all his mail. Nothing.'

'Unless it went to the office, I suppose. But why?'

Lucy was looking down, sniffing and polishing her sunglasses. 'Well, Caro, *I* wondered whether someone on your side was trying to spread muck.' She put her dark glasses back on again and stared across the table.

'Respectable commercial lawyers like me don't *do* that

sort of thing. And I can't believe my client would have either. I don't think they even know about detectives.' She considered her friend. 'Do you believe me?'

'Yes. I'm sorry, Caro, I've had such an awful morning; it's the *shock* more than anything else. But I knew it couldn't be you really. I mean you knew about me and Clive; you could just have told Matt, or sent him an anonymous letter. Or you could have told the DoE, and you never have.' She blew her nose, delicately, and indicated to the waiter that he might approach. 'I'll have a gin and tonic, please. What's yours, Caro – water as usual?'

'No, gin and tonic, please.'

The waiter left and Lucy took her glasses off again. 'What do I *do*, Caro?'

'Take a deep breath and think.' Caroline was furiously concentrating on the present problem, suppressing rigidly all other concerns. 'If these pictures weren't sent to Matt, it's a message to you personally, isn't it? What does it *say*?'

The two women considered each other. 'I've no idea,' Lucy said, helplessly.

Caroline hesitated. 'Darling, I've never liked to ask, but this is an emergency. Is it possible that Matthew already knows and has chosen this way of telling you to stop?' Lucy looked at her blankly, and she blushed. 'I'm only asking. I mean, has he ever told you to stop before?'

'Oh, yes. He bangs around dropping things and saying that he really can't stand that shit.'

'Something really subtle,' Caroline suggested, acidly, and quailed under her friend's reproachful stare. 'Sorry. So it isn't a message from Matthew. So he doesn't know.

What if it is someone else and he or she did tell Matt about you and Clive. Would he – well – would he be very much upset? I mean, of course he would, but what would happen? Would he want to divorce you?'

'No.' Lucy spoke with flat certainty. 'I mean he never has before and I don't think he'd see Clive as enough of a rival.'

'You mean if you had an affair with the chairman of a rival company that would upset him, whereas a senior civil servant doesn't bother him?'

'A bit like that, yes.' They stared at each other. 'Aren't men the *end*?' Lucy said, interested, and Caroline compressed her lips.

'Some of them. Let's try again. Why would anyone pay quite a lot to have you watched? Costs a fortune.'

Lucy sipped her gin and tonic thoughtfully, tears forgotten. 'What if it is Clive they are watching, not me?'

Caroline looked at her, disconcerted. 'Oh yes, that's more likely, isn't it, given that letter to the Department.' She had told Lucy about it, having assumed that Clive had too. 'And you got caught in the net, as it were. Well, who is after Clive, apart from your dear husband?'

Their salads arrived and both women fell silent as waiters fussed around them efficiently with black pepper and oil and vinegar. Caroline gazed at the resultant glistening plate and understood that she was not going to be able to eat any of it. She looked away and clenched her hands together in her lap.

'Caro? Are you OK? You've gone green. What is it?'

She pushed her plate aside. 'Sorry, I'm feeling a bit ropy. Lu, when were those photos taken? Can you tell?'

'Oh, yes, I'm sure. One was taken on Thursday the

week before last – I had lunch at San José with Clive . . . look, that's San José . . . look at the leaves on the trees.' She passed the envelope back to Caroline who took it, clumsily. 'And we had lunch at the flat on Thursday last week, and you can see the leaves there too.'

'Yes, yes, I see. Very horrid for you.'

'Yes, it is. You aren't being very sympathetic, but it is absolutely beastly, the feeling that you are being watched.'

'What are you going to do?' Caroline asked, finishing her gin and tonic in one gulp and feeling her stomach churn in protest.

'*Well*, that's the irony, you see. That picture – the one in the bedroom – well, we were saying goodbye. I mean it's over. So I don't really have to do anything, do I? I mean I can't do anything about those photos, but I've stopped anyway.'

Caroline sat unmoving, looking at the beautiful face opposite her, unmarred even by swollen eyes and a reddened nose. 'You must warn Clive.'

'I'd better, hadn't I? It's only fair.'

'Yes. It's only fair.'

'Caro, you really don't look well. Can't you go home this afternoon?'

'No.'

'It's awful, isn't it? I suppose anyone can hire detectives. I mean, would you know how to?'

'Not personally, no. But I would know who to ask.' She concentrated on the tablecloth, counting the squares.

'Shall I eat your salad? If you're not going to. I *do* feel better having talked to someone. It was *so* terrible this morning when I was alone at the flat. Caro?'

It was no good, Caroline realized, helplessly, as tears

dripped slowly down her cheeks, there was no stopping this.

'What *is* it, Caro? What's happened?' Lucy's hand covered hers. '*Tell* me.' Her hand tightened. 'Oh God, I've got it. I *am* a selfish bitch. What about you and your man? Oh, Caro, you haven't had photographs sent to you too?'

'No, but anyone can hire detectives. And since we know someone has, I must warn him.' She pulled a hand away from Lucy's grip and fumbled for a handkerchief.

'What will he do?'

'Stop. Instantly. He has to.'

They looked at each other, recognition of the stark truth between them.

'Who is it, Caro?'

'I cannot tell you. But he will not want to lose his job.'

'How absolutely awful.' She signalled, economically, for coffee. 'But Caro, perhaps in a few weeks' time, when all this dies down?' She stopped, realizing that her friend was not listening, her blue eyes focused on the tablecloth.

'I just hope it isn't already too late,' she was saying, obsessively, 'but I haven't seen him for two weeks, because he's been away, so if the watchers were on to it for only the last two or three weeks, as the pictures suggest, then with any luck in the world they missed him.'

'What would happen if they – whoever they are – were on to you? Might it force the position? I mean might he leave his wife?'

'No. No, it would just be a disaster.'

'Oh, Caro, I am sorry. Bloody, bloody men. We've got caught in the middle, haven't we?'

512

'Between awful Matt and my customers. Yes.'

'Matt is my husband. I know he's not behaving well about this, but neither are you. That leak about Bartholomews, that was you, wasn't it?' She took her glasses off again and stared myopically at her friend, who slowly turned red.

'I didn't *start* this war,' she said, defensively. 'And Matt is at it again in Dorrington over the Marsh Lane contract. I'll have him for that.'

Lucy sat back, considering her friend of twenty-five years. 'You look just like your father.'

'That is all I need. He would, if present, be reminding me that no end, however good, justifies the use of crooked means to achieve it. Why did I have to have a moral philosopher for a father rather than a thug-like businessman?'

'Like mine,' Lucy suggested, unoffended.

'Exactly so. Have you eaten my salad?'

'Yes. Are you hungry now?'

'Yes. God knows why. Pass me that bread and I'll have an omelette. And we'll both go back and sort out our lovers. Lu, I'd just like to sit here and think, by myself, do you mind?'

'I'm staying with you, Caro. I won't talk but I want to see you through lunch.' She picked up a magazine and buried herself in it while Caroline doggedly ate an omelette.

'Better. Thank you,' she said, briefly, putting her fork down.

'Good, I've paid.' Lucy rose and kissed her. 'I'm sorry,' she said, gently, and Caroline pressed her cheek to hers, unable to speak.

*

At the DoE, Clive Fieldman was working without inspiration. He was feeling wretched over the loss of Lucy and his misery was compounded by feeling distinctly unappreciated at work. Winstanley, informed about Watson's letter, had received explanation and apologies grudgingly, and Clive had not felt comfortable with him since. It was to be hoped that Winstanley did not think him responsible for all the difficulties clogging the Prior sale, from the leak in the *Financial Times* that had destroyed the possibility of a group sale to the unexpected bump in the Friern share price, but his experience was that ministers tended to blame advisers for everything that went wrong. And enough had gone wrong; the closure of Davecat and O'Brien was still causing headlines and the sales of Carrs and SLG were proceeding sluggishly, quite apart from the troubles with Prior. The weekend was coming up; and he would have the children, but, of course, he could not join forces with Caroline Whitehouse and her family. No prospect pleased at all and he had just better keep his head down. The phone rang, startling him.

'Mr Watts for you.'

'Richard! How are you?'

'Well, thank you. I've just been talking to John Martin at Gruhners. Offers will be received from Shaw and Waltons, but are unlikely to be over about £45m. So you've got the management team in, still offering £50m down and £10m deferred, and Friern at wherever they are at now, probably around £57m down.'

It would, Clive thought, grimly, provide the perfect conclusive rebuttal to Michael Watson, if Friern were to win this particular competition. He pulled himself together, remembering Caroline and her grittily determined team, who were politically more attractive than Friern.

'A damned close-run thing, to coin a phrase.'

'Yes.' Richard Watts, Clive realized, was bursting with news. 'But there seems to be a complication. The management offer is apparently conditional on their getting – as they expect – a major contract which is about to be awarded.'

'You mean they'll withdraw, if they don't get it?'

'No, no. But they will reduce their offer and that will put them definitely below Friern.'

Clive considered the scenario. 'Don't tell me that Friern is in the bidding for this contract too.'

'That's right.' Richard Watts sounded mildly surprised at his grasp of the situation. '*And*, what's more, Clive, there is apparently a furious dispute going on up there about the way this contract adjudication is being conducted.'

'Dear, oh dear, oh dear.'

'Yes. Sorry. Difficult for you chaps, I know. Might not have mattered but these two are obviously the only serious punters.'

'I wish you hadn't told me all this, Richard.'

'Well, I suppose it is really the NEB's pigeon.'

'They'll be here weeping on my man's shoulder by tomorrow.'

'John Martin did indicate that his clients were intending to consult your Department, yes.'

'They're wonderful at consulting us when the wheels come off. Thank you anyway, Richard.'

He put the phone down and sat, staring into space and counting his blessings, such as they were, the chief and only one being that his affair with Lucy had been sufficiently discreet or sufficiently long-standing, or both, not to have attracted Michael Watson's notice. His phone rang again.

'Lady Friern would like to speak to you, Mr Fieldman.'

He felt the hair prickle at the back of his neck and nearly dropped the phone. 'Put her through,' he said, hoarsely, clearing his throat.

'Clive. We have to meet for half an hour. Not here.'

'What's happened?'

'I'm not going to explain on the phone. We need to meet somewhere crowded and very public, and be very casual.'

'Sounds dramatic,' he said, dry-mouthed, trying for a light touch.

'It is. I had lunch with Caro and she says I must warn you. I'll meet you at the Carlton, in the bar, as soon as you can get there.'

'I'll just tidy up here and I'll come now.' He felt cold all over.

He packed papers away, mechanically; whatever horror he was going to have to face might as well be faced sooner as later, he decided, steadily. Now that he let himself see it, he'd been bloody lucky to have stayed out of trouble as long as he had. Very indiscreet to continue the affair with Lucy once Friern emerged as a contender. Madness not to have backed off as soon as he had understood the ferocity of the competition between Matthew and the Prior Systems team. He cursed himself steadily, as he cleared his desk with the in-built discipline of the long-standing civil servant, making sure that no confidential documents were left outside the safe. The irony of what he was doing suddenly struck him full force, and he had to stop, winded. He put both hands flat on the top of his desk, leaning his weight on them and was standing bowed when his secretary came in.

'Would you like a cup of coffee, Mr Fieldman?'

'No, thank you. I have to rush off. Would you tell the press office that I can be reached at home after about seven? That should give them time if he needs to talk to me.' Or, if by then, I have no choice other than to talk to Sir Francis, he thought numbly, staring at Miss Williams.

She considered him and whisked out, returning with the coffee he had refused, which she left in front of him. He drank it, gratefully. It was stiff with sugar which ordinarily he disliked, but he could feel some energy returning. He locked the safe, and shut his office, then stood watching his secretary, who was apparently lost in concentration, eyes fixed on a long draft clipped on to a board, as her fingers moved unerringly over the keys. That is an extraordinary skill, he thought, arrested; it ought to be more highly paid. She did not look at him, and he understood that she would not probe, or comment, or speak unless and until she was asked, just as she hoped others would leave her alone.

'Thank you, Miss Williams,' he said, in acknowledgement and recognition. 'See you tomorrow.'

'Good night, Mr Fieldman.' Her hands stilled momentarily, and she looked up at him with the civil, constrained smile with which she always greeted him.

Please God, he thought, scooping up his coat, with the quick neatness returned to him by the shot of caffeine and sugar, please God, let me be here to receive that inhibited familiar welcome tomorrow and all the other tomorrows.

25

Mark Dwyer hesitated outside the firmly closed door of Caroline's office; it was 6.30 p.m. and her secretary had gone home, so there was no one to ask for guidance. He stood, doubtfully, looking out at the bright evening, then heard a footfall behind him and turned to see the senior partner.

'I was just hoping to see Caroline,' Mark said hurriedly. 'About the Voulos deal,' he added, remembering that the Voulos family had originally been introduced by Michael Appleton.

'Was she at the meeting?'

'For some of it. It is still going on.'

'Mm. I was just going to have a word about something else. But perhaps you need her first?'

The answer was that he did: they had got stuck, and Caroline's capacity to move a discussion on by sheer energy and conviction was badly needed. But he was not about to admit to the senior partner that he could not manage without Caroline. He would have to find some resource of his own to disentangle six increasingly irritable men from clauses fifty-six (iv), (v) and (vii), having to do with voting rights for institutional investors. Progress had been blocked for a couple of hours while the Voulos team stormed, in Turkish, at their supporting advisers who then translated their views into thickly Chicago-accented English. It was just the sort of situation in which Caroline's gender and looks, combined with her fearsome directness and lack of respect for the wealth represented in that room had been effective earlier that afternoon, and was now needed again. He trailed regretfully away.

Michael Appleton pushed his way in through the closed door, having knocked, and stopped short. His usually dependable, tough Caroline gave him the haunted stare of a creature at bay. He had seen her look like this after her husband's death; withdrawn to some inner misery which no one could reach, all the lines in the lively face straight and heavy like a child's drawing, or a death mask.

'Yes, Michael,' she said, dead-level, beyond offering greetings, defences or excuses.

'Can I help?' he said, sitting down, errand forgotten.

'I shouldn't think so.'

'What's happened?' He watched, as she considered, unselfconsciously, the best way to offer him the facts. He understood that he was not particularly an intrusion; the trouble she was suffering – whatever it was – was so enormous, and had exhausted so much of her resources, that it really did not matter who was there. Like someone dangerously ill, fighting for their life, he thought, suddenly; witnesses had become irrelevant. 'Is it Prior Systems?'

'Yes. I am waiting for a phone call but I know what it will say. Then I will have to go and have a very difficult conversation head to head. Excuse me, Michael, this will be the phone call.'

He stuck, doggedly, to his chair deciding that she would not care whether he stayed or went.

'Ah. That's brilliant. It's got all the wrong numbers in it? Good. No, don't give it to anyone in Dorrington until I say so. Something has gone wrong there,' he heard her say. 'I'm not trying to stand in your way, but I have one more bell to pull. Hold off your meeting with the editor till twelve noon tomorrow and refuse to consider any earlier.' She listened, unmoving, to what was evidently a statement of protest. 'Do it this way, Peter. We've done all right so far,' she said, with the true finality that always carries conviction.

That, Michael Appleton thought, was a grown-up speaking, a whole category away from the gifted, but idiosyncratic young star he had once had. She put down the phone, gently, made a note and looked over to him, not seeing him except as an object, and he understood that the phone call had in no way solved whatever the problem was.

'Caroline,' he said, 'this is what partners are for. Will you please tell me enough so that I can help?'

Her eyes focused on him and he kept absolutely still while, with the unselfconsciousness of emotional exhaustion, she thought about whether he could be of any use.

'Friern have, by illegal means, put themselves into a situation where they are rebidding on a contract which is critical to Prior Systems' future,' she said, finally. 'The rebid has to be dealt with and we are now in a position where Prior's last throw looks to be a public row – which may not work.'

'Depends on the local political set-up,' he said, cautiously.

'Exactly so. I am having one more shot at disentangling this politically. I have some excellent ammunition now, thanks to my good client.'

The phone rang and he waited, stolidly, for her to answer it.

'I'm sorry, Michael. I have to take this call by myself.'

It was not an appeal, but a statement, and he rose to go.

'I'll come back in ten minutes if that is long enough.' He left before she could answer and shut the door on her. He stopped to look at the new pictures in the hallway by the lift, and had decided that the art committee was being seriously over-influenced by its senior member's predilection for brightly coloured bits and pieces, by the time he heard a step behind him. He turned to see Caroline, looking oddly undressed without a briefcase. 'Michael,' she said, shrugging on a scarlet Burberry, which made her look even paler, 'I have to go, now, in order to sort this.'

'Where are you going?'

'The Reform.'

'I'll come with you. To catch you afterwards. You need someone.'

She looked as if she would crack at a touch, he thought, anxiously. She was dreadfully pale, no light in her blonde hair, like someone going into a major operation. 'Thank you,' she said with none of her usual privileged impatience. 'But please don't. It would make me self-conscious. There is nothing else I can do and I shall run for home afterwards.'

He discarded several questions and offers. 'How are the kids?' he heard himself say.

'Awful,' she said, matter-of-factly. 'It is my fault ... what I am doing is unsettling them. It will be over soon.'

He watched her go, not hurtling down the corridor, as she usually did, with everything – hair and coat flying – but quietly, contained and heavily, head bent, shoulders rounded, in the incongruous bright red Burberry.

*

Caroline walked into the familiar portals of the Reform Club, nodding to a couple of acquaintances. She thought, carefully, about what she was doing, and went down to the ill-lit basement where ladies' coats were hung and into the much better-lit modernized ladies' powder-room, where she deliberately took enough time to repair her make-up and comb her hair. It was, she thought, stoically, a day when there was nothing else to do other than put on armour and pray to survive until the end of it. She emerged again upstairs and looked around; no sign of him yet, so she went over to look at the latest print-outs from the press tapes pinned on the big notice boards near the door, for something to do while she waited.

'Caroline?'

She felt her heart thud, then settle. 'Sholto. What are you doing here?'

'It is my club, you know. I'm meeting Peter Jellicoe – you remember him?'

'Not with any pleasure.'

'Then there is no need for me to introduce you to him again. Who are you meeting?'

She opened her mouth to tell him and was suddenly overwhelmed. She looked hopelessly at her father, at the familiar craggy, over-large distinctive features, so like her own but on a larger scale, topped by her own thick hair, his white now, rather than blond, and she felt tears just behind her eyes. His face changed, sharply, telegraphing emotion in the way he always did.

'What is it?' He was sounding irritable, but this time she heard the anxiety behind the surface, and stood her ground.

'I'd rather not tell you about it.'

He reached out tentatively and straightened the collar of her jacket for her, and she stood frozen, recognizing the driving, frustrated love in the awkward gesture.

'I might be useful,' he said, carefully. 'It is a rigorous discipline in which I am trained.'

She looked back at him and at last saw him properly, a big man, a little stooped, but with the intellectual and emotional energies that had inspired generations of students totally undimmed by time.

'Dad, I'm in trouble.'

He stopped fidgeting and stood absolutely still, his full attention bent on her. 'Tell me.'

'I don't have much time.'

'Just the outline.' He turned her gently round and walked with her, an arm heavy on her shoulders, to a quiet corner. She told him, baldly, about Prior Systems and their problems. 'It has been a dirty fight, Dad, and the bad men are winning.'

'Your side does not have clean hands either.'

'The others started it.'

'That is irrelevant, as you should know.'

She stiffened, but discipline held her back. 'This is true. But there is in my mind no doubt that this contract is rightly Prior's.' How useful, she thought, dazedly, to know that she was talking to a man whose definition of right would agree with hers, because he had taught it to her.

'Yes, but you cannot enforce this view by doubtful means.'

She felt the old impatience overwhelm her. 'What do you mean "cannot", Sholto? I think I can. I'm about to.'

'You do surely know that moral rules are a set of

statements about what works, not an imposed system? The axiom that the ends do not justify the means is essentially a practical warning. If you use corrupt means, your ends are thereby corrupted. That is a fact rather than an exhortation.'

He wasn't, she thought, sounding cross, more slightly impatient, as if she was being unexpectedly slow, and she remembered across nearly thirty years his ill-concealed surprise when she had failed, at the age of eight, to grasp instantly the principles behind the simultaneous equation. She returned, doggedly, to the present, finding that she was holding his hand. 'So, Dad, your view is that the only way out is to make people behave properly, in accordance with the best principles.'

'Yes. And this is not my view, as you put it. It is the basis of moral philosophy; it is the only way you get the right end, by using the right means.' He looked seriously down at her. 'This may not be helpful,' he said, tentatively.

'Yes, it is, Dad,' she said, a weight somehow shifting from her shoulders, and she straightened an aching back. An instinct made her look over to the tapes and there was Gerry, bent in fierce concentration on the notice boards and, as usual, drawing sideways glances, even from the sophisticated Reform audience. 'I am meeting Gerry Willshaw, Dad. For a drink. Come and say hello.'

'Junior Minister at Transport? Going up, they tell me.'

That too, I have managed to ignore, Caroline thought, behind her stoic mask: the fact that my father is consulted by lots of political leaders, and for good reasons. She kept a grip of his hand, like a kid, she thought, but then she was afraid at this moment.

'Gerry.'

He turned, with the politician's ready smile, and came towards them, eyes on her father. She distracted him by kissing him in easy social greeting; he needed a shave, she thought, irrelevantly.

'Dad, do you know Gerry Willshaw? Gerry, my father Sholto, who is here having a drink with another professor, but I thought I might introduce you.'

'I've heard a great deal about you, Sir Sholto,' Gerry said. 'From my Chief Whip.'

'David Craddock. Yes. A student of mine.'

Like half the country, Caroline thought, with belated recognition, watching Gerry fidget under her father's unselfconscious, serious and interested questioning. She lifted a hand to Professor the Lord Jellicoe, remembering regretfully that the reason she had taken a dislike to him had been his informed critique of right-wing transport policy, which had turned out to be absolutely right. Not perhaps the moment to tell him so, with Gerry there. She understood that she was postponing the moment of truth, and took a deep breath.

'Perhaps we had better get on, Gerry?'

He blinked momentarily, but agreed, and said a courteous farewell to her father.

They walked stiffly, side by side, into the big library, sparsely populated with the Reform's usual group of well-known faces. Gerry provided them with two gin and tonics and they sank, awkwardly, into deep, uncomfortable armchairs.

'How are you?' He took a gulp of his drink, not doing more than glance at her, and her heart sank. She waited deliberately until he had to look at her, and she watched him brace himself for a scene, looking around anxiously to see if there was anyone he knew close at hand. 'Why are we here?' he asked, impatiently. 'I mean why are we in quite such a public place?'

'Because I needed to talk to you somewhere where we could not be overheard, and where, at the same time, we were absolutely innocently in the public eye. We have problems, Gerry. It is possible that I am being followed.' She watched, hopelessly, the drink jerk in his glass, and waited, unable to think how to go on.

'For how long?'

A good question, she thought, straight to the point. 'I believe only for the last two or three weeks. Which means I could have been followed once to the flat, but if you remember, we only spent an hour there – less – and it was at some respectable hour, like 8 p.m. So that should be OK.'

'Bugger.' He never swore and she watched him, warily. 'How do you know? I mean, who is doing the watching?'

'Oh. It is connected with Prior Systems. They were also watching Clive Fieldman, it appears.'

'How did you find out?'

'A girl Clive was having an affair with had photographs sent to her.'

'Oh, God.'

'There are of course no compromising pictures of Clive and me,' she went on steadily. 'And no one has communicated with me at all, except Clive's girl.'

'Who is she?'

'I can't tell you. But she is a friend.'

He put his glass down, heavily, on the table in front of him and she watched him, the familiar dark, springy hair, cut unbecomingly short to stop it from curling, and the green eyes narrowed in thought.

'Does she – does Clive – does anyone know about me – about us?'

'The only person who knows – and he guessed, I did not tell him – is the brother to whom I am closest. He will not rat; he disapproves but wishes to protect me.' She could not resist this stab and Gerry winced as it went home.

'Not your father?'

'No. We aren't – we weren't – particularly close. It was purely a chance meeting tonight.' There was another leaden, painful pause, while he looked into his glass, and she decided to plough on. 'So that is why we are here. Difficult for anyone to make anything out of a drink at the Reform. Or of the very swift phone conversations we have had recently.' Ouch, she thought, I had better stop while I can.

'I need another drink,' he said, and shot to his feet, moving with the contained light athlete's neatness, and picked up her glass. She watched him across the room, stopping to talk to a man who had hailed him, head bent in the way she had so often seen him, and for a moment she could hardly breathe. He came back, swiftly, face impassive. 'Sorry. I just got you the same again, I hope that's all right.'

'Yes. I'm sorry, Gerry, I can see this is a shock. I've had since lunchtime to think about it, and I am still all over the place.' She stopped but he was still not looking at her. 'Gerry?' He looked at her, defensive and startled. 'I *do* know we'll have to stop.' She watched as the tight lines in his face insensibly relaxed.

'We will, won't we, my love?' he said, his eyes meeting hers for the first time since he had arrived.

She hunched forward, folding her arms against the

pain, and he bent anxiously towards her. 'Not for ever, presumably – this will blow over – but for a bit,' he said, anxiously.

'No,' she said, knowing where she was. 'No, we can't say that. What this has done is to put a flare over our position. Or your position. You can't afford an affair, and an affair is all you wanted.'

'I've been married a long time,' he said, steadily, the lines round his mouth tightening. 'And there are the children.'

'I do know. I don't actually approve of men who leave their wives and children, I really don't.' She stopped and clasped her hands together and looked at them, thinking that no one had told her that the twenty minutes in his bed almost two weeks ago had been the end, the final act, and that she would never feel the length of him against her again; all that was gone, and she had had no warning, no time to say goodbye to any of it. She could not even touch him in these surroundings. For a moment she was unable to speak, then she remembered what she was here to do. 'Gerry, we are still under threat, and that is also why I had to see you today, not tomorrow. Your Tim Bailey has let me down – in the sense that he has not been prepared to persevere against the latest Friern villainy.' She stopped, alerted by his expression. 'You've talked to him? And he said I was hysterical? Well, I was a bit OTT, I concede.' She took a deep breath and looked at her hands. 'But the problem remains, and the Prior chaps have a date to talk to *Private Eye* tomorrow. I don't think I could hold them back if I tried, and in any case it would be improper to do so. They are in the right.'

'What can they say?' The question came very swiftly,

and she looked back at him, carefully, understanding that she was in enemy territory.

'That Friern substituted a tender document with a lower price for the one they initially offered. That this substitution was probably effected by three councillors, one of whom is a Conservative close to you, Ted Malvern.'

'Can they prove it?'

'Perhaps not in a court of law. But they found a copy of the contract that was originally submitted by Friern, with a date stamp on it, in the council office that your man Malvern shares with a Liberal. It'll sound terrible.' She was watching him, steadily, and after a long pause he looked up from his drink and met her eyes.

'Don't,' she said, painfully.

'Don't what?'

'Don't sit there working out how to handle me, Gerry. We're past that. This is the Archangel Gabriel and staff here. The Prior lads are right, so am I, and nothing can stop us. Presumably it is your Mr Malvern who is bent, but it doesn't matter who it is, we have to go on.

'Caroline,' he said, looking at her straight, 'if I intervene, it's going to cause appalling amounts of gossip. Tim Bailey isn't in any doubt about us as it is, but he's reliable. I've got enemies there.' He watched at her unyielding expression. 'You don't want your name in the papers either.'

'No,' she said, steadily. 'I would as soon not. But our positions are not the same. I am not currently married to anyone.' She looked down at her hands horror-stricken, and listened to the thick silence, and watched as Gerry's long fingers closed round his glass. 'Sorry,' she said, between her teeth, 'that was just because I am unspeakably miserable and angry at having to give you up.' She stopped and drew a ragged breath. 'I would not want to put you at risk because I love you. But separate from all of this is what is due to honest men trying to run a straight business, and that must come first, or nothing makes sense.' She stopped. 'This is what you get for pulling the daughter of the country's foremost moral philosopher,' she said, hopelessly.

'What makes you think I don't agree with you?' He was, she saw, extremely angry.

'Well, no one would disagree with the principle as stated. But I'm watching you decide whether you are prepared to afford it. Shit. I shouldn't drink gin. This one you have to do, Gerry.'

'I didn't go into politics to see shady cover-ups in local authority administration, Caroline. Get the copy contract to Tim.' He put his glass down hard, and looked around for his jacket.

'You have only till noon tomorrow, Gerry – sorry,' she said, with the last of her strength. 'Then I have promised the lads they can go ahead.'

'I've understood all that.' He stood up, reaching for his jacket and she watched him, realizing that his automatic good manners had deserted him. He looked down at her, recollecting himself. 'Sorry, can I get you a taxi?'

'That would be kind,' she said, struggling to her feet. They walked silently out past the notice boards and an older man started forward to speak to Gerry but was repelled instantly by something in his face. At the top of the long steps he and Caroline turned to face each other, like rival lawyers who have fought bitterly but who know that life has to go on and the deal be cobbled together somehow, she thought wearily.

'I'll get my coat, it's downstairs.'

'Your father is over there,' he said, suddenly gentle. 'By himself, pretending to read the notices. Is he waiting for you?'

'No. I mean he shouldn't be. I didn't arrange that.'

'I think he is.'

'You were always more observant than I,' she said, sadly. 'You go. I'll stay and talk to the poor old man.'

'Curious – neither of those adjectives seem to me appropriate.'

'Oh, Gerry,' she said, involuntarily, gripped by the speed of his reaction. She hesitated. 'Can you ring me to tell me what's happening?'

'Tim Bailey will,' he said, promptly, looking away and she saw that he was set on a course which would take him right away from her.

'Right. I'll go and collect Dad. You're right – he reads as fast as I do, he must know that board by heart. Bye, Gerry.' She looked at him suddenly, understanding what was happening, that she was saying a necessarily casual goodbye in full public view to the first man she had loved since Ben, and whom she would never see again, except in similar public conditions. She saw that Gerry understood the same thing, and for a moment they looked at each other, appalled.

'I'll ring you,' he said, urgently. 'In a few weeks' time, when all this is over.'

'That would be nice,' she said, steadily, recognizing instantly the soft option which led to exactly the same place as the hard one. 'Kiss?'

He kissed her ceremonially on both cheeks, and just for a moment the familiar smell and feel of him nearly broke down the careful performance, but she held together and even managed a smile as she waved him off. She turned to find her father and the huge hall suddenly blurred around her, and she felt sick. She stopped unsteadily, then her father was beside her, holding her elbow.

'I can't see,' she said to him, conversationally, 'but I need to make one phone call.'

'Where is your coat? In the basement? I'll get it, you make your call.' He guided her to a phone and sat her down.

'Dad, you're not allowed in a ladies' cloaks.'

He vanished, leaving her to ring Peter Burwood and reflect dazed, what a silly thing that had been to say to Sholto, and then he was back, helping her into her coat, down the steps and into a taxi where she finally collapsed, weeping uncontrollably down his coat and beating his shoulders in helpless anger. He sat stoically through it all, as the taxi sped through the London evening, occasionally mopping her face, or blowing her nose for her, and by the time they got to her parents' house she had stopped, but for an occasional hiccough. Her father sat her down at the kitchen table and made her eat soup while he sat beside her.

'I must go home. The kids . . .'

'No. I will go and stay there tonight and keep order. You've had enough. Or your mother will. She's at a meeting of her women's group.'

'Not before time.'

He looked at her carefully, and cut some more bread. 'You don't understand about your mother and me, but never mind. Or perhaps we do need to explain ourselves. I don't oppress her, you know.'

'Actually you do, but she contributes.'

'Well, I don't mean to. And I haven't managed to oppress you. Quite the contrary.' He passed her the bread. 'You notice I am not asking you anything.'

She gazed at her bowl, feeling herself turn scarlet. 'I would guess you don't need to.'

'No.' Sholto ate a piece of bread, thoughtfully. 'I liked him, in fact. I've heard others speak well of him. A much better man than those young Conservatives often are. Growth potential there. Oh, darling, I am sorry – here, don't cry.'

'I don't think I have anything left just now to cry with,' she said, drearily. 'We were saying goodbye.' Her father's mouth quirked involuntarily. 'You realized?'

'Oh dear, yes. I've been there myself.'

'Dad!'

'Now that did *not* oppress your mother. I was excessively careful not to let her know.'

'And that made it all right, did it?'

'All moral philosophers need a daughter, like a cross. Of course it wasn't all right, adultery and deceit never can be. It pervaded everything else in my life and I did very bad work that year as a consequence. Now, are you ready to go to bed? You look as if three days' sleep would not come amiss. I'll ring Appleton for you.'

'All these years I have managed to forget that he was another of your students. Is he the reason they took me as an articled clerk?

'No. It was Hewson, the then senior partner who decided to take you.'

'Another of yours?'

'Yes, I'm afraid so. Now what about Appleton?'

'Don't ring him. I have to be there tomorrow to see the end of this, and I'll talk to him myself, afterwards.

Michael was there – I mean, tonight, before I left. He offered to come with me to the Reform, although he has no idea what the matter is. A good man.'

'So I thought when he was a student.' Sholto was filling a hot-water bottle and she watched him, realizing how long it had been since she had looked at him properly.

He looked up, feeling her eyes on him. 'Come on,' he said, gently, 'it'll still be there tomorrow, but not so sharp, not quite so painful.'

'Or it may be all over the newspapers. All of it.'

'I don't think so.' Her father sounded casually authoritative. 'I think your Mr Willshaw will find a way. A tough. Something very ruthless in the face. He knows what he cannot do, or have.'

'He shouldn't have seduced me, if he couldn't afford me,' she said, from the depths she was in, then saw her father's face. 'Sorry, I *do* know about personal responsibility, how should I not.'

'I must say however that I agree, darling. Women are much more vulnerable than men, sexually, and men should not forget that. Sorry, darling, I'm getting old, wittering on like this.' He reached over and enfolded her hand in one of his and she noticed with a pang the brown spots of old age on the back of the huge paw enclosing hers. 'You *will* survive this,' he said, firmly. 'And next time you must pick a good man who hasn't been married to someone else for twenty years. It never can work. I'll shut up. Come on. I'll run you a bath.'

Two miles away, Clive Fieldman was sitting, unseeingly watching the *Nine O'Clock News* go past him on the television, the taste of the whisky he had drunk with

Lucy sour on his breath, still trying to digest the catastrophe that was threatening to overwhelm him. If I get out of this, he thought, I will never be such a bloody fool again, but it all happened so *fast*. He pulled himself up sharply; please God I'm not going to find myself saying *that* to anybody. The issue was simple: did he owe it to his permanent secretary to tell him that those pictures of Lucy and him existed, in order that the Department and the might of HM Government Service might be forearmed against trouble from whatever quarter? And given the trust reposed in him, and the way the Secretary had accepted his assurances, there was only one answer to that question; he could not, possibly, conceal the threat represented by those photographs, given that he had no idea of their provenance. He had, a hopeful little voice in his head said, told Sir Francis he knew Lucy Friern better than he knew Caroline, but this careful statement in no way covered the situation made explicit by the photographs. So shut up, you silly bugger, he told the voice, and get the words together to see Sir Francis pronto – tomorrow. He spent twenty minutes trying to draft a note, then in a flash of sense realized that there was no way he could tell Sir Francis other than face to face. Relieved by this decision, he managed to have a bath and get himself into bed, and with the aid of another stiff whisky, he fell into an uneasy sleep.

Lucy Friern scowled near-sightedly at her mirror. John had for once done something not quite right with her hair, which was looking stiff; she had lost an eyeliner and had had to use a substitute which did not work as well; she had broken a nail, because she had been in a rush after seeing Clive; and she was generally seriously ruffled. She gave it up, took two or three deep, careful breaths, and surrounded herself with a cloud of Diorissimo before sailing into the kitchen to tell the help to go home. She checked, remembering that Matthew's best black socks were in the drier and diverted to fetch them, dropping them on his side of the bed.

'Matt, we ought to go in ten minutes. I'm *not* going to stand about watching Act One on the screens again. Andrew and Emma will be too polite to go in, and we'll ruin everyone's evening.'

She got a growl from the bathroom and the sound of running water for her pains, but she knew he would hurry; he had been late before at Covent Garden, had been politely but implacably forbidden entrance until the interval and had had to sustain the realization that no one there was even faintly impressed by Matthew Friern. He was unlikely to let that happen again.

The Friern driver got them there with seven minutes in hand. Andy and Emma Eames Lewis were waiting with immaculate, trained merchant-banker patience and the Walzheims' tickets. Like most of the accepting houses committee, Walzheims were subscribers and patrons, finding it well worthwhile to have four stalls tickets for every Tuesday during the main season with which to entertain existing and prospective clients. Lucy, ruffled by the day's events as she was, was cheered by Andy's expression, and she felt him draw a deep breath as he kissed her.

'Have a programme, Matt?' Emma, who was alarmed by Matthew, was saying, anxiously.

'Bless you, Emma. Is it the singing or the dancing we're having tonight?'

He was very tense, Lucy thought, scowling, while

Emma and Andy laughed obligingly, but it actually didn't seem to have anything to do with her. She had fished carefully round the subject of Clive on the way in the car, starting by telling Matt that she had just had a drink with him, but Matt had not seemed particularly interested, his mind plainly somewhere else. Clive had been no use to her at all; openly worried about his own position, he had, she thought crossly, really not been very interested in her worries. Not very helpful at all. They slid into their seats just before the lights went down and she found herself between Andy and Emma with Matt on Emma's other side. She considered Andy, wondering whether he would be any use, and by the time Count Almaviva was making advances to Susannah, she had decided what to do. At the first interval she waited until they had found the drinks booked for Walzheims, then appealed prettily to Andy to come and help her find a souvenir programme for the boys.

'Andy, I've got something very difficult indeed to tell you. Oh, good, here are the programmes – I need two.' She noticed with pleasure the speed and efficiency with which he paid for them and extracted her from the throng to a quiet spot by the door. 'It's frightfully embarrassing.' No longer particularly embarrassed, she told him about the photographs. 'The really stupid thing is, Andy,' she said, looking up at him, 'that that was the end. I mean, it was all over. So I don't need to stop doing anything, I've already stopped. And it wasn't Matt who sent the pictures. He wouldn't do that. What worries me, you see, is those photographs. Ought we to stop trying to buy Prior Systems? I *can* stop Matt.'

She watched Andy's profile, interested to see that he had turned white and his jaw was clenched.

'Oh, God,' he said, furiously.

'What, Andy?'

'No, it wasn't Matt and no, we don't need to stop trying for Prior.'

'Why not, Andy?'

'*I* sent you the bloody pictures. It was Matt who put detectives on to Clive Fieldman, but the firm was introduced to Friern by us. So they came back to me rather than going to Matt when they recognized you.'

Lucy stared at him.

'You are a sod, Andy. I've had a dreadful day. Why didn't you just tell me?'

'Because I thought, silly me, that you'd be embarrassed. I was trying to warn you anonymously. I didn't mean to frighten you.' He was scarlet now, not looking at her. 'And I was so fucking jealous, I couldn't bear it,' he said, ferociously, to his shoes. 'There's that too. But you don't have to worry. All reference to you got taken out of the report. I'm the only one who knows about you and Fieldman and I wish I didn't. It feels like the second time this has happened to me. Why him, Lu?' He turned his head to look her in the face and she saw that he was both furious and wretched. 'You still didn't want me this time. You had Fieldman.'

A silence fell between them while Lucy's blue eyes slowly filled with tears. 'We ought to get back to Matt and Emma. They've got the tickets. And they don't get on,' she said with dignity, feeling for a handkerchief, and he found himself reluctantly, painfully focusing on the problem.

'They don't, do they? Emma's frightened of him. Oh, Lucy, I wish I'd never taken Friern on, either.' He nodded, distractedly, to a fellow banker, who was obviously dying to meet his companion and pressed firmly back through the throng, with Lucy, beautiful and self-contained as ever, following him towards Matthew and Emma who were sitting with their drinks in constrained silence. 'You have nothing to worry about, Lu,' he said, miserably.

'So it was Matthew who hired detectives.' Her mind was working again.

'Yes. Merchant banks don't do that.'

'You just recommend them. Who else are they following?'

He hesitated. 'God knows.'

'Caroline?'

'She is, after all, the main adviser to Prior and she's getting a lot of political help from somewhere.'

'I had lunch with her. She knows about the photographs. She knew about Clive. She could have used that any time she liked, and she never did. So you'd better all understand, Andy, that I have warned Caro – you won't find anything.' She was so angry that she could hardly speak and he looked down at her, hangdog.

'I understand, Lu. I wouldn't have done this, you know, it was Matt's idea.'

'Matt does what he thinks he has to,' Matthew Friern's wife said, crisply and dismissively. 'And if he wants to waste his money, let him, but I'll tell Caro the whole story.' She hesitated, looking so beautiful and so stern that he caught his breath. 'No, I can't do that, but none of you men will get what you want.' She swept on, apologized prettily to Matt and Emma, and left Andy to follow behind her, with the five-minute-warning bell ringing in his ears.

26

'I'll come and get you at one o'clock. I'll take you home, if you've finished, and buy you lunch, if you haven't. Sit still. That door opens from the outside.' Sholto Henriques bumped the Volvo's scarred tyres against the kerb outside Smith Butler, ignoring the watching pair of traffic wardens, and walked round the bonnet to open the passenger door.

'Very significant, Professor Henriques. You wish to entrap your passenger? Like ze spider,' his daughter said, climbing cautiously out.

'No, darling, really not. I just haven't got round to getting that handle fixed.' He looked at her anxiously and she managed a smile. She felt as if her face had been stuffed, and the skin around her eyes artificially inflated. She had slept and woken weeping, slept again and got up at one point to find her father at her door instantly with tea and a wet flannel for her face. She had gone back after that to an uneasy sleep, dropping into a sound one at 6 a.m. from which she had been woken at 8.30 a.m. with a headache which had started the moment she took her head off the pillow. Her father had tried to persuade her not to go in to the office, but had yielded promptly when she had started to cry in panic and distress. She plodded up the steps, looking neither left nor right, failing to greet the receptionist, and making blindly for her office.

'I'm not well, Susie,' she said, in minimum explanation, to the concerned face. 'But I have to hang on to sort out Prior. My Dad's coming by at lunchtime for me. Could you find me an Anadin?'

She sat, holding her aching head, and waited for Susie to come back.

'Mark Dwyer says to tell you he's in if you need him. He has a meeting at eleven. Your father's ever so good-looking,' Susie said, interested, as she put the coffee down.

Caroline coughed into her coffee. 'Yes, but how do you know?'

Susie stared at her. 'He was with Mr Appleton. He introduced me just now, in the corridor.'

Caroline tried to summon up the familiar resentment but found she could only feel the most profound relief that someone was making the explanations for her that she could not possibly make herself. She remembered, sharply, a family holiday in Cornwall. She must have been about eleven and skinny; having won the under fourteens' swimming race handily, at the Helston Fair, she had entered herself for the eighteen and under, which was to be swum on the high-tide course over 400 yards. She had been waiting, shivering, frightened, among adult-sized competitors, watching uneasily the heaving grey sea under a sodden grey sky, when her father had descended, pausing only to scratch her from the race and to get back her two-shilling entry fee, and had carried her back to the car. 'I could do it,' she had screamed at him, kicking furiously, determined not to show any of her gratitude and relief, and they had fought and bickered all the way home, until her mother had stopped it by bursting into tears. Well, she had learned a bit since those days, and she was not going to burst kicking and screaming into Michael Appleton's office. Her dad could get her two shillings back and get her out of at least one bit of the mess. Only, of course, she was grown-up now, and would just have to endure most of it.

The phone went and she picked it up before Susie could, her heart beating painfully.

'Tim Bailey here, Mrs Whitehouse.'

'Yes.' She felt sick but told herself steadily that she should have known. Gerry had said it would be Tim Bailey who rang, not he.

'I understand that the opposition are withdrawing their tender bid for the contract.'

'How solid is that understanding, Tim?'

'Solid. The council surveyor has been notified.'

'Will he tell my people? I mean, how will they know that they need not take action?'

The silence on the line was eloquent but she was unimpressed. She would have this one gift-wrapped and hand delivered – it had cost her enough.

'I will ensure that the council surveyor tells them. Would that do?' he said, with barely restrained temper.

'Nothing less will convince them,' she said. 'It isn't you they don't trust; they don't know you exist. It's Friern – and for good reason.'

'Better not use names on the phone.'

'My end is clear. I had it checked yesterday. I hope you did the same.'

'Yes, I did, as a matter of fact.' He hesitated. 'You all right?'

'No. But I am grateful to you, Tim, and I am sorry I yelled at you last time. Stress.'

'I shouldn't have lost my rag either. Those buggers were crooks. And they'd involved one of ours.'

'I was sorry to hear that.'

'Yes.' There was a grudging pause. 'We faced him with it – me and the sub agent. We had the document by then of course, your lads delivered it to me, and we told him where it had been found. It took a while but he gave up in the end. He's resigned on health grounds, and Friern withdrew their second tender.'

'Thank you for telling me,' she said soberly, understanding his rage.

'Gerry was fit to be tied. He stuck his neck out for you last night, and made a few enemies up here.'

'My old father would say that to be on the side of the angels must pay long-term.'

'I hope he's right. Well, this'll not buy the baby a new bonnet. Ring me if you need anything else. For Prior, I mean.'

'Thank you, Tim,' she said, steadily. 'I hope I'll not need to.'

She put the phone down gently and looked at the papers on her desk, noticing with mild academic interest that the Voulos clan were coming in at noon for a meeting scheduled to go on all day. There was, she thought, calmly, no way on God's earth she could cope with any of that; she had better tell Mark Dwyer he was in charge. She reached for the phone but it forestalled her and she found Michael Appleton on the other end of the line.

'I'll take that Voulos meeting, Caroline. They're my introduction and it sounds as if they are being extremely tiresome. Dwyer's going to brief me.'

'Thank you, Michael.'

'Anything I can do on Prior?'

'No. It's OK now. Are you still harbouring my father?'

543

'He's gone but will return soon. He's left me in charge.'

'Don't call us, we'll call you.' She hung up on his relieved laugh and sat, watching the telephone, mind deliberately in suspension, waiting patiently until the Prior lads rang her and she could go home. She considered the blinking light which told her that Susie had taken a call and waited for it to be transmitted.

'Caroline. It's Lady Friern.'

'Oh. Well, put her on, Susie, but interrupt me if any of the Prior people come through.'

She braced herself and picked up the phone, gingerly, wondering whether Lucy was going to try to get back at her for the defeat which had just been inflicted on her husband.

'Caro? It's all right.' She was sounding light-hearted. 'The photographs, I mean. I know where they came from. I've just told Clive that he doesn't have to worry – that's all over.'

'Where *did* they come from?' She heard her friend hesitate. 'It *was* Matt then?'

'Well, sort of. The thing *is*, Caro, that the people – the detectives – reported first to Andy Eames Lewis.'

'*Walzheims* hired detectives?'

'No, no. I'm afraid that *was* Matt, but the thing is Andy knew these people and the head of the firm came straight to him when they realized it was me they were photographing – if you see what I mean. So *he* sent the pictures to warn me.'

Caroline stared disbelievingly at the telephone, her own state momentarily forgotten. 'Why didn't the silly bugger just tell you? Oh, wait a minute, I know why not . . . you took him on and dumped him for Matt, didn't you, all those years ago? They *never* forget things like that. He thought you could sweat a bit.' There was an offended, thoughtful silence from the other end and she understood, without caring one way or the other, that she had been less than tactful.

'Yes, I expect there was a bit of that,' Lucy acknowledged, finally, interested but not apparently distressed. 'Also he was wildly jealous, he said.' She sounded innocently pleased with herself.

Caroline sighed. 'Better get the negatives, Lu.'

'I have. They arrived this morning.'

There never had been any flies on Lucy when it came to looking after herself, Caroline thought, resting her aching head on her spare hand.

'Sweet of Andy though, don't you think?'

'Up to a point.' Caroline thought, coldly, about Matthew Friern's banker, and decided that all her precautions had been necessary. 'Are they still watching me, Lu?'

'That's one of the reasons I rang you. I don't know. But Matt is truly not quite sane about this Prior deal, Caro, and he's been non-stop on the phone at the office this morning – I wanted to ask him about the holidays and Mrs W. says she just cannot get him off the phone.'

'But I had better assume that I am being watched.'

'You knew that though, didn't you?'

'Yes, I did. No need to tell him you warned me, Lu; let him waste his money.'

'Yes, I will,' Matthew's wife assured her, in tones of simple pleasure. 'Perhaps you could manage a few red herrings.'

'I may not be able to rise to that. But thank you, Lu. I'm going home at lunchtime.'

'*Darling*, are you ill?'

'I suppose so.'

'I'm sorry. I'm a pig, I didn't quite think about it. I've been so *upset*, Caro. And Andy has been sweet.'

'Don't do that,' Caroline roused herself to advise. 'Comes in the category of sleeping with the help.' That one, she realized, had got right home and she decided just to nail it. 'Like men knocking off the nanny.'

'Really?' her friend said, coldly, sounding like a child whose secretly favoured toy had been abstracted.

'You haven't already, have you, Lu?'

'No.' Lucy was sounding both irritable and regretful, and Caroline felt a moment of pure vengeful pleasure, then repented. 'It really isn't a good idea, Lu, and I don't often say that to you. Matt would find that pretty difficult. So would Andy, because Matt would give up using Walzheims, and Andy wouldn't like that. Ambitious creature – always was.' She massaged the back of her neck, unavailingly. 'Lu, thank you for telling me. I am just waiting for an urgent call, about Prior, as it happens.'

'You're as bad as Matt, Caro.'

'Absolutely not true,' Caroline said, firmly, and they were both managing to laugh, as Lucy rang off.

Caroline spared a fleeting thought for Clive but decided that he, like her, was probably left alone to digest the experience of rejection. She drew breath against a stab of pain as she thought of Gerry, but just then the call she had been waiting for came through. All three of the Prior management were gathered together, wildly over-excited.

'Caroline? Friern have withdrawn their tender for Marsh Lane. How did you make them do it?'

'I'll never tell you. But you gentlemen produced the bullets – I just fired them. So what about the rest of the competition?'

'There was only Maceys, and they came in above us – well above. We'll buy you the biggest bottle of champagne you've ever seen come next week.'

'That would be nice.' She might, she thought drearily, conceivably be around and working by next week since life went on, whatever else was happening. The good bits seemed to last about ten seconds; the rest, the grub work, endured for ever. She listened for a few minutes more to the cries of joy coming from the other end, and managed to find an adequate response, or at least one whose inadequacies went unnoticed. They rang off and, exhausted, she looked at her watch; it was still only eleven fifteen and the day stretched endlessly before her. She was packing papers mechanically into her briefcase when she looked up and saw Michael Appleton, silently considering her. She burst anxiously into speech. 'My lot got that contract. Or rather Friern have withdrawn, leaving them well in the lead. How are the Voulos gang?'

'Unimproved. I came out because I had a distracting view of your father, sitting in that awful car, holding two traffic wardens in parley. If you are finished here, it would be a kindness to take him away.'

'Yes, I am.'

'We're not expecting you next week.'

'Prior need me. Tuesday is the final day for the bids to the NEB. Ours is in, but all the others probably won't get there till the last minute.'

'Close of play, Tuesday? Then they cannot need you until Wednesday. Go home till then, Caroline, get some rest. We all need you back in good order. I can't manage the Voulos clan indefinitely, you know.'

'Wednesday today, isn't it? All right. Tell me. I can see from your smiling faces that the news is good,' Winstanley said, ferociously, considering his assembled advisers. 'So what did happen when they opened the bids last night? I'd rather know now.'

'We did put a note in your box, Minister.' Clive was still feeling like an uncertainly reprieved convict, even four days after Lucy had told him that the photographs of them both were destroyed. She had reached him at the office a bare ten minutes before he was to see Sir Francis and confess to their affair and he was still turning cold all over when he thought about his escape. The experience left him exercising positively invalidish caution in all his dealings with his seniors or his ministers; and the minute the words were out of his mouth, he cursed himself for showing such serf-like anxiety. Richard Watts, to his left, looking pale with exhaustion as usual, cast him an inquiring glance.

'I missed it.' Winstanley, unlike many ministers, never minded admitting he had failed to read something, and Clive, as senior official present, took on the task of explaining. 'The management team are maintaining their bid of £50m down and £10m deferred, subject to various conditions, one of which is that they actually sign up a substantial local authority contract. I understand that the council has agreed to accept their tender. Shaw have bid £50m, subject to conditions.'

'What about Friern? Don't tell me they did not bid.'

'Friern put in a bid of £55m, nothing deferred, but accompanied by a confusing letter saying they might be prepared to pay a bit more. Their intentions are being probed now, I understand.'

Winstanley stared at them. 'Isn't that rather odd? Richard, do we know what is going on?'

'I have spoken to John Martin at Gruhners. He is baffled too, but he thinks Friern are hesitating because of the fall in their share price and the fact that Prior rather than they got the local authority contract. But it is a confused signal, and John was going to talk to Walzheims.'

'Tell them to get their client to shit or get off the pot.'

'That sort of thought, yes, Minister.' He looked up in surprise as a secretary padded in and deposited a message in front of him, which he read in one comprehensive look. 'Christ! Sorry, excuse me, Minister.'

'Is it about Prior?'

'No, about Friern. They have shat, to use a legal expression. Agreed bid for Harrison, cash and shares at £85m. On the screen at my shop, apparently.'

He reread the note, hopefully, as if it would tell him something different the second time, then looked cautiously sideways at Winstanley and the surrounding civil servants, none of whom could think of anything to say at all.

'Well, bugger me,' Winstanley said, finally, and the men round the table laughed in relief and recognition, moved their hands and straightened their backs.

'Sums up the feeling of the meeting, if I may say so, Minister,' Clive said, deeply and incredulously relieved.

'After all that,' Winstanley said. 'All that fuss and lobbying . . .' His voice failed him; and the group around the table made noises indicative of agreement and deprecation. 'Well, they can whistle for the next piece of help they want from us.' He was moving from incredulity to thoughts of revenge. It would not take more than a few hours, Clive thought drily, before this perfectly sensible man recalled that it was not the policy of the administration of which he was a minor cog to give any part of industry any help at all. And on that basis there was not a lot that could be conveniently withheld to signify ministerial displeasure with a particular bit of industry. Moreover, on calm consideration, Winstanley would not wish to alienate an important contributor to party funds. The trick now was to prevent him from speaking in haste what he might have to repent at leisure. Beating back his own feelings of overwhelming relief that Lucy Friern and their affair could no longer be perceived to be in any way relevant to the conduct of government business, Clive bent to the task of damage limitation, and turned to Richard Watts.

'So, Richard, sorry to state the absolutely obvious, but this means that Friern can't possibly be going to bid for Prior, despite what they said last night.'

'That's right. What they put in was a holding bid. A good deal that, buying Harrison, by the look of it.'

The secretary padded in again and handed Clive a message which he read carefully. 'Friern *have* now formally withdrawn their offer for Prior, Minister. The message is from Jenkins at NEB.'

'So who have we got left? The management team.'

'And Shaw.'

'At less money.'

'Yes, Minister.'

'Richard, what do we do?'

Richard Watts kept his head and reacted methodically.

'Well, Gruhners will be talking to Shaw. It is their client after all. But assuming they don't raise their offer, I expect Gruhners will advise the NEB to go for a negotiated deal with the management team, with Shaw up their sleeve, as it were. However I think I did advise the Minister that I was doubtful about how strongly motivated Shaw was.'

'You mean they were put up to it by Gruhners?'

'It seemed possible, yes, Minister.'

'So we've really only got one bid. My God, this won't look good.'

Clive pulled himself together, feeling rusty, intellectual muscles flex. 'Minister, we – or rather the NEB – went through a full public offer process and these are the results. It may seem a bit of an anticlimax, but everyone had a fair and equal chance and if we've ended up with only one client, then that is a statement about the market for this company.'

'Absolutely right.' Richard Watts came in promptly, on cue, heroically abstaining from reminding anyone that he had said all along that this would come to a negotiated deal with one customer. 'And if the NEB don't like it, well, they can hang on to the company for another couple of years and see if they can do better.'

'Is that what a commercial organization would do – withdraw and start again in two years' time?' Winstanley inquired, horrified, as Clive, anxiously, opened his mouth to speak, then decided that the representative of commerce here present could bat first.

'Not if they had received a fair offer – one which gave them a decent price for the company.' Richard Watts had seen the pit beneath his feet.

'In any case, Minister, this sale is part of a continuing

policy initiative. It is not taking place in isolation. It would be very difficult to allow the NEB to back-pedal.' Clive decided to put his tuppence worth in and was rewarded with some authoritative help from Richard Watts.

'Thing is, Minister, the NEB is really in the same position as a private sector group, which has announced publicly that it has decided to sell off a couple of divisions. Provided that they aren't being offered silly prices, the market then expects them to go ahead, not stop in their tracks. In fact, it would probably damage the share price if they did stop.'

Winstanley visibly relaxed at this endorsement from the heart of the private sector, and Clive nodded gratefully to Richard Watts.

'So we tell the NEB to get on with it?'

'Yes, Minister.'

'Do I need to make a statement?'

'Not yet.' Clive and James Mather spoke together.

'I think the right moment to tell the House is when the NEB have reached outline agreement with Prior, assuming, as I do, that Shaw drop out,' Clive added, carefully, having thought this one out well before the day. 'The NEB can issue a press notice saying that they are in negotiation, if they see the need.'

'Well the management aren't going to drop out. And it oughtn't to take them more than three weeks to get to heads of agreement,' Richard Watts contributed. 'The full legals take a bit of time. Lot of documentation in these deals.'

All present consulted diaries.

'Plenty of time before the end of the session,' James Mather said, reassuringly.

Winstanley closed the file, firmly. 'Right. Good. Well, I must tell the PM. Could someone do me a note? Splendid. Thank you for coming, Richard. Thank you, gentlemen.'

'Ye'll have seen, Caroline, that Friern have bid for Harrison. On an agreed basis.'

'What? Hamish, are you sure?'

'It's on the screen in front of me, Caroline – I suppose you solicitors don't have such things. Did you not know? I thought the Lady Friern was a friend.'

'She would know better than to tell me before an announcement,' Caroline said automatically, still dazed by the news. She sat, clasping the telephone, staring into space. 'I wonder when they decided to do that deal,' she said, drearily, thinking of Gerry. 'Jesus Christ, it would have saved a lot of grief if they had done it two weeks ago.'

There was a pause in which she remembered who she was talking to, but it no longer seemed to matter very much.

'Ye'd still have needed that contract – what's it called?'

'Marsh Lane.'

'Aye. So whatever you did to see Friern off was needed.'

'Hamish, do *you* believe that the ends justify the means?'

There was a thoughtful pause. 'Mostly, aye, yes I do. We'd not have been prepared to support a bid at that level without the Marsh Lane contract. And losing it may have been the final straw that made Friern decide to go with Harrisons rather than Prior. Which brings me to what I called you to ask. Caroline, can we not reduce our cash offer up front a wee bit?'

'Hamish, *no*, we don't reduce the bid. Remember us? The ones who make the right offer and stick to it. We just make sure we never have to pay very much of the deferred price. There's still Shaw around, remember, and if we chisel others might come in. It's a bloody good deal in anyone's terms. I'll call you back when I know a bit more.'

Caroline had spent the intervening four days at home, mostly in bed, intermittently trying to reassure her children that she was not ill. The boys had fussed and broken things; Susannah, using some different level of understanding, had simply taken to joining her in the big double bed, getting up to play or to fetch cups of tea or to go for walks with her grandparents. And after a bit, the boys had relaxed and joined her too, so that finally she had been forced to get up herself, crowded out by her children. She still felt most days as if she had been thrown from a moving car and was treating herself very carefully. The days ahead seemed to hold no prospect of pleasure or entertainment, but she knew in some part of her that she would move out of the shadows again.

'Hello, Dad,' she said, into the phone. He had been at her side for most of the past four days and she had come, insensibly, to take his restless, dominating presence for granted.

'Darling, I'm at the Reform. I've just looked at the boards.'

'Thanks, but I've heard about Friern and Harrison. That was good news. I mean, it removed our fiercest competitor.'

'I hadn't seen that. That's good. No, it's something else. There's a reshuffle.'

'A what?'

'Of the Cabinet. Leader of the House to the Lords – well, that was coming. Secretary of State for Trade and Industry takes his place. Brown from Employment to Trade and Industry, and Gerry Willshaw to replace him at Employment. So he's in the Cabinet. I thought I'd better tell you before you saw it in the papers.'

She could not speak for a few seconds, thinking of Gerry talking about employment law, Gerry sitting with long legs stretched out as she had seen him in the House, Gerry buttoning his shirt, restlessly. She felt all her wounds exposed. 'I was more or less told something like this was in the wind,' she said, bravely.

'So you would have had to stop anyway.'

'Yes. Oh, Dad, I am absolutely miserable without him. And it didn't last all that long or take that much time, really. Not if you wrote it all down on a sheet of paper.'

'True of a lot of emotional experience.'

'Thank you, Professor Henriques. Do you have any more words for our listeners, or can I get on and phone the lads?'

'I'll come and drive you home when I'm finished here. About five. You'll have had enough by then.'

Three weeks later, almost to the day, Mark Dwyer worked his way out of the public gallery at the House of Commons against a steady incoming polyglot stream of tourists and found a telephone.

'Mr Burwood, please? Peter, it's Mark Dwyer. Caroline is on her way up to you but she asked me to call and say that the statement has now been made in the House and you may now talk to the press.'

'An hour later than they said. We've nearly missed the front page.' Peter Burwood was sounding outraged and Mark Dwyer sighed, inwardly. He was exhausted but justifiably pleased with himself, having negotiated the heads of agreement for the sale and purchase of all the shares in Prior Systems virtually single-handed in two and a half weeks. Caroline Whitehouse, whose client this was, had taken very little part; apparently she and the senior partner had agreed that in view of the insinuations made about the relationship between her and Clive Fieldman, it would be politic if someone else took the lead in dealings with the Department. Michael Appleton, nominally in charge instead of Caroline, had, of course, been much too busy, so the full load had fallen on Mark. Mercifully, he had always liked Clive Fieldman and James Mather, and found them easy to deal with. He had indeed, with some surreptitious help from Caroline, drafted half the statement to the House which John Winstanley had just delivered, in order to make sure that any references to the legal terms were right. And he and, finally, Caroline had explained several times, in several different ways, to the Prior Systems team individually and as a group that any announcement of the deal ahead of the ministerial statement would result in the Prior Systems management, flanked by their legal advisers, being hung in a row on gallows erected outside the House of Commons for the purpose. 'It's called breach of parliamentary privilege,' Clive Fieldman had explained, patiently, 'and ministers are incredibly touchy about it because they have to apologize to the House. No worse fate can be imagined, and we here will be for the chop too, so get a grip on your customers, Mark.'

The Prior Systems team had remained, to the last, incredulous and inclined to ignore all the words, and only an appeal by Caroline, in which she had grittily reminded them of the political debts they owed, had kept them in check. Mark tried to say a civil farewell to Peter, who could be heard on the other line talking to the local newspaper, but had to content himself with telling a secretary that he too would be with them for the presentation to employees that evening, though on a much later train than Caroline. He raced for a taxi to take him to Kings Cross, deciding that he bore Caroline no grudge for delegating to him the task of going to hear the statement. She wanted, she had explained, for once in her life, to get to a party in time to have a bath and get herself organized, rather than having to put on full make-up in a train lavatory. He considered this explanation again, as he relaxed in the taxi and decided it had an element of disinformation. Caroline White-house had thrived on split-second timetables and changing in cubbyholes for years, but his was not to reason why. Her withdrawal from most of the final stages on Prior had enhanced his partnership prospects not a little; he had worked directly with Michael Appleton and that had done him no harm at all. He was paying off his cab when someone tapped him on the shoulder and he looked around to see Clive Fieldman, dark and neat and self-contained, as usual, carrying his own briefcase and a red box, the strong lines in his face emphasized as he grinned.

'We should have given you a lift. I was in the box. Minister, do you know Mark Dwyer of Smith Butler, the Prior team's solicitors? He is also going to the Prior presentation.'

Winstanley shook hands with him. 'Mrs Whitehouse not with you?'

'No, she went up earlier. She wanted time to change.'

'Right, right.' Winstanley nodded importantly. 'See you at the party,' he said to Mark and bustled off followed by Clive and his private secretary, each carrying another red box, the crowds parting respectfully for the cavalcade.

'Now, you're *not* going to fight with Caroline, are you, Matt? I'd rather not go if you are, and I mean that. Why are we going anyway?' Lucy Friern, elegant in dark-blue linen trousers, hair still wet from the pool, plugged in the electric kettle.

'Because John Harrison and I reckon that in two or three years' time all the investing institutions and some of the managers will be looking to cash their shares and take the profit and we want to be there to pick up the company.' Matthew Friern was wearing his preferred weekend gear of wide outdated linen trousers and an out-of-shape sweatshirt. 'So we're going to show our faces to the investors and we're all going to be good friends, and you and I and John and Vicki are going to watch Burwood greasing up to his employees to get them to buy shares.'

Lucy considered her husband. 'Darling, sorry, but will you want to buy a company where the employees have shares?' She was genuinely puzzled, Matthew's views on employer/employee relationships being based firmly on a model of the feudal system in its full twelfth-century glory.

'Oh, they'll all sell out. At a price. Assuming any of them can sign their names or spare the cash from the boozer to buy shares in the first place.'

'Mm. Well, we needn't stay late, need we? Caroline says the main party ends quite early, but her team are reckoning to go on all night afterwards. She was trying to work out how to creep away without causing offence.'

Matthew grunted and she looked at him sideways; he was probably never going to forgive Caroline for having so comprehensively defeated him. 'Winstanley's coming,' he said, 'and your friend Clive.'

'Oh. It'll be nice to see them both.' She poured water into the teapot, decisively.

Caroline Whitehouse looked at herself in the mirror of the hotel bathroom and decided that she was at last looking better. She had finally started to be able to sleep again in the last week. After three weeks of broken nights when the pain was so bad that she had often had to let herself out of a sleeping house and walk round and round the quiet streets, she had understood that she must live to a strict regimen of exercise, plain food and a rigid avoidance of the television on which Gerry's image might at any moment appear. Economic crisis was threatening, and meaningless television footage of the Cabinet trooping into Number Ten, looking worried, had appeared on every version of the news for days, Gerry, his natural bounce subdued for the cameras, looking concerned with the best of them. She winced at the thought and resolutely turned her attention to her clothes: a vivid green silk suit against which her newly washed blonde hair shone. 'Right,' she said, firmly to herself, and immured her briefcase in the wardrobe. She hesitated in front of the TV, but passed it by, deciding not to test her fragile equanimity and went down to find Peter's driver, who was taking her to the auditorium of the local polytechnic to join in the fun.

On arrival she waited for the driver to open the door for her which he did blinking in surprise since she normally hopped out before he had got his own door open. He watched admiringly as she went up the long path covered with carpet for the occasion, straight-backed, and vanished into the arms of the company's finance director who was on duty to greet guests. 'Graham,' she said, with pleasure, kissing him. 'Oh my God, there's a programme with gold tassels on it.'

'Got to put on a bit of a show,' he said, grinning at her. 'You look wonderful.'

She smiled at him, gratefully, hearing the faint note of relief in his voice. That lot were smart, she reflected, as she moved down the line, greeting familiar faces among the senior staff; they could not have failed to notice that she had dropped back out of the front line. They had not altogether believed the explanation they had been offered, but they had not pressed. Like all really good businessmen, they were sensitive to negotiating nuance. And they had been very well served professionally in the final stages, thanks to Mark Dwyer. She noticed that on the other side of the vast hall there was a cluster of people, and others were streaming from all sides towards it. She walked over, chatting civilly to one of the salesmen and his wife, and stopped, blinking, at the sight of a group of girls in fishnet tights, silk leotards and black bowler hats, all jostling to meet someone she could not yet see.

'They are meant to be City bowlers, I am told,' a familiar Glasgow accent said in her ear.

'What?' She turned to consider Hamish, square and tidy in a dark suit. 'Hamish, to what are we come?'

'I thought you'd written this presentation, Caroline.'

'I thought so too. I did write all the sober words about how to buy shares, and warnings about them going down as well as up. But I really did not understand that they were going to be spoken by young women in fishnet tights.'

'Sung rather than spoken, as I understand it,' Hamish said, gloomily. 'It is a musical, Caroline, with actors as well.'

'You're having me on.'

'Not at all. I'm surprised to find you didn't know. The wee girls there are just being presented to the minister – Mr Winstanley – and then the whole thing starts. I've brought Sir William, and all the rest of the investors, Caroline. I hope this is going to be all right. You're looking very beautiful – are you appearing too?'

'Not so far as I know.' She was watching, fascinated, as the line of girls surrounded Winstanley, who was looking bemused but pleased with himself, a wary eye on the local photographer. The line shifted and she suddenly saw Clive, framed between two girls, looking self-contained and amused, laughing with the girls, and she saw as his head turned that the black hair was showing grey at the side and that he had grown into a distinctively good-looking man. His head went back as he laughed at something the prettier of the two, a bouncy blonde, had said, and as he turned to his minister, Caroline waved to him: a tiny companionable gesture, such as she used for the children at a school play, meaning I am here, ignore me if that is what is best, and she saw his face split into a huge smile. His minister called him and he went over, waving to Caroline to indicate that he would catch up with her. She found that she was smiling as broadly as he, insensibly cheered by the sight of him, and she turned to give her attention to the Frierns who were approaching her crabwise, Lucy moving towards her determinedly, bringing a visibly reluctant Matthew with her by sheer force of character.

'Darling, how nice to see you,' Lucy said, firmly, kissing her. Caroline hugged her back, touched and amused, and considered her friend. She was looking dazzling in petrol-blue silk, her black hair tidily piled on the top of her head, totally unconscious of the fact that all the Prior employees and their wives in the vicinity were watching her out of the corners of their eyes.

'And Matthew, how nice,' Caroline said, resolutely, standing on her toes to kiss him, mindful of the City rule, drummed into her by older partners, that you were always, always gracious in victory against the day you might need a little grace in your own defeat. 'Many congratulations on your Harrison deal. That looked very good.'

Matthew, in the tones of one eating broken glass, was managing to express similar congratulations when Andy Eames Lewis appeared, silently, at Lucy's shoulder.

'Where's Emma?' Lucy asked him, prettily, while Caroline considered them both, wondering whether Lucy had taken her advice, but decided that she absolutely could not tell, and never had been able to, she remembered, soberly.

'She was on a later train. She'll be here in a minute,' Andy said, registering nothing other than bankerly civility. 'I must go and have a word with Hamish Brown, who I see over there. I believe that was the five-minute bell, as it were.' His glance swept disbelievingly over the crowds of people working their way towards the entrance to the auditorium, and he headed off towards Hamish.

'Where are you sitting, Caroline?' Matthew asked into an awkward silence.

'In the pound seats, with the management. I'll be the only one paying attention since they've already seen the show twenty-five times in rehearsal.' Caroline was belatedly savouring the fact that this gathering of 2000-odd people was to celebrate the work of her hands, along, of course, she reminded herself, with that of many others. She allowed herself finally to feel the creator's joy, and beamed on Matthew, who raised a small, reluctant smile.

'Well, I hope it all works for you and the team, Caroline. If it doesn't, you know where to come.' He nodded, tight-lipped, while Lucy behind him cast her eyes to heaven.

'Oh, I do.' Caroline grinned piratically, but virtuously forwent any swift and vengeful response, contenting herself with murmuring, 'Dear Matthew, always so kind,' and reducing Matthew's wife to stifled giggles.

She turned and found herself face to face with Peter Burwood, pale, sweating and wearing lipstick. He hugged her warmly and she smelt face powder. 'Dearest Peter, are you appearing in this entertainment? What as?'

'As myself of course, Caroline. It's the story of how we did the buy-out.'

'Ah,' she said, ominously, 'why aren't I in it?'

563

'You are,' Graham appeared, grinning. 'You're the tall one, over there.'

'In the blue fishnet tights? And feathers? And not a lot else. Thank you very much indeed.' She started to laugh, helplessly, and went up the stairs, with the comfortable weight of Graham's arm on her shoulders, to take her place in the middle of the management and investors' enclave. As she settled herself, Peter appeared from nowhere and sat firmly beside her.

'I'm not on till the end,' he explained, signalling to Hamish to sit on his other side.

'What about the Minister, Peter?' Caroline asked, quietly.

'Only popped in to wish us luck. He's going on up to Edinburgh for something. Nice of him to come.'

'A signal honour,' she agreed.

The lights went down a notch and the rest of the Prior management scrambled for seats so that as the lights dimmed again she found herself surrounded, Peter to her left, his shoulder touching hers, Martin to her right and Graham just behind her, his long legs cramped so that she could feel his knees as she bent back. She saw out of the corner of her eye Clive edge his way along to Martin's other side, climbing over coats, and she leant forward to smile at him. He grinned back and reached across Martin to grip her hand and congratulate her. The lights went down, and the girls in fishnet tights bounced on to the stage with a cheerful introductory song about the City, waving bowler hats neatly in unison. She sat, torn between laughter and admiration as the show progressed, interspersing song and dance with actors portraying various bits of management and contriving to make the words she had so

564

ruthlessly amended sound reasonably real and spontaneous, as they explained to each other how a company worked and what a share was and how you bought it. She looked carefully round the rapt faces just beyond the management block, and touched Peter's hand. 'Brilliant,' she said, quietly. 'I would never have believed it.'

He clasped her hand firmly in his, and they sat, both of them like children, until the final song when he leant towards her and said he had to get backstage.

'Good luck,' she said, and watched him climb over Hamish. Whatever else had gone wrong, this was all right; he was a happy man, it was the start of a success story and it would not have happened without her. For a moment, as she sat surrounded by her allies, she saw past her present grief and remembered that tomorrow all this would be in the papers and she would be in receipt of the congratulations of her partners.

The girls were dressed by now in brightly coloured tutus, personifying, presumably, individual shares, she thought, hazily, realizing that she must have lost concentration, but as she tried to work it out, they danced off stage and the spotlight came up on Peter, pale and obviously nervous. He spoke the epilogue, explaining that the dream had come true and the company was theirs (except for the seventy-five per cent that belonged to Hamish and his confrères, as she could just hear Hamish observe), and said the rest of the words about how to buy shares that had been given him to speak. A final burst of song and the lights on stage died down, while the lights in the auditorium came up, and the audience stood up gratefully, straightening their backs and looking for the exits in order to find the promised champagne supper. Caroline stood with them, found that one foot had gone to sleep and grabbed at Martin to avoid falling into the next row.

'Damn. You go on, Martin, I'll follow.'

'I'll bring her along,' Clive said, cheerfully. 'After all there has been between us, it's the least I can do.' He waved off the Prior management and held her firmly by the elbow. 'You OK?'

'Very nearly. Weren't they good?'

'Bloody marvellous. I wish my man could have stayed – he'd have lapped it up. And you were pretty good too, Caro, you really hung in there. You did well.'

She looked at him sharply, and saw that he was looking tired. 'Are *you* OK, Clive?'

'A bit battered,' he said, straightforwardly, deciding not to avoid the question, 'but we'd have stopped some time.'

'Yes. Yes, that must be so.' She looked away from him, around the auditorium where the last of the audience, the men in dark suits and the women in their best dresses, were pressing towards the exits.

'Your foot all right? Come on, let's find the champagne.' He took her hand firmly and set out pulling her behind him and she followed him, amused and respectful.

They emerged into the huge hall and made their way into the room reserved for the visiting dignitaries, where they were greeted by Peter and a waitress with a tray of champagne. 'Caroline, come quick.' She looked at him inquiringly, as she picked up a glass and saw, ten feet away, a dark head utterly and painfully familiar bent to listen to someone. 'Your friend, Gerry Willshaw. He wasn't going to come, but managed to get here after a dinner somewhere.' Peter was alight with joy and relief, secure on the bridge of his ship, freed from care, surrounded by friends.

'How very nice,' Caroline managed to say, as the room turned momentarily dark. Peter rushed away but someone took her glass from her and then she felt Clive's steadying hand.

'You feeling faint?'

She took a deep breath and looked into the familiar dark brown eyes, level with her own. 'I didn't realize he'd be here. Stupid of me,' she said, as if to a brother, and saw his face change as he realized what he was being told.

'That's him?' he said, holding her hand. 'Your chap.'

'Was. Like you. We had to stop. I have to get out of here.'

His hand tightened on hers. 'No, you don't,' he said, urgently, the flat northern accent very marked. 'This is your triumph, it's your night, everyone here wants to talk to you and wants you to have a good time. You stay here.'

She stared at him, trying to frame a protest, and he pulled her towards him and kissed her on the lips. 'That's a good girl,' he said, firmly. 'You've done a brilliant job. You enjoy it.'

Suddenly it seemed possible to laugh back at him, to find her glass and to stand, squarely, as investors and managers came up to congratulate her. She looked up from accepting tribute from McMurray, Hamish's right-hand man, and there was Gerry, with half the room watching him, wearing a dinner jacket and looking tired and tense around the mouth.

'Caroline.' He kissed her on the cheek. 'Peter Burwood very kindly invited us, but Susan has flu.'

'I know he is delighted *you* could come,' she said, steadily. 'He was – we all were – very pleased when you got into the Cabinet.'

'I've been very lucky.'

She felt her stomach clench at the familiar dismissive formula, and looked away from him to see Clive standing on the outside of a group, watching her as he talked to Graham, and she drew a steadying breath.

'We all need luck,' she said, lightly. 'Thank you for your help with all this. They deserved it.'

'So do you,' he said, adding so quietly that for a moment she did not realize what she had heard, 'I'm sorry I couldn't go on.'

A fair statement of responsibility, she thought. 'Neither of us could,' she said, accepting her share and watched the lines around his mouth soften as he smiled at her, relieved.

'We could have lunch?'

'Or you could come and lunch with my partners. They'd be thrilled. When you have time.' She managed a smile herself, and they looked at each other.

'Half the room is waiting to talk to you, Gerry,' she said, as lightly as she could. 'You'd better circulate.'

'I have. I was due home twenty minutes ago.' He kissed her again, and she was aware momentarily of envying glances from other women. Then he was gone, efficiently making his way to the exit, bustling, smiling, talking to this one and that as he passed, touching an arm here, or kissing a cheek with the politician's ease, and she watched him go for a few seconds until Clive arrived at her side and hooked an arm round her shoulders.

'Come on. We'll drown our sorrows together.'

568

'Yes. Let's do that. Unless you want to finish working your way through the chorus line?'

He considered the point, seriously. 'No, I think I've had enough of them. I must talk to the Frierns, though.'

'I could hold your hand this time,' she suggested, and he grinned at her.

'It's not necessary. We had a good run.'

'More than we did.'

'Yes. That must be hard.'

'It is. But it will pass – one day.'

He looked at her steadily, and started a sentence, then visibly thought better of it. 'Come with me to the pictures tomorrow?' he suggested.

'I'd like that. But I've got the kids.'

'So have I. We'll take them all.'

She hesitated, but he took her hand and towed her over to where Peter, Hamish and Sir William Eyre were engaged in mutual congratulations and pious statements about the future of the company. Peter, his fair skin flushed with drink and excitement, was assuring his audience that in three years' time his company would be the brightest star in the north-east, an inspiration to its friends and a lasting grief to its enemies.

'It won't be quite like that in real life,' Caroline said quietly as they joined the group.

'But he's got a chance, hasn't he?' Clive said, sharply. 'I mean he's engaged with real life – there aren't any impassable barriers to getting where he wants to be. Don't knock reality, it's got advantages.'

'This from you,' she said inimically, kicking at the carpet.

'This from me, who has no right at all to bang on. Come on, pluck up, back to the future.'

There was an uneasy moment, then she laughed, kissed him and waded into the party to make quite sure that Sir William and Hamish got interviewed by the local paper.